Jutland! A Yank's tale

Tim Concannon

Copyright © 2018 Tim Concannon
All rights reserved.
ISBN: 978-0-9576688-2-9

CRANDRU PUBLICATIONS
29 North Lane
Buriton
GU31 5RS

DEDICATION

This book is dedicated to all of those officers and men of the Royal Navy who served in the Great War

ACKNOWLEDGMENTS

I have to acknowledge the invaluable help of Heather Johnstone of the RN Museum Library, The Imperial War Museum and the staff of the Royal Naval Club and Royal Albert Yacht Club in Portsmouth who have put up with the author setting up camp for long periods in the library and to all family and friends who have assisted and contributed to the work, especially Janet Rawson, whose critical eye has been ever helpful and encouraging.

I have to thank too, those serving and retired officers and men of the Royal Navy who have had an input into this work, especially Commodore Berry Reeves for a crash course in navigation and the perils of the Pentland Firth, Stephen Saunders for access to the archives of Janes Fighting Ships, Commanders Crosbie, Mitford and Wright for battleship memories and especially someone only known to me as "Old Tom" whose tales of the destroyers of the Grand Fleet left a great impression on a young eighteen year old more than forty-five years ago

JUTLAND: - A YANK'S TALE

1. **The Beginning** 11
   Mare Island Navy Yard, California, February 1916 11
2. **A Sensitive Matter** 19
   Washington DC, February 1916 19
   Washington DC, Office of the Director of Naval Operations Monday February 22nd 1916 20
   Western Approaches, March 1916 29
   Liverpool Docks: Monday 20th March 1916 34
3. **The Journey North** 39
   Euston Station, London, Thursday 21st April 1916 39
4. **In the Northern Mists** 51
   Thurso Railway Station, 21st April 1916, 09:00 (Good Friday); 58°35' N, 3°32' W 51
   Wardroom, HMS Warspite, 21st April 1916 (Good Friday) 1230 hrs 58°52" N 3°8" W. Outer Battleship Line, Scapa Flow 67
5. **Night Departure** 79
   HMS Warspite, 21st April 1916 79
   Saturday 22nd April 1916, North Sea, 57° 15' N, 1° 57' E, HMS Warspite 1100 92
   Saturday 22nd April 1916, North Sea, 57° 45' N, 6° 04' E, HMS Warspite 2000 98
   Sunday 23rd April 1916 (Easter Sunday) North Sea, 56° 42' N, 6° 26' E (To the West of the Little Fisher Bank), HMS Warspite 1015 107
6. **A New Flap** 123
   Scapa Flow, forenoon Monday 24th April 1916 (Easter Monday) 123
   Later that day 126
   Tuesday 25th April 11:00, HMS Warspite, 5th Battle Squadron 55°5' N 0°7' E 135
   SS Borodino, Scapa Flow, Wednesday 26th April 1916 142
   A few days later 144
   Sunday 30th April, HMS Iron Duke, Battleship Line A Scapa Flow 150
7. **A Seaplane Raid** 165
   The Firth of Forth, Monday 1st May 1916, afternoon 165
   Thursday May 4th, 55° 36' N, 7° 54' E. Danish coast 50 Nautical Miles North West by West from the Tondern Zeppelin sheds. 0400 180

    Saturday 6th May 1916, HMS Iron Duke, Fleet Flagship, forenoon *186*

8. A Concert Party **193**
    Wednesday 10th May 1916, HMS Warspite, outer battleship line Scapa Flow. Forenoon *193*
    Saturday 13th May, SS Ghourko, Outer Battleship Line, Scapa Flow, Afternoon *197*
    A little later *204*
    Sunday 14th May 1916, 3rd Sunday of Easter, Roman Catholic Chapel HMS Warspite, Outer Battleship Line Scapa Flow *210*

9.   Gunnery Practice and Reorganisation **219**
    Monday 15th May 1916, Gunnery Practice Area, Scapa Flow, Forenoon *219*
    Rosyth, Saturday 27th May 1916 ....*226*
    The North British Hotel, Princes Street, Edinburgh, Saturday 27th May 1916, 9:30 PM *229*
    Aberdour House, Monday 29th May, Forenoon *234*
    The Wardroom, HMS Warspite a little later *251*

10.   A New Sweep **253**
    Wednesday 31st May 1916, 1400 HMS Warspite, 56° 47' N, 4° 40' E *253*

11.   Battle **281**
    Wednesday 31st May, HMS Warspite, 1740, 56°40' N, 5°48' E *281*

12.   Aftermath **311**
    Wednesday 31st May 1916, HMS Warspite, 2100, North Sea, position uncertain *311*
    HMS Warspite, 31st May 1916, 2130, 57°30' N, 5°3' East *319*
    The Wardroom a little later *320*
    HMS Warspite, North Sea, 0330 Thursday 1st June 1916 ....*322*
    HMS Dreadnought, Rosyth Dockyard, Friday 2nd June 1916 ......*327*
    Admiral's day cabin HMS Iron Duke, Scapa Flow, Forenoon Monday 5th June 1916 ....*331*

Report of Lt. Jonathan J Marston USN **335**

Author's Note **349**

Notes **353**

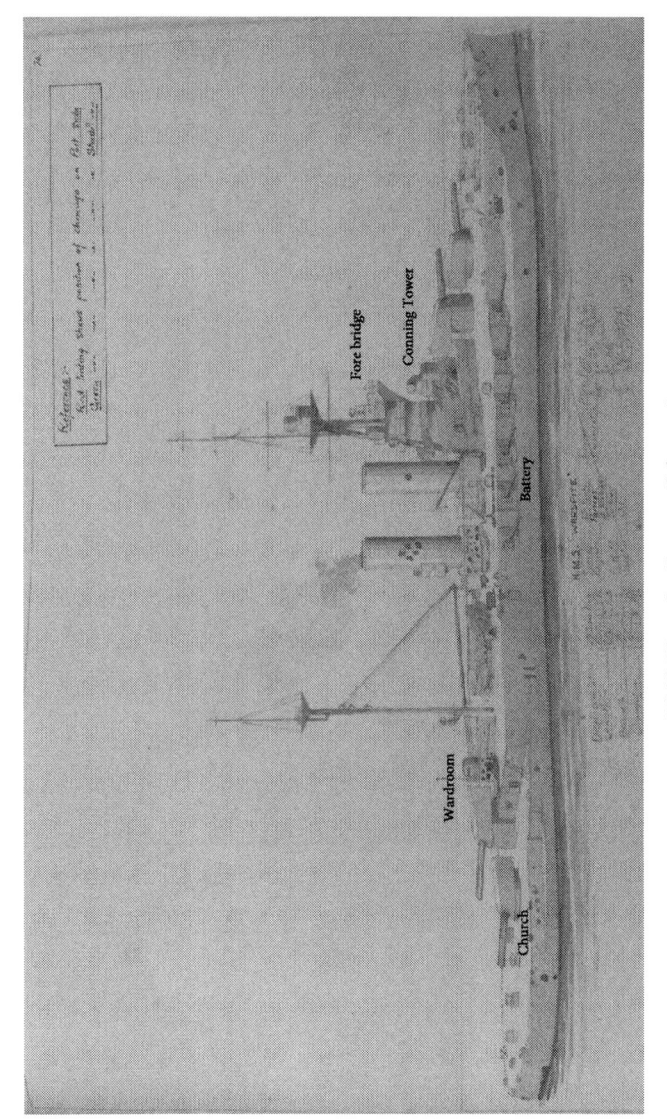

HMS Warspite Damage Schematic
Courtesy of the Royal Naval Museum

1. The Beginning

Mare Island Navy Yard, California, February 1916

The spring air was really quite warm in that sheltered corner of San Francisco Harbour. The Napa River wound gently through the flat marshy lands of Napa and Sonoma Counties before entering San Pablo Bay between Vallejo Town and Mare Island. This was the harbour that Sir Francis Drake had discovered in his voyage round the world in 1579. Richard Dana[1] had described it as one of the most beautiful in an immensely beautiful coastline eighty years back. It was surrounded by a fertile and well-wooded country. Not sixty years before it had been the preserve of trappers and traders in hides. Nowadays it was a rather more organized place and possessed a real live modern naval dockyard and a fine naval establishment.

Experiencing the balmy air that forenoon was another Bostonian seafarer, Lieutenant Jonathan J Marston USN.

Jonathan's vessel was rather less picturesque than Dana's tiny brig *Pilgrim*, which had loaded hides not very far from here in 1835. Indeed she was a wholly different class of being. USS *Wisconsin* was 12,000 tons of steel, carrying powerful engines that made nonsense of Dana's two-year epic journey from Boston and back. Armed with massive guns protected by impenetrable armour she was the mistress of all she surveyed.

Sporting a sinister dark grey colour scheme with two huge basketwork masts, she was a force to be reckoned with. The ninth of the modern battleships built for the Navy, BB 9 had been laid down in February 1897 in San Francisco, just across the bay. And yet, not twenty years after that proud day, she was already obsolescent. Newer, faster behemoths had been conceived and brought to life thousands of miles away in Drake's homeland, which had made *Wisconsin* and all her ilk into has-beens[2].

And now, in the spring of 1916, with troubled times ahead, this once proud flagship of the Pacific Fleet was gainfully employed as a training ship for the United States Navy, part of the US Naval Academy practice squadron. Famously, Josephus Daniels, the Secretary for the Navy, described it as 'a Great University, with College extensions afloat and ashore – every ship being a school, and every man having opportunities to improve his mind and fit himself for promotion'.

Jonathan, a lean and tanned thirty year old, was her gunnery lieutenant, charged with that noble aim. Specifically his task was to inculcate the finer points of gunnery practice into a mixed bag of cadets. He was taking a class now, on the battery deck, beside the long 6-inch quick firing guns.

"So," he said, "The effective range of your gun is 10,000 yards at twenty degrees of elevation. Your ship is travelling at twelve knots. The enemy bears ninety degrees on your beam at 12,000 yards on a converging course bearing thirty degrees to your line of travel. How soon will he be in range of your battery?"

A hand shot up, Radford[3], one of the brighter ones. "Sir. What is the rate of change of bearing sir?"

"Bearing steady" said Jonathan. It was a good question, but Jonathan intended the sum to be a simple matter of geometry and assumed that both ships would hold their course until they met at a point 24,000 yards ahead of the class's ship at the start of the calculation.

1. BEGINNING

Once one started factoring in rates of change of bearing (which meant that there was a significant disparity in speed or course between them) the calculations became more complex.

As a teacher, Jonathan preferred to ensure that his pupils caught the basic idea first, before adding all the bells and whistles that they would encounter in real life. Radford was clearly thinking ahead but Jonathan needed to know that the rest of the detail was keeping up.

Some minutes of agonized wrestling with the class's slates and their books of tables produced a response within a gratifyingly short time. Out of a class of ten, seven hands were up. Of the other three, two were still writing but one was staring at his slate in a picture of misery.

"Having trouble Hornton?" asked Jonathan.

"Oh, I am sure I can do it sir, just as soon as I have worked out the drift..." The answer was nonsense.

"You don't need to concern yourself about drift Hornton. Work it out without!"

Hornton stared at his slate, his misery, if possible, increasing. The other members of the class were becoming restive, some, one in particular were almost reduced to schoolboys saying, "Me sir! Me sir!"

Jonathan was not having any of that. These boys were training to become officers in the United States Navy and that meant, above all, maturity and self-control. "Be silent! Put your arms down gentlemen! This is an academy, not Grade School!"

By the same token, a naval officer could not afford to indulge in nonsense, not when there were lives at stake. Turning to the lad he said, "Tell me how you approach this, Hornton."

Agonized silence.

Hornton looked so pathetic that Jonathan took pity on him. Some instructors would bark at the unfortunate wretch but that would not help in this particular case. It may very well be that Hornton was not cut out for this life and would eventually flunk the course. But if he did, Jonathan would make sure that it was not for lack of any effort on his part.

"OK, son." He said, adopting a rather more avuncular tone, "Look at it this way. Break it down into a number of steps. Step one. You are travelling at twelve knots. That is 24,000 yards in an hour. There are sixty minutes in an hour. How far do you travel in one minute?"

"Uh, that would be 24,000 divided by sixty."

"Good"

"Four hundred yards sir."

"Correct. For every minute your vessel travels, you move four hundred yards. We need to know when we are ten thousand yards apart. Suggestions anybody? Radford?"

" When we are 10,000 times the cotangent of 30 degrees from our intersection sir!" That was correct.

"Which is?"

Radford looked it up in his book of tables, "1.732051 sir!"

"And 10,000 yards times 1.732051 is?" he didn't bother to wait for an answer "17,320.51 yards. The current distance to intersection is 24,000 yards. The difference is 24,000 less 17,320.51, namely 6,679.49, say 6,680 yards which will take how long?"

"Sixteen point seven minutes sir! 6,680 divided by 400 is sixteen point seven. It was Radford again. Time to

1. BEGINNING

bring home the wider picture, thought Jonathan, "And what do you do in the meantime?" There were blank looks all round.

Jonathan sighed, "Make sure your guns are tested, your ammunition supply secured and your men alert! Keep them busy and their mind off the events to come. " Jonathan was not really being too much the old soldier, but he had learned from the Veracruz operation the year before last[4] and he well remembered the sense of apprehension that he had felt. As it happened the fighting was limited in scope but Jonathan had smelt powder and knew what it was like to have people firing at him in earnest. He also knew what it was like to be sailing for a war zone with its mixed emotions of excitement and.... well not fear as such, merely a desire to do his best for his country.[5]

Jonathan became aware that a messenger was approaching him from the gangway. He returned the sailor's salute.

"Order for you sir. You are to report to the Captain as soon as is convenient."

"Very Good!"

That sounded interesting. Jonathan had been in post for eighteen months, and he considered that he was very good at what he was doing. He liked to teach and enjoyed the challenge with pupils like Hornton.

The international situation was very confused. The old world of Europe was locked in a death struggle between rival empires, which had already been going on for eighteen months with no sign of any early conclusion. As a naval officer, Jonathan had followed the naval parts of the campaign with eager attention: - the sinking of three British cruisers by a single submarine in the matter of a few hours in the North Sea,[6] the annihilation of a British squadron by the Germans in the South Atlantic last year and the annihilation of THAT squadron by British battle cruisers shortly thereafter[7], not to mention the carnage that had happened in the Dardanelles where no less than six allied battleships similar to *Wisconsin* had been sunk by mines or torpedoes. On the other side two Turkish battleships (albeit of older design) had been sunk by British submarines.

America was very much piggy in the middle. On the one hand her commerce was being disrupted by the British, who insisted on searching all merchant ships heading for Europe, with an arrogance that had brought them to war with the United States once before. On the other, it was being threatened by German submarines, which had adopted a shoot to kill policy that had cost American lives. On the British liner *Lusitania* alone, 128 American citizens had died in this way when she was sunk without warning.

The position was complicated and frankly Jonathan didn't know what to think. He did know that the United States was falling over backwards to remain neutral, but that resulted in the ridiculous situation whereby any training for war (which was, of course the business of any armed service) was prohibited by the politicians as being a potential breach of that neutrality.

Like many of his contemporaries, Jonathan was finding that position rather irksome. It was as if America was a man walking around with his arms tied behind his back in the middle of a free-for all roughhouse.

Once the class was finished he made his way aft to the captain's quarters. Pausing outside the curtain, he rapped on the bulkhead.

"Come" came the voice. Jonathan entered, saluted and closed the curtain behind him. The captain's quarters were tastefully panelled in mahogany and the scuttles at the extreme stern of the ship were covered with lace curtains. In times gone past, these had been the quarters of admirals but in accordance with established tradition, once the admiral had gone ashore, his quarters became the purlieu of the captain.

Admirals were a fairly new innovation in the United States Navy, which had managed very nicely with nothing higher than commodores for its first fifty years of existence. It was yet another example of an emerging class system in what should be an egalitarian service, whose officers were selected on merit alone.

Captain Sellers[8] sat in his chintz armchair. He was a rangy Texan with a direct gaze. To his right was his desk, laden with ship's books, signal flimsies, reports and all the trappings of a warship in commission in the age of rapid communication. There was a pot of coffee on the table to his left and leather bound volume on his lap.

"What in hell have you been up to Marston?" he said, "I have a telegram here from Washington. Seems they want to see you about something."

Jonathan was mystified. "I don't know sir. I haven't a clue."

"Do you know Benson?[9]" Admiral Benson had been an instructor at the Naval Academy when Jonathan was there and was now the Chief of Naval Operations He was a friend of Jonathan's father and had known Jonathan since he was a boy.

"Why yes I do sir. Quite well."

"He is asking for you by name. He don't say why, simply that I am to pack you onto the next train to Washington."

"I see sir. Perhaps I had better go then," said Jonathan.

"Indeed you should. Good luck in that snake pit!"

Jonathan turned around and left. His mind was in a ferment. He understood Sellers' reference to the snake pit.

Currently, there was a domestic war going on in the Navy with the politicians. Reformers such as Rear Admiral Fiske, the recent Aide for Naval Operations and now an incumbent at the Naval War College and his successor, Benson wanted a proper naval staff along British lines, with professional naval officers in charge of operations, whereas Secretary Daniels, the Naval Secretary and President Wilson were determined that the Navy should remain under civilian control and seemed to be totally opposed to anything which would imperil the neutrality of the United States. They thought that professional staffs were a Prussian idea, which would allow the military too much power, without any political accountability.

Jonathan agreed with his naval superiors. He had extensive experience of the political world in Boston, where the Marstons were wooed by politicians of both sides and did not rate any of them particularly highly. His natural inclination was Republican but he considered that his duty was to follow the civilian administration, whatever the cost. He did, however, resent being unable to prepare his service for doing its job properly.

2. A Sensitive Matter

Washington DC, February 1916

Washington's Union Station was a busy place. Jonathan dismounted from the train and managed to obtain the services of a porter to deal with his sea chest. Jonathan had taken the view that if he was to be in Washington for any length of time, he should have the bulk of his possessions sent on to his parents' home in Boston, retaining only a small sea chest for uniforms and other possessions.

The journey across the continent by the overland route had been an adventurous one. It was extraordinary, in Jonathan's view, that the journey, which had taken the old pioneers months, could now be accomplished in comfort and safety in a matter of days. Even as grounded a soul as Jonathan had been impressed with the vastness of the Old West as the railroad ran along what had once been the Santa Fe Trail across the Rio Grande, through Santa Fe, Dodge City, Topeka, Atchison, Kansas City and St Louis Missouri.

Taking a hansom cab, he realized that it was some time since he had been in Washington. It was quite busy but would soon, no doubt, be shutting down for the beginning of the 1916 presidential campaign. No one had yet been adopted as the candidate for the big parties but Jonathan was pretty sure that Wilson was a shoe-in as the Democrat. Roosevelt probably wouldn't run again but his would be a powerful endorsement. As for the rest of them, no doubt someone would emerge and Jonathan would look at them as and when they sorted the nominations out.

As it happened it was a horse drawn hansom, which meant that as he journeyed down 1st North East Avenue towards the Navy Yard, he had nothing but the clop of the horse's hooves to distract him from the magnificence of the White House, the Supreme Court Building and the other specimens of monumental architecture that made Washington such an impressive, if impersonal, place.

It was ironic, he thought, that a Frenchman had originally designed Washington. The system of avenues and boulevards gave it a wonderfully spacious feeling. The British had burned it to the ground in 1812 and it had taken a German architect, to rebuild it.

Washington DC, Office of the Director of Naval Operations Monday February 22nd 1916

Benson was a contemporary of Jonathan's father and very much the Southern gentleman, with an iron-grey moustache.

"Good morning my boy" he said, getting up and shaking Jonathan's hand. "Thank you so much for coming. I have something of a conundrum in front of me and I think that you might be able to help me through it. Sit yourself down and lets see where we can go. Smoke if you wish." Gratefully Jonathan sat down and began to fill his pipe.

Lighting a cheroot, Benson said "I am afraid that it is all a bit unofficial and I ask that you keep our conversation private for the moment."

"Of course sir" said Jonathan.

"Tell me Marston, do you love your country?"

Jonathan was completely taken aback. What sort of question was that? He lit his pipe, drew on it and hazarded, "Well I am as patriotic as the next man sir."

"My country right or wrong eh?" said Benson, looking at him directly.

"I am a serving officer sir and I have taken my oath, so I guess the answer must be yes, sir" Jonathan's puzzlement became even more acute at the next question.

"Do you have any extreme prejudices?"

"Uhhh.....I would say not sir."

"What about those who would wish your country harm?" Had the Director completely lost his mind?

"Well I guess it's OK to be prejudiced about them, sir. Broadly speaking, I'm agin them." This was turning into one of the most extraordinary interrogations that Jonathan had been subject to since the very early days of College.

"What do you make of the war in Europe?"

That was safer ground. "Well sir, it looks as though the Old World has completely taken leave of its senses. It is tearing itself apart and God only knows what will emerge."

"Who do you think will win?" That was a much trickier question. Why would Benson be interested in Jonathan's take on a question that had, quite literally, divided the world? Well the question had been asked and it had to be answered. The schoolmaster in Jonathan told him that a glib answer would not do and how he answered was important.

"That is very hard for me to say, sir. I am a naval officer, not an economist. In military terms, it seems to me that the Germans and Austrians are a match for the French and Russians, which is why there is stalemate on the various fronts. I can only assume that something, perhaps new weapons, will break it, or else they will have to go on until one side or the other can no longer sustain the effort. The casualty lists are unbelievable."

"And at sea?"

"Well sir, I would have thought that the British would have been an easy match for anyone else, with all that that implies but the Germans do seem to be doing rather well, certainly in terms of cruiser conflicts.

"Thinking about the sinking of *Aboukir, Hogue* and *Cressy,* I do not think that we have really taken on board the damage that a torpedo can do. I must say it is very difficult to know what the main battle fleets are doing, we simply don't hear about them. I guess they must be sitting in harbour most of the time, waiting for an opportunity. I would guess that when they do meet, whoever wins, would win the war."

"Why?" asked Benson.

"Well sir, as we know from our War [10], whoever commands the sea commands the trade. As long as the British can blockade Germany, they have the upper hand, whereas if the British are defeated, the Germans can do the same thing to them. In addition, whoever commands the sea can cover troop landings wherever he wants. The British are supplying the French and the Italians by sea but as far as I can see, no-one is able to trade with Germany, so they are purely dependent on their own resources. I am afraid that I do not know enough about the resources of Germany to be able to say whether or not they can manage without an overseas trade. The reports would seem to suggest that they couldn't. I simply don't know." The answer was straight out of Mahan[11].

"Do you know anything about any of the navies in detail?"

2. A SENSITIVE MATTER

"Well I have met the British, of course, they are everywhere you go around the world. I did see something of the German Pacific Squadron some years ago. I am afraid I know nothing about the French, Austrians or Italians. I have seen some reports of the damage to the Russian ships in the war and of course I have read all that I could about the Japanese."

"Your assessment?"

Jonathan reflected. "The British are supremely confident. Their ships are efficiently run but they vary tremendously in age and capability. I would guess that some of the officers I have met are rather hidebound, lacking in flexibility, plus, of course they believe the world revolves around them."

"You don't like them very much do you?" said Benson, looking sideways at Jonathan.

"Well that's putting it a bit strong, sir. I don't like their arrogance, or being treated as some sort of performing monkey but to be fair, they do have style. Of course, the fact that their navy is everywhere does give them some justification. The Empire on which the Sun never sets and all that.

"The Germans are a different animal. From what I have seen, they are playing the game very well. The ships I saw in the Pacific were pretty good and pretty smart. I was impressed with Von Spee at Coronel. That was a very good piece of work. Of course his ships helped him: - I saw *Scharnhorst* and *Gneisenau*[12] in 1913. Beautiful, well balanced ships, carefully designed and well manned."

"What languages do you speak?"

"French, sir and a little Spanish."

"Any German?"

"No Sir" said Jonathan, "most of the officers I met spoke very good English."

There was a pause and then Benson said, "We have something of a situation here. It's a bit tricky to explain it." Jonathan realized with some surprise that Benson was embarrassed. "You know that the President's father was a leading minister in the South during the war?"

Jonathan did not know that and said so.

"Well he was, and he saw something of war up close and personal. He don't like it and he don't want anything to do with it."

"Well I guess that's understandable sir."

"Trouble is," said Benson, "that it's durned difficult for us. Folks are getting restless here. Some people think that we shall have to get involved. The President is dead agin that."

That made Jonathan think. He had been following the newspapers with close attention. After the *Lusitania* two former presidents Roosevelt and Taft called for war. Many voices were raised in support of the 'preparedness' movement and Senator Root,[13] one of the front-runners, was actively campaigning for entry on the side of the allies. He was strongly supported by Jonathan's fellow Bostonian, Henry Lodge[14]. Even his main rival Weeks[15] another New Englander, well known to Jonathan said that he was not averse to joining the War.

"Fact is" said Benson, "some folks think it's our patriotic duty to go to war. The British navy stops ships and sometimes seizes property, but the German navy sinks ships and kills people."

"What does the President make of that?" asked Jonathan.

"Nobody knows," said Benson. "He don't see nobody but Colonel House[16]. What we do know is that he won't even let us send observers to see how they're doing. 'Too proud to fight' is what he said last year, so I guess he's still of the same mind. He reckons that as a nation, we're so right that we don't need to convince others by force that we are right! 'Course all that might change come November if we get a new President. We may have to change our mind sharpish." It was very true.

"We have a number of problems facing the US Navy at this point," Benson went on, "We're weak, deficient in manpower, inefficient and in no shape whatsoever to enter into the greatest war the world has ever seen. We don't have the ships, the equipment, Hell we don't even have the reservists!" Benson ground out his cigar.

"The Royal Navy may have control of the sea but the Imperial German Army control the French industrial heartland. Both sides say that victory is just around the corner and one more push will do it."

Jonathan nodded.

"This coming summer may very well be decisive, one way or the other. What will happen then? It will be a whole new world. If the allies win, who's to say that Britain and France might want to have a go at their old colonies?"

That made Jonathan think. On balance, he didn't think that it was likely, but clearly some people in Washington did.

"And if the Germans win, sir?"

"The Kaiser might want a slice of the British and French colonies in the Caribbean and the West Indies. Given what he has done in the rest of the world, I don't think that he's likely to stop there. D'ye fancy Uhlans in Ontario?[17]

"And then we have the Japanese ambitions in the Pacific, which are not dependant upon the outcome of the European War. Hell! We could find the United States with a serious problem in the near future. In the worst-case scenario we'll have an Imperial German Empire in the west and an Imperial Japanese Empire in the east, with no check on them from the rump of Europe."

Jonathan was shaken to realize that this nightmare might actually take place and that it might be as soon as the following Fall. It was a very frightening thought.

"What about the Navy Bill sir?" asked Jonathan. That bill, currently wending its way through Congress would mean that by 1922, the US Navy would be one of the two largest in the world, getting close to the British. It would outrank any other navy (be it German or Japanese) by a considerable margin.

"That's a long term project, Marston. It will take five years, and some people don't think that we have five months."

"What can we do sir?" asked Jonathan

"The better question" said Benson, "is what are we going to do." He paused.

"I have had a letter from a 'highly placed naval personage' in the British Admiralty. It has reached me through....unusual cannels. It is a bit of a hot potato really. He wants us to appoint a US Navy officer of sufficient seniority to carry out full liaison duties with the Royal Navy.

"The President vetoed the idea. He says that it is highly provocative, which, of course it is." Benson paused again to let it sink in.

2. A SENSITIVE MATTER

He went on "Some people in the Administration don't agree with the President; some quite senior people in fact. They think that it could and should be done and I agree with them."

"But sir," said Jonathan, putting down his pipe, "if the President vetoes it isn't that it? The end of the matter I mean? He is the Commander-in-Chief"

"Not necessarily, Marston. The Commander-in-Chief doesn't normally concern himself with individual postings, especially if they are lieutenants." That was true.

"There is, for example a demonstrable need for an extra Naval attaché to the American embassy in London in view of all the problems with the blockade. What use the attaché makes of his time is within the purlieu of the senior officer on station. And his hosts of course.

"I would like you to be that attaché."

So that was it. Jonathan was being asked to carry out what was, in effect a clandestine mission, clean contrary to the wishes of his Commander-in-Chief. It was a troubling thought to someone of Jonathan's mindset.

"What would I be asked to do sir?" he said.

Benson said "I want you to do three things; first to observe and report on how the British Royal Navy operates on a day by day basis, second, review their tactics and know-how and last, but equally important, give me a steer on the morale of the country generally and the armed forces in particular.

"In the nature of things, your written orders would be bland and uncontroversial for obvious reasons"

In other words, thought Jonathan, 'plausible deniability.' He would be doing a very valuable, even vital, job but if he were caught overstepping the mark, he would be hung out to dry. Benson clearly knew that and was uncomfortable with it. It did not sit happily with his sense of honour and he obviously knew that Jonathan would have the same doubts.

"I have to say," said Benson "I am not happy with the whole concept of going behind the President's back, but I do think that the needs of our country take precedence. Administrations may come and go but the country will still be there, still with the same needs.

He was right there, thought Jonathan, It was very difficult territory.

"I appreciate that this will be a hard decision for you to make. It took me a while to get a handle on it. Why don't you take a fortnight's leave to think it over?"

Jonathan was very grateful for that. Whilst the proposal was highly sensitive and desperately secret, he got the leave of Benson to discuss the matter with The Commodore, as Jonathan's father was known at home. A wise old bird and a well-respected officer, Jonathan really wanted to get his input on what to do. On the one hand, he was bound by his oath to defend the Constitution of the United States against all enemies, foreign and domestic, which was fine, but he was also bound to 'bear true faith and allegiance to the same'. President Wilson had been lawfully elected by a considerable margin and was the head of the armed services. His word was, quite literally, law.

As against that, a new President could very well supplant Wilson in November, who may have other views entirely on what was in the best interests of the United States. That was the essential problem with a democracy as opposed to an autocracy but it was that very democracy that Jonathan was oathbound to defend.

2. A SENSITIVE MATTER

Western Approaches, March 1916

Of course Jonathan had taken the mission: his father reminded him that his duty was to the United States and not to the President personally. "Remember Jonathan going into the garrison at Michmash in the Bible? 'If they say come unto us, we shall go up'.[18] I guess you should go." So he did.

The journey over in *SS New York* had been eventful. Somewhat to his surprise, he had found himself sharing space with a Japanese delegation, accompanied by a full Commander of the Imperial Japanese Navy who had taken a liking to Jonathan.

Geymjio Sasai was an amusing, if somewhat disturbing companion. Jonathan had been travelling in civilian clothes masquerading as a Marine Consultant. Sas had seen through that very early and they had become companions.[19]

The rest of the passengers were a mixed lot, including Enrique, a Spanish composer and his wife Amparo, returning from a triumph at the New York Metropolitan Opera,[20] and Jamie Hall, an American adventurer heading for France to 'observe' a squadron of American volunteer flyers.[21]

Sas had served in the naval battles of the Russo-Japanese War [22] and regaled the company with his stories ("I don't mind telling you, old fellow, but I was asking the ancestors to get the drinks in on more than one occasion!")

Approaching European waters, Jonathan had been struck by how tight the British blockade was. They had been challenged by armed merchant cruisers and other blockading vessels on a regular basis.

As the *New York* had approached the war zone, the Royal Navy was even more in evidence. On the day after a party organised by the Japanese, they had encountered *HMS Adventure,* which was a rakish destroyer leader, with a bevy of mean-looking destroyers in company. Ignoring *New York* they had swept across their course at twenty knots or more, intent on some other goal.

After that, they had encountered another British cruiser squadron, this time of *Town* class ships, which were capable of twenty-five knots carrying a powerful armament of six inch and four inch guns. These were the very ships that Billy Sims[23] had said that the US Navy was lacking.

Jonathan knew that the Royal Navy had a numerous class of even faster cruisers attached to the Battle fleet. There were at least sixteen thirty-knot *Arethusas*, with God knew how many more completed since the beginning of the War. Each of them had almost as many guns as the *Towns* and was five knots faster to boot.

As if that wasn't enough, as they got closer to their landfall in Northern Ireland, they encountered a squadron of battleships, albeit of an older pattern similar to *Wisconsin,* ploughing majestically through the restless North Atlantic with contemptuous ease.

Approaching the gap between Northern Ireland and Liverpool, Sas had drawn Jonathan's attention to a mist of smoke moving across the northern horizon at very high speed.

"Look at that!" he had said, "Oil fuel, for certain and probably thirty knots by my reckoning!" He passed his binoculars over and Jonathan focused on the base of the smoke (which was fairly sparse, compared to the

2. A SENSITIVE MATTER

thick plume that one would normally expect from a coal-fired vessel) and saw a long, lean greyhound of a ship, with two funnels and a built up bridge structure before the fore funnel.

To Jonathan's surprise, he saw that the foremast was a tripod, with a bulky fire control centre at the top which meant a capital ship with big guns, "Good God!" he exclaimed involuntarily, "it's a battle cruiser!"

"Yes!" said Sas, "and look at those turrets!"

As he spoke, the weather cleared briefly and a ray of sunlight threw the distant ship into Jonathan's focus, like a theatrical spotlight.

Jonathan gasped. The thing was absolutely beautiful, speeding through the ocean with a deceptively small bow-wave and a positive plume of white water rising behind the neat counter. She was moving extremely fast and such a low bow-wave argued beautiful lines.

In the sunlight, her light grey paint stood out perfectly against the darker clouds behind her. Jonathan counted, one, two and then *three* turrets, at least one fewer than he had expected. The latest British battle cruiser that he knew about, the *Tiger* had four twin 13.5" turrets on the centreline.

Fewer turrets could only mean bigger guns.

"Have you noticed anything about it?" asked Sas.

Looking again, Jonathan had a sudden *frisson*, which made him shiver physically.

"It is a battle-cruiser *Queen Elizabeth*," he said flatly.

The *Queen Elizabeth's* were the largest, fastest and most heavily armed battleships in the world. They carried eight fifteen-inch guns, which fired a shell weighing close on a ton fifteen miles. They had a top speed of twenty-five knots, which was five knots faster than anything in the US Navy, apart from a few torpedo boats, which would be blown, away by the twelve or sixteen six-inch guns shipped as a secondary armament. There was really nothing like them. They could run rings around either *Nevada* or *Fuso*[24] or even both together, with their bigger guns and faster speed. Neither the American nor the Japanese battleship would be able to touch them.

And the British had five of them.

Over the past ten years, the Brits had concentrated their innovative skills on new classes of battleships and then added battle-cruiser equivalents a year or so later. Thus *Invincible* and *Inflexible*, which had annihilated Von Spee's Pacific squadron in 1914, were battle-cruiser derivatives of *Dreadnought* carrying two fewer guns but with much higher speed.

The *Queen Elizabeth's* broke the mould, by sacrificing two guns for higher speed. A battle cruiser equivalent would, logically, have even higher speed. It would also mean that the three turrets he was looking at were at least fifteen-inch guns.

A ship capable of outrunning the fastest warships in the world, armed with the most devastating gun in the world was truly to be feared.

Struck by a sudden idea, Jonathan thrust out his left hand, thumb up and hand held blade wise in front of his eyes. "Mark me Sas," he said, as he lined up his hand with the bow of the ship. "Time, Now!"

Sas had instantly realized what he was about and took out his watch.

"Wait" he said, "ready..... Now!"

2. A SENSITIVE MATTER

Jonathan instantly realigned his hand to the bow of the vessel and then pivoted with the bow as it moved westward.

"Halt!" cried Sas a few moments later. "Ok, let's think about this. *King George V* [25] is six hundred feet long. *Lion*[26] is seven hundred feet. She is therefore 1.167 times the length.

"*QE* is about six hundred and fifty feet long. If they apply the same rules, that ship is about seven hundred and sixty feet long. Shall we say seven hundred and fifty for convenience?

"Can you get the angle between bow and stern?" he asked "I'll have a go," said Jonathan. Again, pivoting slightly, with his hand outstretched, Sas, crouching behind him, measured the angle with a pocket compass. After a number of trials the two men came to the conclusion that the angle was about three quarters of a degree

Thus, by way of approximate measurements, they decided that the ship was about 18,000 yards away and proceeding at something in excess of thirty knots, indeed faster than anything else in the world.

For Once Sas did not have a great deal to say. 18,000 yards was a mile greater than the distance that the Russians had been straddling his ship in 1904 with shells that were less than half the weight of those that could be thrown by a 15" gun and that ship, now disappearing over the horizon, was moving at twice the speed of the Russians twelve years ago.[27]

Both of them had been struck silent at this demonstration of what they presumed to be the very latest British warship's capabilities.

"Well" said Sas after some moments, "I always said that the British set a pretty high bar."

"Indeed" Jonathan agreed. There was nothing in either of their Navies, which could cope with the ship they had just seen.

Liverpool Docks: Monday 20th March 1916

The arrival in Liverpool was a shock. The place was absolutely teeming with ships of all kinds, and as a result, the water was black with coal dust. He had never seen dirtier water. His welcome, however, could not have been chillier. He had been treated with the deepest suspicion by the authorities, and when he protested that he was an American citizen, he was reminded that America had not always been a friend to the British Empire. He had, grudgingly, been allowed in to His Majesty's realm, but had been under virtual house arrest in his London hotel (which was no real hardship) ever since.

To make matters worse, he found that he was not particularly welcome at the American Embassy either. The Ambassador would have nothing to do with him. As far as he was concerned, Jonathan's mission was not approved by the President and that was it. He couldn't call himself a Naval attaché or even wear his uniform.

Jonathan had been left to the Second Secretary, Ed Bell,[28] who was clearly a spook. The only bright spot of his miserable experience was the presence of Cliff Carver, who was a friend of his brother's on the embassy staff.[29] Jonathan was reduced to the absurd pretence of being on furlough, taking advantage of Cliff's presence to visit wartime London.

2. A SENSITIVE MATTER

He had spent the next four weeks as a frustrated tourist, seeing the sights of London whilst Ed Bell was pulling various invisible strings.

That had resulted in a discouraging interview at the British Admiralty; where a charming RN Commander, Brandon[30] gulled Jonathan into setting out exactly want he wanted to do. "So what you are really asking is for us to tell you exactly how we are conducting this war, including our tactical methods and command structures so that you can learn from them?" he had said.

Jonathan had answered "Well I guess it does come down to that, now that you put it that way but..."

"No, that's fine Lieutenant, I appreciate your candour. It makes things much easier. The answer, of course, must be 'no'."

It transpired that Jonathan's invitation had been sent by a politician, with American relations.[31] He had been removed in disgrace and was currently serving in the Trenches. In his absence, Jonathan's mission was not looked upon favourably.

To try and cheer himself up, he had followed the advice of an advertisement in his morning paper. War or no war, the Brits were not giving up their Easter holidays. "Southsea, on the silvery Solent" it ran "Handsome piers and grand sea front. Best military band and high-class concerts. Safe, select and sheltered." In a cartouche over a drawing of a pier against a distant shoreline was a drawing of a barge sailing past what appeared to be an old time three-decker ship of the line.

Jonathan had been homesick for the sea, and he knew that Southsea, on the Solent was immediately adjacent to Portsmouth, Britain's premier Naval Port. He took a day excursion. That too had ended in disaster.

Overwhelmed by a trip round the harbour (in wartime? The Brits weren't letting that get in the way of earning a living) and unfamiliar with the strength of British beer, Jonathan suddenly found himself up close and personal with the provisions of the Official Secrets Act 1911, by courtesy of a senior Scotland Yard detective, ironically called Savage.[32] After another, very uncomfortable interview, Jonathan was discharged. The detective had, with dogged effort, made his enquiries and had discovered the original invitation from the then First Lord of the British Admiralty.

Everything changed when Jonathan found himself co-opted into a US Enquiry into a mysterious explosion, which had damaged an unarmed passenger ferry, the *SS Sussex*. Unusually, it had not been sunk, but the bows had been blown off, killing several people, including, to Jonathan's distress, Enrique and Amparo Granado. Enrique had taken Jonathan rather under his wing, on the voyage over, and had occupied the time giving him a master class in the guitar, which, up until then, Jonathan had played indifferently. The sight of the vibrant Amparo dancing flamenco to Jonathan's guitar was a memory that he would always treasure.

The enquiry demonstrated with all possible clarity that *Sussex* had been torpedoed without warning by, Jonathan presumed, someone who called himself an officer and a gentleman. Jonathan would like a few minutes alone with that gentleman. Poor Amparo and Enrique, caught up in a war that was nothing to do with them, and now dead, through no fault of their own.

He also experienced a zeppelin raid, which appeared to have done little damage, and had cost the Imperial German Navy one of their aerial cruisers, shot down by ground fire.[33] More pointedly, he had read news of airplane attacks in which children going to Sunday school were killed. It was not the sort of war that he was used to.

Immediately after the *Sussex* enquiry, Jonathan found that the attitude of the British establishment had changed towards him. From being a pariah, things started to happen. In short order he was invited to lunch with Brandon (in a gentleman's club, where else?) that turned seamlessly into an interview with the British Director of Naval Intelligence, Captain Hall. The DNI was a sprite of a man with whom, after some verbal fencing, Jonathan got on very well indeed.[34]

After that he was kitted out with an hybrid uniform, of British cut, but with US buttons and badges, which Symington, the US Naval attaché authorised with a straight face.

3. The Journey North

Euston Station, London, Thursday 21st April 1916

It was Maundy Thursday, three days before Easter and the day on which Jesus had celebrated his last supper with his disciples. Jonathan's last supper was going to be a little different.

Shortly after his interview with Hall and Brandon he had received a note from Brandon saying

"Dear Marston

The job has come up. Please be at Euston Station, Thursday 21st April at 1030 hrs with full kit. Be prepared for sea duty in foul weather. Present the enclosed travel warrant to the ticket office and await instructions.
Yours

Brandon"

Jonathan had immediately sought the opinion of Ed Bell. Bell had been very interested in Jonathan's lunch. "'Blinker' Hall is a perfectly marvellous person but the coldest-hearted proposition that ever was – he'd eat a man's heart and hand it back to him! If you've impressed him, the job is done but God help you. The man is perfectly capable of tying you to a torpedo and launching you at the German High Seas Fleet telling you that it's a reconnaissance mission!"

When he showed him the note Bell whistled, "Phew! Euston! That sounds like a 'Jellicoe' to me. God! What an opportunity!"

Not for the first time, Jonathan realized that the London Embassy sometimes spoke a different language to that which he was used to.

"Jellicoe?" he queried.

"Jellicoe special! A train headed straight into the Northern Mists where the Grand Fleet hangs out. There are special trains several times a day from Euston and other places which head north, no-one's saying where. They take sailors up and back from here and coal, one way from South Wales. They're called 'Jellicoes' because that's the name of the Admiral and he has organized the whole thing."

So here he was, at another railroad station, wearing his unfamiliar uniform and his US pattern overcoat. He was actually delighted with his uniform, which had an air of sophistication to it. The tailoring was impeccable and he felt very dashing. The station was absolutely crowded with uniforms. Having reconnoitred the previous day, Jonathan had left plenty of time to get to the ticket office, a task that was easier than it sounded. Most of the men were in organized groups and it was not difficult to get served.

He presented his travel warrant, which simply said "Lieutenant Marston for special service" with an illegible signature and a stamp. The booking office clerk took the warrant and consulted a ledger. Going to a series of pigeonholes behind the counter he reappeared with a large manila envelope, which was addressed to Lieutenant J. J. Marston and marked "to be opened no less than one hour after departure of train".

"There we are sir, Platform 5, first carriage, fifth compartment seat 37. Here is your ticket. The seat is marked on it. Departure is 11 o'clock sharp. Please

3. THE JOURNEY NORTH

arrange for your luggage to be transferred to the trollies marked J5." And Jonathan was left to his own devices.

Given the volume of travellers, he figured that it would be better to get snugged down on the train sooner rather than later, so he made his way to the barrier. The cabbie had transferred his sea chest to a porter's trolley but there was no porter to operate it, so Jonathan had to attend to it himself. That did not seem unusual, as he saw several other officers having to do the same thing.

Just by the entrance he saw that there was a mini train of carts, laden with luggage each labelled with a cardboard flag. Locating J5 was a matter of moments and it was not too difficult to get close to it, although it was seething with men. As he was approaching, a group of bluejackets were stowing their own kitbags with cheerful care.

Seeing Jonathan pushing his own sea chest one of them said cheerily "'Old up mates! This 'ere hofficer needs an 'elping 'and! 'Ere you go sir, let us deal wif that for you!" And they laid hold of the sea chest between them and slung it onto the trolley without effort.

"Why thank you men" said Jonathan, "Real kind of you."

"No bother sir, we'll 'ave to unstow it when we gets there anyway, so we might as well do it now. Canuck are you sir? If you don't mind my asking?"

"No, I'm American."

"Cor lummee! A yank! That was quick! Pore little *Sussex* barely dried out and the Yanks are 'ere already! God bless you sir! You're very welcome!"

"Why thank you" said Jonathan

"Know where you're going sir?" asked the other

"I have orders to be opened on the train."

"Well that's a turnup for the book and no mistake! Real 'ush 'ush then. Well good luck sir and if ever you needs an'elping 'and you can find me on the old *Warspite*. Arthur Bond is the name sir, AB." And with a cheery wave he was off with his mates.

Tickled with his first encounter with the famous Jolly Jack tar, Jonathan made his way up the Platform towards the front of the train. He swung up into the first carriage behind the locomotive and immediately heard a riot going on inside. A young male voice (yet unbroken) was screaming "Get off you beasts!"

Another voice was saying loudly, "Come on Smith! All junior officers under five feet tall have to travel in the luggage rack!"

Another voice was shouting "scrag him! scrag him! And there were all sorts of other noise from other voices, which settled into a chant "In the bag! In the bag! In the bag!"

The young voice shouted, "There's no such rule Single! And you know it! Leave me alone! Gettoff me!" He was clearly not going quietly.

As Jonathan slid back the door of the compartment, the participants froze in their actions as if they had been turned to stone, looking at him aghast.

There was a group of three or four midshipmen holding a very small boy in a midshipman's uniform over their heads. It was clear they were trying to place him in the luggage net over the seats. A young sub-lieutenant (which Jonathan knew was an Ensign in British usage) was directing operations. The boy was yelling at the top of his lungs. He didn't notice Jonathan at first but was alerted to his presence by the stillness of his attackers.

"What's going on here?" asked Jonathan sternly.

3. THE JOURNEY NORTH

The sub-lieutenant looked at him and took in the American greatcoat and the unfamiliar cap-badge. "Kings' Regulations sir, all junior officers under five feet tall have to travel in the luggage rack in wartime." He essayed a wink, trying to get Jonathan onside.

"Don't listen to him sir! It's not true!" shouted the boy, writhing in the grip of his fellows "anyway I'm not under five feet tall, I AM five feet tall! Don't let them do it sir!"

Jonathan was amused. He was actually delighted to see that the stuffy Brits were as addicted to horseplay in the junior ranks as the Americans were.

"Well that's a poser, I guess." He said slowly, looking round the compartment. "Has anyone got the instructions?"

"Well it may be a Custom of the Service, sir," said the sub-lieutenant. Truth to tell, my copy of the KI &AI are in my sea chest in the baggage train.

"I see," said Jonathan, ruminatively. "Well I guess the first thing to do is to see if the younker is actually under five feet tall. Put him down you three and let's see.

The three mids deposited the boy on the floor, with exaggerated care. The boy faced Jonathan directly, with courage in his eyes. "Now let's deal with this properly" said Jonathan. "Anyone got a ruler?" They had not.

"So" said Jonathan, "How are you going to prove he is under five feet tall? *Quique assertit, onus probandi inculcit.* He who asserts must prove." He didn't have a brother as a lawyer for nothing.

"Ooh sir!" said one of the older Mids. "That's not fair, topping it the sea lawyer!"

"And why not?" asked Jonathan "the Law is there for everyone. I guess this officer is entitled to it as much as anyone else." Addressing the boy he said, "How tall are you son? Think carefully before you answer?"

"Five feet and a bit, sir"

"A bit?"

"Almost half an inch sir. In my socks."

"Anyone able to disprove that?" Silence was the answer.

"Then I guess you get to travel in a seat son."

"Thank you sir! You're a brick! You really are! Smith is the name sir, Edward Smith, Midshipman"

"Jonathan J. Marston" said Marston. And the turning to the sub he said "Fair enough sub-lieutenant?"

"Aye sir!" said the sub-lieutenant smiling. Some other officers might have dealt with the matter differently but clearly he appreciated Jonathan's good-humoured sense.

"Frank Single, sir and that's Dick Fairthorne Bill Fell, Goddard and Hanwell. All on our way North to various destinations."

"Very good" said Jonathan, locating his seat in the corner, which was distinguished by a ticket ticked into the elastic holding the antimacassar to the seatback. "Carry on then" taking off his coat, abstracting his poetry book from the pocket and sitting down.

Slightly shamefacedly, the boys took their own seats. Jonathan had Brown beside him and Single opposite with the other three disposed among the other seats. Jonathan removed his hat and placed it on the table under the window.

Looking at it, Single said, slightly hesitantly, "Is that a US Navy cap badge sir?"

3. THE JOURNEY NORTH

"It sure is" said Jonathan, relaxing. He felt that he had been hiding his identity forever and of course there was no longer any need for subterfuge.

"Does this mean that America is in the war sir?"

"Not quite yet, sub. We are still, officially, neutral." He could see Single turning it over in his mind.

"I don't quite understand sir. If America is neutral, why are you on a 'Jellicoe' going north with us?"

It was a very good question. The boy would go far.

"I don't know sub but we shall find out when we are an hour into this journey." He tapped his breast pocket. "Instructions, to be opened when the train has been going an hour."

"Phew!" whistled Fairthorne, "secret orders! That must be very exciting!"

"Do you know where this train is going?" asked Jonathan.

Fairthorne and Single exchanged glances. "Well yes, sir, we do," said Fairthorne. "We have our own orders of course and we know exactly where we are going but, well, we don't talk about it."

"Does this train stop anywhere?" asked Jonathan.

"Only to take on water," said Fairthorne.

"Yes it does, Fathead!" said Single. "There is a change of engines at Perth, they need two engines to get this lot up the mountains!"

"How long does it take to get to Perth?" asked Jonathan. It sounded exotic.

"Oh six hours or so." It was an appreciable journey.

"Well in that case, I guess I am going to the same place as you guys."

At that point there was a whistle and a judder and the insistent chuffing of the locomotive began as the heavily laden train began to move, the chuffing began to accelerate as the train picked up speed. The diddley-dee, diddly-da, diddley-dee of the railroad began to make itself felt. In no time the town was rushing past the windows at quite a rate. The locomotive whistled and the insistent rhythm of the rails took over.

The ride was smooth, but looking out of the window, Jonathan realised that this train was really flying. If it was doing sixty miles an hour, it meant a journey of three hundred and sixty miles or so. That was the same distance as Washington was from Boston. Perth had to be in Scotland. He knew from 'Janes'[35] that the Brits maintained a base at Rosyth and another at Cromarty but he was not quite sure where these were in relation to each other, or indeed Britain as a whole. He did remember that they both faced east, which meant that they were on the front line.

Indeed, the sheer numbers of service personnel getting on this train meant that they were headed somewhere significant. Come to think of it, *Warspite* was one of the latest British Dreadnoughts. Jonathan thought that she was a *Queen Elizabeth,* which meant fifteen-inch guns and twenty-five knots. If AB Arthur Bond was headed on the same train as Jonathan, the chances were that they were headed for the Grand Fleet. It was an exciting thought.

The journey passed pleasantly. The youngsters were amusing companions. Smith was learning German and had been reading the famous Karl May books about the Wild West[36] and Fairthorne's parents had actually attended Buffalo Bill's Wild West Show twenty years ago and had seen the great Hunkpapa Chief, Sitting Bull, who had been reduced to playing himself in a circus.

3. THE JOURNEY NORTH

Young Smith was completely fascinated and asked how many Indians Jonathan had killed and what he did with the scalps. Jonathan told him that the number of Indians he had killed was a State secret and that scalps were only worn with full dress, on which he elaborated by saying that the most dramatic part of a parade was the counting of scalps, in which the officer with the greatest number gained the most honour.

As they were getting on for an hour into the journey, Jonathan checked his wristwatch. His young companions fixed him with an expectant gaze. They too had been surreptitiously timing the journey and were watching Jonathan from behind hooded eyes to see what, exactly was going to happen.

With the habit of a schoolmaster, Jonathan had been observing this process and had decided that he rather liked these lads, who were in such high spirits. There was certainly no lack of morale in the younger members of the British Royal Navy.

He decided to have some fun.

"Mr Single" he said

"Aye aye sir!" said Single.

"Would you be kind enough to indulge me a little?" said Jonathan.

"Of course sir, anything."

"What time did we leave London?"

"Just gone 1100 sir."

"How much just gone 1100 Mr. Single?"

"1105 sir." Jonathan was not convinced about that but had, himself been so taken up with the company that he had not checked their exact departure time.

"Then please be kind enough to let me know the time by your watch."

Consulting his own watch, Single said "1202 hours sir"

"Really?" said Jonathan, whose own watch said 1205 precisely.

Jonathan's wristwatch was another indulgence, albeit one that was readily justifiable, given his calling. It was the latest model from the latest watchmakers, the Rolex company and it had the distinction of being the first wristwatch to be awarded a "Class A" precision certificate from the Royal Observatory at Kew, which meant that it was on a par with most marine chronometers used in navigation.

It was a dime to a dollar that his watch was right and Single's was wrong. Nevertheless, notwithstanding his own impatience, he said, "In that case Mr Single, since my own watch is in advance of yours by three minutes, I shall wait on your count."

It was dramatic but very rewarding.

Single entered into the spirit of the thing, after all, he was hardly more than a boy himself.

"Two minutes"

"One minute"

"Thirty seconds"

Jonathan took out the envelope and prepared it for opening with his pocket penknife. Single began to count down and the boys joined in

"Ten, nine, eight, seven, six,"

Jonathan opened his penknife and slipped the blade under the fold of the envelope,

"Four, three, two, one, OPEN IT SIR!"

Jonathan began slitting the heavy manila. He extracted a sheet of typescript, with the embossed fouled anchor of the Royal Navy heading it.

3. THE JOURNEY NORTH

He read silently

From the Office of the Second Sea Lord
The Admiralty
London
WC   *19th April 1916*

To Lieutenant Jonathan Marston USN

Please be advised that your nomination as an Observer of His Majesty's Royal Navy has been approved by the Lords Commissioners of the Admiralty effective under my hand from the instant date for an indefinite period until lawful or mutual termination shall take effect from an agreed or appointed date.

Your substantive rank and seniority is recognised in the said Royal Navy in the same manner as it is in your own service, save and except the executive functions of your rank are not to be exercised over RN personnel unless in exceptional circumstances, when you are authorised to give orders, lawful under Admiralty Instructions for the preservation of life, the safety of any ship or vessel of His Majesty's Navy or any personnel thereof in accordance with that rank and seniority.

As to which you and any so commanded by you, shall answer at your or their peril.

Accordingly, you are directed to proceed to join HMS Warspite, *wherever she may be lying, there to report to Captain Philpotts of the said vessel and place yourself under his command save and except any action which in your discretion shall impact negatively on the interests of your Country.*

(Signed)
Hamilton
Vice Admiral.

Jonathan was screaming inside. The newest, fastest dreadnought in the Royal Navy! A *Queen Elizabeth*! And he was joining her! As an observer!

He was aware of five faces watching him expectantly. Schooling his features into imperturbability, he folded his orders and returned them to his pocket.

Looking around, he said, slowly "It's *Warspite*. I am sorry gentlemen but I am joining you!" and he broke into a grin, despite himself.

The compartment erupted in a roar of approval.

4. In the Northern Mists

Thurso Railway Station, 21st April 1916, 09:00 (Good Friday); 58°35' N, 3°32' W

It was an extraordinary scene. The railway station appeared to be nothing much more than a single story granite construction that resembled a cowshed. There were, however, multiple platforms, which would not have disgraced the vast metropolis they had left the previous day. The station gate opened out into a street where a queue of motor lorries was waiting to pick up the train's passengers.[37]

Jonathan realized that the train had brought several hundred people north with minimum fuss to this tiny little town, which was really little more than a fishing village, now completely subsumed into His Majesty's Royal Navy.

The old hands were formed up by efficient petty officers and embarked on the lorries in short order.

Jonathan would have been something at a loss but of course Single and some of the others were heading for the same destination as he was.

"Don't worry about the dunnage[38] sir" said Single, "provided it's properly marked it will find us. This way sir." On the other side of the station were a number of smaller motor vehicles for the officers, Crossley tenders[39]. He swung up into the back with the boys. The driver started the engine and set off through the town and along a road that wound its way beside a cliff, which gave them a very good view of the sea.

It was indeed a very pleasant morning. Dry, sunny but for all that, not very warm. The air smelt fresh and the seagulls' cries were oddly soothing. There was something about the light that was unfamiliar to Jonathan: - a sort of clarity and breadth that he had not seen before. He realized that he was probably about as far north as he had ever been.

It was about ten in the morning and judging by the height of the watery sun, they must be nearly sixty degrees north: - on a par with Cape Farewell which was the Southern tip of Greenland, a good twenty degrees north of New York. Twenty degrees equated to twelve hundred nautical miles. More specifically, New York was twenty degrees of latitude north of Vera Cruz, which meant that Jonathan was as far away from New York as he had been in Vera Cruz the previous year but in the opposite direction.

More dramatically, the diametric opposite position on the globe of where he was standing now, sixty degrees south, was the latitude of the Great Southern Ocean, below Cape Horn, which encompassed the worst weather in the world. This was truly the margin of civilization.

The road wound round to a cosy little harbour with a large enclosed basin. Dominating the northern horizon was a sheer cliff rising out of the sea, with some low-lying land beside it. It was clearly part of a sizeable island.

Again the harbour seemed to be an accretion to a small village, which was wholly out of character with the handful of granite buildings that made up the rest of it.

And it was busy.

4. IN THE NORTHERN MISTS

At the quay alongside was a rather pretty passenger ferry, with lines resembling an old tea clipper. She had, in happier times, transported people on cruises into the Northern Fjords but was now pressed into service with the Royal Navy for the greater good. The transport was heading straight to it.

"That's our ride, sir," said Single "*SS St Sunniva*. She's on her way to the Shetlands but dropping us off in Flotta on her way." Jonathan knew that the Shetland Islands were British but much closer to Norway than Britain, part of the archipelago of ancient islands in the North Eastern Atlantic, bordering on the Arctic Sea.

Jonathan and the boys embarked with several hundred matelots and in no time the ferry had cast off and was heading out of the harbour.

Once they had cleared the heads the ferry headed out to sea. Jonathan would have loved to have his Jane's with him but, learning from his experience in Portsmouth, he had left it in his baggage, which he hoped was somewhere nearby. He literally had no idea where he was.

Apart from the island cliff, there was no land visible to the east or west.

"Pentland Firth, Sir" said Single, "Nasty bit of water at the wrong time. Spin a dreadnought around in its own length if you let it. Should be OK at this stage of the tide though."

The sea state was low but indeed very lumpy in the middle, for no apparent reason. The sun continued to shine, which was rather disconcerting with such a sea state. It suggested that the sea had a turbulence all of its own, independent of the weather.

Notwithstanding that thought, the Ferry thumped its way across without incident. Jonathan could imagine that this strait of water could indeed be an absolute pig in bad weather.

As they approached the low-lying land to the east of the cliff, Jonathan noticed that they were, in fact approaching a small island, which turned into two. They began to pass between ever narrowing bluffs with batteries on the top of them. The guns looked like six-inchers to Jonathan and he counted at least four of them per side.

He could also just make out some camouflaged barrack blocks, which were really quite hard to see against the bright green of the grass covering the grey rocks.

"You must be important sir," said Single who had attached himself to Jonathan since they boarded "We're using the main entrance rather than the tradesman's entrance. This is the way the fleet comes and goes. Service boats like this normally use the Switha Channel over there to port."

There was a rapid flicker of Morse from a signalling lamp mounted on one of the cliffs by the battery. It was answered from the ferry's bridge and reinforced with a blast of her siren. Jonathan suddenly saw that there were two lines of buoys stretching from one side of the channel to the other. He deduced that they must form part of a barrage. They were attended by a number of trawlers, two of whom now blew off steam and began to move, opening the gate for *St. Sunniva,* which passed through, unhindered. Looking aft, Jonathan saw the busy trawlers shutting the gate after them. No one was getting in here uninvited.

4. IN THE NORTHERN MISTS

Rounding a headland they were suddenly in another world. The bay was immense, surrounded by low, treeless green hills, tinged with purple. That was not, however, what caught his attention. The bay was filled with the largest number of ships that Jonathan had ever seen, stretching away in line after line into the misty distance, the watery sun lighting up the innumerable grey hulls.

It was the British Grand Fleet.

The image was so overwhelming that Jonathan couldn't fully take it in. Picket boats and trawlers moved busily across the lines and there was a gentle waft of funnel smoke from the anchored ships as they kept their generators going on a couple of boilers. There were battleships, cruisers and light cruisers all together and overlapping each other.

St Sunniva came round the point and proceeded down the coast of the nearest island, passing close to the nearest line of ships. Jonathan recognized the distinctive shape of an *Iron Duke* class Dreadnought, with its piled bridgework, single mast and improbably thin funnels. They were close enough for him to read the name *Marlborough* on the quarter. She flew the white ensign with one ball from her mast, which meant that she was the home of a Vice Admiral. Next forward was a surprise, a massive bridge with a huge spotting top, a single funnel and a pole main mast. This couldn't be the *Royal Sovereign* that he had seen fitting out in Portsmouth but was clearly a sister ship. He counted eight fifteen-inch guns and seven smaller guns per side, presumably six inchers. This was the very latest Dreadnought in the fleet. The name he read was

Revenge, which was the name of Drake's flagship in the Battle of the Armada.

Jonathan wondered what the old admiral would make of the latest incarnation of his ship's name.

After a slightly older dreadnought (*Hercules*) there was an even greater surprise. An immensely long ship with no less than seven gun turrets all on the centreline.

"Now sir, there's a sight" said the faithful Single, "Originally built for Brazil, then sold to the Turks, we took her over on the outbreak of war and she's now *HMS Agincourt* otherwise known as the 'Gin Palace', Dago officers being so particular about luxury and all. We had to decommission the Royal Yacht to man her. Cocktails on board are a real treat, I'm told. A very fast set." He sounded half envious and half disapproving.

As they were passing, a bugler on the quarterdeck started a cheerful little tune, which was instantly echoed somewhere forward. Some of the matelots on the ferry began to cheer.

Jonathan looked quizzically at Single, who looked at his watch. "Just gone 1150 sir. Grog."

Jonathan was about to enquire further when he noticed that they were then passing a squadron of light cruisers, which were very smart looking ships with flared bows and two or three funnels. Jonathan estimated them as being about 4,000 tons and noted six-inch guns fore and aft.

"4th Light Cruiser Squadron, sir" said Single "'C'class ships, all pretty new and all capable of 30 knots." Jonathan realized that these were the very ships that Sims wanted and which he had been looking up in

4. IN THE NORTHERN MISTS

Jane's. They were very impressive to Jonathan's mind. It was quite clear what they were designed to do: - find the enemy battle fleet, get close enough to report it and then retreat at high speed, fending off all attempts to stop them reporting. At thirty knots[40] there was almost nothing in the world to touch them. Some torpedo boat destroyers may be able to keep up with them but were no match for those six-inch guns.

Jonathan was a fan of the school of thought that said that if a ship looked right, it probably was right. These ships looked right. He noted that they were belted with armour, which was presumably quite light but even two-inch armour would keep out most splinters. It would be no good, of course if hit by an eleven or twelve-inch shell but it was pretty difficult to hit a ship which was shifting a thousand yards – half a sea mile – every minute and no doubt jinking at the same time.

A passage was opening up on the port bow and *St Sunniva* headed straight for it, leaving the immense fleet stretching away to starboard. As far as Jonathan could see there were six or seven lines of dreadnoughts, flanked by cruisers and light cruisers. He could not see any battle cruisers and had to assume that they were elsewhere. That begged the question, if the battle cruisers were elsewhere, what else was elsewhere?

As they passed through a narrow passage between the islands and turned to port Jonathan suddenly saw a new wonder: - in the narrow leads between islands was an immense number of torpedo boat destroyers of the latest design. "Eleventh and twelfth Destroyer Flotillas sir" said Single, "Twenty-one inch tubes and thirty knots."

Their black paintwork made them look particularly threatening. Jonathan was reminded of the Japanese attack on the Russian fleet ten years ago and then remembered that these vessels were three times the size of the Japanese boats and carried four-inch guns as opposed to twelve-pounders, twenty-one inch tubes as opposed to eighteen inch and, more importantly, were much more weatherly than the small torpedo boats, which meant that they could be used in the open ocean rather than being confined to coastal waters.

The Destroyer leaders were even more impressive. They passed *HMS Tipperary* which had no less than six four-inch guns and boasted four funnels, one tall one in front and three squat ones following on.

For once, Jonathan felt that the US Navy could be proud of itself: - the US equivalent of these ships carried eight twenty-one inch tubes, as well as four four-inch guns. They could give a good account of themselves against these vessels, ship to ship but of course the Brits had so many more of them, so that eventually the Americans would be overwhelmed.

Holding that thought, Jonathan suddenly realized that it had a wider implication. Jane's suggested that the Brits had at least forty Dreadnoughts compared to the German's twenty-eight, which meant that, in brutal terms, the Brits could afford to lose a third of their dreadnoughts and still be a match for the Germans.

He felt awed by the sheer might of the British Royal Navy. At that point the recently developed cynical side of Jonathan's character began to make itself felt.

4. IN THE NORTHERN MISTS

When he had first arrived, he had been, in the eyes of the British establishment, an unknown, slightly dubious, tourist. He had progressed to being accused of spying, with a fighting chance of being shot and then, suddenly, became the new best friend of the United Kingdom's Royal Navy. He was in the place where any hostile spy would give his right arm to be, assigned to one of the most powerful battleships in the world. Now, he was passing the greatest fleet the world had ever seen as if he was some sort of reviewing officer. His senses were so distorted that he wondered if Single's throw-away comment that he (Jonathan) must be so important as to pass through the main gate (where he could not avoid seeing the massiveness of the fleet) rather than the 'tradesman's entrance' where he would not, was true.

He could not discount the power of Hall and his cohorts and it actually sounded very much like the Captain's *modus operandi* to divert a ferry to show him (Jonathan) the might of the Royal Navy at its best, solely to make an impression.

Well, thought Jonathan, to himself, it darned well worked!

The ferry began to make its way up yet another lead between lines of service ships. Dominating the scene was a tall black hull with an incongruous single funnel and a stump mast, from which flew a Vice-Admiral's flag. Her stern was towards the approaching ferry and she exhibited a gallery of white-painted windows across it. She was clearly an old ironclad of some sort.

"*Imperieuse*[41] sir," said Single. "Base flagship. We shall send the mail over when we dock."

Fussy drifters and a large tug surrounded the old warrior. Ahead of her was another shock. Apart from the lack of lattice masts, he could have been looking at *Wisconsin*. The guns had been taken out of her and the after bridge had been filled in and provided with windows, so it resembled nothing less than a block of flats. There were a pair of Samson posts fore and aft with derricks and a lazy drift of coal smoke was coming from her twin funnels. "Oho!" Said Single "That's a new one. Wonder why she's here? Looks like an old *Majestic*. Heavy repair maybe, we certainly need that."

The ferry slowly made its way to a pier on the shore and Jonathan became aware of a number of picket boats heading for the same spot. Behind the piers was a collection of buildings and some oil tanks. As the lines were thrown ashore, the parties of matelots began to assemble in their groups. Single rounded up the *Warspite* party and Jonathan saw the cheerful face of AB Bond with them. "'Ello sir!" He said to Jonathan happily, "joining us are you sir? Cor blimey that's wonderful! It's an 'appy crew we are and no mistake!" And then noticing Single he said "Good morning sir. Mr Single ain't it? Pleased to see you got our Yank with you. Look after him for us won't you sir?"

"Of course I shall, sailor, no question of it."

"Oh look sir, 'ere's Mr Donald with the pinnace! Step lively lads, let's hope they've saved our tots!"

It was ever so subtle but Bond had made it clear that although Single was a ranking officer, he was too junior to count for much.

The pinnace was an elegant vessel, fifty feet or so long with covered cabins, a funnel and two prominent ventilators, painted red inside which almost

4. IN THE NORTHERN MISTS

looked like ears. Although she was painted a wartime grey, the upper works were white and the handrails, porthole surrounds and wheel were polished brass, as was the top flare of the funnel. The woodwork was varnished, apart from the deck planking, which was scrubbed. Jonathan noted the mounting for a small gun on the foredeck. A wooden box on the after cabin displayed the name *'Warspite'* in illuminated letters. A cheerful looking Mid was at the helm and brought her alongside the pier opposite the ferry with considerable dash, much to the annoyance of some of the other boats which were not quick enough and had to lie off until the berth was vacated.

Stepping aboard Single said to the mid "well done Donald[42], although God help you if you bend it again!"

"Shan't do that Single, you know me, once beaten, twice shy!"

The *Warspite* party rapidly transferred itself to the boat, with Bond and his mates heading into the forward compartment and the young officers settling down in the wooden saloon. Jonathan elected to remain by the wheel, which was protected by a canvas 'dodger' and sat on the roof of the after cabin, which was a convenient height. Single and Fairthorne took the other side. Flanked by the three of them, Mr Midshipman Donald gleefully rang the telegraph to go astern and back out of the throng.

Once clear, he pushed the telegraph right forward and the boat fairly leaped off down the fairway beside the destroyer lines. Single introduced Jonathan, saying "This is Lieutenant Marston, of the US Navy, come to see how it's done."

"Good morning sir, welcome to our merry band!"

Jonathan was in something of a quandary. In his dash to impress, Donald was going all out on the engine close to lines of anchored ships, which, whilst considerably larger than the pinnace, were still disturbed by its extravagant wash. Had this been a US base, he would have told the youngster to slow down but he felt it was not really his place to do that at this time.

Happily, he was forestalled. On the bridge of a light cruiser, which was acting as a destroyer leader (*Castor* Jonathan noticed) a four ring captain hailed them furiously "Slow down you bloody idiot! 'Ware wash!"

"Do me a favour you two" said Donald, cutting the engine room telegraph dramatically, "cover the name board will you?"

Single immediately moved aft on the cabin roof as if he was trying to get a better view and keep out of the way of the con. Fairthorne leaned back and his greatcoat artistically obscured the name board in a quite satisfactory manner.

"What ship?" demanded the four ringer peremptorily.

"*Malaya* sir. Sorry sir" said Donald.

"Very Good" was the answer.

"You won't half cop it Donald, you prize chump" said Single, amusedly in a low tone.

"You can't lie to a Captain 'D' and expect to get away with it."

4. IN THE NORTHERN MISTS

"Well they'll have to catch me first. Anyway, you're the senior RN Officer in the boat, it's your responsibility!"

"Oh shut up young Donald and get us aboard quick before anything else happens!"

They came out between another two low headlands back into the main fleet anchorage. This time the *Queen Elizabeth's* were the first squadron they saw. At this stage of the tide they were stern on to the approaching pinnace. Jonathan drank in the sight. From this angle, the size of the guns and the effect of the mass of directors, bridgework, masts and tops were impressive.

As it happened the first they approached was *Malaya* with *Warspite* ahead of her. They were passing down the starboard side and Jonathan was close enough to get a very good look at his new home. Painted dark grey with two substantial funnels, she was a very impressive looking vessel. She was longer and lower than *Nevada*, with a forecastle lasting only to X turret and a dropped quarterdeck aft of that. Right aft, almost at the waterline were a pair of embrasures for what would appear to be six-inch guns but they were plated in. Jonathan imagined that they would have been a nightmare to serve in a seaway.

What the embrasures did allow was easy access by the pinnace, which Donald brought alongside with a dash. The bowman stepped onto the deck with the line and held it as Jonathan and Single stepped aboard. An accommodation ladder led to the quarterdeck. Single gestured and said "after you sir."

Mounting, Jonathan found himself confronted with the largest gun turret on the largest quarterdeck he had ever seen. To his eye, used to the clutter of an older style battleship, this deck looked neat and clean of unnecessary obstructions.

He saluted the quarterdeck automatically.

A duty Lieutenant, attended by a midshipman, saluted him.

"Lieutenant Marston, USN, come aboard to join" he said. "I hope you are expecting me"

"Marston, you are very welcome. Hammill, fourth liuetenant at your service. We have indeed been told to expect a Very Important Yank so I assume you must be him!

"I guess I am" said Jonathan, "Although I'm not quite sure how important I may be. I am directed to report to Captain Philpotts."

"Yes, so I understand. The Captain thought you might like to get settled in for a bit and then he'll send for you to talk matters through at some convenient moment. Meanwhile this is Griffiths. Not bad as warts go."

The Midshipman grinned and saluted Jonathan.

"Wart, take Lieutenant Marston to the guest cabin. Hope to see you when I come off watch Marston. Very pleased to have you aboard."

"Aye aye sir" said Griffith the wart "This way please sir, follow me." He led Jonathan forward past the bulk of 'X' barbette to an inviting looking door into the after superstructure.

Entering, Jonathan was suddenly aware of the feel of a warship in commission. It was partly sound, the gentle hum of machinery somewhere, and partly scent; an amalgam of warm oil, corticene,[43] electricity and a faint whiff of cabbage.

4. IN THE NORTHERN MISTS

The door led into a spacious passage with doors either side. "Wardroom to the left sir, correspondence office to the right." There was a large wooden notice board with a glass front on the bulkhead opposite the wardroom. "Ships notice board sir, that's where all orders and events are posted". Beyond the wardroom door, to his left was a business-like rack of rifles nestling against the bulkhead.

Jonathan could see the curved bulk of X barbette to the right, partially screened by a ventilator and a pair of key cabinets. An armed sentry stood beside them. Opposite was a watertight hatch with its armoured lid propped open.

Griffith, lead him past the hatch and down a passage with yet more rifle racks against one side. He opened a sliding door between the rifle racks and a shelf of bugles that led into a comfortable cabin " I think that they have assigned you an orderly. I'll pass the word. He'll see to your dunnage. Welcome aboard sir." And with a quick salute he was gone.

Jonathan began to examine his new home. There was a bed settee, with a shelf over it, a desk and a wardrobe. There was also a suspicious piece of major trunking aft which looked like some form of vent trunk. In such a high - powered vessel that might be intrusive at speed.

There was suddenly a knock on the door. Jonathan opened it. The Brits obviously believed in doors to cabins, unlike the US Navy. It was Griffith. "Sorry sir, forgot to say, officer's heads[44] up the companionway the other side of the engine room vent on the other side of the flat, sir."

"Thank you Mr Griffith. Carry on please."

"Aye aye sir." And he was off again.

Shortly afterwards there was another knock at the door. This one sounded rather more discrete, almost apologetic. "Come" said Jonathan.

It was a Royal Marine in Khaki.

"Brown sir" he said, "I have been allocated as your orderly sir."

"Good to meet you Brown. I guess I am going to need a little bit of assistance, this is all new to me."

"That presents no difficulty sir, I was in service before I enlisted. I have your dunnage sir. Shall I stow it for you?"

"Please" said Jonathan removing his overcoat. Brown eyed his uniform and said, approvingly, "very fine sir, if I may say so. An excellent piece of tailoring."

Almost immediately there was yet another knock at the door. Jonathan was clearly very popular. This time it was Hammill. Jonathan had been vaguely aware of the watch changing, with the faint sound of a bell.

"Are you settling in alright Marston?" he asked. "Indeed I am" said Jonathan.

"Lunch in the wardroom at 1300. You may like to come a little early and have a snifter and meet some of the chaps. The drill is to come in through the lobby by the companionway. I shall be there myself in a jiffy. Hope to see you then."

Jonathan was charmed. This was a far cry from the stuffy, standoffish Brits he was expecting.

4. IN THE NORTHERN MISTS

Wardroom, HMS Warspite, 21st April 1916 (Good Friday) 1230 hrs 58°52" N 3°8" W. Outer Battleship Line, Scapa Flow.

The wardroom anteroom was a very comfortable space, filled with officers; it boasted a cheery stove with leather settees and chairs. There was a comfortable fug of tobacco smoke and a buzz of conversation. Jonathan made his way in through the door and looked around him. He was very conscious of his new uniform and of course, being below decks, he was carrying his cap with its telltale badge under his arm. He did, however, make sure that its US Navy Eagle was prominently to the front.

Hammill was waiting for him near the door and immediately turned when Jonathan opened it.

"And here he is!" he said loudly, "Gentlemen, I give you Lieutenant Jonathan Marston of the United States' Navy, our latest acquisition!"

There were cheers and suddenly everyone wanted to shake his hand or slap him on the back, "Very well come old boy!" "How lovely to see you yank!" "Come and have a drink."

There was no doubt what the officers of *HMS Warspite* thought of the Americans.

"Stow the cap behind the door," said Hammill and Jonathan saw that there was a series of hangers for caps and coats. "We don't really wear 'em below deck unless on duty." That too was a refreshing change from US practice.

After doing so, Jonathan turned and suddenly found himself in the middle of a cheerful group of officers; a glass of something was thrust into his unprotesting hand. A detached part of him noticed that

Hammill had pronounced lieutenant in the American fashion. He suddenly felt very welcome.

"Well, gentlemen, it is an honour to be here. May the guest be worthy of the welcome!" and he took a swig from the glass. It was clearly spirituous but had a refreshing sparkle to it.

"We'd heard that you were coming," said one officer, "but it's absolutely spiffing to have you here with us. That's one in the eye for the flagship!"

"Oh?" Said Jonathan, "is there some problem with the flagship?"

"Too bloody right" said a two-ringer, vehemently "we had a difference of opinion last year, in which they cocked up the signal and if the skipper hadn't done what he did the B would have been at the bottom of the deep blue sea!"

"Tell me more," said Jonathan.

"Well there we were, proceeding at sixteen knots in line ahead. *Barham,* as Flag was leading, we were next astern at two and a half cables. Bloody idiots hoisted G8, reduction in speed to 8 knots, which was plain ridiculous. Our signal party read it as 18 knots and we damn near sank her. Skipper went hard astern and reduced the impact tremendously."

"What happened in the end?" asked Jonathan.

"Court of enquiry and censure for the Skipper. Bloody unfair in my view. Bloody stupid orders!"

The other officers reacted with shouts of "here here" and "damn' shame" with one even going as far as to say "disgraceful". It was clear that the Flagship was not the toast of the day in *Warspite.*

Suddenly, Jonathan became aware of a pair of eyes boring into him. Following their gaze he saw, to

4. IN THE NORTHERN MISTS

his surprise, a Commander who was incidental in his arrest for spying in Portsmouth. The Commander was looking at him in a manner that was far from welcoming. He was standing a little way away and clutching a glass of something clear. He was looking straight at Jonathan.

"What the Hell do you think you're doing here?" He asked. It was not a friendly enquiry.

"Orders, sir" said Jonathan, evenly. "Appointed as supernumerary US Naval Liaison Officer to this ship."

"You can no doubt produce them Lieutenant?" He asked.

"Indeed sir." He said reaching into the breast pocket of his RN style reefer jacket.

The Commander looked at the proffered orders for some time and then folded them and handed them back to Jonathan.

"I shall check these with the Captain. Keep him under close observation gentlemen, please." And he left without further ado.

"What was that all about?" asked Hammill, clearly bewildered.

"Oh, we met in Portsmouth," said Jonathan. He thought I was a spy and I was arrested on his say so.

"Really?" Asked Hamill. "Hodgson is a bit preachy but he's a decent fellow for all that."

"Anyway" said another, "delighted to see you, Yank. Tell us about yourself"

"Well" said Jonathan, "not much to say really. I'm a gunnery man, just posted here from a training squadron. I'm really looking forward to seeing how the Royal Navy operates."

"Pretty much in the dark for most of it old boy" said another, perched on a comfortable red leather club fender around an electric fire, "kept in the dark and fed on bullshit, for the most part. We might as well be the mushroom service."

"How do you spend your time?" Asked Jonathan.

"Trying to get the Hun to come out mostly" said Hammill. "The trouble is that the buggers won't play. We do a sweep most weeks but get sod all. Father is at the end of his tether. Everything he tries ends up without a result. We've made two sweeps this month, as far as the Norwegian Coast but we've seen nothing. We try and attack the zeppelin and submarine stations with our light forces but the Germans sit in harbour and do nothing. It is, as Dickens would have it, werry wexing."

"Father, that is the c-in-c, is trying all sorts of things. We even have a big aircraft carrier, which joined us last month. Officially she is an armed liner but they have put a huge deck over all, which means that they can fly off airplanes without having to stop to lower 'em but simply drop them off down a trolley, into the wind."

"I'm sorry," said Jonathan, who was trying to keep up.

"Simple really" said Hammill. "She's an ex-Cunarder capable of nineteen knots. She only needs a wind of twenty knots and they can just let the airplanes take off on their own!"

It sounded fascinating. His thoughts immediately went back to Admiral Fiske and his idea of aerial torpedoes. It turned out that Admiral Jellicoe was thinking along the same lines. He had pressed the

4. IN THE NORTHERN MISTS

authorities to provide a flying off deck and there were already torpedo-carrying airplanes in service. "Sank a couple of Turks in the Aegean last year" he was told.

The session developed seamlessly with Jonathan's glass being constantly refilled, something, which he did not notice.

He suddenly became aware of a bugle being played outside the flat. Everyone stopped and listened. After the short call, everyone brightened a little.

"Orders, Marston" said Hammill, delighted, "now you'll see something. Hang on and we'll find out what's going on" and he stepped through the door. Other Officers began to move in various directions. Jonathan heard someone say "probably another bally sweep, still, it gets us out of this place."

"Preparatory" said Hammill stepping back into the wardroom. "Raise steam for eighteen knots at two hours notice. There will be a time signal next."

"Time for lunch in any event. Better than bowls" said someone. Jonathan remembered the old story of Sir Francis Drake finishing his game of bowls before setting off to fight the Spanish Armada. Of course, the unromantic part of his Northern soul reminded him that the sort of ships that Drake commanded were dependent upon the tides and wind, so that it was perfectly possible that Drake's fleet couldn't sail at the time the Spanish were sighted but would have to wait a couple of hours for the tide and wind to be right but it wasn't worth spoiling a good story for an over literal appreciation of the alternatives on offer. Although they were not normally dependent upon the tide, modern dreadnoughts needed at least two hours to raise steam from cold boilers. Before that they were pretty powerless. The intervening time might just as well be spent in having lunch as playing bowls.

The lunch was another congenial affair and to Jonathan's surprise, wine was served.

He was just enjoying his pudding, when the Commander from Portsmouth came in. He had not been lunching with the other officers and Jonathan hadn't seen him since their conversation. He made his way directly to Jonathan and said, "It seems that I owe you an apology Marston, your appointment is indeed regular. No hard feelings I hope?" And to Jonathan's surprise and embarrassment he had out his hand. Awkwardly, Jonathan half got to his feet to shake it. "No problem, sir, I guess you were right to be concerned. I was acting a little suspiciously."

"Too right you were but at least it was all sorted out in the end. May I stand you a drink?"

That seemed like a good idea to Jonathan, in the warm glow of company. "Well that's mighty handsome in you sir but are you going to join me?"

"Not today, I am afraid Marston but you go ahead. Simmonds, a drop of Nelson's blood for this officer! On my tab."

"Aye aye sir. One tot coming up." And then enquiringly, "Neaters sir?"

"Oh definitely, I should have thought." said the other. "Have you ever had rum Marston?"

He had not, but when the thick, dark liquid was brought the scent instantly transported him back to the gun deck of *HMS Victory*. "Traditionally, of course" said Hodgson "it is downed in one but that is hardly fair on a novice. Enjoy it Marston. Treat it like a decent

4. IN THE NORTHERN MISTS

brandy. Anyway, must dash. See you soon." And he was off.

The rum was indeed delightful. Smooth and satisfying it went down very well.

After lunch, various officers left and Jonathan found himself sitting in a comfortable armchair by the fire with a comic paper. He was in that happy state of relaxation when he knew that he had had just a little too much to drink, was replete with a decent meal and had a well-filled pipe to enjoy.

His reverie was interrupted by a knock on the door. It was a midshipman with a message. The captain wanted to see him at 1420, which was, he noted in ten minutes time.

Not for the first time Jonathan cursed his easy-going nature. He knew that the captain was going to be summoning him. He knew that he had the opportunity of a lifetime to serve his country but most importantly, he knew that as a result of the alcohol that he had drunk, he was not in the best shape to meet a senior captain in the Royal Navy or to act as an ambassador for his country.

He looked at the servery to see if he could grab a coffee but the servery was empty and there was no one around that he could ask.

In an ideal world, he would like to have blamed his warm welcome; his hosts and in particular Commander Hodgson who had virtually forced the stuff down his throat but he realized that was an abnegation of responsibility. He should have known better.

He dropped the comic paper on the table and got to his feet with the intention of getting some fresh air on the quarterdeck. Going through the door in the superstructure, Jonathan suddenly realized that that was a big mistake. The chilly air cut deeply into his lungs and far from soothing his intoxication, it appeared to increase it. Worried about his breath, he began to breathe through his mouth, which only resulted in a semi-frozen tongue and an even more heightened sense of dizziness. The sheer strangeness of the anchorage to his eyes did not assist. The low, treeless, green hills, the grey ships and grey-blue water, with the omnipresent trawlers going about their business was not a familiar sight. In short it was seriously disorientating.

A midshipman was approaching him. "Lieutenant Marston?" he enquired.

"Yes," said Marston.

"Captain requests the pleasure of your company, please sir."

"Aye aye" said Jonathan

"Follow me please sir," said the youngster,

There was no alternative. The youngster led him through the door and along the passage past the wardroom and the office to a door, which, to Jonathan's surprise, was just round the corner from his own cabin. The mid knocked and a voice from within said "Come". The Cabin was large and well lit by two scuttles, which opened out onto the quarterdeck. Captain Philpotts was seated at a round table directly opposite the door.

He was an intimidating man. Seated at his table, the first thing that Jonathan was aware of was that the captain was wearing a wing collar, unlike most of his officers. He had neatly parted dark hair with flecks of grey over the temples. Lean features were coupled with a direct, no nonsense gaze from under level eyebrows.

4. IN THE NORTHERN MISTS

"Do come in, Marston. Sit yourself down," he said, as Marston was ushered into his presence,

Jonathan took a seat on the other side of the table.

"Push off wart" said the Captain, shortly and the midshipman vanished instantly, leaving Jonathan alone with the Captain, who was looking at him through clear grey eyes. It was not a comfortable experience. Jonathan hadn't much experience of Captains RN, but if this man, who exuded competent authority, was typical, they were a force to be reckoned with.

"So Lieutenant," said the Captain, "You are here to observe us

"Yes, sir" said Jonathan, carefully.

"What have you seen so far?"

"A great deal to impress sir" That was true.

"In what way?" This was worse than his previous examinations, including those by Savage, the Scotland Yard detective. The Captain was clearly very perceptive and after his lunchtime session, Jonathan felt that he was simply not up to this level of questioning.

He took refuge in obfuscation.

"In a many ways sir. The Royal Navy is clearly a formidable force." To Jonathan's ears, something was not quite right about that phrase. It came out as "frmidble-ble frce".

" I see Lieutenant," said the Captain. "And what does the US Navy make of this conflict?"

It was a very challenging question, which required an answer that Jonathan was not, in his present state, prepared to even consider. His first, irrational instinct was to tap his nose and say words to the effect of "never you mind, we have it all sorted in

75

Washington" but some vestiges of decency reminded him that this was a very unwise course of action.

What he did say was " The RN is very good but there have been some – problems."

"What do you mean Lieutenant?"

"Well...Coroneal and ....things." He wanted to say "Dardanelles" but he was wary about trying to pronounce it. He thought he might have pronounced Coronel incorrectly but tried to move on. As he opened his mouth he was overtaken by a hiccough, which he tried to stifle but of course that only made it worse.

"Are you quite alright Lieutenant?" asked the Captain.

"Yes sir, I'm absolutely fine" and he found that he was treating the Captain to a beaming smile. "Been made very...welcome sir." His rebellious system interposed another hiccough

"I can see that," said the Captain dryly. "I suppose my officers have been entertaining you?"

"Yes, sir"

"Did the entertainment include rum by any chance?"

"Yes, sir"

"And no doubt they told you that it was quite innocuous?"

Jonathan beamed and hiccoughed again.

"No doubt they also told you that it had to be drunk down in one?"

"Yes, sir."

"I thought so," said the Captain. "Navy rum, Mr Marston, is one hundred and forty percent proof, which means that it is roughly twice as strong as whiskey. That is why it is always served with three parts water. I shall be having words with my officers but in the mean time I suggest that you retire to your cabin for a lie down. We shall be departing at midnight. If you join me in my sea cabin at 2330, we can resume our little talk.

"Meanwhile, could you ask my messenger to pass the word for Commander Walwyn as you leave?"

"Aye aye sir" Jonathan managed.

"In the office opposite."

"Thank you sir"

In fact he didn't have to go to the office. As he shut the cabin door he saw a Commander hovering outside. "Hello" said the Commander in a friendly way "You must be our Yank. Walwyn's the name; I hope we can give you something of what you want. If you need anything, feel free to ask me directly"

"WALWYN!" came a shout from within. "In here. Now!"

With a nervous smile, the Commander straightened his tie and squared his shoulders as he stepped up to the door.

Jonathan followed the bulkhead round the corner until he reached his own cabin. Carefully he removed his jacket, tie and shoes and lay down on the bed. It felt as if there was a rough sea outside and the bed was moving in a decidedly odd fashion.

Notwithstanding that, Jonathan fell asleep almost straight away.

5. Night Departure

HMS Warspite, 21ˢᵗ April 1916

Jonathan woke quite naturally. The ingrained habits of fifteen years watch keeping kicked in immediately, nurtured, no doubt by the hum of machinery and the odours of a warship. He noticed that there was a jug of water by the bunk, with a glass, ready for his awakening. He also noticed that there was a twist of white paper beside the glass.

Looking at his watch, Jonathan saw that it was 2000, just at the end of the last dogwatch.

He was aware of the bustle of the change of watch and the ache behind his eyes as well as a slight discomfort in his stomach. "Oh Hell!" He thought. "What a first impression to make!" Thinking back over the whole episode he realized that he had been guilty of a solecism worthy of the greenest of greenhorns. He had, he supposed, been overwhelmed by his welcome, not to mention the sheer relief of finally getting close to what he was here to do.

The Captain had been a model of understanding - towards Jonathan – (who was, of course, his guest) but remembering the summoning of Walwyn, Jonathan doubted that he would like to be in that officer's shoes.

There was a discrete opening of the door and Brown entered quietly. "Good evening sir" he said. "I have taken the liberty of providing you with some water and some liver salts."

"Thank you Brown. Very thoughtful of you."

"Yes sir. I had heard that the wardroom had made you welcome."

"They sure did."

"I believe that words have been had. In the mean time, may I recommend the liver salts? There will be scratch supper in the wardroom before evening quarters, in view of the fact that we are sailing tonight" and he was gone.

Jonathan was in that wobbly state whereby he was no longer intoxicated but was not wholly sober. He suspected that there would be a headache in the offing if he allowed it to happen.

Opening the paper twist, he emptied the white powder into a glass of water that resulted in a reassuring fizz.

After downing it and washing his face, Jonathan felt ready to face the wardroom.

As he entered the first person he saw was Hodgson.

"I say old chap," he said on seeing Jonathan. "I'm frightfully sorry about this morning, I simply wasn't thinking. You must think me a terrible oik."

"Oh that's alright, sir," said Jonathan, "I should have been thinking myself. We haven't had liquor aboard ship for some time and I am not, what you would call a drinking man much anyway."

"Frank, please, when we are in the Mess. It looks like we got off to a bad start and I've made it worse since. Anyway, have a sandwich and a cup of tea and get yourself set up for tonight's little jaunt."

Jonathan thought. This man could be a useful friend, so he put out his hand and said "Jonathan. Will you join me?"

5. NIGHT DEPARTURE

"Not just now, I'm afraid," said Frank, "I've had my ration for the day but I shall happily accompany you and watch you eat."

There were plates of thick cut sandwiches on the mess tables and groups of officers were gathered round engaged in various activities.

To Jonathan's surprise he saw that a fairly large group was engaged in rope work. Seeing Jonathan's quizzical look, Frank said, "Making rope grommets for shells. The army needs thousands of the things, so most of the officers in the fleet spend some time making them in their spare time. Every so often we pack up a load and send them across to France."

"Aren't there factories for that?" said Jonathan.

"Oddly, no. Making them by hand is by far the best method and who better to do it than otherwise idle NO's?"

"Are you idle?" asked Jonathan, curiously.

"Well no, not really" said the other. "We are perpetually out on sweeps here but we never see very much. The Army is suffering so many casualties, that it makes us feel that we are doing something useful at least."

"How often do you sweep?" asked Jonathan.

"Well for the first couple of years we never spent any time in port at all. There were no proper defences and Father would only allow us to spend enough time in harbour to coal ship. It was pretty tough, believe me."

"And now?" asked Jonathan.

"Well, Scapa has some decent fortifications now and we spend a little more time here but truth to tell, we may as well be at sea. There's precious little here apart from some golf, a bit of stalking and plenty of hiking for them as wants it."

"What about the men?" asked Jonathan, "How do your keep them amused?"

"Bread and circuses mostly. That is, lots of sport; football, boxing, cricket. Regattas, pulling races, all the usual stuff. Why we even have our own theatre ship for our sods' opera."

Jonathan was familiar with the term: - it usually meant a scratch show put on by the ships' company for their own amusement.

"Actually," said Frank, "Some of this theatrical stuff is really rather good."

After his supper, Frank showed him the way to the conning tower and something of the upper deck. He said that he was going along to the charthouse to make sure all was ready for sailing and invited Jonathan to accompany him.

"There are really two ways to go" he said "Along the forecastle deck past the boats and funnels in the open air, or else through the battery. Open air can be cold and wet, battery can be crowded. It's not too bad tonight, so we'll take the foc'sle. They'll pipe hands for leaving harbour shortly, so the battery will be pretty busy with bodies checking the guns and so on."

Jonathan's overwhelming impression was that of size. This ship was half as long again as *Wisconsin* and considerably longer than *Nevada*. Again the upper works seemed much less cluttered than either of those ships. The massive funnels and elaborate bridgework dominated everything. Jonathan's professional eye noted directors for the secondary battery as well as the main battery. This was truly state of the art.

Frank, it would seem, was the Commander (N) or Navigating officer. It was a mark of the importance of that

5. NIGHT DEPARTURE

branch of the service that British ships had no less than three senior officers under the Captain; the Commander (which corresponded to the Executive officer in American parlance) the Commander (N) who was responsible for navigation and the Commander (E) who was responsible for the machinery. Each had a staff of more junior officers under them. In the US service, these posts were typically held by more junior men.

Obviously an enthusiast for his specialization, Frank took Jonathan up a series of steep ladders and into the bridge structure itself. It was, apparently, the chartroom, which was a comfortable space near the top, where the charts were kept and the navigation was worked out.

The Captain's sea cabin, he learned was on the same level and on the opposite side of the platform.

A lieutenant and an attentive mid were poring over a well-used chart and a ring binder. There was a chronometer in a prominent position on the bulkhead. Jonathan checked his wristwatch and was pleased to see that his watch was living up to its reputation: - spot on. He recognized the Lieutenant as one he had met that morning. "Oh, hello Marston" he said as they came in "Sorry about this forenoon, we all got a frightful rocket from the Captain. No hard feelings I trust?"

"Well, I guess I'll survive" he said. Indeed the decidedly cool air of an April evening was beginning to have its effect. Besides, he was far too excited to feel hung over.

"Tidal stream?" asked Frank. "Slack water at 2145, sir" said the Mid. "Flow will be maximum in the Firth at 0110 sir."

"Time of clearing Swona?"

The Mid consulted the pilot and made some calculations in a pocket book. "0045 Sir" he said.

"Bugger!" said Frank "That means we'll hit the tide rip just at the wrong moment. Slap bang in the middle of it. Still, can't be helped. Pass the word to the cox'n would you wart? Tell him to be on the *qui vive* for the tide rip."

"Aye aye sir" he said, slipping out of the charthouse.

"There are some of the strongest streams in the world around here Jonathan," said Frank "eight knots straight across our course and the trouble is that it hits you suddenly, just as you pass Swona. Look at this" and he pulled out a smaller chart with tidal streams marked on it. It was a nightmare, resembling nothing less than the scrawlings of a lunatic. Some of the whorls were annotated with rather worrying names like the "Merry Men of Mey" the "Duncansby Race" and the "Swelkie".

"That's the difficult one" said Frank, pointing to an elaborate swirl to the north of Stroma, a little way to the south of the entrance to Scapa Flow, which, Jonathan realized looking at the place on the chart, was an immense bay surrounded by islands.

"The Swelkie, which, I am reliably informed, is Old Norse for 'The Swallower'. Legend has it that it is caused by a Sea Witch grinding salt to keep the seas salty. Get caught in that and you are in real trouble.

"We, however, will have more trouble with that one," pointing to what looked like a wall running north to south slightly to the west of the island called Stroma, "the 'Merry Men of Mey' which, you will see forms a natural breakwater. Slack water to the east of it and 10 knots to the west. We are tasked east of Swona and then north of the Skerries, here, and then out through the Firth to the east.

5. NIGHT DEPARTURE

We will go from nothing to an 8-knot tiderip at 90 degrees and back again in a few seconds. Then we hit the eddy around the Skerries, which takes you the other way. You can look a frightful fool if you end up doing a pirouette in full sight of the flagship!"

Indeed, looking at the chart with a professional eye, Jonathan realized that this anchorage, marvellous though it was, was a navigator's nightmare. The combination of fierce tidal streams and rocky shores was not a good one.

Frank looked at his watch and said "I expect we shall go to Harbour Stations about 2200. I shall stay here but you are very welcome to explore a bit if you choose to. I should keep away from the Mess decks though, Bad form after rounds and just before going to sea."

Jonathan took the opportunity for a stroll around the bridge and the upper deck. The bridge was much more elaborate than that of *Nevada*.

In that ship there was a conning tower, a charthouse and bridge wings. The conning tower was officially the armoured position from where the ship was worked. In this ship, however, abaft of the conning tower was a tower construction of three decks with solid looking cabins on them. At the lower levels there were searchlights, searchlight directors and some bunker-like structures with sinister looking sighting slits in them as well as a clutter of vents, tanks and hoists of various sorts.

The intake vents below the funnels were taking in the cold night air with an audible rushing sound.

In contrast to the rest of the ship, the bridge structure was crammed with equipment, some of it wholly unfamiliar to Jonathan. The structure was also filling up with various people of all grades even though to Jonathan's knowledge no formal sounding of quarters had been made. There was a definite air of expectation about them. It was not exactly excitement, indeed quite the reverse. It was more a sense of professional readiness. He saw lookouts cleaning binoculars and fitting them to their mounts, the same was being done with telescopes, which appeared to be attached to some sort of bearing indicator (of which there were several). After a circuit of the lowest level, which was the flag deck, where the signalling party was preparing the flag lockers under the supervision of a warrant officer, he thought he would climb to the top of the edifice, a good forty feet above his head.

As he ascended the ladders giving access to the top, he was aware of a tremble underfoot as some piece of machinery was tested.

When he eventually reached it, he was in a different world. At the very top was a platform that had the gyro repeater compass, a magnetic compass and a rangefinder. There were banks of voice pipes on either side of the island, which suggested that the officers directing operations preferred to be here. Jonathan could understand that, as the visibility was far superior to the slits in the thirteen-inch armour of the conning tower. Thinking about it, he was actually nearly as high above the water as the fighting top of an old time sailing frigate like the *Constitution*. Again, it reminded him of how big this ship actually was.

He saw that there was a shelter for the watch keepers, telegraphs and various range taking instruments.

In contrast to the dim blue light below, here he was illuminated solely by the stars that peeped out between wisps of cloud. The night was cold but clear enough. There was a large binnacle on a raised platform in front of him,

5. NIGHT DEPARTURE

with a gyro compass repeater aft of that. There were neat ranks of voice pipes against the port and starboard rails. It was an indication of how complex a machine this ship was. Stepping onto the platform, he found that he had a good view of the foc'sle below, which seemed to be bustling. Every so often there was the reflected glow of an electric flashlight. Above him to the rear he was aware of the tripod mast with yet more platforms on it. There was a brief whiff of funnel smoke and up here the subdued roar of the ventilating fans below was very apparent. The ship trembled again and seemed eager to be off.

Looking around him Jonathan realized that the starlight illuminated the next ship ahead and the adjacent ship in the neighbouring column. The mast and funnels masked his view aft. He realized that this scene was being repeated on half a hundred warships simultaneously. Moving forward, he grasped the rail that, he noticed, incorporated a glass screen, which could be unfolded to provide some protection from the elements to the watch keepers up here.

Looking down, he wondered what it would be like to be in charge of this monster of a ship.

"Enjoying yourself Marston?' came a voice behind him. With a start, Jonathan turned to see Commander Walwyn behind him, looking quizzically at him.

"Indeed I am sir," said Jonathan. "This ship is mighty impressive".

"She is that," said Walwyn moving forward companionably, lighting his pipe.

"I like to come up here myself for a bit of peace before sailing" he said, drawing on his pipe, with the glow illuminating his rather handsome face. "Sometimes it's the only place no-one bothers you. And if they do, you know that it's pretty important!"

"It is rather a long way up," agreed Jonathan.

"We shall be weighing in three-quarters of an hour. Scheduled to be at midnight plus six. Four minutes after the flagship and two minutes after *Valiant*. *Malaya* will be two minutes after us. Then the Second Battle Squadron, the Fourth with Father, followed by all the rest. All done by stopwatch. With two orders. Pretty straightforward really."

Not for the first time, Jonathan found himself seriously impressed. One of the most difficult exercises was to get a fleet to sea in an orderly manner. To do it with such a large fleet was nothing short of a miracle, especially in darkness.

"Do we know what we are doing, sir?" Asked Jonathan.

"Oh, another flap" said the other. "Usual stuff. Some bod in the Admiralty has a sniff that the Bosh are coming out, so we'll set off and see if we can spoil his fun."

"And shall we?" asked Jonathan

"Who knows old boy? They're pretty leery of us and won't engage if they can possibly help it. Damned upsetting really."

He knocked his pipe out on the rail and said "Shouldn't really be smoking on the upper deck after lights out but rank hath its privileges sometimes. Rules are for the obedience of fools and the guidance of wise men. Still, wouldn't do for some busybody on another ship to report it."

"Would that be possible sir?" asked Jonathan.

"Oh indeed" said Walwyn "you wouldn't believe how far away you can see a match flare and of course it only requires one idiot to give away the position of the

5. NIGHT DEPARTURE

entire fleet. In the right circumstances I would report it myself if I saw it in another ship. Should be OK tonight though. Too damn' bright for my liking."

"Do you have much trouble with submarines sir?" Asked Jonathan, interested.

"Not really at this stage, the entrance is too difficult for 'em but that doesn't stop some other people panicking. I believe that there was a right to-do up here in '14 with the whole place chasing an imaginary submarine. No, the trouble is when we get towards our rendezvous. The Hun tries to lay his submarines across our course in the hope of hitting one of us."

"And does he succeed?"

Walwyn smiled. "Not often, Marston, not often. We are usually too fast and zigzagging. Buggers up his aim a treat!"

"May I ask what we are rendezvousing with?" said Jonathan.

"I don't see why not," said Walwyn, "we do have instructions to accommodate you as far as we can. It'll be the 3rd Battle Squadron from Cromarty and the Battle Cruiser Force from Rosyth."

Jonathan briefly did the math. That would amount to about to about twenty-eight or twenty-nine dreadnoughts plus nine or ten battle cruisers and scouting cruisers and torpedo boat destroyers.

"Wow!" said Jonathan, unintentionally.

"It does mean that you have to keep your wits about you, that many ships in that small area can be pretty hairy but everyone knows their place. Probably sounds worse than it is."

They were interrupted by more another bugle call and a flurry of bos'uns pipes with shouts of "Special sea duty men! Special sea duty men!"

"Right" said Walwyn. "It's the foc'sle for me and you for your chat with the Captain. He was in his sea cabin when I left him ten minutes ago. Know where it is?"

"One platform below, starboard side?" queried Jonathan.

"That's the ticket," said Walwyn. "Don't be put off. He's a decent enough cove underneath it all."

Jonathan made his way down to the sea cabin and knocked on the door.

"Come," said a voice and Jonathan entered. It was quite a contrast to the grandeur of the cabin aft. This was a no-nonsense sleeping place, with a bunk, a chest of drawers and nothing much else.

"Sit down Marston" said the captain, indicating a stool by the chest. "Feeling better?"

"Aye sir. I would just like to apologize...."

"Oh don't worry about it Marston. You aren't the first to be gulled by the wardroom and no doubt you shan't be the last. Just don't let it happen again. There's a good chap."

"No sir. Certainly not sir."

"So tell me about yourself Marston. What makes you tick?"

"Well sir, I am a gunnery man basically, but I have done some teaching and a bit of research into the war"

"Have you indeed?" said the Captain, clearly interested.

'Aye sir, you see, when this job came up I didn't really know what it was and I thought it might be some sort

5. NIGHT DEPARTURE

of staff job, so I read all I could about it. No substitute, of course, for the real thing."

"And what do you make of it so far?"

Jonathan was far more clued up on the war since that similar conversation back in the States, which seemed ages ago. He had formed a much better evidenced view of the belligerents, particularly the all-important morale aspect.

"I am very favourably impressed by the allies sir. I crossed by steamer and saw the blockade at first hand. I have experienced an air raid and the aftermath of the torpedoing of a merchant vessel without warning. I have seen some of the RN's new materiel which is impressive."

"Ah yes" said the captain, "Hodgson told me about that. Said you were taken up as a spy on his say so."

"Well I was making notes about the *Royal Sovereign* and a new large submarine which nearly sank me. I can't really blame him and he has apologized since."

"He is a good man, in that way. Damn fine navigator too. Lucky you weren't shot, the way things are."

"Well sir, I seem to have made some impression on the spooks. I met Captain Hall in London and we seemed to get on pretty well."

"Did you indeed?" said the Captain. "Did you count your fingers after shaking hands with him?"

It seemed that Captain Hall's reputation preceded him.

"Not quite, sir but I did make him laugh."

"Must have been someone else's misfortune then."

The conversation continued and Jonathan found, to his surprise that this rather forbidding looking man was actually immensely human and appeared genuinely to care about Jonathan and his mission. He learned that he had the run of the ship save for the Transmitting Station far below, where the guns were directed and the Wireless Telegraphy shack between the funnels. "All pretty secret, Marston but no doubt if you have to know someone will tell you."

Saturday 22nd April 1916, North Sea, 57° 15' N, 1° 57' E, HMS Warspite 1100

    The scene was one of the most extraordinary that Jonathan had ever seen. From horizon to horizon the sea was filled with ships in ordered columns. Jonathan had been on the compass platform at the very top of the fore bridge for the departure and had found it exhilarating. As he had anticipated, the Captain had chosen to oversee the operation from there, rather than in the more restricted conning tower forward. Jonathan could appreciate the wisdom of that as the ship ahead hauled in her anchor and got under weigh. The only light that could be seen was a dim blue one at the base of the ensign staff right at the stern. Frank, who was actually taking *Warspite* out, had told him that it was only visible for a narrow arc across the stern, so that if the following ship was out of position by much, the column was likely to be lost.

    Warspite's own anchor came home with the familiar clanking sound and as soon as a red light was waved from the forecastle, to show that the anchor was free, Frank gave orders for engine revolutions bringing the ship speed up to eight knots on the engines. The vagaries of the tidal stream meant that the ship was facing the way that they were leaving which meant that she picked up weigh smoothly in the wake of the next ahead.

    Frank was standing by with a stopwatch, timing everything. The manoeuvres required to come round the tip of the anchorage (the island of Flotta, Jonathan now knew

5. NIGHT DEPARTURE

from looking at the chart) were carried out in accordance with his mark, passed down the voice pipe.

Once they had come round the tip of Flotta they started to move down the fairway at twelve knots, increasing to fifteen as they approached Swona.

"Stand by Quartermaster," said Frank leaning into a voice pipe "Passing Swona in two." then turning to Jonathan he said, "Just watch *Valiant's* stern light now and you'll see something."

With his eyes firmly on the dim blue light bearing steady dead ahead, Jonathan was astonished to see it suddenly twitch and dance around like a firefly. He realized that it must be as the tiderip caught the battleship. He was watching 26,000 tons of steel tossed around a like a cockboat.

Almost as suddenly it steadied again. "Pretty fair" said Frank. "Now it's our turn" and leaning forward he said into the voice pipe "passing the lee now" and almost instantly, Jonathan felt his own ship twitch like a startled horse as the moving mass of water caught it. Jonathan felt the instant press of the wheel as the quartermaster turned into the flood and then back again. Then they too steadied once more.

"Well done QM" said Frank, looking at his watch. "Starboard thirty in four minutes." Turning to Jonathan he said, "Now it gets interesting. We have a ten-knot tide stream under our backside with fifteen knots indicated speed through the water; we are doing twenty-five knots over the bottom. It means that things happen very quickly." As the manoeuvre was executed Jonathan was aware of the stern light of *Valiant* swimming back into focus ahead of them. "Got him QM?" asked Frank down the voice pipe.

Obviously the answer was in the affirmative as Frank then said "Well done. Keep on him."

He then turned aft and called to the lookouts stationed on either side of the platform "Keep on him men. Watch for any bearing change." Turning to Jonathan he said, "We're fine now but the problem is keeping station. At this state we are twelve and a half cables apart, two thousand five hundred yards. These ships are three cables long, which means that *Valiant's* stern is just under nineteen hundred yards ahead of us, or about ninety seconds steaming at this speed."

"How do you keep an eye on that?" Asked Jonathan, fascinated.

"Mostly by mark 1 eyeball but I do take the occasional rangefinder fix if I can get the loom of the funnels or bridge." The rangefinder was a wonderful gadget, which showed whether the viewer was approaching or receding from an object instantaneously.

And now, some hours later they were proceeding at seventeen knots in a column of four dreadnoughts, five hundred yards behind *Valiant* which was five hundred yards behind *Barham* in the lead. Looking aft, in the misty light of a North Sea forenoon, Jonathan could see the fourth member of the squadron *Malaya* five hundred yards astern of them.

A mile away to starboard was another column of four battleships, which Jonathan recognized as being of the *King George V* type and beyond them was another column of ships. Beyond them, he was told, there were another four columns but they were lost in the pearly mist. That meant twenty-four dreadnoughts in company. The figure was extraordinary.

5. NIGHT DEPARTURE

To port were the screening light cruisers, looking low and racy, with destroyer squadrons outlying them.

Ahead were the distinctive shapes of big four-funnel heavy cruisers spread out like markers ahead of the columns.

Just in sight, ahead of them was another set of large ships with flanking cruisers and destroyers: The battle cruisers. They were too far away for Jonathan to make out much of them but he thought he could distinguish the gap-toothed look of an *Indefatigable* in the last of the line right astern and therefore closest to the Grand Fleet. It was difficult, because of the angle but Jonathan was pretty sure. They were, after all, fairly unique ships, which were really not much more than a hull, with three funnels two masts and four turrets.

"*New Zealand*" said the officer of the watch seeing Jonathan with his binoculars on her. "A gift from the Kiwis. They gave the Captain a Maori kilt and pendant and made him promise to wear them whenever they are in action, which will ensure that they don't come to any harm."

"And does he?" Asked Jonathan

"They tell me he does. In any event, they weren't hit in either Heligoland Bight or Dogger Bank. Spooky if you subscribe to that sort of thing."

Looking at the scene, Jonathan was surprised at how little funnel smoke there was compared to his experience of American warships. He remarked on it and was told that it was as a result of the Welsh steam coal favoured by the Brits, which gave much less smoke than other varieties.

After the departure, Jonathan had retired to his bunk when 'cruising stations' were sounded and found that he slept very well indeed. The ventilating fan was not nearly as intrusive as he thought it may be, quite the reverse, the continual hum was soothing and the noise of the turbines was quite different to the clank and thump of reciprocating engines that he was used to.

Turning to at 0800, he had enjoyed a splendid breakfast in the wardroom and had been up here ever since.

The weather was cold, with some misty patches, so he was glad of his greatcoat.

God help anyone who meets this lot, thought Jonathan, to himself, no wonder the Bosh[45] don't want to tangle with them.

He was told that this was an operation to keep the Germans occupied. They were trailing their coat tails across the Heligoland Bight, close to the German bases. The idea was to distract them from the Baltic, where the Russian ports were thawing, meaning that the minefields needed renewing. The Kiel Canal allowed the German High Seas Fleet to travel rapidly between the Baltic and North Sea, as required. This show was designed to keep them on the North Sea side.

After lunch, the battle cruiser fleet was sent on ahead and the battleships altered course to the east to close the Danish coast. He saw that the signals were given by flag, reinforced by light from repeating ships.

Jonathan returned to the compass platform where he encountered Walwyn once more. "Ah Marston!" he said, "I am just about to do Rounds. Would you care to join me? You can see something of the ship and her men. Quite informal at this time, just want to make sure everything is OK before Sunday."

"Delighted sir, if that wouldn't discommode?"

5. NIGHT DEPARTURE

"Not at all, old boy, happy to show you round our little world. Besides, the men are very curious about you, real live Yank and all that. You seem to have made an impression on AB Bond at least."

Jonathan was struck by the fact that his presence had been noticed and more to the point that the executive officer knew what an Able Seaman was thinking.

For the next hour, Jonathan was taken all over the ship from stem to stern. Walwyn was obviously a popular officer and was greeted with affection from the upper deck, where men were greasing hawsers, through the batteries where practice was carrying on ("they drill with wooden shells and we try to make it interesting for them by throwing the occasional spanner in the works") down through the various compartments to the engine and boiler rooms.

In the starboard six-inch battery, Jonathan encountered AB Bond once more. Bond was delighted to see him in the company of the Commander. "'Ere, look sir, you in't 'alf been good luck fer me!" he said "I got me second gun, see! Gunlayer first class now!" And he pointed proudly to his sleeve where Jonathan could see crossed gun barrels embroidered in red.

"Well done Bond" said Jonathan, "well deserved I'm sure."

"All we need now is for Jerry to come out and give us a bit o' target practice now."

"Are you looking forward to it Bond?" asked Walwyn.

"'Course I am sir" he said "'s wot we trained ter do innit? Bring it on, that's what I sez anyway."

There was clearly no lack of Morale in His Majesty's Royal Navy.

Saturday 22nd April 1916, North Sea, 57° 45' N, 6° 04' E, HMS Warspite 2000

Dinner in the Wardroom was a semi formal affair, notwithstanding the fact that they were at sea. Jonathan found that members could sit where they liked on either of the two tables, save for the Commander, who always took the head of the principal table. Jonathan found himself between Frank and Walwyn. This was his first formal meal since joining. Again, wine was in evidence but he noted that Frank and some other officers were not drinking. Jonathan asked the steward if they had such a thing as coke, only to be met with incomprehension. Frank came to his rescue and suggested tomato juice, which is what he was having. "When we get back to Scapa, I'll take you to the Army and Navy, they'll get some sent up for you. In the meantime have some blood with me. Try it with a bit of Worcester sauce, it makes it a bit more palatable."

"Thank you" said Jonathan. "You don't drink at sea?"

"Indeed I have been known to indulge in that vice but not at the moment. It's still Lent you see." That made a certain amount of sense. Guiltily, Jonathan realized that he had been so preoccupied with his mission that he hadn't given very much thought to the season. He didn't usually go to the length of giving something up but he did like to remember the forty days with some extra piece of worship.

Walwyn and Frank were pleasant companions and he found that the dinner was very good; roast beef, roast potatoes followed by suet pudding with currents in custard. "Special night tonight. Schooner on the rocks, shrapnel and plum duff with yellow peril for afters." said Walwyn, "Easter Sunday tomorrow. Is your padre doing his usual Frank?"

5. NIGHT DEPARTURE

"Yes, I believe so. We have a course alteration at 2200 to close the Horns Reef and the BCF at daylight, so there will be time after that."

"Frank's a left footer" said Walwyn amicably, "Got their own sky-pilot, who's a decent bloke for a padre."

Jonathan recognized the expression 'sky pilot' from his lunch with Blinker Hall (who had mentioned it as a possible career move for him) but didn't know what a left-footer was. "Left footer?' he queried.

"Roman Catholic" said Walwyn; "Ruddy ship's rotten with 'em. Surprised we haven't shipped the bloody Spanish Flag with all the Tikes on board."

"I didn't hear you complain when we put on Monteverdi's vespers the other day" said Frank. "It's part of our mission to civilize the Heathen, especially *fratribis nostris disiunctibus*!"[46]

"Music's different," said Walwyn. "The rest is all my eye and Betty Martin if you ask me."

"*O mihi Beate Martine*, 'come to my aid Blessed Saint Martin' as you ought to know. Anyway, I *don't* ask you, wise though you be in other matters. You're a complete chump when it comes to matters spiritual."

"That may be Frank, but at least I am a member of the Church of England, by Law established, so I'm in pretty good company."

"Man's law, that is, established by an adulterous thug to cover his own sins!" said Frank.

"Thug, I'll grant you" said Walwyn, equably, "but at least he established the good old RN. We shouldn't be here without him."

"Nonsense" said Frank "The RN was established by Alfred the Great, who was as good a Christian as you could ask for. Henry just built on his foundations. By the way, do you know why we salute the quarterdeck?"

"Of course!" said Walwyn. "Respect for the King"

"Rubbish!" said the other.

"Saluting the life raft as a pseudo Crucifix?"

"Again, rubbish. The real point is that in Henry's day, before the iconoclasts got a hold, we used to have a statue of the Blessed Virgin Mary there and all the sailors would make their duty to her. They would sing evening prayer at 'lights out' which always finished with an '*ave*' or two."

"Well there you go!" said Walwyn, "You learn something every day!" and addressing Jonathan he said "He's actually a very learned cove for an NO, even if he does march to a different drum to the rest of us!"

After the last course had been finished, the cloth was drawn and small glasses were placed in front of each officer. A decanter appeared in front of Walwyn, with another at the bottom of the table. The same process was repeated on the second table outboard of where Jonathan was sitting, headed by Hammill. The buzz of conversation gradually died away and all eyes turned to the Commander. With a conscious theatricality, Walwyn drew the stopper of the first one, held it aloft and placed it carefully in front of him. At the foot of the table, the junior officer did the same with the other decanter. Walwyn passed his decanter to Jonathan, saying quietly "The drill is to help yourself to a glass and pass it to the left." Jonathan did so and passed it to Frank, who poured a glass for himself and then passed it on.

"I thought it was Lent" said Jonathan to Frank.

"Indeed it is old son but there's a special dispensation for the toasts."

5. NIGHT DEPARTURE

The decanters did the rounds and one finished up back at Walwyn. With equal theatricality, he lifted up the stopper and placed it elaborately back in the decanter. The same was done at the other table.

Walwyn stood up and said. "Gentlemen, we have a distinguished guest with us tonight, from one of our earliest colonies, now thoroughly grown up. All stand please and I give you 'The President of the United States of America'."

All the officers got to their feet with a scraping of chairs and toasted the President. As far as Jonathan was concerned, it was, indeed, a pretty compliment to his country. As a representative of the recipient of the toast, Jonathan elected not to drink and remained seated nodding and smiling, leaving his glass in front of him, untouched. The assembly sat down.

Walwyn then looked down the table to the bottom and said' "Mr Vice. 'The King'."

The junior Lieutenant at the foot of the table lifted his glass whilst seated and said "Gentlemen, The King."

Jonathan was about to get to his feet but was conscious of a restraining hand on his arm. It was Frank. "King's health is drunk seated in the RN old boy" he murmured quietly.

The officers all raised their glasses with a muttered 'The King" with some adding "God Bless him" or "Long to reign over us".

Jonathan took a sip of the ruby red liquid in his glass and found it very pleasant indeed, sweet with a sense of strength to it.

"Decent spot of port this," said Frank. "Graham's 1904. One of the blessings of being wine treasurer is that one has some sort of control over what is bought. Some of these fellows would drink any old rubbish."

Walwyn then rapped on the table. "Five minutes have passed. Gentlemen may smoke, those already doing so, please carry on." In fact no one had been smoking, it was clearly a well-established custom. Jonathan was reaching for his pipe and tobacco when Walwyn leaned across and said "we have a decent stock of cigars if you'd care for one?"

"I sure would," said Jonathan and a large box was brought in response to Walwyn's signal. Jonathan selected a Romeo y Julieta in its own humidor. Walwyn took another as did Frank.

He was rolling it and sniffing it with relish when he noted that Walwyn had put his own cigar down and that fresh decanters were appearing. Walwyn removed the stopper with less ceremony and passed the decanter again. Jonathan filled his glass again and handed the decanter on. Once the decanter was back under Walwyn's control he put the stopper in it and rapped the table again.

"Gentlemen" he said, standing up and raising his glass, "Saturday night at sea. I give you 'Sweethearts and wives'." This time the entire assembly got to its feet again and repeated the toast. Beside him Frank said, "May the former become the latter and the latter never cease to be the former" as he drank.

After that the atmosphere lightened and the conversation became general.

Frank excused himself and left to attend to the course change, leaving Jonathan with Walwyn. "It was getting a bit misty this afternoon and the met doesn't look too hopeful for tomorrow. Have you thought of how you would like to play it if we do run into a spot of bother?"

5. NIGHT DEPARTURE

Jonathan had not. He had never been in a ship in action and didn't quite know what to expect.

"Probably the best thing is if you stick with me" said Walwyn. "My principal station is 'B' Turret but if we do have any problems then I like to take charge of damage control myself, so an extra pair of hands and eyes is sometimes useful."

Jonathan was flattered. Walwyn had no idea of his capabilities; indeed Jonathan didn't know them himself. He had, of course been under fire but in a landing party that was quite different. Indeed, thinking back over his career, he had never had a 'spot of bother' in any of his commissions. "I'd be delighted if you are happy to have me," he said.

"Right." said Walwyn "That's settled then. I'm off for a final prowl around before I turn in. Sunrise is 0548 but it will start getting light about 0440. We should meet the BCF about 0500 if their navigation is up to snuff. Up to you when you appear. See you then!" and he was off.

After finishing his port and enjoying a cup of coffee, Jonathan realized that he still had almost half of the cigar left. He was tempted to take a turn round the quarterdeck and was just making his way towards the door through the darkened passage when he remembered the rule about lights on deck after darkness. Regretfully he ground out the cigar in a nearby ashtray and put the remains in his reefer pocket.

Settling his cap on his head he opened the screen door through the blackout curtain and stepped out into the moving darkness.

He felt the cool breeze, which was not unpleasant at this speed and was immediately conscious of the rushing wake alongside, gleaming in the dark. He could hear the noise from the funnels and stepped over to the port rail and stared at the sea. Here the breeze was rather more obvious and he was glad that his hat was well fitted.

He could see nothing that suggested that he was surrounded by such a large collection of ships. Struck by a thought, he moved right aft by the ensign staff and looked astern at where he knew *Malaya* was following them, not four hundred yards off. Straining his eyes, he thought he could just make out a hint of phosphorescence slightly to one side of the luminous wake, with a darker shape behind it. There was a man stationed by the staff as lifeguard. Jonathan was not going to disturb him but the man said, without looking round, "Evening sir. Lamp burning, *Malaya* in sight. Distance steady and all's well."

"Thank you sailor" said Jonathan without thinking. The man looked round immediately "Oh hullo sir. You must be the yank. Welcome aboard sir. Glad to have you on board the old Weston."

"Glad to be here" said Jonathan as the sailor returned to his vigil.

"She's going to be a good'un this'un. She's got a right personality already and she's only been in commission for a year." The sailor could clearly watch and talk at the same time.

"Are you enjoying her?" Jonathan asked.

"Too right I am, sir. Good scran, good owner, good bloke, good mates and no bobbery." Jonathan understood about half of what the man said.

Watching him, Jonathan was conscious of the old lookout's trick of looking in one direction, stopping and looking away and then back to where he was looking before. He seemed to be covering the quarters in turn.

5. NIGHT DEPARTURE

"Never know when you might see some evil-intentioned Jerry trying to get a sly one in. This sea state should show 'em up though, even with the mist rising."

Jonathan, alerted to the fact, could see now that there was a grey fuzziness occasionally obscuring the faint bone in the teeth of their next astern.

"Going to be a right to-do if it carries on thickening sir. 'Scuse me a second." He turned to a cabinet by the lifebelt adjacent to the staff, located a phone and rang it, keeping his eyes outboard as he did so. Jonathan could hear the tinny tones at the other end "Fore bridge?" they said.

"Fore bridge. Lifeguard here sir. Mist is thickening."

"Very good. Can you still see *Malaya?*"

"Aye sir but occasionally obscured. Getting worse I think."

"Thank you lifeguard. Keep on it."

"Aye aye sir."

That little exchange told Jonathan a great deal about the Royal Navy. The lifeguard was awake and intelligent enough to know that when an officer appears, he will want to know how things stand and he had covered the necessary ground economically. It was also clear that the officers had a habit of checking up on the lookouts, who, in their turn were prepared to make an unprompted report when it was warranted.

"How long before you are relieved?" asked Jonathan.

"Four bells sir. Half hour tricks these sort o'conditions." That made sense. Jonathan knew from bitter experience as a youngster how tedious watching the same piece of sea could be. Tired men made mistakes and mistakes in wartime could be fatal.

He returned to his cabin and turned in and fell asleep.

He was awakened suddenly. Something was different. What was it? The fans were going, the turbines were humming quietly but there was something else as well. Just at the edge of audibility there was a strange sound. It was very faint, wafting up from somewhere below. He couldn't quite make it out but it sounded like some sort of singing. No, not singing exactly but some sort of chanting. He could hear one voice intoning something and then a reply by a different voice. Occasionally there was what could only be described as a murmur of voices, a considerable number of them from the sound of it.

He swung out of his bunk, padded to the door in his pyjamas and opened it. He had no idea of the time. The flat was deserted and in darkness. Apart from the hum of machinery and the distant noise of the fans, there was nothing to be heard out there.

He wondered if he was imagining things.

Back in his cabin, he could still hear something, including the unmistakable tinkle of a bell, being rung three times. That was followed by the first voice singing something unfamiliar. Locating his watch, he looked at the luminous dial and noted that it was 0045, a quarter to one in the morning. Who would be making such a noise at this time of night?

Then he had it. Today was Easter Sunday and someone was celebrating the fact. It was oddly comforting, that here, in the middle of the North Sea, approaching a hostile coast, men still had time to remember their Redeemer.

5. NIGHT DEPARTURE

Settling back in his bunk, Jonathan offered a brief prayer of his own, in concert with whoever was commemorating the Resurrection somewhere below him.

Sunday 23rd April 1916 (Easter Sunday) North Sea, 56° 42' N, 6° 26' E (To the West of the Little Fisher Bank), HMS Warspite 1015

The mist had turned into thick fog. Nothing could be seen from the fore bridge and the fog siren was sounding mournfully. To Jonathan's surprise, *Warspite* was still proceeding at fifteen knots. He could hear other fog sirens around him but could see nothing.

Frank was on the bridge, looking a little strained. He didn't look as if he had had much sleep. The officer of the watch was unknown to Jonathan, but looked quite young. He was attended by a very self-conscious midshipman. There was a distinct tension in the air, which was not surprising under these conditions.

"Morning Jonathan" said Frank, with assumed brightness. "Bit of a kerfuffle last night. *Australia* and *New Zealand* [47] collided in the fog and both of them are heading home u/s. We've had our own problems too. Father had us turn north in the early hours, which was entertaining. We have had a couple of destroyers running athwart each other's hawsers, so they're on their way home as well. We're only waiting to hear that they're OK before we start back ourselves. Can't be soon enough for me."

Jonathan couldn't even begin to understand how you could handle such a fleet in these conditions.

"Do you slow down in fog like this?" he asked.

"Not without orders I don't" said Frank. "Provided everyone keeps the same speed and course we're safe. As soon as some idiot starts thinking independently we're in the deep mire. My bet is that's what happened to *Australia* and *New Zealand*. The BCF is renowned for its BF's[48]."

A signalman came running up to the bridge, saluted Frank and said "WT message received sir, *Ardent* under tow and clearing the area at six knots."

"Very good. Have you told the Captain?"

"Not yet sir"

"OK, I'll do so. Keep me informed please."

"Aye aye sir. Keep you informed"

"I'd better tell Philpotts what's up." Addressing the Officer of the Watch he said "Keep your eyes open. Any trouble, sing out." And he was gone, down the ladder, leaving the Officer of the Watch with the duty mid. Both looked uneasy, but were trying not to show it.

Jonathan could sympathize. He would have been extremely worried himself if the responsibility was his. Proceeding at this speed, in these conditions in this company was, in his opinion, a recipe for disaster. One false move and there would be a horrible collision, in which, no doubt lives could be lost. The thought of *Warspite* being rammed by her next astern was terrifying, let alone the prospect of ramming a smaller vessel, which would undoubtedly be sunk.

Thinking about it, Jonathan realized a number of things in sequence. The lookouts were doubled. That meant extra pairs of eyes. The compass repeater was steady. That meant there was a competent quartermaster at the wheel. He couldn't see a log, but he assumed that there was someone equally competent in the engine room that could be relied upon to keep the revolutions to that ordered. That meant station keeping was as good as it could be. Frank did not keep a regular watch, which meant that the officer of

5. NIGHT DEPARTURE

the watch was deemed competent. It was, however, a severe test of his abilities.

What was going on was quite mad and clean contrary to anything that he had learned about safety and best practice as a Naval Officer. But the Brits were doing it anyway, regardless of the consequences. It was like a blind man leading a cavalry charge across unknown country at full gallop. If there was going to be a reckoning, Jonathan thought that it was going to be a considerable one.

Idly, he was running through all the possible scenarios that could occur. The worst thing he could think of would be seeing a ship on a collision course. In this fog, they would have almost no time to react. He decided that if there was no choice, he personally would go for a glancing blow, which would mean turning towards the vessel, ideally passing it port to port in accordance with the international rule of the road.

The next possibility was running into the next ahead. He remembered from last night that *Malaya* had not been exactly in *Warspite's* wake. He asked the OOW "Excuse me, I can't help but be interested. Is *Valiant* dead ahead of us?"

"No, she is two points on our starboard bow" was the short answer, which meant that the ships were actually in a shallow echelon. That made sense. If there was trouble, *Warspite* could starboard her wheel and hope to pass down *Valiant's* port side. "I don't mean to intrude," he said to his tense companion, "but this looks damn dangerous?"

"Indeed it is" said the other shortly.

"Is this normal?" asked Jonathan innocently.

"Yes it bloody is. Now if you don't mind I have a ship to look after. Please shut up." The strain he was under was obvious.

Jonathan considered. He couldn't find it in his heart to condemn his hearer.

His rebellious thoughts went on. What else? Were the men ready for a possible collision? If it were up to him, he would have been moving at five knots with the men at collision stations. He didn't want to ask that.

What about possible enemy action? He had no idea what to do if an enemy appeared. Presumably the ship's company knew what to do, so he would simply sing out and see what happened.

One blessing was that the fog was beginning to clear a little. He began to get tantalizing glimpses of a white wake ahead and then, through the swirls the stern of *Valiant* coming and going with increasing persistence.

He was suddenly aware of feet on the gangway and looking aft he saw the same messenger coming up at the double. Looking around he saluted the OOW, "W/t message from Flag sir, 'Squadron is to alter course in succession to port at 1100, new course South 26 East' Sir."

"Very good" said the OOW. "Have you told the Navigating Officer?"

"No sir. Its 1055 already."

"What?" exclaimed the OOW, with a squawk "How in hell did that happen?"

"Delay in transmission sir. *Barham* was adrift in her w/t procedure. Again." It was clear that the rivalry between the two ships was not confined to the wardroom.

"Well never mind that now. He's in the Captain's sea cabin. Tell him now and also tell the conning tower. At

5. NIGHT DEPARTURE

the double please." The voice had a slight overtone of hysteria.

The wheel order was a simple one but the complication was the timing. Jonathan knew that the separation between the ships in the column was two cables – four hundred yards, compass platform to compass platform. *Warspite's* compass platform was, or should be eight hundred yards abaft that of *Barham* the squadron flagship. Turning in succession meant that each ship would turn on the same spot as they reached it. The squadron speed was fifteen knots, or five hundred yards a minute, which meant that *Warspite* would reach the turning point exactly one minute thirty-six seconds after the Flagship.

"Mid!" said the OOW, "Work out the timings please, double quick!"

Leaning forward to the voice pipe that Jonathan had seen Frank use as they were leaving Scapa he said "Wheelhouse? Fore bridge, do you hear there?"

"We are to turn starboard onto course South 26 East in approximately seven minutes."

"New course South 26 East in approximately seven minutes, aye aye sir."

"What does the log show?" he asked.

"Indicated speed fifteen knots exactly" It was interesting to have a sailor who not only answered the question but also knew why it was being asked.

"Very good. Stand by."

"Standing by sir."

Jonathan looked at his watch; it was still a couple of minutes before 1100. The Mid was looking at the officer of the watch with a frozen expression

There was a clatter on the companionway and the Captain appeared at the run, closely followed by Frank.

The OOW was heavily engaged with his binoculars looking out, and did not notice the intrusion. Jonathan saluted and said, formally "Orders to alter course to South 26 East in succession from 1100. Speed fifteen knots, time of turn 11 plus 1'36" exactly. Weather clearing. Wheel alerted and acknowledged, Sir."

Philpotts and Frank exchanged glances.

"Thank you Marston" said the Captain. "Very helpful. All set Jenkin?"

The OOW looked back from his binoculars, distracted. "Aye Sir" he said.

"When do we turn?" asked Philpotts."

"In about two minutes sir" said Jenkin.

"No sir, sorry" said Jonathan, who was getting sufficiently worried to be concerned. The estimation was too far out for him to keep silent. "Time of turn is one minute thirty-six seconds by my reckoning, sir, 11.01.36, any later and we will run into trouble." It would mean that they would be rammed by their next astern *Malaya* with disastrous consequences.

"Jenkin?" asked the Captain evenly. "I...don't know sir," the wretch replied, "the signal only came in a minute or so ago. I haven't had time to work it out."

"I have" said Jonathan, "I haven't been so weighed down as Mr Jenkin, sir. I think this will serve."

"Are you sure?" asked Philpotts.

"Yes sir" said Jonathan. There was really no other acceptable answer.

"Very well then. You had better carry on and make the turn."

"Aye aye sir, carry on and make the turn." Jonathan was apprehensive. He was going to make the turn. If his judgment was out by very much, he was going

5. NIGHT DEPARTURE

to pile up one of His Majesty's latest battlewagons. God only knew what Benson would say if he got this wrong.

Philpotts said "The protocol is to give the wheel order in points followed by 'midships' as you're coming onto the course. In this ship at this speed I would do that just after passing southeast. Then give the new course. Standard turn such as this is ten points."

"Aye aye sir" said Jonathan. "Helm order ten points, ease after south east, new course South 26 East."

"Oh and remember in the RN its the *helm* direction not the turn direction." That harked back to the days of sail, where turning the wheel one way turned the rudder the other.

"Aye aye sir, port ten it is sir."

"Very good."

The mist was clearing quite quickly now and *Valiant* was almost continuously in sight. Looking at his watch, at just before 11.01 he saw the stern begin to move to starboard with an obvious movement.

"*Valiant* turning to starboard sir!" the lookout sang out from behind them. "Very good" said the Captain.

Jonathan was counting down. He had time to alert the wheel and did so "Fore bridge, turning on my mark in approximately thirty seconds" and had the response "Fore bridge, turning on your *order* in approximately thirty seconds. Aye aye sir" and then as an aside he heard the quartermaster talking to someone below without closing the voice pipe "Bleedin' 'ell, they've put the bloody yank in charge! Gawd 'elp us all!" Jonathan chose to ignore it. Struck by a thought, he turned to the Captain and asked, "Do you use siren sir?" The ship's siren could be used to indicate a change of course.

"No, not on this occasion"

"Very good sir" and he turned back to the task in hand. The second hand of his watch was reading twenty seconds, then twenty-five and then at just before thirty-five he leaned into the voice pipe and said "Helm, Fore bridge, port ten" and the voice from below said "Fore bridge, Hellum. Ten of the port wheel on."

"Very good' as he watched the compass repeater begin to swing around as the great ship turned. For such a large ship, she seemed to turn pretty well. As they were passing through South East Jonathan said "Mid ships" remembering to pronounce it as two words. "Steer South 26 East, steady" and heard "Mid ships. Steering South 26 East, Steady as she goes" and then the aside from the comedian below "Collision stations next I shouldn't wonder! Save yourself first Taffy and keep a raft fer me!"

Again Jonathan chose to ignore it. He was not yet ready to impose his authority on this foreign crew and anyway the remarks came within the broad ambit of legitimate grumbling, not to mention leg pulling.

Philpotts was looking at him. "Manoeuvre well executed," he said. "Do you fancy taking the rest of the watch? I shall be here but Hodgson had a bit of a rough night and could do with a zizz."

Jonathan thought about it. "I would be extremely happy, sir but I am not familiar with your standing orders, or what to do if we encounter an enemy."

"That doesn't matter Marston, that's why I'm here. Of course Jenkin will remain here for form's sake, but I should like to see how you manage. If we see anything of Jerry there's a duty bugler within earshot, all you have to do is sing out 'Action Stations' and he'll do the rest. Other than that, there is a standard zigzag that I'll help you with.

5. NIGHT DEPARTURE

You have already proved that you can think and handle a ship.

"Is that OK Jenkin?"

"Of course, sir" said the erstwhile officer of the watch in an unreadable manner.

"Well sir, I should be delighted," said Jonathan. "Thank you for your confidence" he said. Inside, he was thinking with delight, that he was about to take the watch in the latest British battleship in wartime conditions. He couldn't think of a higher accolade. His delight was not diluted even when Philpotts remained on the bridge and directed Jenkin to do the same. Something must have shown on his face, because the captain said: -

"Don't worry about it Marston, it's not wholly altruistic, we can always do with an extra watch keeper, you never know when you might need one. Besides, what better way of learning about our methods than taking a watch?" There was no arguing with that.

The Captain moved to the voice pipe and said "Captain here. Lieutenant Marston has the ship." Then turning to Jonathan he said, "There we are Marston, She's all yours."

"Aye aye sir. I have the ship" he said formally and moved forward to the bridge screen. Philpotts settled down in his chair, which was an elaborate affair fixed aft of the binnacle and began staring out over the quarter. Jenkin moved awkwardly to the lee, and stared moodily over the waters to the next column.

To Jonathan, it felt good. He took his binoculars and swept around the ship. The mist was definitely lifting now and *Valiant* was clearly in sight with glimpses of the next ahead. Looking aft, he could see *Malaya* following them sedately.

The starboard lookout sang out "2nd Battle squadron in sight sir! *Ajax* and *Centurion*. On station Sir"

"Very good" said Jonathan and turned to see two of the battleships of the next line ploughing majestically through the sea, a mile on their starboard side. As he watched the mist cleared further and he could see two more, one ahead and one astern of the ones he was watching and then another column beyond that. "There's the old *Tin Duck*! said the lookout and then reported formally "Fleet flagship in sight sir!"

"Very Good" said Jonathan and then reported to the Captain as protocol dictated, even though he must have heard the lookout anyway. "Fleet flagship in sight sir."

"Very good" said the Captain. "Keep an eye out for signals. She'll use flags for preference, reinforced with lights."

"Aye aye sir" said Jonathan.

Being on watch was a return to normality. It was a simple pleasure that reminded him of who and what he was. There were a couple of course changes, 'zigzags' Jonathan realized, to put off any hostile submarines but they were easily managed. The drill seemed to be a signal from the Fleet Flagship *Iron Duke* (which the lookout had referred to as the *Tin Duck*) repeated via the squadron Flagship, *Barham*.

Whilst he was aware of the presence of the Captain, Philpotts was not intrusive and kept to his chair, almost ostentatiously looking over the side.

By the end of the watch, the weather had virtually cleared and Jonathan had a good view of the fleet once more. *Warspite* and her column were on the extreme eastern edge of the battle fleet, closest to Germany, somewhere out there over the horizon, which made sense

5. NIGHT DEPARTURE

as they were the largest and fastest battleships in the world and thus best suited for meeting any trouble from the Bosh. Outside them was the 4th Light Cruiser Squadron and elements of the 4th Destroyer Flotilla. As before, the bigger cruisers and their attendant destroyers were ahead of the battle fleet deployed like military pickets.

With the aid of his binoculars, Jonathan was able to get a good look at his neighbours.

They were all handsome ships that looked right, especially the light cruisers, which were lean greyhounds, yet with a powerful punch. Looking at the nearest (which rejoiced in the distinctly unwarlike name of *Caroline*) he could see that she had three funnels and at least two six-inch guns together with a collection of four-inchers. She was cutting through the oily sea leaving very little wake. As a seaman, he found her to be beautiful, combining form and function perfectly.

By contrast, the next column of battleships, on his starboard side, was impressive for a wholly different reason. Not the latest British design, they were still massive. Ten thirteen point five-inch guns coupled with a handsome profile, set off with two large funnels and the piled up bridgework characteristic of the later British dreadnoughts, they were handsome ships.

Astern of the third was an oddity. She didn't look like any British Battleship Jonathan was familiar with. Noticeably shorter than her squadron mates, she had two close-set funnels, as well as a full battery of six-inch anti-torpedo boat guns. She was too far aft to be able to read her name but he assumed that she was one of the battleships building for foreign countries at the start of the war, which the British had taken over, like the old *Gin Palace* he had been shown on his way into Scapa. Whatever she was, she

117

too had ten large guns, which looked like thirteen point five-inchers.

Beyond them was another column of two funnelled, single masted ships and at the head of the third column from where he stood was the fleet flagship, with the Admiral's flag prominent on the mast three miles away. Beyond that, the columns were an indistinct jumble of ships.

It made sense for the C in C to be in the centre column, where he could see the entirety of his fleet, provided that conditions were good enough. It needed at least five miles visibility, which, Jonathan was learning, was not guaranteed in the North Sea.

He wanted to know where he was, exactly. Well, he was officer of the watch and was entitled to, no, expected to know. He still didn't know the midshipman's name; so, ignoring Jenkin he said, "Mid, I'm just going to the Charthouse. Keep me informed of any developments."

"Aye aye sir. To keep you informed of developments."

Going down the ladder into the charthouse, there was another mid, who was Frank's assistant ('Tanky' was the curious word for it). He looked at the plot and saw that they were cruising south by south east about sixty miles from the Danish coast. If they carried on this course they would be in the German port of Bremerhaven in sixteen hours. The Grand Fleet was nothing if not bold. He was reminded of the Blockade in the Napoleonic wars, where the British inshore squadrons habitually anchored almost inside the French ports.

Struck by a thought he said, "When was the last fix taken Tanky?"

5. NIGHT DEPARTURE

"Here sir, we managed to get a fix at 1030 yesterday. We have been following a line of bearing ever since."

"And who worked it out?" working out a position at a time other than noon required a more sophisticated technique and some additional calculations.

"Mr Hodgson sir but I helped."

"I'm sure you did son. Would there be, by any chance a sextant that I can borrow?"

"Yes sir, just here in this cabinet" opening it and handing it to Jonathan. He checked the chronometer on the bulkhead against his wristwatch and was pleased to see that they agreed exactly. It was 1120. Normally, sun sights would be taken at local noon, which, in this area would be around 1133 ships time.

"Thank you son. Tell me, what's the drill about noon sights on this ship?"

"Officer of the watch passes the word for the Navigator and the Schoolie[49] about fifteen minutes before local noon sir."

"Very well" said Jonathan, "Consider the word passed."

Examining the sextant he found that it was a superior instrument of reassuring solidity. He took it up to the Compass Platform by way of the Captain to whom he reported "Local noon in approximately ten minutes sir. Navigator and Schoolmaster alerted."

"Thank you Marston, carry on."

Jonathan located the sun and took a sight. It was still climbing. There was the familiar clatter of the companionway and Frank hove into view, holding his own sextant. To Jonathan's surprise, Frank saluted him and said "Permission to take a sight from here?" Feeling slightly foolish, Jonathan returned the salute and said "Granted, sir. Sun still ascending. I anticipate local noon in three minutes or so." Of course, on reflection it did make sense. Jonathan was Officer of the Watch and as such he had charge of the ship unless or until he was relieved. Notwithstanding the fact that Frank was senior to him, he still needed the permission of the Officer of the Watch to come onto the fore bridge.

"Thank you" said Frank, "Height above water at this draft is seventy-five feet as near as makes no difference. No refraction." he addressed his own instrument towards the sun. "Still rising" said Frank. Jonathan took off his wristwatch and handed it to the duty Mid. "Hold onto that son and when we call noon, make a note of the exact time will you please?"

"Aye aye sir."

Both officers addressed the sun with their instruments. The Captain was watching intently. It was Frank's duty as navigator to take the initiative and he said "Noon." Jonathan agreed and said so "I agree" and turning to the Captain he said "Noon sir!"

"Very good" said the Captain, "make it so."

"Aye aye sir" said Jonathan and turned to the voice pipes. He didn't know which one to use but chose the conning tower, which seemed sensible. "Fore bridge, Conning Tower. Local noon" he said. It was clearly the right thing to do as the voice on the other end said "local noon. Aye aye."

"46° 54' 36.6"" said Jonathan to Frank. "I have 46° 54' 36.4"" said Frank. Time of noon?"

"11.32.01 sir" said the snotty. "Thank you" said Frank. "I'll just nip below and work this out. Send the snotties' observations down when they come up will you?"

5. NIGHT DEPARTURE

"I shall," said Jonathan.

A couple of minutes later Frank's tanky appeared with the observations of his fellows. Glancing at them quickly Jonathan saw that they were mostly within a second or so of each other with a couple of wild ones. "Take them to the Pilot please" said Jonathan, who was acting automatically now. He was back in the world in which he belonged, doing a job that he loved.

Within a very few minutes Frank was back with a slip of paper. He went to Jonathan first and said "Our position is 56° 35' North, 6° 36' West as near as I can make it. Forty-five Miles off the Danish coast, sixty odd miles from the Horns Reef which bears South East. The DR was out by five miles." 'DR' meant 'dead reckoning' and was used when ships were unable to take a proper sun or start sight to fix their position. If there were long period without being able to take a sight, the estimated position could be out by many miles, which in these waters could be serious. "Thank you sir" said Jonathan, "I shall inform the Captain" and stepping over to the chair he did so. "Thank you Mr Marston" was the response.

The rest of the watch passed uneventfully and it was an extremely satisfied Jonathan who returned to the wardroom for some well-deserved lunch and a look at the comic cuts, as periodicals were known in the Royal Navy.

6. A New Flap

Scapa Flow, forenoon Monday 24th April 1916 (Easter Monday)

"Steady on" was the call from the fo'csle as the ship's weigh died, "approaching bearing now....Let Go!" and with a noisy rush the anchor cable ran out ahead of the ship. "Slow astern!" ordered Frank into the voice pipe. "Still!" and then "Finished with main engines!" and turning to Philpotts he said "Anchored as directed sir!"

"Very good!" said the Captain and His Majesty's ship *Warspite* was anchored 500 yards astern of *Valiant* and 500 yards ahead of *Malaya*. Once more they were at the extreme outside edge of the battleship lines.

To their starboard, the 2nd Battle Squadron was anchoring too, with *Centurion* abreast them, not five hundred yards distant. Each ship had its assigned colliers waiting for them to anchor to allow them to coal as soon as they dropped their anchors.

The 5th Battle Squadron, however (of which *Warspite* formed a part) were oil fired, so their attendant ships were oilers.

"Rig deck cloths and screens for oiling" ordered Walwyn and the bosun's mates started their energetic routine as the oilers approached.

An enthusiastic party of sailors turned to to connect the hoses. Walwyn said to Jonathan "I'm going to take a turn around the ship by boat. Would you care to join me?"

"Delighted, sir" said Jonathan. He was beginning to understand that Walwyn was obsessive about his ship, which was, he decided, about right for an Executive Officer.

In a pulling boat a few minutes later, Jonathan was privileged to witness the Royal Navy's standards as currently practiced. There was a select crew, which, he understood, consisted of the Mate of the Upper Deck (a commissioned lieutenant), the officers of the seaman divisions, the Boatswain and a couple of assistants. It was a new evolution to Jonathan, who would not have dreamed of taking enlisted men on an inspection but a little thought showed that it made sense. These men had a special interest in making sure their ship passed muster in this enormous fleet.

Walwyn had said to Jonathan "Some people think that there is no place for bull in wartime. I disagree. If the ship's company has a ship to be proud of, it gives them a better sense of responsibility. The ship is their home after all. Who wouldn't want to be proud of his home?"

The logic was difficult to refute.

"Jerry doesn't live on his ships, so he don't have the same sense of home as we do" said Walwyn.

"Fore funnel guys need attention Wardlow," said Walwyn. Lieutenant Wardlow noted that down in a notebook. "Foc'sle guardrails are a disgrace."

"Aye aye sir"

"Starboard lower platform 40 inch searchlight needs to be square. I want them at 90 degrees to the line of travel, not on the platform centreline. Clear?"

"Aye aye sir" said the dutiful Wardlow "Square to the centre line, not the platform."

"We could do with a lick of paint on the bow at the waterline if we get a chance."

"Aye aye sir"

6. A NEW FLAP

"This bloody weather plays havoc with the paintwork. WHAT IN HELL DO YOU THINK YOU ARE DOING?" The last was addressed in a roar to a picket boat, which was being lowered in a less than seamanlike manner. "HOLD THOSE BLOODY GUYS TAUGHT YOU IDIOT!"

"Aye aye sir" was the shamefaced reply from the side.

"IS THAT DONALD?" shouted Walwyn.

"Aye sir"

"SEE ME AT EIGHT BELLS!"

"He's a good lad at heart," said Walwyn to Jonathan as an aside. "But he needs the occasional shake up. I had a complaint about him from some destroyer officer who said he was going too fast in the anchorage."

"Really?" said Jonathan innocently.

"Young rascal claimed to be from another ship. As far as I am concerned hard lying is what destroyers are paid for. I'd prefer to see smart boat work rather than pussyfooting around wreckers."

"What will you do with him?" asked Jonathan.

"For the speeding? Nothing. I heard about it unofficially so shan't investigate. Some lad in *Malaya* took a beating for him but that's no concern of mine. That's a snottie's life."

"And the sloppy seamanship?" asked Jonathan.

"Personal explanation to me. Make sure he understands what he's done wrong. In many ways, a picket boat damaged by a mid may save a more important vessel damaged by the same man as a lieutenant."

Like so many other things, it sounded strange to Jonathan's ears but made a lot of sense.

Later that day

Jonathan was appreciating the benefits of oil-fired ships. The battleship lines inshore of the 5th Battle Squadron were surrounded by a fog of coal dust, with hammering steam cranes lifting great bags of the stuff, which was being deposited down the coal shoots with a rattle and roar clearly audible across the water. By contrast, in *Warspite* there was just the throbbing of pumps as the duty working party filled the tanks. The rest of the duty watch was engaged on other tasks.

This also meant that the officers were engaged elsewhere (Jonathan had learned that in the Royal Navy even officers took part in coaling along with the men). Jonathan was at leisure. It was after lunch and his mind was turning to his report. He needed to give Benson a heads-up and it would be nice to get a letter home. He was acutely conscious that he had left one Clementina Fessenden with the impression that he had two weeks leave, so that they could see something of each other. Whilst they were not exactly 'walking out' they were friends and companions. In normal circumstances he would have written to her by now but could not do so easily. A motorcar driving, emancipated young woman, she was not the sort of person to treat in a cavalier manner, such things could be dangerous.[50]

Frank walked into the wardroom and, taking a picture paper, sat down in an armchair beside Jonathan. "You look pensive old chap," said Frank "Penny for them?"

"I was wondering what to do about mail up here. After my last bit of bother I don't want to upset anyone but I need to at least tell my boss and the family that I am alive. I shall be discrete, of course. Any suggestions?"

6. A NEW FLAP

"Well normally our mail is censored by one of the Padres and then sealed up and sent off in the normal way. Return mail is usually posted to the ship, or to the British Forces Post Office dealing with ships, they call it BFPO Ships. Why not do that?"

"The problem with that is that I am not supposed to be here, apparently. I can't tell my family that I am on a British warship in the middle of a war. I can send a note to my boss via the Naval attaché but I am damned if I can see how to do anything else. The stamp alone would be a give away." Jonathan had been puzzling over that very point.

"Tell you what" said Frank, "let's see if Father Anthony has any ideas."

"Father Anthony?" Queried Jonathan.

"Father Anthony Pollen, the RC Chaplain. He has a first class brain and oodles of experience at solving problems. Since he's one of the censors he'll know the ropes. Come with me and we'll find him."

Jonathan was far from sure about any of this but he got up and followed Frank out into the lobby along the quarterdeck and down a hatch abaft the guns of Y turret into the stern flat. This part of the ship was reserved for senior officers and was fitted accordingly, which is to say that the decoration and fit was identical to the other parts of the ship, with the usual jumble of pipes, wires and equipment crammed into the available space but the space available was rather greater. Another clue was the dark red boot topping to the white bulkheads was a good eighteen inches lower.[51] The hatch gave out into a lobby with cabins on either side, the bulkheads converging aft to the bulkhead of the admirals' quarters themselves. It boasted two doors either side of a ladder way leading below. Against the forward bulkhead was a pair of fan motors that presumably fed the air conditioning. A line of steel pillars ran down the centre of the space and there was a concertina curtain that ran on rails, which could divide the lobby into two flats.

On the starboard side there was a door marked "RC Chaplain" on which Frank knocked. "Come in," said a voice and Frank opened the door and went in. "Hello Father" he said, "I've brought our Yank to see you. Jonathan, this is Father Pollen.[52] Father, this is Lieutenant Jonathan Marston of the US Navy. He has a slight problem which you might be able to help with."

The cabin was sparsely furnished. There was a bunk, a desk with books over it and a crucifix. An officer's hat without a cap badge was on the bunk. On the after bulkhead between the door and the desk was another bookshelf, which was empty apart from a statue of a saint. On the opposite bulkhead to the desk (the forward one) was a locker with a pair of fine brass candlesticks on it and a folding table. Above the locker was a painting of a woman on a rock with her arms out towards the beholder, palms up, in gentle entreaty. She had stars around her head and was standing on a snake, which was writhing in agony under her feet. With a shock, Jonathan realized that it was a depiction of St Mary, the mother of Jesus, the 'popish idol' so hated by his co-religionists. It didn't look so bad to him, in fact it was really rather lovely. The face, carefully and naturalistically portrayed radiated compassion. There was a lot of symbolism to the painting but Jonathan couldn't work it out at the moment.

There was no other furniture save for a curious contraption, which looked like a very low seat, with the back facing the locker in front of the painting. Above the bunk, to the left of the scuttle (which gave out onto the

6. A NEW FLAP

embrasure for the after six-inch gun) was a small religious icon.

The whole feeling was of deliberate austerity.

Getting up from the chair by the desk was an older man, with striking looks, a noble Roman nose set off with a shock of thick grey hair. It seemed that he had been writing something. He was dressed in a dark civilian suit with a soft collar. A black tie was partly covered with a navy coloured pullover.

Holding out his hand the man said "Lieutenant Marston, a pleasure to see you in the flesh at last" the voice was warm and the handshake was firm. "Please make yourself comfortable. How can I help?"

Apart from the bunk and the low chair, there was nowhere else to sit. Catching his glance, Father Anthony said, "Please, perch on the bunk. It is not luxury but it suffices." He resumed his seat at the desk and swivelled to face the two officers.

The bunk was, of course quite high and perching was an uncomfortable procedure in which the cleft under Jonathan's buttocks lodged in the wooden edge to the bunk. Frank did the same and said, "Back on the misericord then father?"

"Is the story going to be that long?" asked the priest.

"I shouldn't think so Father but it is somewhat ticklish," said Frank

"Tell me about it" said the priest addressing Jonathan.

Jonathan pondered. It was clear that the British Authorities knew who he was and why he was here. It followed that this man, who, whatever else he was, was a censor of the ship's mail, should know that as well. The problem was the politics at home. He was about to articulate that when he suddenly realized that he did not know how to address this priest of a foreign religion. Frank had called him 'Father' but he was not Jonathan's father and that form of address seemed wrong. He settled for 'sir'.

"Well sir" said Jonathan, "I am here to liaise with the Royal Navy and understand its methods. The British Authorities seem happy with that and have, to be fair, given me all the help that they can. The problem is that in my own country, the President would not approve of what I am doing."

There was a silence, which Jonathan felt impelled to fill, "I am personally satisfied that the orders I am acting under are lawful and legitimate." He went on "I have to report to those who sent me in an unobtrusive manner and I am not quite sure how to do it. Also, I should like to let my folks know that I am well and happy but because what I am doing is kind of secret I'm not sure how to do that either."

Once it was out, it suddenly seemed simpler.

"I see the problem," said the priest after a moment or two. "Tell me" he said looking directly into Jonathan's eyes "what, exactly do your family know?" His priorities were interesting, family first and superiors after. His gaze was uncomfortably direct.

"Well" said Jonathan, slowly "My Father knows where I am and why I am here but he is sworn to secrecy. My mother won't press him but she will know that I am involved in something secret and, perhaps, dangerous. My Dad is not so good at hiding things from my Mom. I should like to reassure her."

More silence, and then "I see. May I inquire how you are to report to your superiors?"

6. A NEW FLAP

"The instruction is to use uncoded cable, that is to say by cable not formally encoded."

"Does anyone *officially* know that you're here?" It was a perceptive question.

"Well yes, sir, they do now you mention it. The Ambassador knows that I am here on furlough, or at least that's what he chooses to believe."

"Your problem is solved then, as far as the family is concerned. You can write to them perfectly normally. If you use an accommodation address, for example the American Embassy, they will be happy. I presume that someone in your organization knows where you are?" It was strangely easy talking to this man. He had a knack of helping to focus things and leading the thought process to sensible conclusions. "The Second Secretary knows that I have come north but he doesn't know exactly where I am."

"I can't see that would cause a problem. If he knows you have come north then he will guess you're with us. All you need to do then is tell that person to forward your mail to "*HMS Warspite* BFPO Ships" and the organization will do the rest. Provided you're discrete it shouldn't provide too much difficulty. Now" he said, steepling his fingers as he looked at Jonathan, "how are we going to get your report back? I take it that part of your brief is to report on how we're doing?"

Taken aback Jonathan asked "How do you know that?" it sounded rude to him as soon as it came out. The priest was unfazed. "I suspect that if *I* were a senior officer in your Navy at this moment I should want to know exactly what the odds were. It is reasonable to suppose that this person, whoever he is, has some *nous* and as such it would, logically, form part of your brief." Jonathan was not quite sure what *nous* was but it's meaning was obvious in context.

The priest thought for a minute and then said, "Are you a racing man Mr Marston? Do you follow the horses?"

Jonathan was about to answer 'certainly not' but thought better of it. Betting was anathema to his Northern soul but this strange clergyman seemed to have a different view. He settled for "No, not really. I've never really thought about it."

"And would your superior know that?"

Thinking about it, Jonathan thought that Benson probably would. He knew pretty much everything else about Jonathan. "I guess he might," he said.

"Well there you are then," said the priest, "You are visiting your grandmother who is taking you to the races. You can report the odds. You may even enjoy it. Would you like me to be your censor? It may make matters easier, you can just drop your letters in here or in the Sacristy opposite. No-one else will interfere with them."

Jonathan was beginning to understand why the Catholic Church had a reputation for subterfuge. This deceptive man seemed to be a master.

They were suddenly interrupted by a knock at the door. It was Frank Single "Oh hello sir" he said addressing Jonathan, "I hear you've settled in nicely."

"I have, thank you Mr Single. I trust I see you well?"

"Indeed you do sir, capital, in fact. Mr Hodgson sir, the Captain would like to see you ASAP. As the Army says, the balloon has gone up; Ireland's gone up in flames and there's Hell to pay! Oh sorry Padre, begging your pardon!"

6. A NEW FLAP

The priest flapped his hand in a dismissive manner and addressed Hodgson. "I was worried about this Francis. Do keep an eye out for our flock, there are a couple of hotheads in it who may not take this too well."

"I shall Father" said Frank "I'd better go. Thank you Single" and they were off, leaving Jonathan alone with Father Anthony, who looked grave. "Mr Marston" he said, getting up, "I need to say a few prayers. You are very welcome to join me."

Jonathan was nonplussed.

"Oh nothing formal and not for very long but those poor people don't know what they've started. Please use the priedieu if you wish, I shall take the floor," and he moved over to the bulkhead under the painting and lowered himself to his knees, signing himself with the Cross as he did so.

With a flash, Jonathan realized what the low chair was, it was a kneeler and was intended to be used back to front. He had some idea what a rebellion in Ireland would involve and he was reminded of Ed Bell's prophetic words, "If you're going to take on the British Empire, son, you had better make damn sure that you win."

On the train coming down from Liverpool, he had passed some time with an Irish officer in the British Army, and had been treated to a crash course in Irish politics. He realized that a lot of people were going to die. And it was going to happen quite soon.

That decided him. Getting off the bunk himself, he turned to the priedieu ('of course' he thought as he knelt down in front of the painting, 'priedieu' meant 'pray God' which is exactly what he was doing.')

He was not quite sure what to say. He had no connection with Ireland or England but he did have common humanity with their inhabitants. Wondering, he examined the painting in front of him. He could imagine any number of preachers shouting "Idolatry" at what he was doing but the picture was extraordinary. There was compassion in the face and the gently entreating arms seemed to reach out to comfort him. At once he was conscious of all the misery in the world and the thousands of men, even now, dying in agony on a hundred battlefields as he knelt there in that extraordinary space. Some would be crying for their mothers and here she was, the epitome of all of them, feeling their suffering and soothing it away.

Instead of a formal prayer, he thought about things. He had never thought very much about St Mary, or indeed any of the other Saints before. His was a simple, no–nonsense Biblically based Faith. In his simplistic view it was set of rules and an expected code of behaviour set out by a distant but loving God. Popes and Virgins and all the fol-de-rol of Roman Catholicism was quite foreign to him and, he had always believed it was for other people, foreigners and suchlike, not for rational, reasonable men like himself.

Now, in front of those compassionate eyes, he was a child again. The painting did not physically resemble his mother in the least but there was the same feel about it. Before he knew it, he was addressing....well not the painting but the woman behind the painting, 'Be a mother to those poor people' he articulated internally. It wasn't much but it was enough.

Beside him, the priest was wrapped in his own devotions. Kneeling on the bare deck, he opened his eyes and looked up at the painting and began to sing softly in Latin.

6. A NEW FLAP

As he listened he realized that was it! That was the sound that Jonathan had heard on Easter Morning. Father Anthony had a beautifully modulated voice and the tune was otherworldly. The last phrases were almost a moan, leading up to a satisfying caesura.

The priest crossed himself again, saying audibly *"In nomine Patris et Filio et Spiritu Sancti"* and got, somewhat stiffly to his feet and said to Jonathan "I'm sorry about that but you have no idea what misery these people are likely to unleash on the Innocent. They need our prayers."

"Actually, Father," said Jonathan, "I rather think I do. I shared a train journey with an Irish officer and his men, most of whom were Nationalists. It was….thought provoking."

Tuesday 25th April 11:00, HMS Warspite, 5th Battle Squadron 55°5' N 0°7' E

The four battleships of the 5th Battle squadron were crashing their way south at twenty-three knots. It was not a comfortable process. The seas were heavy and the ships were taking it green over their forecastles. The forward gun turrets had been rotated aft to provide some protection from the weather. Jonathan found that these ships had a deep and slow pitch, which was most disconcerting in these short, steep seas. Every time *Warspite* dipped her nose, there was a hollow boom, which echoed through the ship as if it was the inside of a bass drum, closely followed by a noisy explosion of spray, whipped aft with the speed of their passage, spattering the bridgework like hail. It struck exposed flesh with the force of bullets.

There was then the slow pitch up, followed by a sickening fall, sometimes so deep that the racing propellers were exposed shaking the ship with a mad vibration, followed by another crash as the labouring bow pitched down again and the whole procedure was repeated.

Added to that was a slow corkscrew motion as the ship rolled.

The four ships were in an arrow formation, with the flagship leading. *Valiant* was on her port quarter. *Warspite* was on the starboard quarter and *Malaya* was on *Valiant's* port quarter in turn. Together, they formed probably the most powerful arrowhead the world had ever known.

The sight from the bridge shelter immediately abaft the open fore bridge was breath taking, quite literally in the teeth of the gale, which was raging outside. The conditions were far too much for the destroyer escorts, which had been left behind. A four-funnel light cruiser abreast of them was porpoising through the sea, only distinguishable from the surrounding murk by the flash of her wake as she cut through it under the shadow of her smoke. To Jonathan's way of thinking, the North Sea was either murky or rough, and frequently both. Today was typical. Characteristically, the Brits ignored the conditions and carried out their sweep anyway. That little ship on their beam somehow represented the spirit that he had seen since his arrival in the Grand Fleet: - purposeful, efficient, and ready for anything.

The Irish rising yesterday had been followed by a simultaneous attack in England by a force of zeppelins. The conditions today, however, were far too severe for those vessels to fly, so that at first light this morning, the German battle-cruisers had bombarded the coastal towns of Lowestoft and Yarmouth, doing considerable damage. It

6. A NEW FLAP

was clear that the Irish rising and these raids were coordinated. The British were good and mad.

The Grand Fleet had been ordered to sea as soon as it had completed coaling.

The 5th Battle Squadron had been sent on ahead, as their refuelling was finished long before their coal-fired sisters. They were about seventy miles south of the rest of the Fleet. The British battle cruisers were further to the southeast, trying to cut off the raiders. There had been an engagement between British Light Cruisers based at Harwich and the raiding German squadron. As far as anyone knew, nobody had been sunk and the Germans had fled.

Jonathan had eschewed his favourite post on the fore bridge, which was virtually uninhabitable, even though it was seventy-five feet above the waterline and more than two hundred and fifty feet aft of the bow. He was in the watch shelter, from which he had a limited view of what was going on through the clear view scuttles forward. He was conscious that there was not much space and he was probably in the way but he would not have missed this for the world. It was exhilarating.

"I bet we've missed the beggars," said the officer of the watch, between crashes. "If they bombarded at daybreak they'll be nearly home by now. It's werry waxing as Sam Weller would have said." Sam Weller was, of course the archetypal cheery cockney in Dickens' Pickwick Papers, which Jonathan had always enjoyed. "Werry waxing" seemed to be the default position of the Grand Fleet officers. He had heard those very words in his first visit to the wardroom. He felt the pressure on his soles as the ship rose up the next crest, only to fall back with a sickening crunch into the troubled sea. The racing screws made themselves felt as the ship rolled uncomfortably in the gale.

Sure enough, by the middle of the afternoon they received the recall by wireless. The enemy had got away and could not be caught. Grimly they reversed their course (a tricky evolution in itself in that sea) and headed back to Scapa at reduced speed. Jonathan began to appreciate the perpetual frustration of the blockade. That was the disadvantage of having part of the blockade being maintained by one's own, vulnerable, coast when there were people ruthless enough to shell innocent civilians in the hope of attracting a part of the British fleet which could be overwhelmed by numbers locally. "That's what they're after, old boy," Walwyn had told him "draw out a squadron or two and then wipe them out with locally superior numbers. Damn' clever but damned un-English."

Jonathan was not quite so sure of that, given what he had read of the Allied war aims and the effectiveness of the Blockade.

They arrived back in Scapa Flow the following forenoon. Jonathan decided that it was time to start his report. The priest had a good point. In many ways it gave him a great deal of freedom.

Dear Admiral Benson, he wrote

I am sorry that it has taken me so long to get in touch and give you the latest news but a lot has happened since we last met.

Grandmother has made me very welcome, thank you. We had a few difficulties to start off with but they are

6. A NEW FLAP

sorted out now. I have to say that she has been very generous and has given me the free run of her stables.

That was suitably obscure, he thought. He found that he was tempted to chew his penholder as he was composing like a schoolboy. Stables should be a good enough metaphor on which he could expand.

She has given me a mount of my own to use; she is a powerful brute (the mount that is) with a tremendous kick on her. I must say, for so heavy a beast she is pretty quick.

What next? Ah! He had it. If the stables were hunting stables rather than racing stables the analogy would be more exact.

We have had a couple of frustrating days out. The country, as you know, is quite rough for hunting and the fox is pretty leery of coming out but when he does, he is very elusive. Everyone is very keen to have a go, especially when he keeps on raiding the henhouse. He doesn't do very much damage but it is very annoying.

I have to say that the estate is very well organized and the...

He paused. He wanted to say that the head of the hunt had it all in hand but he was not familiar enough with the business to know what the proper term was. He was actually chewing his pen when there was a knock on his cabin door.

"Come in" he said. The door opened and there was Frank with a newspaper in his hand. "I say" he said, "you're in the ruddy paper!"

"What?" said Jonathan "How can I be?"

"Look, here it is, amongst all the diplomatic guff about the sinking of that ferry 'The evidence is then adduced of Captain Smith and Lieutenant Marston of the United States Navy together with Major Logan of the US Embassy who examined the *Sussex* and themselves discovered and retained 15 pieces of metal. The American officers gave technical reasons for the belief that the *Sussex* was torpedoed and expressed "the firm opinion that the pieces of metal were not part of a mine" Among them were two screw-bolts which Lieutenant Marston, whom we understand to be a specialist, fortuitously on a private visit to friends, says showed the effect of the explosion.' Here you are, see for yourself!"

Jonathan took the thing and read the article. It was a pretty fair summary of the official report under the headline "Evidence in the Sussex Case". Beside it was the full text of the note from Wilson to the Germans. Well, that was one of his problems solved. If that article were repeated in the States, as it may very well be, there would be no need for secrecy. He could write a perfectly normal letter home and to Constantina.

"Well I'm blowed," said Jonathan "At least it solves one of my problems. Father Anthony was right. By the way, what do you call the OIC of a foxhunt?"

"MFH, Master of Foxhounds, or just the Master. Why?"

"I'm writing to my Boss. Here, have a look at it and see what you think" passing over the sheet to Frank, who had taken a seat in the guest chair. Frank skimmed the

6. A NEW FLAP

document and said "Sounds OK to me. I presume you want to refer to Father as the Master?"

"Yes, I have been impressed with what I have seen over the past few days and I want to pass it on. He seems to have everything buttoned down pretty well."

"Well" said Frank, lighting his pipe "If he runs true to form, you'll get the chance to meet him soon. He hates journalists but he won't want to pass up the chance to meet a Yank. Apparently, he got on well with your lot in China in the year zero."

"I know about that," said Jonathan, re-lighting his own "A friend of my father's mentioned that he knew him just before I came over. Says he is pretty sound."

"He's actually pretty terrific" said Frank, "Personally groomed by Fisher from an early age, he is our best hope of dealing with the Bosh. He's a gunnery man. Was the Commander of the Flagship of the Mediterranean Fleet in '93 when she was sunk by her own squadron mate, Flag Captain in China in the year zero, got badly wounded, recovered and was promoted rear Admiral, then Third Sea Lord, C-in-C Atlantic Fleet as Vice Admiral and then took over the Grand Fleet in 'fourteen. He really is the best we have."

"I shall look forward to it when it comes" said Jonathan. "Do you normally work at this pace?"

"Sorry?" said Frank

"Well, two flaps, one after the other and no time to fuel in between."

"Depends," said Frank, drawing on his pipe. "We do spend a bit more time in port than we once did but there's no guarantee either way."

"That must be awkward"

"Well, on the one hand, we want to have a bash at the Bosh but on the other hand this is a damn' miserable anchorage. Sheep and stones mostly. Oh, that reminds me. Father Anthony is threatening to take us off on a cultural trip to look at some old stones. Do you fancy it?"

That sounded intriguing. "What sort of stones?" asked Jonathan.

"Well there are some strange stone circles up by Stromness which have caught his interest. He says they are pagan temples."

"Sounds exciting," said Jonathan.

"It'll be bloody wet, that I'll tell you for nothing. Place is full of ruddy bogs. Have you got any suitable gear?" Jonathan thought about this. In addition to his uniforms, he only had his civilian suit, which didn't seem suitable for bog trotting. "No" he said, "not really."

"Tell you what" said Frank, "I promised to get you sorted with some Coca-Cola. Come with me and we'll take a trip to the Army and Navy and see what they have in stock. It's Wednesday, so they'll be in Gutter Sound with the Destroyers."

SS Borodino, Scapa Flow, Wednesday 26th April 1916

SS Borodino was an unprepossessing merchantman of about 2000 tons. There were a number of boats surrounding her but the presence of Frank, as a Commander gave them some priority as they came alongside. Once aboard, however, everything was different. A door in the superstructure led down into a complete department store. The compartment was lined with sales counters manned by staff in white coats. The counter front displayed the words "Junior Army and Navy

6. A NEW FLAP

Store" and at the end was the address 15 Regent Street, London, Aldershot, Dublin, Malta, and Gibraltar.

The shop was crowded with officers and mess men, making various purchases. To Jonathan's surprise he saw *Warspite's* own wardroom mess man there ahead of them. "Hullo Simmonds" said Frank "What are you getting for us?"

"Oh a few bits of this and that sir. Mr Marston sir, they don't have coca cola today but they are having some sent up overnight, so you'll be able to have some tomorrow." That was incredibly thoughtful and Jonathan said so. It was really impressive that a special supply could be sent up overnight to this remote location.

"Whilst I am here sir, is there anything else I can get for you? Anything particularly American?"

Jonathan thought. Hotdogs and hamburgers! He had an idea. "Well yes, now you mention it. Do you know about frankfurter sausages and hamburger buns?"

"Are they a special sort sir?"

"Yes," said Jonathan. "They are thin and meaty, with a specially flavoured filling. They go in long buns with mustard and fried onions. Hamburgers are meat patties in round buns. And American Mustard!" he was really flying now. Then struck with a thought, he said to Frank "How do I pay for these? What's the norm?"

"Oh that's easy old chap. Open an account here and settle up monthly, that's what most people do."

"Great," said Jonathan. "Simmonds, I shall see to it, charge it to my tab"

"Very good sir" said Simmonds and, excusing himself went on to the next compartment, with a list in his hand.

Opening an account was a very simple process. He simply saw the clerk and gave his name. He had made an arrangement with a British Bank whilst he was in London and realized that he had a check book in his cabin. That presented no difficulty to the clerk who said that he would be billed monthly and therefore had thirty days credit.

Once that was sorted out Frank took him into another compartment, which did service as a tailors shop. "Local tweed sir" said the assistant "extremely hard wearing and quite chic sir. Many of the gentlemen like it."

Looking at the selection, Jonathan found that it was quite different to the sort of thing that he was used to. Subdued greens, shot with reds and yellows predominated. The cloth was fine and soft rather than the scratchy, hairy tweed he knew. He settled for a very fine green suit with a subtle red and dark green stripe in its herringbone weave. At the assistant's suggestion, he chose knickerbockers rather than conventional trousers, which he was told were likely to get wet in this climate. "May I suggest some cavalry twill for shore going in towns sir?"

The cavalry twill was a pleasing light tan colour and again the cloth was sturdy but comfortable.

They spent a happy couple of hours on *Borodino* where they met all sorts of people from other ships. They even took coffee in the ships saloon, which did service as a coffee shop cum restaurant.

Examining his purchases back in *Warspite* Jonathan found that he was now the proud possessor of a tweed knickerbocker suit, a matching tweed cap, several twill check shirts, some cavalry twill pants, a selection of stout woollen stockings and tartan ties. He had even bought a pair of oxblood brogues. He felt that if he was attired in that get up, he would look like a proper Scottish gentleman.

A few days later

Jonathan was very glad of his new clothes as he picked his way gingerly across a damp field. Brown had applied dubbin to the brogues and they were satisfyingly waterproof. He also appreciated the virtues of the knickerbockers. The grass and heather were quite long and very wet. As it was, his socks were wet but the rest of him was dry. Hamill, who had worn flannels, was wet up to his knees.

Father Anthony was dressed in a similar manner to Jonathan and was making use of a thumb stick. Not that he needed it; indeed for an older man he was really quite spry. All of them had knapsacks on their backs with their packed lunches. They had taken the dinghy from the ship, which Frank sailed with evident enjoyment. It was an exclusive group, just Father Anthony, Frank, Jonathan and Hamill, who had come along at the last moment.

"Should've taken some of the youngsters I suppose" Frank had said "but frankly I could do with a rest from them."

The trip was a wonderful break. There was heavy fighting in Ireland, with British gunboats shelling rebel positions in Dublin. The Irish men in *Warspite* kept discipline, but they were subdued. Father Anthony and Frank were working hard to reassure them that the fighting was limited to Dublin; the rest of the country appeared not to have risen. They deserved their holiday in Jonathan's opinion. He was seriously impressed with the way both men dealt with their charges.

The weather was overcast but clear, and the strange landscape of the islands was visible on all sides. Green and treeless, it could have been oppressive but there was a grandeur to it, especially the low heather clad hills. "A Fairy archipelago set in a summer sea, on a good day, someone once said" said Frank.

It had been a stiffish sail, up between the islands. The breeze was lively and the dinghy light, which meant that Frank had his hands full for most of the time. To Jonathan, who was enjoying himself, it was really quite striking how big the place was. Up here, at the top of the Flow, the fleet was an indistinct blur of misty smoke lost against the low island of Flotta but the evidence for its presence was clear. They had to negotiate gates in various submarine booms and nets and right up close to their destination was a lonely cruiser at anchor in the sound.

Frank headed up a shallow inlet, which led to a stone bridge. "OK you fellows" said Frank, "Drop the mast and we'll scull through." Between them, Jonathan and Hammill had the mast down and they took an oar each and rowed under the low arch. "Bet this is a bugger in the tide," said Hamill and Jonathan had to agree. The loch ahead of them looked large and the entrance was narrow.

Once through the bridge, a vista opened up ahead of them. There was an instant contrast to the openness of the Flow to the south. In this almost enclosed loch, the water was a slate grey colour, flecked with foam, surrounded by green and purple hills that stood out against the lowering grey sky. If Scapa Flow was a secret base, this place was its secret heart. The hills formed a wall around it, making it almost look like a cauldron.

6. A NEW FLAP

They re-set the mast and sail and set off north again. It was quite lively sailing and the wake of their passage bubbled happily behind them.

They saw that there was another low pair of green headlands dividing the loch again. On one of them was an extraordinary sight, a large, obviously artificial mound and beside it a series of huge stones, set upright in the ground. "That's it!" said Father Anthony "The Ring of Brodgar! An ancient sun temple!" Frank took the dinghy up onto the narrow pebble beach and Hamill jumped ashore with the painter and an iron spike, which he hammered into the soft ground. The others followed and made their way across the field to the extraordinary structure.[53]

The stones were slabs, about ten feet high set in a large ring with a ditch around them. It had a curious, otherworldly feel to it. Father Anthony had a map in his knapsack and consulted it carefully. Orientating himself he looked around. "Over there" he said, pointing "are the stones of Stenness, the Temple of the Moon. In comparatively recent times, young people used to come here to plight their troth. According to some, they would first go to the Temple of the Moon, where the woman, in the presence of the man, would kneel down and prayed to the god Woden. They would then come here and the man would do the same in the presence of the woman. There used to be a stone with a hole in it and they would have their hand fasting there."

He looked at the map again and turned the other way, "And over there" he continued "is the Ring of Bookan, the Temple of the Stars."

"Good heavens!" exclaimed Frank "I didn't realize it was so ruddy pagan."

"Well, there are some as would say that it wasn't as pagan as all that," said Father Anthony. "You see that there are some stories about Noah's wife, Tythea. When the Ark came to rest on Mount Ararat, she was the one who was told to teach the courses of the stars to her children. Seth was her best pupil and he founded the town of Araxim from where the Sages came.

"So what are they doing right up here?" asked Hamill

"Samothes, the son of Iapheth taught the Gauls and the Britons when they were still in Spain and when they came here, they brought their traditions with them. Some would say that this religion was as pure as any prior to the coming of Our Saviour."

"So no human sacrifices then Father?" asked Frank.

"Well, I don't know much about that," said the priest. "We are talking a good couple of thousand years BC. We know that the Jews strayed from the path often, so why not the Britons and the Gauls?"

They spent a happy half an hour poking about the ring and then at Father Anthony's suggestion they took the boat across the passage to the Temple of the Moon. Here the stones were much bigger, Jonathan estimated that they were about twenty feet high but there were only four of them. In the centre was an altar-like construction. "What price Human sacrifice now?" asked Frank.

"Well it certainly looks strange," said the priest. "I don't think we'll be having our picnic here though. Let's head over there" indicating another large green mound nearby.

There followed a completely surreal experience. At the priest's insistence, they went into the very centre of

6. A NEW FLAP

the mound, which was entered by a very low passageway, flanked by a white painted picket fence. Father Anthony had brought a flashlight and some candles in anticipation. To their astonishment the low passageway gave out into a great space with a high, corbelled roof. There were niches, which on further investigation gave out into small side chambers in the three walls away from the entrance. There were three stones on the floor, which appeared to be fitted for blocking the passages.

Father Anthony took out his candles and set them up on the stones and lit them with a cigarette lighter. The soft candlelight exaggerated the space. "Here we are," he said, "snug as a bug in a rug. Now let's have some lunch."

There was something strange about the acoustics. Although Jonathan was close to him, his voice seemed to be coming from a very long way away.

"I say, that's damned queer!" exclaimed Hamill. "I got a huge echo from you over here. Sounded like you were shouting."

"Oh?" said the priest, quietly. Jonathan couldn't hear him. "Well I can't hear a thing," said Jonathan. "Try a sound Father and let's see what happens."

Opening his mouth, the priest began to intone in Latin. The effect was an extraordinary wall of sound. By experimenting, they found out that when the hearers were close to him, they could barely hear him, whereas when they were out by the walls, the echo sounded as if he was singing from the side chambers.

"I say, can we stop, please" said Hamill after a while, "it's making me feel dashed odd." Obligingly the priest did so. "Thanks Padre" said Hamill, "It was giving me the collywobbles. It's a dashed spooky place in here."

"Apparently a group of Vikings took shelter from a storm in here years ago. Two of them went mad," said the priest.

"Well I'm not surprised," said Jonathan, "there's heap big medicine here, as our Indian friends would say. What is this place?"

"Technically, it's a tomb," said Father Anthony, "but I think it's much more than that. Do you know, at midwinter, the setting sun lights up this chamber?"

"Must have been built by a Navigator!" said Frank. "If its midwinter, it must be…what do you call this place Father?"

"Maeshowe"

"Well there you go. Now I'm famished and I could really do with a drink." They sat on the floor and opened their knapsacks and put their supplies together. There were sandwiches, cold chicken, a bit of salad and a couple of bottles of beer each.

Before eating, Father Anthony said a brief grace and Frank and the priest crossed themselves. Somehow, the ritual seemed fitting in this place, which must count, he thought, as one of the strangest meals Jonathan had ever had.

On the way back he asked Father Anthony why he had done it.

"Sometimes" said the old priest "one has to confront ones fears."

Jonathan thought he was beginning to get the measure of this man and was becoming aware of a bond between them. "What did you fear, Father?"

The priest thought for a few moments. "I suppose fear itself, really. It is the weapon of the Enemy. It distorts our view and can be very dangerous. Much evil can be done through fear. There is power in that place and it is not wholly benign. I wanted to face it."

It was a decidedly odd conversation to be having on a boat sailing back down Scapa Flow but no odder than the experiences he had enjoyed that day.

Sunday 30th April, HMS Iron Duke, Battleship Line A Scapa Flow

On their return from their trip up the Flow, there was a message waiting for Jonathan from the Captain. They were invited to the Fleet flagship for drinks on Sunday after church. Jonathan had not seen a normal Sunday in harbour before and found it an interesting experience.

It started with Divisions, where the whole ship's company was inspected by the Captain, accompanied by a train of officers, Walwyn, Russell the Paymaster and Keir the Fleet Surgeon together with the heads of department. To Jonathan's surprise, Philpotts invited Jonathan to join them, which he did with alacrity.

The whole thing was accompanied by the Royal Marine Band, which was playing a selection of tunes including, Jonathan noted dryly, 'Yankee Doodle' and a selection of Sousa marches. All the men were drawn up in their Sunday best. There were so many that the quarterdeck alone was not big enough to accommodate them and some had to muster in the batteries and on the forecastle. They were, on balance, a smart bunch.

The news from Ireland was that the fighting was reduced to street sniping of a sort that Jonathan was familiar with from Vera Cruz. Apart from 'disturbances' in Clonmel and Enniscorthy the rest of the island seemed to be quiet. To Jonathan's surprise he saw that General Maxwell, Cliff Carver's prospective father-in-law had been dispatched to Ireland with 'plenary powers'. The men were still settled, and there appeared to be no underlying problems.

After inspection they were allowed to stand easy but the Captain and his party carried on round the ship from top to bottom. Philpotts had a keen eye and missed nothing.

On his return to the quarterdeck, boatswains' whistles sounded for the rigging of Church. The actual order was " Rig for Church! Roman Catholics and Jews Fall out," which sounded rather odd to Jonathan's ears but, on reflection made a certain sort of sense. Jonathan was surprised to see how many men did actually fall out and descended the after hatchway to their own service. Those who remained brought up stools and chairs and set them up in a hollow square around a lectern, which had been set up aft. Jonathan saw and heard that the neighbouring ships were following the same routine.

When all was ready, the Anglican Chaplain, Mr Carey appeared and the order "off caps" was given and obeyed smartly. The service consisted of some hymns, accompanied by the Band, some readings from the Book of Common Prayer, which Jonathan recognized and a lesson read by the Captain. Another hymn and it was over. "On caps! Dismiss!" and the men were free to amuse themselves for the rest of the day.

After the bustle, getting ready in his cabin Jonathan could hear something of the RC service below. There was clearly something peculiar about the acoustics. Now he knew what he was listening to, it was clearer than last time. In contrast to the short and simple service that he had just witnessed on the quarterdeck, this was an elaborate affair, with chanting and bells. Some of the

6. A NEW FLAP

melodies that he half caught sounded beautiful. He made a mental note to ask Father Anthony if he could attend himself some time.

And now he was alongside the Fleet Flagship.

HMS Iron Duke was a similar size to *Warspite* but had two more big guns instead of *Warspite's* more powerful machinery. Jonathan knew that there was always a trade off in dealing with ships of war. Higher speed meant fewer guns, or else less armour. Heavier armour meant less speed or fewer guns. In essence, you could have higher speed and heavier armour, but fewer guns or else lower speed, more guns and heavier armour, but not more guns, high speed and heavy armour, at least, unless you wanted a much bigger ship.

The guns that *Warspite* did have were much bigger than those of *Iron Duke*. The 13.5" gun threw shells weighing half a ton more than twelve miles, whereas the 15" gun threw shells of three quarters of a ton up to seventeen miles, that was well over the horizon from the highest fighting top.

In short, *Warspite* and her sisters had a greater weight of broadside than the *Iron Dukes* and were four knots faster. Jonathan was reminded that the ship he was serving in was a pretty unique piece of kit.

The pinnace that brought them was Donald's and Jonathan had been amused to hear Philpotts urging the young officer to keep his speed up. Clearly the demands of the Fleet were not the same as the demands of peacetime propriety. In any event they arrived alongside *Iron Duke's* companionway without difficulty.

Philpotts was piped aboard and warmly welcomed by the Captain of the Fleet. He introduced Jonathan as "Our Yank." To Jonathan's surprise, he found that he was in the company of Captain Dryer of Fire Control fame who was now the Captain of the Fleet. Jonathan could not think of a better person to occupy that position. He was a highly scientific officer who had written many papers on fire control and Jonathan had read every word this man had written. He was, not to put too high a label on it, awestruck.

Below decks, the Admiral's quarters were identical to those in *Warspite*. The ladder led down into a large lobby. Captain Dryer knocked at a door in the after bulkhead, which was opened by a Flag Lieutenant-Commander. In the cabin, Jellicoe rose from behind a desk to greet them. Jonathan was surprised how small he was, and idly wondered if all British Admirals were small. Jellicoe smiled and shook Philpotts' hand warmly, "Edward" he said, "How nice to see you again, it's been really too long!"

"Hello sir!" said Philpotts beaming "Well you do keep us rather busy."

"Sorry about that" said the Admiral, "but it can't be helped." He turned to Jonathan, putting out his hand "and you must be Lieutenant Marston, here at last! You're very welcome. Thank you for taking the time to come and see us. I trust Captain Philpotts is treating you well?"

He made it sound as if Jonathan was doing him a favour rather than the other way round. Instinctively Jonathan took the hand and shook it, noting abstractedly that this was the first time that he had shaken the hand of a flag officer rather than saluting him.

"Sir, I'm delighted to be here" said Jonathan "thank you so much for having me. Indeed he is, I have been made very welcome."

6. A NEW FLAP

"So I heard," said Jellicoe "Has your coca cola arrived safely?"

Nonplussed, Jonathan said that it had.

"I bought some myself," said Jellicoe. "I don't drink very much at sea and it serves admirably, although it is a little sweet for my taste. Now, do come in and let's have a yarn" and he ushered them into what was clearly his sitting room. It had the air of a formal, front room designed for visitors, which did not, in general get much use. It was not a welcoming space. Philpotts, Dryer and the Flag Lieutenant-Commander followed on. As they entered Jonathan was surprised to see a large slobbery bulldog, which heaved itself to its feet and waddled over to greet the visitors on its bandy legs. "Hello Patch" said Philpotts, ruffling its floppy ears, for which he was rewarded with a series of wet licks.

"This is Patch," said Jellicoe to Jonathan, "I am afraid that in my position one is really expected to have a dog, and if one is going to have a dog, it really ought to be a bulldog. Or at least that is what I am told." The dog moved over to Jonathan, clearly expecting to be petted. Jonathan was not a doggy person, so he patted the grotesque head in a distracted fashion, which seemed to suffice.

"Do sit yourselves down gentlemen," said Jellicoe. "We shall be joined shortly by the commanders of the aircraft carriers, but in the meantime what can I get you?"

Jonathan sat on a convenient sofa and, to his surprise the dog collapsed at his feet and then rested its head on his ankle. As time went on, it fell asleep and began to snore. Jonathan was increasingly aware of dog drool all over his sock, but decided that it was better to say nothing and endure a soggy ankle. The more irreverent part of his brain wondered if there was a market for socks, which had been drooled on by the bulldog of the Commander in Chief of the British Grand Fleet.

Philpotts, Dryer and the Flag Lieutenant-Commander (whose name was Fitzherbert) settled for gin, but Jonathan asked for coffee, which duly arrived in a silver pot with two cups. It would appear that the Commander in Chief was going to join him in a cup. To Jonathan's surprise, it was really rather good.

"I acquired a taste for decent coffee in the Med, years ago." Said Jellicoe, "Most of the stuff that's served these days is absolute rubbish! This one's Columbian Arabica, I hope it will remind you of home. Boston isn't it?"

"Indeed it is sir."

"Captain Sims told me you were coming. I understand he knows your father"

"Yes sir, he does."

"A very good man. We met in China years ago and have corresponded ever since. In fact, he wrote me a very kind letter the other day," turning to Fitzherbert he said, "Herbert, what did we do with it?"

"I'll get it sir," said the Flag Lieutenant-Commander and putting his drink down he ducked out of the cabin.

"How is he, by the way? He never says in his letters"

"Well sir, when I saw him, he was about to commission a new dreadnought. I managed to get a look around her. She was mighty impressive" As he spoke, Jonathan was suddenly struck by the incongruity of what he had just said. This man had charge of more than thirty Dreadnoughts, including some of the very latest type.

6. A NEW FLAP

The dog emitted a loud snore and shifted position, wetting some more of Jonathan's ankle. He became conscious of an unpleasant smell, and realized that the animal had also broken wind.

"Ah yes" said Jellicoe, ignoring the rising fetor, "*Nevada* isn't it? I should be very interested to see how he manages those triple turrets. We looked at that idea a little while ago when I was Director of Naval Ordnance, but we could never get a satisfactory mounting. There is also the problem of putting too many eggs in one basket. If a turret with two guns is knocked out, it is better than a turret with three guns."

The officer returned with a letter.

"Thank you Herbert" said Jellicoe as it was handed to him. "Here we are, dated 13th of April 1916

'USS Nevada, Navy Yard, New York

....hardly a day has passed since this war began that I have not thought of you and the great responsibility that you bear, and I have wondered what have been the tactical conceptions which, according to Mahan may be expected under such conditions....wishing you every possible success'

"It was very thoughtful of him to remember me at such a time."

With a slight lurch, Jonathan realized that the letter must have been written immediately after commissioning, which he remembered was due to be March 11th. On reflection, it was not surprising that Sims was thinking about his friend at such a time. It must have been in that letter that he had mentioned Jonathan.

"He speaks of you in glowing terms and asks that I should do anything that I can to facilitate your mission."

Jonathan changed position slightly, which resulted in the dog shifting its own position, grunting and licking his ankle with a large wet tongue a couple of times in its sleep.

"Well sir, with all due respect, you seem to be at the cutting edge of Naval tactics at the moment. It is not really surprising that he was thinking of you. No-one else is doing what you are at the moment." Jonathan felt that he was being jejune, but what he was saying was absolutely true. This was the largest fleet the world had ever seen and this unassuming man was in charge of it.

"Not necessarily, Lieutenant" said Jellicoe, "There's a chap sitting five hundred miles south east of here who is doing exactly the same thing. It never pays to underestimate the other fellow." It was very true.

"Do you know what you are going to do sir?" It was out before Jonathan could think about it.

Jellicoe smiled a sad little smile as if to say "nice try" but said "I'll tell you what I shan't do. I shan't be following in the wake of a German battle squadron dropping mines! If he turns away, I shall assume that he's trying to lead me into a trap and I shan't be drawn."

"Even if it means he gets away sir?" Jonathan was the most junior officer there, but he had been made so comfortable, he was not aware of any strangeness in questioning the C-in-C.

"Of course. You have to understand that our margin of superiority isn't guaranteed. Scheer would like nothing better than to reduce our strength by a ship or to. As long as I am in command, he won't be allowed to do it."

6. A NEW FLAP

Jonathan realized that there was real steel behind the charming manners.

"Might that be misunderstood sir?" Jonathan was too engrossed to worry about seeming to be rude.

"Well if it is, it can't be helped. It is far better to do the right thing for the right reasons than do the wrong thing simply because some ignorant people want you to. I do have a few strategies of my own."

There was a discrete knock on the door. The dog draped around Jonathan's ankle woke instantly, sat up and began barking in a regular rhythm. It was a surprisingly deep sound. "Down Patch" shouted Jellicoe, "Get down Sir! Behave!".

The dog, hearing the word of command stopped its' barking and looked at its master, grumbling in its' throat. "Down Patch" said Jellicoe "Come here boy". The dog looked at him sideways and then went over to him and collapsed again as the Admiral ruffled its' ears. "Come" he said to the knocker.

The door opened and a Captain and two Lieutenant Commanders were ushered in and made welcome. "Delighted to see you gentlemen" said Jellicoe, restraining Patch, who was still interested in the newcomers. "Come and have a drink and tell me all about how things are with you at the moment."

The Captain said, "Well sir, I think that I had better let these two answer that. You know all about my flotilla I trust?"

"Indeed I do Edwyn," said Jellicoe. "The 1st Light Cruiser Squadron is always close to my heart. The fastest and the best!"

"You are too kind sir. Gentlemen?" He looked expectantly at the two junior officers.

The two officers exchanged glances. The older of the two, Robinson, said, "well sir, we are all ready and raring to go, but no-one seems to know how to use us. They got rid of us from Harwich and now, officially I'm with the 3rd Light Cruiser Squadron by way of the Battle cruiser Squadron. Apparently attached to the 1st LCS. My friend here is even more lost."

Jellicoe resumed his seat and looked at him thoughtfully.

"We'd really like to help sir. I am sure that we can."

"Sit yourselves down, have a drink and unwind" said Jellicoe, "tell me what you can do."

Nothing loth, the two junior officers settled down on either side of one of the admiral's sofas with a glass of gin each and began to expand. The Captain took an armchair and steepled his fingers as he listened to his juniors.

"As we have said before sir," said Robinson, "the problem with the zeppelins is that in general they fly too high and too fast for our machines"

Jellicoe inclined his head in acknowledgment.

"Well sir, they are vulnerable on the ground."

"Indeed" said Jellicoe in agreement.

"But their bases are too far away from our airfields for our aeroplanes to attack them."

"I had heard that," said Jellicoe.

"Well sir" said Robinson "we can launch aeroplanes from the sea, well within range of Cuxhaven and Tondern and burn the beasts in their lair. And what's more, our new aeroplanes can bomb the blasted things as they're flying. We nearly got them last month, here Gerry, you take over, it's your story!"

6. A NEW FLAP

The other officer took a sip from his drink and went on. "As you know sir, we were asked to attack the zepp base at Hoyer. We went well inside the Vyl light vessel, with the Harwich force in support and the Battle-cruiser force in support of them. We got our planes away by 0530. It was pretty foul, with heavy snowstorms, but we were able to operate OK. Trouble was that there were no zepps at Hoyer, they were at Tondern instead, a bit further inland."

"It ended up with a bit of a mess as I recall," said Jellicoe, "collisions and the loss of some aeroplanes?"

"Indeed it did sir, but we did get the High Seas Fleet out. And some zepps. I think we can do it again and rather better if we get the chance."

"Go on" said Jellicoe.

Jonathan was fascinated. This is exactly what Fiske was advocating back at home. The Brits were actually doing it. For real.

"What do you need?" asked Jellicoe.

"Not much really sir, a calm-ish sea, some escorts in case Jerry finds us whilst we are launching and that's about it."

"What do you think Edwyn?" Jellicoe asked the captain. The man was covering every base.

"I think it can be done sir. Indeed I think it should be done." The overall commander was clearly someone who had serious vision. More to the point, Jellicoe clearly trusted his judgment, which spoke volumes.

"Very well then" said Jellicoe. "Get it done. Give me a draft plan and let's get it underway. The sooner the better."

It was a perfect illustration of the way that the man worked. Jonathan was impressed. He was surprised, however when Jellicoe turned his eyes onto Jonathan. "What do you think lieutenant? Do you like the idea?"

Nonplussed, Jonathan said, "Well sir, I have no experience of such things. I simply don't know what aeroplanes can do."

"Well, now is a good time to find out" said Jellicoe. "Do you want to go with them and see what's going on?"

Jonathan was overwhelmed. This was access to the cutting edge of Naval warfare. No one, but no one knew what this weapon was capable of, and here he was being allowed in to watch it in action. He realized that he was incredibly privileged, and also, at the same time, he was being trusted with some of the greatest secrets than any Navy might have. Jellicoe had clearly taken a decision that he was prepared to share these incredibly private moments with the US Navy in the person of Jonathan J Marston esq. The analytical part of his brain told him that meant that Jellicoe was sure that the US would be coming into the war on the side of the allies, and pretty soon. It was a momentous moment.

There was only one answer. "I should be delighted sir."

"Excellent" said the Admiral. I'll get a travel warrant sorted out and you can go south with them this evening. Can you get back here for 1800?"

"Of course sir." There was no other answer.

The rest of the encounter passed off in a very pleasant fashion, and as Jonathan returned to his ship to get his things he found that he completely understood why the Fleet called him "Father". He was charming, and approachable, but there was never any doubt as to who

6. A NEW FLAP

was in charge and what was to be done. He felt that he had been in the presence of greatness.

Back in his cabin he just had time to finish his report to Benson: -

"The Master is a splendid chap, who really knows what he is doing. I had coffee with him today and was very impressed. I daresay that he will surprise us all. He has asked me to go on a very interesting trip, which will involve some hawking. I cannot tell you how much I am looking forward to that. He is a serious friend.

Incidentally, our other mutual friend is right about the harriers. I saw a group at full speed over rough country the other day. We really need a pack of our own

Yours ever

Marston"

Frank had told him that there was a special breed of hunting dog, designed to catch hares, called a harrier, which was smaller and faster than the usual hunting pack, and he thought that was an excellent simile for the light cruisers.

Leaving the letter, open, in the Sacristy, he packed a bag and went on deck to get a boat back to the flagship to pick up the other officers

7. A Seaplane Raid

The Firth of Forth, Monday 1ˢᵗ May 1916, afternoon

His Majesty's Seaplane Carrier *Engadine* was a channel ferry, bearing an uncomfortable resemblance to the *Sussex*. Just abaft her second funnel a large box-like structure had been added on with a stout pair of cranes aft of that. Jonathan was with Lieutenant-Commander Robinson who was in command of this unlikely looking warship.

"We're a bit basic old boy," Robinson had said, but we can offer you a corner of the wardroom for your own. We have pilots and aircrew to accommodate as well as seamen, so we all have to rough it a bit, but we shan't be out very long and there are some decent hotels in Edinburgh. Mind you, I think we're going off tonight or tomorrow, so perhaps you had better stay with us for the moment.

As they came on board, the only mark of respect was a brief pipe from a Petty Officer and a salute from a single lieutenant. "Hello Sir!" said the latter, throwing a surprisingly smart salute. "How did you get on with Father?"

"Pretty well Fred"[54] said his commander. "Looks like it's on. By the way this is Lieutenant Marston of the US Navy, come to see how we're getting on."

"Hullo there!" said Fred, saluting him. "Pleased to meet you Lieutenant. Welcome to Fred Karno's Army. Are you a flyer yourself?"

"Jonathan, please" said Jonathan. "And no, not at all. I have barely seen an airplane, let alone been in one."

"Well we'll soon fix that for you" said Fred. Turning to Robinson he said "Sir, I should like to test 8359 if I may, the carb's giving a bit of trouble. Is that ok?"

"Of course Fred, get 'em closed up and you can have your jaunt. Do you fancy it Marston? Quick trip around the Firth? See some things you have never seen before?"

"I'd sure like that sir," said Jonathan, who was intrigued. There had been a couple of aircraft at Vera Cruz, but apart from a distant buzz, he had seen very little of them.

"Will you take him Fred?" asked Robinson. "You'll need some ballast won't you?"

"Delighted" said Fred, "Come with me and we'll get you kitted out. PO? Call the flying party would you. Get them to get 8359 out and unfolded: - we'll be along shortly."

"Aye aye sir" the PO responded.

"Oh, and we'll use the port motor boat. Get her alongside would you? There's a good chap."

"Port motor boat alongside. Aye aye sir." He saluted and turned aft towards the big box structure, piping and shouting alternately "Flying party to Flying Stations! Flying party to Flying Stations!"

Fred led the way to the main ladder that led down to what was once the forward saloon. It was eerily like the one on *Sussex* with the same smell of leather, old tobacco and stale beer. The difference was that this ship was uncompromisingly alive. Opening a door he said to Jonathan "dump your stuff in there and we'll see to it later. Do you have anything valuable on you? Just in case

7. A SEAPLANE RAID

we get a dunking? If you have, you may like to leave it here, it will be quite safe."

Jonathan left his billfold, pipe, tobacco and after some reflection, his watch on the bunk in the small cabin. Fred led him aft to the sheer wall of the box which rose high over their heads. Passing through a pair of double doors they were suddenly in a different world.

The space seemed enormous, and it was filled with…things. Jonathan's first impression was of a forest of struts, wires, radiators, motors and wings. It was lit with a garish white light from the ceiling high overhead. Looking further, he could see that the white painted frame of the walls and ceilings carried racks filled with all sorts of strange items of equipment. Beyond that through the open doors the misty Firth was bathed with a greyish light. In the hangar it was noisy and there was a strange, stirring smell of oil, petrol, warm machinery and something else, rather like pear drops.

High above them, a couple of mechanics were doing something to the engine of the nearest machine. The engine was at the front of a box-like fuselage on stilts mounted on what looked like a pair of small wooden boats on a trolley. The wings of the contraption were folded back against its body like some hulking great moth. At the very front was a large wooden airscrew, behind which was something that resembled nothing more nor less than the front of a domestic cooking stove, with slits cut in it. Presumably that was some sort of ventilation for the motor. The whole machine appeared to be straddling a hatch of some sort. There were wire braces everywhere.

Beside it was another, similar machine and aft of that was a raised coaming with a small capstan and a ladder aft of that leading down into the bowels of the ship. The iron deck, which was painted a deep blue, had a series of sunken ringbolts, presumably so that the machines could be tied down in a seaway. The smell of machine oil was very strong.

There was really not a lot of room for anything.

Fred had stopped just inside the door and was taking it all in. "Pretty impressive eh? No matter how many times I see this it never fails to get my heart racing!"

Jonathan had to agree. The machines appeared enormous. Jonathan was not a small man, but at full stretch he would only just be able to touch the bottom wing of the nearest thing as it sat on its trolley. There was another set of wings above that almost as high above the lower ones. Two men were working on the engine one standing on the wing, and the other on the float.

"Ok Stevens?" Fred asked the one on the float who was wearing a dirty overall, covered in oil. His hands were black and he had clearly been wiping his brow with them as his face had a comically streaked look.

"Naw sir" said the mechanic, who appeared to be chewing tobacco. "The bleeder's still losing power and I don't know why. Plugs keep oiling up for some reason. I'm guessing some bugger's sent us the wrong oil. Too thick I reckon."

"Have you tried thinning it with some petrol?" suggested Fred.

"Well if'n I do sir, will you fly it?"

"I'd fly anything you certified Stevens, even that bloody workbench!"

"And that, sir, is why you is a bleedin' hofficer and I ain't!" The witticism seemed to go down well with the

7. A SEAPLANE RAID

rest of the men. "I'll keep on it a bit, sir, afore we tries that'un. Some machine oil mebbe. Are you taking 8359 up sir?"

"That's the general idea Stevens, I want to see if you've fixed that carburettor. Did you sluice it out as we agreed?"

"Indeed I did sir. Full of sludge it were. I think the petrol's been sitting too long in those big tanks and going bad. Going ter have ter filter it I think. Better safe than sorry. She's last one in line sir, we're just pushing her out now for you." It was clear to Jonathan that both officer and man knew exactly what they were about in this novel environment. He was impressed, but then thought that if he was going to trust his life to this unlikely contraption the officer had a vested interest in what was going on in it.

Fred led the way aft past the first machines to a much smaller one with a cheerful chequered pattern in red and white on its front. "Now these are the beasts!" said Fred, "based on a racing plane before the war, these will sort out those blasted zepps. Ninety knots and 10,000 feet. That'll get the beggars!"

Against the massive size of the other machines, this one looked small, neat and very dangerous. There was a business-like machine gun mounted on the diminutive top wing. "Only one seat though, more's the pity. Now here's *our* ride" and he indicated another large machine which was being wheeled out through some very large doors onto the quarterdeck by what seemed to be lots of men.

To Jonathan's surprise, all of them seemed to be wearing officer style caps, but were clearly enlisted men. Then he remembered that the British Army favoured that style of cap before it was replaced by steel helmets of a sort that would not have looked out of place at the Battle of Agincourt.

With considerable to-ing and fro-ing the thing was finally positioned to the satisfaction of the senior Petty Officer right under the cranes, one of which was turning in. A ground crew man swung up into the pilot's position. As the hook was lowered he fitted it into a loop fixed to the top wing of the airplane.

The crane whirred and the whole package was picked up and swung clear of the hangar onto the diminutive quarterdeck, steadied all the time by its attentive crew.

Once it was in position, the wings were unfolded. To Jonathan's fascinated eye it looked exactly like a butterfly emerging from its chrysalis. The bracing wires were attached to the floats by the crew, and the leading edge of the wings were locked in position. The butterfly image was so powerful that Jonathan almost expected the wings to flap occasionally as they extended. They did not.

There followed the performance of starting the engine. The man in the cockpit said in an audible tone "Switches off!"

"Switches off" came the reply from the deck.

The man seemed to be pumping something. "Dope, three pumps" he said.

"Dope three pumps" was the echo from below

"Throttle open one tenth, ignition retarded"

"Throttle open one tenth, ignition retarded." To Jonathan's ears it sounded like some strange religious ceremony.

"Pressure 3 pounds"

7. A SEAPLANE RAID

"Pressure 3 pounds." The litany continued. Jonathan had the irreverent thought that the crew of the airplane was invoking the gods of the air. It certainly fitted with the magic of the idea that this contraption could actually fly!

"Contact!"

"Clear!"

The man in the cockpit began winding something, which whirred and at the same time there was a hiss and the airscrew began to revolve. There was a cough and then a roar as the engine caught. It was a much more certain catch than the fuss and palaver experienced starting Clementina Fessenden's automobile. The engine was throttled back and settled down to a comfortable rumble. It sounded powerful to Jonathan's untutored ear.

Fred said, with satisfaction "225 horsepower. Sweet![55] Now Jonathan, let's find something to fit you. In here" and he opened the door of a locker, which to Jonathan's surprise was full of leather coats and large boots. Flying helmets and goggles were hanging on pegs.

"Not too cold today" said Fred. I should just use a coat, mittens, goggles and helmet. No need for boots."

Jonathan selected some garments and felt vaguely foolish getting into them. The coat was lined in sheepskin and surprisingly warm.

"Coat's not as long as we use on land, but we're better to be able to swim if we fall into the oggin, I always say." It sounded ominous.

"Do you often fall into the oggin?" asked Jonathan as they were walking out of the big doors towards the machine, which was trembling, ready for the off.

"Not often, flying these buses, but trying to fly off THAT lot is another thing altogether." He gestured

171

towards the other seaplane carrier anchored alongside them. It was very similar to *Engadine* but had a sloped platform over the bow flanked by a pair of masts with derricks attached to them.

"Do you mean that you can actually fly off the deck?" asked Jonathan, astonished.

"Piece of cake" said Fred. "Well, that is if you don't mind your cake wet and soggy occasionally. It's the occasionally that reminds you that you don't want to be wearing heavy boots and a big coat!"

They were now back at the seaplane, which looked even more intimidating with its wings unfolded and the engine running. The wings overhung the narrow ship's beam by a considerable margin. It looked altogether far too big for the small and crowded quarterdeck on which it sat. No effort had been made to make the space suitable for its current use save for removing the wooden benches that had previously occupied it. By contrast, and almost to offset that, a pair of 12 pounder guns had been added to the ship right aft. The whole business looked seriously incongruous to Jonathan's eyes.

"Better mount up" said Fred. "I am just going to take a walk around and make sure everything is where it should be."

To Jonathan, the cockpit seemed impossibly high up from the deck. There were some obvious footholds, but they appeared to be inaccessible. Apart from anything else every access seemed to be obstructed by wires "Err, how do I….?" asked Jonathan diffidently.

"On the floats, knee in the step, Hands on the longeron, pull yourself up, other foot in the step and swing over" was the slightly unhelpful reply. There were indeed two slot-like affairs at the bottom of the fuselage

7. A SEAPLANE RAID

that were, apparently additional footholds. He put his knee into the slot and tried to pull himself up, but couldn't get any purchase and slipped back onto the float.

Looking around for help, Jonathan saw that Fred was engaged elsewhere, checking that the wings were properly locked. A mechanic said, "Use the bomb gear sir. Get your left foot on that and you'll find it easier." Indeed, there were a couple of substantial rails running below the fuselage, supported on solid looking metal struts. Once he had got his left foot on the rail, it was easy to get his knee into the slot, shift his left foot into the foothold and swing his body up into the passenger place. He was slightly concerned that he had grasped the fabric fuselage harder than was good for it, but a surreptitious examination showed that no damage had been caused by his mittened fingers.

Once inside, Jonathan found that he was presented with a wicker seat with a leather cushion on it and not much else. The hull of the thing was made up of a wooden frame braced by yet more wires. It was trembling under the power of the engine and the wash from the prop. A square of plywood was fixed to the bottom frame that did service for a floor. It was small and flimsy. The frame was covered in translucent fabric that was clearly not strong enough to step on. Jonathan felt quite vulnerable, but there was nothing he could do about it.

Sitting down, he saw that there was a rudimentary wooden desk affair in front of him. It reminded him of the sort of desks that he sat in at school. There was even a plywood panel in front of his knees. On one side was a wireless set with various dials and a Morse key. This airplane could obviously communicate with whom it needed to in the most modern fashion

In front of him, he could see the pilot's cockpit, which appeared to have a large wooden steering wheel in it, together with several dials on a dashboard and some levers on a quadrant. It looked not unlike a simplified version of the steam control panel of a ship. He was reminded that operating gas motors was a complicated affair and was instantly transported back to a hair-raising trip with Clementina in her motorcar. She was an accomplished motorist, albeit with a tendency to prefer speed to caution. Starting her vehicle always seemed to involve much fiddling with knobs and enthusiastic cranking of the motor

He could also see a large compass on top of the coaming, right in front of the pilot. It was on gimbals. It was reassuring to see something so familiar in such strange surroundings. Looking over the side of the contraption he realized that he was a long way up above the deck.

A sailor in overalls swung up beside him and leaned over the padded cockpit rim. "Here you go sir. Let's just get you strapped in." To Jonathan's surprise he found that webbing straps were produced, one over each shoulder and two more coming from the region of his hipbones.

The man flicked them out with practiced ease. Jonathan was fascinated to see that the system was almost fool proof. The strap coming over his left hip ended with a brass fitting with a tapered spindle on it. The other straps had holes in them surrounded with brass eyelets like a belt. The procedure was that the straps were placed over the tapered pin, as tight as was comfortable, and then they were secured in place by a cotter pin that

7. A SEAPLANE RAID

slipped through the tapered spindle and kept all the straps in place.

"If you need to get out in a hurry sir, all you need to do is pull this lanyard" indicating a lanyard attached to the pin "and you're free immediately. If you go over, wait until the aircraft is stable and then pull the pin. Don't release it until the aircraft has stopped moving."

"Sorry?" said Jonathan not quite following what he was being told, which sounded important.

"Well sir" said the man "sometimes, an aircraft can pitch over on landing. That makes the passenger a bit like a pea in a catapult, so you can be thrown out rather violently. That is generally not a good idea. Hitting the sea at that speed is generally frowned upon. It can break your neck.

"The trick is to keep the belt on long enough to stay in the 'plane until you are about to sink. That's when you want to get out quickly."

It was reassuring information.

Fred by now had swung up into his position like a monkey and was sitting in the front cockpit. Jonathan was conscious of bits of the planes moving as Fred tested the controls. Apparently satisfied he leaned over the rim and gave the order "Haul out." The electric winch whirred and the aircraft was swung up and over the rail.

As it did so, the wind caught it and it began to sway alarmingly. Fred opened the engine briefly and the control surfaces moved so that the machine steadied into the wind. Jonathan suddenly realized that this machine was not a helpless victim of the wind, but actually welcomed it, so that it could be used to its owners' advantage.

It was fended off from the side by long poles with padded ends wielded from the quarterdeck. He became aware of the motorboat coming underneath them, and catching the lines from the rear of the floats that had been, up until then, used as steadying lines from the ship. The only restraints were now the crane hook from *Engadine* attached to the upper plane and the slip wire from the floats held by the motor-boat, which cleared downwind, anchoring the airplane head into wind in a haze of blue exhaust smoke.

Once the floats made contact with the water Jonathan realized just how light the structure was. The sea state was pretty calm, but the airplane bobbed around like a cork Fred opened the engine briefly to get the aircraft under control.

He had been watching the proceeding intently, and once settled he stood up and waved his arms in an unmistakable gesture. "Clear!" he shouted and the winch slackened off allowing Fred to unhook the crane, which immediately hauled the hook out of the way.

The airplane was now bouncing about in the slight chop of the sea in a quick and light motion as the engine continued to turn over. It was quite uncomfortable. Fred raised his right hand in a sketchy salute and then pointed forward, for all the world like an old time general directing people to charge. He leaned forward again and appeared to be doing something with his left arm. Looking out, Jonathan noticed that they were facing the most enormous railway bridge that he had ever seen. It looked frighteningly close. The motorboat released their painter and they were free.

The engine roared again and Jonathan felt a pressure in his back as the machine gathered pace,

7. A SEAPLANE RAID

bouncing over the sea much like a skimming stone thrown by a skilled operator. After a short while the bouncing stopped, the engine note changed and they were literally flying.

To say that it was a novel feeling was an understatement. The overwhelming sensation was the noise and vibration from the engine in front of them. Then there was the wind from the speed of their passage. Snugged down in the body of the machine as he was, it did not impinge too much on Jonathan, but he was well aware of the power of it. In addition to that, the airplane was bouncing around in the air in an entirely unpredictable fashion. At least in a small boat, one could see the sea, and get some sort of idea as to what was coming next. In the transparent air, this couldn't be done, which meant that the bumps and waves were unexpected. That said, the speed was probably twice that of the fastest surface vessel, which meant that the disturbance was shorter by a factor of two. As they climbed higher the bouncing slowed and then virtually stopped. Jonathan was surprised to see that as they gained height, their apparent speed reduced to a point where they were almost sailing serenely over the grey water between the green shores.

Looking over the side of the machine, Jonathan had a clear view of the massive bridge as they passed over it. The construction was like nothing he had ever seen. Three large, red painted lozenge shapes made of latticed iron tubes were joined by conventional bridges. Unlike the bridges that Jonathan knew, this structure embraced the railway that ran across it so that a train was actually steaming through it as they passed over it.

In front of them now was a line of big ships looking like toys from his present elevation. He realized that they must be the battle cruisers and he was surprised at how much detail that he could see.

Fred tilted the machine and flew along the line, giving Jonathan a first class view of them. They were indeed handsome ships, but their size was only obvious because of the smaller boats alongside them. Beyond them was a large basin and some dry docks surrounded by green fields.

Fred appeared to be enjoying himself as he swung around the line of battle cruisers and made the machine climb. As they got higher, Jonathan was able to see a long way. They passed back over the bridge, which now looked much smaller. Jonathan was able to make out the seaplane carriers far below them. Beyond them was the smoke pall from a big city, which must be Edinburgh. Fred turned again and was heading straight for it. Jonathan had a clear view of a solid green hill above the town, which was unfolding below him like a map. As the light changed, he suddenly saw a massive grey lump of rock topped with buildings.

It was a large castle dominating the city from its rocky eminence. Fred tilted the airplane and treated Jonathan to the spectacle of this brooding presence, which appeared to rotate around the wings as the craft turned. Jonathan was fascinated. This view of the world was like nothing else he had ever experienced. To be able to move through the air, and wheel and turn like a bird was extraordinary. Fred descended so that Jonathan could get a better view of the castle. It was incredible. Walls, battlements and buildings seemed to grow out of the living rock. On a flagpole on the highest eminence

7. A SEAPLANE RAID

flapped the union flag of Great Britain. As they passed the flag Fred waggled the wings of the 'plane in salute and then piled on the power and they climbed away towards the Firth again.

All too soon, Fred was heading back towards the moored seaplane carriers and throttled back allowing them to descend. Another turn led them back towards the bridge and a controlled descent ended with them eventually kissing the water gently as they alighted not far from their mother ship. Fred taxied back towards *Engadine* and Jonathan noticed how skilfully he did it. With extraordinary delicacy he manoeuvred the seaplane into a position where the poles could manage it and the derrick could hook on. They were hoisted back on to the inadequate quarterdeck. Feeling tired and stiff, Jonathan found that he could get over the side of the machine and lower himself onto the float without too much of a stretch.

He didn't quite know how he felt. The experience had been extraordinary. Reflecting on it in the saloon that night as he prepared to turn in, he realized that torpedo boats could deliver their cargo at between thirty and thirty five knots, and whilst they were very handy vessels, the machine that he had been treated to could deliver a torpedo at seventy knots, and was infinitely more manoeuvrable than a three hundred foot long torpedo boat. The submarine did not even come close as a comparative platform for the delivery of torpedoes to a hostile fleet.

Based on his experience of torpedo damage to the Russians, one torpedo was worth 13 heavy hits. A torpedo boat could deliver its package at the expense of being seen, and identified as a target by the victim, which was armed to deal with such attacks. This machine could move so rapidly that it was virtually impossible for the victim to identify and neutralize the threat.

He had seen the future.

Thursday May 4th, 55° 36' N, 7° 54' E. Danish coast 50 Nautical Miles North West by West from the Tondern Zeppelin sheds. 0400

The lightening sky revealed the two seaplane carriers proceeding slowly through a lumpy sea. They were in company with a light cruiser squadron and a number of destroyers. A long way behind them was the Battle Cruiser Fleet and behind them, as usual, was the Grand Fleet. Somewhere ahead of them, they understood, some submarines were carrying out their nefarious business. If the Germans did come out they were sure of a warm welcome.

Nothing had been seen, save that a zeppelin had been reported in the middle of the North Sea during the night. A light cruiser squadron had been dispatched to deal with it.

Aboard *Engadine* there was a palpable air of excitement. The large machines had been landed and her aircraft complement now consisted of five of the small Schneider machines, each of which carried two 65lb bombs. The same had been done with *Vindex,* which carried an extra machine on her flying off deck.

Jonathan attended the briefing in the saloon, which was given by Fred. "Right chaps," he said, reading from the orders in his hand.

"The two flights for attacking Tondern will leave at short intervals as soon as possible after 0400, or as soon after that time as light permits a formation being picked up and kept. Don't waste too much time getting

7. A SEAPLANE RAID

into formation though, you don't have that much fuel to spare.

"The attack should be made at low altitude, after which machines of each flight should endeavour to meet at a pre-arranged rendezvous before returning, but only a few minutes can be allowed for this.

"Aeroplanes should pass to seaward of Blaavand point and the neutral territory of Denmark should not be infringed." He looked up, briefly, with a half smile on his handsome face. "It says here." That raised a laugh from the assembly.

"If a zeppelin is encountered on the outward journey, it should be attacked, bombs being dropped beforehand. If encountered on a homeward journey, it should be attacked irrespective of fuel remaining, machine landing in Denmark or Germany afterwards if necessary.

"Fighting with enemy aircraft other than zeppelins should be avoided.

"If visibility on return is so low that an inshore destroyer cannot be sighted, pilots should endeavour to pick up the Fleet by taking their departure and steering North 45 degrees West Magnetic from Lynvig Lighthouse"

"Pilots are to be instructed in the position and movement of ships between the hours of 0400 and 0730. On return of machines, destroyers, when ready to pick up aeroplanes will hoist the affirmative flag. Pilots should land about two cables ahead of a destroyer, selecting the one nearest to *Engadine*, which has this flag flying. The inshore destroyer will not be used for picking up."

"If on return, ships are seen to be steaming away from coast and destroyers are not flying the affirmative flag, pilots should close *Engadine* and read deck signals before alighting in sea."

"Pilots should always be guided by the amount of fuel remaining before trying to carry out the last orders."

He then put the orders carefully back into a buff coloured file and added

"Don't worry too much about formation or any of that stuff. Your true course is South East by South and your distance is fifty miles, so about 45 minutes flying. The sheds are great big things so you can't really miss them. Wind is westerly, so aim a bit south, maybe South South East, or something like that. Countryside is flat, so nothing to run in to. Of course I am not telling you, but if you think it better to ignore a direct order, you can head due east from here when you will hit the channel between the islands of Fanø and Mandø. You will then hit a straight road running north and south about two miles after crossing the coast. There is a railway to the east of that. Follow it south and the third town you see should be Tondern. The first one is Scherrebek, then there's Bredeboro and Tondern. Tondern is the biggest of the lot and the sheds are to the North, in the direction you're travelling. You should have no trouble locating them."

There was a movement from the assembly. An officer raised his hand and asked, "What do we know about the opposition sir?"

"As far as we are aware there is no defensive squadron of aeroplanes anywhere near Tondern. They think they're safe. Nordholz is too far south to worry you, so you ought to have a clear run." After a thought he continued, "In any event, your aircraft are better than anything the Bosh are likely to have in this sector. You can outmanoeuvre them!"

7. A SEAPLANE RAID

There were no more questions and the men dispersed to their machines. In the absence of the large craft, the hangar looked even more crowded. Feeling in the way, Jonathan went up onto the diminutive bridge to watch operations. Robinson was there and they both looked on as the seaplanes motors were started and they were swung out into the sea. Fred, who was not taking part in the raid, joined them,

"Don't like the look of that sea" he said to Robinson. "It's not right. They may have trouble getting off."

Indeed, so it proved. The first machine began to taxi to a take off position. The sea conditions were such that it was pitching and bobbing, and every time it did so the propeller kicked up a cloud of spray and dashed it backwards. As the craft began to move faster there was a sudden splash and the airplane instantly lost way. After a few minutes, clearly audible was a splintering crash, followed by a change in the engine note, which quickly died as the pilot killed the throttle. There was then a silence. The motorboat moved over to pick it up and tow it ignominiously in.

"Broken the prop" observed Fred. "That's a good start!"

Machine after machine opened up its throttle and careered off. Several had to return with some damage or other, some under tow from the attendant motorboats. The remainder seemed unable to progress beyond plunging through clouds of spray.

"This is no bloody good sir!" said Fred who was getting visually cross "can we get the TBD's to make a wash for them?"

"OK Fred" said Robinson "Yeoman, make to flag 'Submit TBD's required to make a wash to assist unstick'."

"Aye aye sir" said the yeoman who moved to the searchlight on the bridge wing. He flashed a rapid message to the light cruiser wearing the flag. There was a brief acknowledgment and then a destroyer changed course and began to gather speed towards the struggling aircraft. Jonathan watched with fascination. He was not quite sure what was intended, and then he saw.

The TBD, moving at speed cut across the track of a machine, which hit the wash with an impressive splash, instantly dashed into spray by the whirling propeller and suddenly it was flying free. Turning to Jonathan, Robinson said "sometimes the damn' things don't unstick so the trick is to provide them with just enough sea to break the hold. The trouble here is that the sea is lumpy, but it isn't breaking. We either need calm, or else a bit of white water. We normally do it with motor boats but TBD's will do just as well."

The TBD turned and headed for another 'plane. This time the captain got it wrong and the wash was not enough to allow the machine to clear. Nothing loth, the TBD turned again and tried with a further struggling aviator.

The rest of the flotilla had cottoned on and two more TBD's joined in. Jonathan began to feel a little worried. The sea was littered with flying machines and TBD's chasing each other at high speed. Sure enough, the inevitable happened, a machine unstuck and flew slap bang into a TBD going the other way. There was an involuntary gasp from Fred as the little machine crashed into the mast and was smashed into matchwood.

7. A SEAPLANE RAID

"What a fucking cock up!" Fred swore, "This is never going to work."

"Was it one of ours?" asked Robinson "I don't bloody know" said Fred "I've lost track." And then, 'Sorry Sir, I didn't mean to be quite so short but I'm a bit distracted.'

That's OK number one. I think you're excused," said the captain.

The TBD slowed down immediately and at Robinson's command the yeoman flashed a query at the ship, "How is pilot?"

The flickering light from the destroyer's bridge told its own story. "Pilot lost. Deeply sorry."

"What was name?"

"Walmesley, Oswald N, Flight Lieutenant, drowned." He was not one of *Engadine's* compliment, but Fred still went off into a perfect passion of swearing, interrupted by the signal yeoman, "Flagship signalling sir. 'Disengage'"

Robinson and Fred looked at each other for a moment. Jonathan felt as if he was intruding in a private grief.

"Very good!" said Robinson flatly. "Acknowledge."

Fred turned to a wooden locker in the wheelhouse and brought out a very pistol, which he proceeded to load with a flare and then stood ready.

"Signal's down sir!"

"Aye aye" said Robinson and nodded at Fred who fired a red flare high over their heads.

Just over the water *Vindex* fired a similar one. Sheepishly the TBD's returned to their stations and the remaining aircraft turned back towards their mother ships. The atmosphere was thick enough to be cut with a knife.

"How many got off?" asked Jonathan after what seemed like an age of uncomfortable silence. "Three." Replied Fred, shortly, "including Walmesley, and one of those flew of *Vindex's* deck."

"Well at least we know that's the way forward" said Robinson. "Fly 'em off the deck. As you see Marston, we're learning as we go here. I am sorry to disappoint Father, but at least we have two off. That'd be four more bombs than would otherwise be the case."

In fact it turned out not to be. After hoisting in the last of the lame ducks they heard the unmistakable sound of an aero engine running roughly and one of the raiding machines appeared coming low over the water towards them, trailing black smoke behind it. There had not been time for the machine to travel the necessary distance and return. It had clearly been turned back by some mechanical mishap. It alighted gently and was picked up by a launch from *Vindex* and hoisted back on board.

It was a sad little expedition that returned to the Firth that evening. The single machine had found its target and dropped its bombs, but was not able to confirm any damage.

The bright spot was that the activity had attracted a zeppelin that was engaged by the cruisers and brought down almost on top of a British submarine, which destroyed it with gunfire.

Saturday 6th May 1916, HMS Iron Duke, Fleet Flagship, forenoon

And so Jonathan was once more in the Admiral's quarters of the fleet flagship. In the fallout from the German raid the previous month and the failure of the

7. A SEAPLANE RAID

raid on Tondern; the Admiral wanted a first hand account. To Jonathan's surprise, he found that Fred in one of the big machines flew him up to Scapa Flow. It had been an awesome journey up the coast, with two stops to refuel. Robinson and the captain of *Vindex* had prepared a joint report, which they commissioned Fred to take up to the C in C by the fastest means possible. Fred and Jonathan had arrived the previous evening after an epic flight, which, even when taking into account the time necessary for refuelling, had taken just an afternoon. A conventional ship would have taken most of the day.

They were both asked to attend the flagship where Jellicoe personally debriefed Fred. To Jonathan's surprise, Jellicoe included Jonathan in the process. After hearing Fred, he turned to Jonathan and said "Well Mr Marston. You are an impartial observer. Tell me what you made of it?"

The question caught Jonathan off guard. He had had so many new experiences in the last couple of weeks that he needed a few moments to reflect. He realized that Jellicoe was aware of the enthusiasms of the Royal Naval Air Service and was using him as a sounding board. It was again a serious compliment. A distant part of his mind noted wryly that he had been asked for his opinion on various matters by a number of senior officers over the past two months, but none of them had the cares of this quietly spoken man, on whom an unimaginable weight of responsibility rested.

"I confess myself impressed sir" he started "I have never seen so many aerial machines used in such a way. It was a bit chaotic, I grant you, but the lessons seem to be clear. Such a raid could work, especially if the machines could be made to rise reliably.

"I am also impressed with the use of airplanes for communication. I never expected to be here so quickly and as a reconnaissance tool, they must be invaluable."

"Thank you Mr Marston that was most helpful. Mr Rutland what are your recommendations?"

"Flying off decks sir. *Vindex* managed to launch her machine from her foredeck easily. I see that *Campania* is back with you[56]. That's what we need sir, fast decks from which we can launch machines without having to put them in the sea first."

"I understand" said Jellicoe, "I have been asking for more flying off decks for some time, but it is sometimes hard to get the message through. What about recovering them?"

"Well sir, not too much of a problem. Most aeroplanes are lighter than a picket boat, so most things can hoist them in. Even a TBD could hoist a folder in on their sea-boat davits, if they trailed the sea boat. In any event, if the worst comes to the worst, most aeroplanes float pretty well. They just need a serious overhaul after a dunking."

"So," said the admiral, "we are agreed that aeroplanes are valuable to the Fleet. They can, and should be launched from flying off decks. Their recovery at sea is possible. Is that the size of it?"

"Pretty much sir" said Fred "and...." hesitantly.

"And, Lieutenant?...." said Jellicoe, quietly.

"Well sir. Most aircraft stall, that is, stop flying, at about 35-40 knots. Sometimes, if the conditions are right, we can have an almost zero relative speed over a deck. If the ship were fast enough and the deck big enough, we might be able to land back on the ship without touching the sea."

7. A SEAPLANE RAID

Jellicoe was silent, clearly thinking about the concept. After a moment he asked, "How would that work, precisely?"

Fred said "There is a manoeuvre that can be accomplished by an experienced pilot, not unlike luffing up in a sailing boat, whereby one can sideslip an aircraft at ninety degrees to its path, and then reduce the speed to allow it to stop flying. Effectively that would allow a machine to sideslip onto a moving deck, where she can be caught by a deck crew and brought into stasis with the mother ship. It's a bit like reefing a topsail in one way. Co-ordination of the crew and intelligent use of the wind."

Jonathan found that his imagination was stimulated by the analogy. In big sailing ships, the topsails were usually the largest sails in the ship. They required careful handling. The trick was to use the power of the wind to subdue the sail into whatever configuration that was required for the use of the ship. One of the manoeuvres was to steal the wind and trade forward motion for movement into the wind. It didn't need much imagination to translate that concept into operating airplanes. Fresh from his recent experience, Jonathan knew that airplanes were creatures of their element. He could readily understand that if an airplane stopped flying at 35 knots, a 30-knot headwind meant that the speed over the ground was five knots, which was a convenient manoeuvring speed. If a mother ship was capable of twenty knots it was clearly not beyond the wit of man to so arrange matters that an airplane could synchronize its speed with a mother ship and hence be gathered in to the ship without difficulty.

"That would surely require landplanes rather than floatplanes would it not?" asked Jellicoe.

"Yes sir, indeed it would be better if they were equipped with wheels, or indeed skids. They have a better performance as well"

"So you are advocating launching and recovering landplanes from ships at sea. Is that correct?"

Jonathan found that he was holding his breath. This was so far outside his experience that he didn't know what to think.

"Aye sir" said Fred "The advantage is the very fact that they don't have floats, which are a serious drag. It means that we can use the latest machines and hence acquire local aerial supremacy. We can bomb from any position up to a hundred miles away from our objective."

It was an exciting concept.

"What about recoverability?" asked Jellicoe. "The mother ship will be moving too. How do the raiders find her?"

"Well, I admit that is a problem sir. The only thing I can say is that visibility is far better from an aircraft than it is from the surface. Perhaps some form of RDF could be used?"

Jonathan recognized RDF as Radio Direction Finding, which was a technique whereby the source of a radio signal could be followed to its source.

"And home in the enemy's cruisers to our carriers?" asked Jellicoe.

"Well maybe not sir, but I am sure we can work out something," said Fred slightly shamefacedly.

"That's alright Lieutenant," said Jellicoe, "a very interesting concept. It would be a great assistance to me if you could think about this a bit more and let me have

7. A SEAPLANE RAID

some submissions about it. I think there is some genuine merit in the concept, and I should like to hear some more. Let me have it in writing would you Rutland?"

He then looked at the clock on the bulkhead and said, "Thank you very much gentlemen. That was most helpful. I am sorry, but I have other things to attend to. Please remain as long as you wish" and without further ado he was gone through the door and off to his next appointment. Once more, Jonathan was seriously impressed with the man who seemed to be conducting the Naval affairs of the British Empire, not unlike a famous orchestra.

8. A Concert Party

Wednesday 10th May 1916, HMS Warspite, outer battleship line Scapa Flow. Forenoon

Jonathan was alone in his cabin contemplating his guitar. A concert party had been arranged and he had agreed to take part. As a result he had had his guitar sent up from the Embassy and had visions of giving a flamenco piece. Now he was not so sure. The last time he had used his guitar was for Amparo's dance on the way over, a performance that was etched into his memory. Now that the lively Amparo and her gentle husband had been killed he felt a deep reluctance to awaken those memories.

He didn't think he could do the piece. The feeling of loss was too raw.

Suddenly, he heard the voice of Enrique in his head saying "You play my frien'. I no teach you for nossing. Play for me an' Amparo. Is better you remember us that way! Els morts són morts. La vida ha de ball. The dead are dead. The living must dance!"

He was right. With a new determination, Jonathan grasped his instrument and began to play.

As he did so, he began to understand flamenco. It was all about sadness and loss, and the celebration of life in the midst of adversity. Yes, Enrique and Amparo were no more, but their memory was vivid. They deserved their song. He played it again, with gusto.

For his second piece he was stumped. He had had ideas of doing the Gettysburg address, but on reviewing it, he thought it would be lost on his likely audience. Frank had told him that it was to be a variety show, and that they would be presenting it on the Theatre Ship, SS *Ghourko*, which doubled as a refrigeration ship for the Fleet's supplies. "It can get pretty chilly, so remember to wear something warm, and give'em something lively."

However noble, the Gettysburg address was not exactly lively. He had looked through his verse book and found nothing suitable for an audience of matelots, who were, if they were anything like American Jackies, sentimental and potentially, vocal. Perhaps a song would be better.

Then he had inspiration. Drake's Drum! It was a favourite of his father's and Jonathan had learned it as part of his contribution to entertainment in the Marston House. He thought he knew it by heart, but wondered how it would work with a guitar accompaniment. There was an extensive collection of sheet music in the wardroom. Putting his guitar away, he went over the flat into the anteroom.

Frank was sitting in an armchair reading a periodical. "Hullo old chap" he said "You have the air of a man on a mission."

"I'm wondering if we have a copy of 'Drake's Drum' by any chance."

"Dunno old boy. Have a look and see what you can see. By the way, was that you playing flamenco?"

Jonathan admitted that it was.

"It was pretty good, I must say. I like a bit of flamenco myself: - always reminds me of Gib, and hunting expeditions into the Sierranía de Ronda. Are you going to sing as well?"

"I'll take that under advisement, as my legal uncle would say."

8. A CONCERT PARTY

"Do you want a drum accompaniment? It could be rather fun."

"Are you offering?" asked Jonathan.

"Indeed I am" said Frank.

"That's settled then," said Jonathan, going over to the piano stool and opening it up. Rifling through the contents he found what he was looking for: - 'Songs of the Sea' by Stanford. Drake's Drum was the first piece. It was quite a well-thumbed copy. Retrieving it, he ordered a Coca-Cola and joined Frank, who was drinking a glass of beer.

Opening the sheet music, his heart sank. The melody was designed for what Jonathan mentally described as 'Heroic Piano'. He had no idea how that was going to work for a guitar. At that point in came Father Anthony. "Good morning Father" said Frank, getting up. "Will you join us?"

"My dear boy, of course I will. Mr Marston, a pleasure to see you as always. How's the horse racing?"

"Going very well sir, as you know! Can I get you a drink?"

"Well I think that it is about that time. An oloroso if you would be so kind." Jonathan's puzzlement must have shown on his face. "A sweet sherry, which, thanks to Commander Hodgson's excellent taste, is stocked behind the bar."

Jonathan ordered one, which seemed to be well known to the mess man. The officers settled down and lit their pipes. Father Anthony did not indulge in tobacco. "Perhaps the occasional cigar after dinner, but by and large I like to enjoy the taste of my wine."

Spotting the sheet music, he said "Stanford eh? He has some very good points about him, despite what they say."

"Does he?" asked Frank. "I had heard that he was a bit on the dull side."

"Oh my boy, that is the moderns for you. They have no idea of discipline, and think that any old row will do, provided one is shocked out of one's seat every few bars or so."

Whilst Jonathan was fond of music, he hadn't studied it as much as his companions clearly had.

"Jonathan wants to transcribe this for his guitar, so he can put it on at the weekend."

"Why would you want to do that?" asked the priest, curiously. "It will never work you know." Despite that, he took the music from Jonathan's unresisting hand and began to examine it, humming slightly to himself. After a few minutes, and a reflective sip of sherry he pronounced, "The problem is the beat. I can see how you could do the melody: - it's very simple really, but I can't see how you could reproduce the underlying motif without more hands than the Good Lord gave us."

"Perhaps with a drum Father?" said Frank.

"Yes" said the priest, "that could work. Pa-parrumph! Pumpf! Pumpf! Pa-parrumph! Pumpf! Pumpf!"

"Hmmh." He said, under his breath.

"So if we were to take out the bass line, the chords could be simplified slightly. You don't need three hands then. How do you tune your guitar Mr Marston?"

"At the moment it's tuned to D, A, D, F#, B and E sir. It's the flamenco tuning."

"I see. That could work."

8. A CONCERT PARTY

In the remaining period before lunch the Priest took some manuscript paper and a pencil and within a very short time there was a usable score.

Saturday 13th May, SS Ghourko, Outer Battleship Line, Scapa Flow, Afternoon

SS *Ghourko* was a sister ship to SS *Borodino* but the cargo deck had been fitted out as a theatre rather than a department store. She was moored close alongside *Warspite* and was crowded with people. They were not exclusively from *Warspite*. To Jonathan's surprise Jellicoe himself was there, sitting beside Captain Philpotts. "He often does that," Jonathan had been told, "it helps him unwind, and of course it helps him to judge morale."

An even greater surprise was the presence of Admiral Oguri, the Japanese Naval Attaché attended by Sas, who was in the Admiral's party. Jonathan had met the Admiral at an Embassy party in London.[57] There was no opportunity to speak to Sas, who clearly hadn't noticed Jonathan in the crowd in his unobtrusive uniform.

The story was that there had been a major conference at Rosyth the previous day to consider the fall out from the Coastal raids by the Germans last month and the rumour-mill ('scuttlebutt' was the picturesque naval term for it) was in full spate. It was well known in the 5th Battle Squadron that Beatty, the Admiral commanding the Battle Cruiser Force was casting envious eyes at the QE's. Jonathan knew from the Grand Fleet standing orders that the 5th Battle Squadron was designated as a special high-speed division, which could be trusted to plug any gaps in the battle line as and where they were required. That didn't sit square with an attachment to the

Battle Cruiser Force, whose duties were primarily scouting.

Opinion in the wardroom of *Warspite* was divided. Some of the younger members were very keen to join the BCF (as it was known) "They're a terrific lot" he had heard said, "that's where we'll get some action. Couldn't come too soon for me."

Frank was less sure. "They're a pretty fast set, the people that is, as well as the ships. I am afraid that there is a considerable amount of unsuitable talk, and some scant regards for morals."

"Oh really?" asked Jonathan curiously.

"I don't want to speak out of turn, and it doesn't do to criticize a lady, but I am afraid that it does come from the top, rather. The Admiral's lady is a divorcée, you see and it shows."

Jonathan did not quite know what to make of that. He had sufficient experience of Frank now to know that his first description as 'a bit preachy, but fundamentally sound' was a good one. Frank wore his faith lightly, but underneath his Naval Officer's persona was a faith of solid rock. Much as he liked him (and Jonathan shared many of his values) he would not like to cross him in matters spiritual. He could see him lighting the fire under a heretic with genuine regret, but doing it all the same.

"Of course it doesn't help that she's American, saving your presence Jonathan, and filthy rich to boot. If we *do* go south I have no doubt whatsoever that she will want to meet you. My only advice is to be careful: - lunch parties at Aberdour House have a habit of degenerating rather."

"Oh?" Asked Jonathan "in what way?"

8. A CONCERT PARTY

"Well I shall leave that for you to find out. Just watch it if you get an invitation."

And now they were about to be 'on'. Frank had secured some Spanish style hats from somewhere, and they wore waistcoats and sashes. Both had applied Spanish-looking moustaches with burnt cork. They were following a young sailor, who sang a comic song, which went down well. Hammill was acting as compere and gave them a big build-up, worthy of the best music halls "And now, wafted to us from exotic shores, the Hispanic Herero, the epitome of Latino lugubrious lucullity, I give you the veritable refried bean from across the Ocean, Don Juan De LOS AMERIGUAS!" and Frank played a rattle on the drum.

Stepping out onto the stage with his guitar, the house went wild. "Our Yank" was clearly popular. Jonathan bowed, and took his place on the single wooden chair that he had asked for in the centre of the spotlight. Frank sat to the side.

Bowing his head over his instrument, Jonathan struck up the first chord and then launched into the falsetta. On stage, in the limelight, with an appreciative audience he found that he was compelled to wail in the Spanish manner. It was not something that would normally occur to him, but in that place and in that company, he felt there was no alternative. The advantage was that as his own letrasero, Jonathan could choose his own cante. Frank was playing a staccato rhythm on the drum, which sounded not unlike the tap and stamp of dance shoes. As he played, he could almost see Amparo dancing in front of him.

Taking his inspiration from wherever it was coming he opened his mouth and surprised himself at the sound that came out. Starting at the middle D he ranged right up to the top E and wavered up and down a few times "Ampa-aa-aa-aa-ah-ah-ah-ro!' and then dropping a third before wandering wildly up the scale again, with attendant flourishes "Aeh-eh-eh-eeh-eh-ehe-eh eh-eh-ey-eh-est" all the time strumming the stirring compás based on the A chord (which Enrique called 'por medio'), before changing gear to the D minor, where sang "Mu-eh-eh-ehe-ehe-uerto!" with energetic strumming of the new chord. He had just announced that Amparo was dead.

He then went on to a few flourishes and refinements that Enrique had taught him. The ever-faithful Frank followed him, and on occasions led.

When he had finished the piece the audience was silent for a few moments and then exploded with applause. Cheers, from a thousand throats, together with shouts of "Good on yer Yank!" "Bravo!" and even, from some balletomane "bis!" which echoed around the makeshift theatre. Jonathan bowed deeply in his chair, surprised at his own virtuosity.

For 'Drake's Drum,' Jonathan had decided to appear as an old time sailor. His orderly, Brown had risen to the occasion and had produced a blue and white striped jersey, a blue vest with gold buttons, some baggy brown breeches and a suitable hat. His original intention was to leave his feet and calves bare, but Brown reminded him that *Ghourko* was a refrigeration ship "You might find the cold distracting sir." So he was wearing some canary stockings and his brogues.

Hammill had decided that it was to be the finalé, immediately following Father Pollen's Choir, who were doing a medieval piece. So Jonathan was to close the

8. A CONCERT PARTY

show. It was quite a challenge. The score was written in a British West Country dialect. At home the Marston family had always adopted a cod pirate accent, but *Warspite* was a West Country ship, commissioned in Plymouth, Drake's home town. All British ships commissioned in one of the three Royal dockyards, Devonport, Portsmouth or Chatham, each of which had their own legendary attributes. Pompey for music, 'Chatty' Chats for talking and 'Guz' (which was the odd name for Devonport, the Plymouth Naval Dockyard) for food and drink. It was quite a challenge to do a convincing West Country accent in a West Country ship.

As always, Father Pollen had come to the rescue. "They will appreciate you trying, Mr Marston, and the music is such that the accent doesn't really matter. Perhaps a slightly diffident introduction might help. Now, let me see" and he pulled out a small black notebook from inside his jacket and leafed through it for a while, noting things down on a blank page with a pencil. After a few minutes he looked up and said

"I think this might work, please try it, after me 'Oi won't keep 'ee longful, moi fore-right vreinds, but chave 'n'atch t'end 'ee a lidden, o' Drake cottening they dawcock Spaniards'."

It was surprising to hear such outlandish words coming from the urbane priest.

"It means 'I shan't keep you long, my good friends, but I have a fancy to tell you a tale of Drake fighting the Spaniards." Going back to his book, he went on, "I could go on if you wish?"

"No thank you Father" said Jonathan, rapidly," let me get my head round this bit for the moment." And he attempted it in his cod pirate accent.

"That sounded rather good, my boy," said Father Pollen. And again?"

"Oi won't keep 'ee longful, moi fore-right vreinds, but ....I'm sorry Father, I have forgotten the rest."

"Chave 'n'atch t'end 'ee a lidden," said the priest

"chave 'n'atch t'end 'ee a lidden" repeated Jonathan

"O' Drake cottening they dawcock Spaniards"

"O' Drake cottening they dawcock Spaniards"

"By George he's got it!" Said Frank, demonstrating his knowledge of contemporary London shows.

Jonathan repeated the phrase a couple of times, finding it more and more easy as it became familiar.

Father Anthony's piece involved doing something very clever with medieval polyphony. Whilst the complexities were lost on Jonathan, it was the perfect introduction to what he wanted to do.

And so Jonathan was ready. The program simply said "A Seaman's Tale" without indicating who was to be performing. When the lights went up, Jonathan was looking down, his features concealed by the brim of his hat. With hitherto unsuspected theatricality, he slowly raised his head. In the crowded theatre, only the first few rows could recognize him, but they went wild when they saw that it was 'Our Yank' again. As he was raising his head he met Sas's astonished gaze. He took quiet pleasure in the shock on Sas's face. That was repayment in kind for his mischievousness in the American Embassy, where he had teased the Ambassador with his knowledge of Jonathan's true identity.

Keeping Sas's gaze, he launched into the first part of his rehearsed phrase, before addressing the wider

8. A CONCERT PARTY

audience. The result was cheers and whistles which took some time to die down. When it did, he nodded to Frank, who started the drum.

> "Drake he's in his hammock
> And a thousand miles away.
> Captain art tha' sleepin' there below
> Slung between the roundshot
> In Nombre Dios Bay.
> Capten art tha' sleepin' there below?

Jonathan's natural voice was a light baritone, but he found as he sang the piece he could feel his jaw relaxing and the sound broadening. The West Country vowels helped. As he sang he noticed Jellicoe's hands beating time to the rhythm, and Jonathan suddenly became aware that he was singing to Drake's heir. The thought made him falter, with the enormity of what he was doing.

Happily it coincided with the line "Drake, he was a Devon man and sailed the Devon Sea" so that his temporary lapse sounded like emotion. He recovered and proceeded to the finale

> "Tak' my drum to England
> Hang et by the shore.
> Strike et when yer powder's running low.
> If the Dons sight Devon,
> I'll quit the Port o' Heaven
> And drum them up the Channel as we drummed 'em long ago!"

The applause was rapturous, and very gratifying. As he rose from his bow he saw, to his surprise, that

Jellicoe was on his feet, applauding vigorously, as were the Japanese.

Hammill closed the show in true theatrical style and Jonathan retired to the Green Room where he was shifting into his normal uniform with all the others when a Midshipman appeared and made his way up to Jonathan who was, at that precise moment, struggling into his pants. Unsure of the protocol, the youngster said "Sorry to disturb you sir, but I have a message from the C-in-C. He says congratulations, and would you like to join him in the bar when convenient."

"Very good" said Jonathan, who decided that in the circumstances a salute was inappropriate.

A little later

SS Ghourko boasted a pair of bars, like any normal theatre. Jonathan finished dressing, made all square and made his way to the Officers' Bar where Jellicoe was nursing a pint of beer in company with Philpotts and the Japanese.

"Congratulations Marston!" he said, as Jonathan approached, "that was quite *a tour de force*. Where did you learn to sing and play like that? Commander Sasai here says that he shared the best part of a week with you coming over, but didn't recognize you at all during the flamenco piece."

"Well sir, I had a pretty good teacher. Do you remember Sas?" he said, half turning to Sas "Enrique and Amparo?"

"But of course!" said Sas, "Such a tragedy!"

"What happened?" asked Jellicoe, apparently in genuine curiosity.

8. A CONCERT PARTY

"They were on *Sussex,* sir," said Jonathan.

"Ah" said Jellicoe, quietly. "I understand. A very bad business."

Admiral Oguri said "How pleasant to see you again, Lieutenant. We met at the Embassy party did we not?"

"Indeed we did sir. A most memorable encounter."

"I see that our British friends are treating you well," said the Japanese Admiral. "It is most gratifying to see you here in the *Sanctum Sanctorum.* You are truly one of the Elect to be here.

"I shall not be so crass as to ask your opinion, but you have clearly made a hit with the men. That 'Drake's Drum' was truly inspired. I have to say that I struggled with the introduction, but Commander Sasai managed to make a decent fist of it for me. Where did you get it?"

"Oddly, sir, from a Catholic Priest!"

"Ah the Church!" said the Admiral, "A truly remarkable organization, you must agree."

"Well sir, I don't know much about them, but this one is a good fellow."

"Would that be your chap Pollen, Edward?" asked Jellicoe, "The one that gave us that penultimate piece? Sounded distinctly ancient"

"Indeed it would, sir. He is quite a fellow, but not to be trusted on the Golf course!"

"Is that because you lose Edward?" asked Jellicoe, playfully. Phillpotts grinned ruefully and said, "I am afraid that I couldn't possibly admit that sir!"

Then almost, for him, petulantly, Jellicoe said, "well I wish he'd control that brother of his. He keeps on writing to me telling me what I should be doing, or trying to get me to buy more of his wretched machines."

"Is that Arthur Pollen Admiral?" asked Sas "He of the Pollen Fire Control system?"

"Indeed it is, Commander. He just doesn't seem to understand that other people have ideas too. I am afraid that it fell to me to turn down a number of his ideas when I was Director of Naval Ordnance. I don't think he has forgotten it."

"Commander Sasai is at Portsmouth at the moment, learning all about fire control" said Oguri to Jellicoe by way of explanation.

"Then you will understand the problem," said Jellicoe.

Jonathan was following this conversation with fascination. Fire control was a tantalizing mystery to him. The essential idea was that all the guns in a ship would be controlled from a central point with a good visibility, usually at the top of a mast. The problem was that the speed of ships today and the distances at which they engaged caused the spotting officer real problems. The enemy's course was not always apparent at the sort of distances that modern guns were capable of. Add to that the extraordinary speeds that ships moved at today and you had a nightmare, much more complicated than the simple problems that he had been setting his classes, not three months ago. Add to that the fact that at these ranges, the time of flight meant that the Earth had turned on its axis appreciably between the time of the shell leaving the gun and its arrival at the enemies position. Even that had to be allowed for. It was really too much for the human brain to cope with.

In the past few years, various people had been working on the problem and the technical press reported all sorts of designs for 'thinking machines' that made the

8. A CONCERT PARTY

complex calculations automatically. Indeed, Jellicoe's own flag captain, Dreyer, had invented a machine, which allegedly achieved the object, but its details were secret. With an uncharacteristic flash of annoyance, Jonathan realized that Sas, as a representative of a 'friendly' power was allowed to attend a course in this very important field, but he, himself, as an US Navy officer was barred from the transmitting station where the machine was located.

Still, he realized that he could not really complain: - after all, he was here, in the heart of the Royal Navy, on the most advanced battleship in the world.

"I am told that you have some full calibre shooting arranged for us Admiral?" said Oguri.

"Yes, indeed" said Jellicoe, turning to Philpotts. "Edward, you and the rest of the 5th Battle Squadron are scheduled for a full calibre shoot on Monday. Would you be kind enough to take the Admiral and Commander Sasai with you?"

Clearly taken by surprise, Philpotts blinked uncomfortably and said, "Well of course sir, but wouldn't the Admiral be better accommodated on the Flagship?"

"Edward, you know that a flagship is going to be overcrowded, almost by definition, even in your class of ship. Rear Admiral Evan Thomas is quite content for Admiral Oguri to be carried in a private ship." Turning to the Japanese Admiral, Jellicoe said, "You have no objection to a private ship do you Admiral?"

"Of course not, my dear fellow" said Oguri, "it is such a privilege to be here, I should be happy with a trawler."

"No need for that" said Jellicoe, "*Warspite* is fully equipped as a flagship. You should be very comfortable."

"Actually, sir" said Philpotts almost diffidently "I have given over the admiral's quarters to the ship's Roman Catholics for a church. I do have rather a lot of them you see."

"Well that isn't a problem," said Jellicoe, "they can clear out for a couple of days, surely."

"Aye aye, sir" said Philpotts. To Jonathan's heightened senses, he seemed uncharacteristically ill at ease. Jonathan could almost see him working out how he was going to tell Father Pollen that he would have to move out for a period.

"Oh my dear chap, I wouldn't hear of it" Oguri said to Philpotts. "The Church must have its church. Do you have many Catholics on your ship?"

"I am afraid that I do, sir," said Philpotts. The Padre is a decent chap though."

"Oh really? I look forward to meeting him," said Oguri. "Does he do High Mass? I must confess that I am partial to a High Mass. Especially if it is sung decently."

Philpotts was clearly out of his area of comfort. "Well I believe he does sir. It certainly appears to involve considerable quantities of music and chanting. The sailors love it. He was the one that gave the piece before Lieutenant Marston's final number."

"Well in that case I wouldn't dream of disturbing him. I have seldom heard Monteverdi, done so beautifully. Any old cabin will do for me and Commander Sasai."

"That's very good in you sir. It will be well received by the men," said Philpotts. "You shall have my own cabin and ancillary rooms, I shall use my sea cabin."

"That seems to be very satisfactory Captain," said Oguri, bowing slightly. "As it happens, I am actually a

8. A CONCERT PARTY

baptized, and allegedly communicating member of the Roman Catholic Church myself."

Jonathan had difficulty in hiding his shock. He had some familiarity with Roman Catholicism as a result of his experiences with Frank, but to find a Japanese, of a different race, from the other side of the world professing the same Faith was astonishing. Jellicoe and Philpotts also looked surprised, demonstrating it in different degrees. Jellicoe raised his eyebrows slightly, without saying anything, but Philpotts opened his mouth in an almost audible "oh!"

"The Jesuits were very well respected when I was growing up" Oguri went on "These days, Christianity is thought of as being so modern and general in my country. It is forgotten that we have had the Jesuits for the best part of four hundred years. They are almost traditional. Unlike here, where they look like black crows, at home they wear saffron robes like the Buddhists. I find their music superb, much better than the Buddhists. When I was younger, some friends were being baptized, they suggested that I might like to join them and so I did."[58]

For once, Jellicoe looked awkward to Jonathan's eye. "H'mm. Well. Jolly good. Personally I am not too keen on saints and Virgins and things, but......."

"Oh my dear chap" said Oguri, "no need to take on so. We shall be just fine. I am a Roman Catholic, but I don't get too carried away by it. Christianity is very useful for the lower orders, 'Render unto Caesar' and all that is very conducive to public order."

"Very good," said Jellicoe and then, over his shoulder "Snotty!"

An obedient Midshipman appeared immediately, "Sir?"

"Compliments to Commander Walwyn from the C-in-C; Please prepare to receive Rear Admiral Oguri and his suite as guests in ten minutes."

"Aye aye sir" said the mid, "To receive Rear Admiral Oguri and his suite in ten minutes" and after saluting, he was off.

Sunday 14th May 1916, 3rd Sunday of Easter, Roman Catholic Chapel HMS Warspite, Outer Battleship Line Scapa Flow

It had been quite a convivial evening. The presence of an Admiral, albeit a Japanese one, meant that Captain Philpotts himself was invited to dinner in the wardroom. Slightly to Jonathan's embarrassment, he found that he was Oguri's favoured companion. He insisted on being introduced to Father Anthony, who dealt with him with his customary urbanity, although the chance of showing off his own Mass setting to an appreciative audience was a considerable draw for him.

That, of course involved Frank as Sacristan, Altar Boy and Master of Ceremonies. At some point, Jonathan found himself nursing a pink gin with Sas.

"Is the Admiral really a Catholic, Sas?" he asked.

'Oh, undoubtedly old boy. Many of us are, you know. We sometimes get carried away with fashion in exotic religions. Why, there is one fellow I know, who was supposed to be baptized a Christian, but it was raining, so he became a Buddhist instead. The temple was closer than the church you see."

Jonathan was slightly shocked that the choice of Religion should be so haphazard and said so.

"My dear chap" said Sas, "if the spirits had wanted him to be a Christian they would have stopped the rain wouldn't they?" The logic was irrefutable.

8. A CONCERT PARTY

In any event, without quite knowing how or why, Jonathan was now seated in the well-appointed Roman Catholic Chapel with the Japanese, and a creditable congregation of sailors waiting for Mass to begin.

An organist was playing something gentle on a harmonium, and to Jonathan's surprise, several of the sailors were telling rosary beads, their mouths moving silently as they prayed. It was a strange sight in this day and age on this, most modern of ships. Sas was looking around with interest. "Some of our fellows use beads like that too," he hissed in a stage whisper.

"Sssh!' said an officer sitting close by.

"Sorry" said Sas and made a little moué at Jonathan. The chapel was decorated just like a church, with a statue of the Virgin Mary to one side, and painted icons with numbers on, depicting various stages in Christ's Passion round the bulkheads. They appeared to be by the same artist (and were certainly in the same style) as the picture of the Virgin in Father Anthony's cabin.

There was certainly no mistaking the altar, which was altogether too grand an edifice to be anything else. It was quite alien to the simple "God's Table" that he was used to. It faced the after bulkhead, and was flanked with six large candlesticks with tall beeswax candles burning in them. Above it, flanked by a triptych was a box-like affair draped in gold cloth: - a motif echoed by the gold altar frontal. Above that was an elaborate crucifix with an agonised Christ figure on it.

In front of the statue of the Virgin was a metal framework, which supported a number of small, lit candles, with a bin of unused ones underneath. As he watched, sailors were coming in and in succession, took off their hats, dipped their fingers in a small water stoup, crossed themselves, genuflected to the altar and moved to the statue, where they took a candle out of the bin, lit it from another, placed a coin in a moneybox and moved to their place. It was oddly moving. There was a low susurration, partly composed of imperfectly vocalized prayers and partly of low conversation. There was an odd aromatic scent, which he couldn't quite place.

As his gaze wandered around the room he mused on just what it was that made this particular faith so different. He had been vaguely aware of the Catholic Church over the years, but it had never featured very much in his experience, apart from the occasional reference by pious preachers to the alleged horrors of Rome, which was identified with the Beast in Revelations. So far, what he had seen in this ship had not demonstrated any particularly bestial qualities, indeed, quite the reverse.

Suddenly, everything was brought to a halt with a tinkle from a small bell, wielded by a Petty Officer beside the door leading into the chapel. The door opened and in came Frank bearing a processional cross, followed by two others bearing candles in tall brass candlesticks. After them came a man carrying a brass pot, suspended from chains from which a thick, aromatic smoke was emerging. That was the scent! Incense! All of them were wearing black, floor length robes, topped with a waist length white linen shift affair, with lace around the bottom.

If that were not outlandish enough, Father Anthony followed them in robes that would not, in Jonathan's opinion, have been out of place in the Temple of Jerusalem itself. A white, floor length garment with lace

8. A CONCERT PARTY

at foot, top and sleeves, was covered with an elaborate gold tabard, with the Gothic initials IHS embroidered on it at front and rear. He was wearing a deceptively simple black hat, folded to represent a cross on the hatband. In one hand he was carrying something concealed in a gold cloth, falling from a square top, which he steadied with the unoccupied hand. A long, stiff, gold cloth dangled from his right wrist.

As the procession came in, the harmonium altered its tune, and Father Anthony began to sing in Latin. Frank answered his phrase in the same tongue.

They made their way to the altar, where they stopped. Father Anthony made the sign of the Cross and intoned something, which Frank answered.

Bowing, the participants moved to their appointed places and the Mass commenced.

To Jonathan's fascinated gaze it was a most interesting experience. Father Anthony made a statement, sometimes chanted, sometimes said and sometimes sung, which was answered by Frank in the same mode. Occasionally the statement went on at some length. The congregation stood up, sat down, or kneeled down at apparently arbitrary intervals. The chanting and singing in an unfamiliar tongue was, quite literally, mesmerizing, punctuated as it was with bells and a particularly impressive ritual, when the wielder of the brass burner (apparently it was called a 'thurible') stood in front of Father Anthony, and lifted the lid by means of a brass chain, which allowed father Anthony to load it with a powder from a brass container that immediately yielded more pungent smoke.

The acolyte would then close the lid and advance to the front of the ceremony, where he would grasp the chains a little above the brazier and then swing the censer, so that it would 'clink' with the slack suspending chain three times. He did this facing to the front, the left and the right. It added to the atmosphere no end.

"Incense" whispered Sas "we use it too. It soothes the Spirits". Immediately Jonathan was reminded of the Temple of Solomon. This, he realized, was what worship in that Temple must have been like, and he realized that he was watching it here, at the northern margin of the world, in wartime. In a machine designed to kill as many people as possible as quickly as possible. It was a major paradox.

He suddenly found that he was humbled. He was partaking in something that was so much larger than his simple world. What he was hearing transcended his personal experience. And yet, he was hearing what thousands, if not millions of people were hearing at the same time today, across the whole planet. He found himself wondering why the preachers that he was used to had such a down on this extraordinary ritual.

There came a time when a man moved to a lectern and began to read in English. Jonathan vaguely recognized the text, but couldn't put a reference to it. He was, however struck by a phrase, "be subject to every human creature for God's sake, whether to the king as supreme, or to governors as sent through him for vengeance on evildoers and for the praise of the Good."

It struck a chord. The attack on the *Sussex* and the death of the Granados was, in Jonathan's book, a deed of the 'evildoers'. He was reminded of the latest British Dreadnought that he had seen, the *Revenge,* which was an appropriate name.

8. A CONCERT PARTY

There was then a further piece of ritual, which involved Father Anthony moving to another lectern, where he was subjected to a vigorous dose of incense, before intoning *"Dominus Vobiscum"* to which Frank replied *"Et cum spiritu tuo"* an exchange that seemed to be very common in this ceremony. The next phrase included the word *'evangelium'* which Jonathan recognized as 'Gospel'.

Everyone stood up with an audible rumble of seats and feet.

Father Anthony commenced the well-known piece from the Gospel of John: -

> *"At that time, Jesus said to his disciples: 'A little while and you shall see Me no longer; and again a little while and you shall see Me because I go to my Father'*
> *.....Amen, amen, I say to you that you shall weep and lament, but the world shall rejoice; and you shall be sorrowful, but your sorrow shall be turned into joy.*
> *A woman about to give birth has sorrow, because her hour has come, but when she has brought forth the child, she no longer remembers the anguish for her joy that a man is born into the world. And you therefore have sorrow now; but I will see you again, and your heart shall rejoice and your joy no-one shall take from you."*

Father Anthony bent and kissed the book and then stood up straight, looking around the flat at his assembled congregation, which sat to a similar rumble to that which had accompanied their rising. He said, in a conversational tone "You shall weep and lament, but the world will rejoice. These words are so appropriate for us at this time. Your brothers in the Army are suffering huge losses, not only in deaths, but also in the wounded, the maimed, the blind, the crippled. All of those who bear the marks of the evil done by man unto man.

"There may come a time when you, in this service may have to suffer the same fate. Our faith is that those of us who may not survive the conflict, so that we are seen no more on Earth, will be welcome into the Glorious Kingdom of God, where we shall live for ever with Him.

"Never forget that our Saviour suffered and died for us, enduring the greatest pain that the human body is capable of withstanding. Whatever we suffer in any forthcoming conflict, Our Lord has suffered, so I say to you, whatever lies in store for you in this ship, however terrifying your fate may be, remember that Jesus Christ, our Saviour is with you. He endured as we may be called upon to endure.

"And in our last hour, remember the Night Prayer of the Church, 'May the Lord grant us a quiet night, and a perfect end.'"

The sermon was shorter than Jonathan was used to, but seemed to cover the ground economically. The theme was the requirement to do one's bit, however humble in the hope that what one was doing was for the greater good. It offered no great thoughts, or noble causes, but simply the very human need to do the task that one was presented with.

He was profoundly moved. All his worries about doing the right thing, his conflicting duties to the President and to the United States, his agonizing over 'his mission' was reduced to the simple task of doing what

8. A CONCERT PARTY

was in front of him. To the best of his abilities and trusting that he was doing what God wanted.

Jonathan finished the Mass in an almost elevated state. He was almost indifferent to Sas's enthusiastic chatter and was filled with a sense of wellbeing that he had not felt for some time.

There was something soothing about the age-old ritual words and music, something quite outwith the real world.

9. Gunnery Practice and Reorganisation

Monday 15th May 1916, Gunnery Practice Area, Scapa Flow, Forenoon

Scapa Flow boasted an entire area dedicated to gunnery practice. The size of it was so great that a squadron equipped with even the largest guns could practice in safety and security. This morning it was the turn of the 5th Battle Squadron, including *Warspite*.

Despite himself Jonathan was excited. He had, of course, had the experience of *Wisconsin's* twelve inchers back home, but this promised to be something else again. It had been decided that they would treat this as a rehearsal for action and so Jonathan was assigned to follow Commander Walwyn, whose primary action station was B turret, the second one from forward, set so that it could theoretically fire over A turret, which was the foremost. There were certain difficulties with that, as the shock from such large guns could do a considerable amount of damage to the structure of the ship itself.

He would like to have been able to watch the director firing process in more detail, but the circumstances by which visual observations and range takers from various stations throughout the ship were converted into a bearing and elevation remained very secret. Even Sas was barred from the nerve centre of operations, called the Transmitting Station, deep within the bowels of the ship.

Jonathan did not really mind, the next best thing to the spotting top was an elevated turret, which contained its own range finding equipment. As Commander of the turret, Walwyn's station was in the cabinet to the rear of the thing, just under the top armour. It was shared with his deputy, Lieutenant Griffiths. They were looking at the massive breeches and complicated loading equipment for the guns that filled the available space. The men, like acolytes to some ancient god, were dwarfed by their surroundings.

The cabinet was equipped with a range finder of its own, which was really a vast pair of binoculars, with the lenses fifteen feet apart. Using that as the base of a triangle meant that one could work out the range to an enemy ship at surprising distances. Each lens showed half an image, and by twiddling a knob it was possible to bring them together so that the image coincided, the range could then be read off from a scale.

"Here you are Marston," said Walwyn, proffering some cotton wool "You'd better shove some of this in your ears. Blast can be quite a bore, especially if A turret is firing abaft the beam too. Another tip is to open your mouth just as the gun fires; it relieves the pressure."

Gratefully, Jonathan took the stuff and packed his ears with it. He noticed that every one else did the same. Absurdly, he was reminded of old time sailors tying their neckerchiefs around their ears before battle.

Walwyn suggested that Jonathan might like to use a periscope to observe things. There were no less than three of them so Jonathan was allowed to use one alongside the port barrel. It gave a surprisingly good view around the turret, and the elevated position allowed a view almost as good as from the fore bridge. *Warspite* was third in line, as usual, astern of *Valiant* and ahead of *Malaya*. They were steaming at eighteen knots, which was two knots faster than *Wisconsin* at her best. This was apparently the battle speed of the Grand Fleet.

9. GUNNERY PRACTICE AND REORGANISATION

Suddenly there was a ringing on the navyphone. A rating answered it and said "Load and train green three oh!" That was transmitted to the training and elevating numbers who had modern-looking headphones covering their ears. Suddenly everything happened at once. Jonathan felt the turret begin to move and the various hoists began to whirr. The Numbers 2 and 3 on each gun operated the gun-loading cage, which came up through flash tight doors that opened with a heavy clang and a rattle of the drive chain. In each of them was an enormous shell and two cordite charges in canvas bags. A move of the lever rolled the whole thing into the loading tray with a thud and a clunk. Another lever unscrewed the shining breech a quarter turn and opened it like magic with a hiss. Number 4 operated the rammer that pushed the shell and charges into the breech with a rattle of chains. The breech closed after it with another hiss and turned back a quarter turn to lock it. The action, prompted by hydraulics, made the sight almost magically surreal. The ramming of the shells and their charges was purely mechanical. The cage rattled back down through the doors. It was not a quiet procedure.

After the noise, each gun captain shouted "Gun Ready Sir!"

"Very good" answered Walwyn and then pressed buttons on a board beside his position that were labelled 'L' and 'R, just below another button marked 'B'. As he pressed them they lit up, and immediately after that the 'B' button lit up on its own. Jonathan realized that this was an electric telegraph system whereby the Gunner in overall charge of the ship's main armament would realize that B turret was ready in both barrels.

"Target in sight sir," reported a Petty Officer, who was on another periscope. "Bearing green three two."

"Very good"

Jonathan turned his periscope onto the bearing and saw, very far away, a plume of smoke, some white wake and then another wake surrounding three small, square shapes. It was the target being towed through the water by a Torpedo Boat Destroyer at some considerable speed. "Report bearing" said Walwyn, and a nearby Midshipman (Walker?) addressed himself to a strange instrument, which seemed to consist of a single dial connected to one of the periscopes.

"Bearing green three four, Sir"

"Very, good. Report." The Mid did something with his instrument and Jonathan saw that in front of him was a brass dial, which appeared to move of its own accord. "Indicated bearing green two niner sir". The target was changing bearing rapidly. This was quite unlike the scenario he was teaching three months ago. Things were happening very quickly indeed, and not in a simple and predictable manner.

"Distance one five thousand yards." That was seven and a half miles away. The range of *Wisconsin's* main armament was not much in excess of 10,000 yards and even then, it was virtually impossible to hit anything.

"Very good, Report and stand by"

The phone buzzed again, "Director Firing sir."

"Very Good."

The turret moved with a whirr as the trainer turned a brass wheel following a similar dial in front of him. Simultaneously, the elevating number at Jonathan's feet moved a lever and the barrel began to elevate. Suddenly

9. GUNNERY PRACTICE AND REORGANISATION

there was the sound of a gong, for all the world as if they were about to go into dinner. *Bong!*

A second or so of silence and then all hell broke loose. Looking through the sighting hood, as he was, Jonathan saw the left hand barrel of the twin 15inch guns just beside him explode in flame and orange smoke as it moved violently backwards against the recoil mechanism. Simultaneously, he felt a hard blast of warm air, incongruously laced with cold spray, hitting him like a fist through the open sighting port. He felt as if he was momentarily in the air. It was a disorientating experience. He did not hear the noise, but rather experienced the sensation of being punched hard all over his upper body. He could almost feel his cheeks being blasted back to somewhere around his ears. His eyes were watering.

To his knowledge, no one in the turret had pressed the trigger, and yet this was clearly not a random explosion, as he couldn't help but be aware of X turret two hundred and fifty feet aft of him firing at the same time. Somehow the concussion seemed to hit him around the back of his head. Clearly this was director firing, controlled from a central position. He felt the ship shake as the guns went off.

A few seconds after the primary explosion there was a puff of blue smoke as the barrel was cleared and moved forward again. The orange cordite smoke dispersed in their wake as the ship continued on her course, followed by the blue smoke, already dispersing into insubstantial wisps.

The gun cages rattled and clattered as they brought the next load of projectiles and charges up, which were loaded in as before.

There was then a period of silence as the projectiles mounted skyward on their lengthy journey. Jonathan suddenly realized that the turret was training even as the shells flew, and more than that, the guns were elevating and depressing in time with the roll of the ship. It was oddly hypnotic.

This was seriously impressive stuff. One of the principal difficulties of this sort of gunnery was the motion of the firing ship. The Brits seemed to have got that one sorted out. Those enormous barrels were fixed on their target, and had every intention of remaining there, whatever the host ship was doing. After a long pause a white pillar of water became dimly visible, streaking the distant grey. It was near the target, but to the left.

The brass dial in front of the trainer moved and he repeated, "right six". Then there was the fire gong and the right hand barrel exploded. Jonathan saw that the splash was behind the target, correct for line, but over.

The left gun, which had already been reloaded and was ready once more, moved downward a fraction, in obedience to the elevating clock and shortly after that the gong sounded again and the gun fired in very short order. The splash this time, when it came, was in front of the target, but still in line. The barrels elevated slightly and then the order came "Broadsides, rapid fire" and the whole scene went mad. As far as Jonathan's dazed senses could make out, they were firing full broadsides of eight guns every twenty seconds or so which shook the ship continuously, with a veritable blizzard of splashes around the unfortunate target. At the same time the other four ships of the squadron were doing the same thing. It was an extraordinary experience.

9. GUNNERY PRACTICE AND REORGANISATION

The TBD towing the target turned rapidly away from his original course, moving very quickly. To Jonathan's surprise, the Squadron kept with the target throughout all the evolutions, and hits were registered continuously until it vanished into the mist and smoke.

Suddenly, Jonathan became aware of the bugles sounding 'Still' and there was just the whine of the turbines with the subdued roar of the ventilators set off by the hiss of the sea. He thought that what he had seen was a pretty impressive piece of gunnery, but it wasn't yet over.

The Flagship veered hard to starboard and Jonathan realized that the Squadron was cutting off the target's putative escape. The speed of these ships meant that judicious handling by the Admiral could do that, notwithstanding the fact that the target had turned away. These ships were fast enough to cut off a retreating enemy.

The dials continued to turn, in spite of the fact that the target was obscured in the mist. To Jonathan's astonishment, after fifteen minutes the target appeared once more in his view. The TBD had not turned far enough and the result was that the 5th BS was effectively crossing his front. The TBD was between the ship and its target.

The fire gong went off again and the ranging shots were directed over the TBD towards the target behind. This seemed to him to be incredibly dangerous, but the shell splashes were gratifyingly close to the target, leaving the towing craft unscathed.

He saw a rapid flicker of Morse from the TBD's bridge, which he read instinctively "I do not know what you do to the enemy, but by Christ you frighten me" it said. Amused, he recognized the alleged reaction of the British General, the Duke of Wellington, to the sight of a highland soldier just before the battle of Waterloo.

He could not, of course see what the response was, but the boat flashed again "Submit you should go away and try it on the Bosh!"

Back at anchor that night, Jonathan reflected on what he had seen. This was a seriously good exercise in which the battleships had done very well indeed under difficult conditions. Frankly, he had never seen anything like it. Whatever the Brits were doing about director firing, it was clearly working.

Putting it in context, he had just witnessed battle practice by a ship going half as fast again as anything he was used to, at twice the range, engaging an enemy moving at similar speed. More to the point, the equipment seemed to have been able to anticipate where the target would appear again, even when the range was obscured. It was seriously powerful medicine.

Rosyth, Saturday 27th May 1916

It had happened. The 5th Battle Squadron had been sent south to Rosyth to join the Battle Cruiser Force. The 3rd Battle Cruiser Squadron, comprising of the oldest ships of the BCF, had been sent north to Scapa for firing practice and the 5th were, ostensibly, replacing them on a temporary basis.

The 5th Battle Squadron and their attendant destroyers were anchored just to the east of the great bridge. The two remaining squadrons of the Battle Cruiser Force were anchored above the bridge. There was a palpable air of excitement among the men in *Warspite*. After so many months of confinement in their northern

9. GUNNERY PRACTICE AND REORGANISATION

base, they were south once more, within sight of the fleshpots of Edinburgh, which was a real stimulus. "Real pubs, real food and real women" Jonathan heard from the lower deck.

"The North British[59] does a really good steak," said Frank, "can't wait to treat you Jonathan. There may even be a half decent show on!"

The joy, however, was not unalloyed. "It'll be full of battle cruiser types," said Hammill, "cocky and full of bull. I was in the old *Cornwall* at the Falklands in '14. The firing from *Inflexible* and *Invincible* was very wild. They didn't seem to hit the Bosh at all half the time. I don't know about others, but as far as I was concerned I was decidedly crestfallen. The Bosh on the other hand were firing fast and accurate salvoes. Damn concerning!" Jonathan did not know that Hammill had served in that battle and made a mental note to speak at length to him about it. It was generally considered to be a victory for the superiority of the Royal Navy. Hammill clearly had other ideas.

"That fits," said another. "Chap in *Barham* was posted to *Invincible* for a while, told me he was just plain shocked at the standards he found."

"I agree, they're no damn good at gunnery: - the Dogger Bank affair last year was a disgrace!"[60]

"And their signalling. Completely hopeless." Clearly there were issues between the squadrons of the Royal Navy.

"Take their welcome, or should I say lack of it. Beatty's been angling after this squadron for eighteen months, now he's got it heaven only knows what he'll do. Was there a signal for Evan Thomas to lay aboard? Not bloody likely."

Evan Thomas was the rear admiral in command of the 5th Battle Squadron. It would normally have been protocol, if not wisdom, for the vice-admiral in overall command to meet his latest rear admiral on joining, especially if that rear-admiral was in command of the most powerful and fastest squadron of battleships in the world. Nothing of the sort had occurred.

That said, if no invitation was forthcoming, it was probably incumbent upon the junior officer to call on the senior. That hadn't happened, either because Beatty hadn't thought of it, or Evan Thomas thought it was beneath him to call upon a vice admiral who was actually junior to him in terms of years of service.

Jonathan had been on the bridge as they came to anchor and had witnessed the exchange of signals between the flagships at first hand. Evan Thomas' signal reporting his presence had been met with a single acknowledgement from *Lion* the flagship of the BCF, with no human word of welcome.

Jonathan had learned that there were politics even in that acronym. The official designation was the Battle Cruiser Squadron, but Beatty insisted upon Battle Cruiser Fleet. The rumour was that Jellicoe objected to that, as giving the impression that the battle cruisers were not part of the Grand Fleet. They had apparently compromised on the acronym BCF, which could mean Battle Cruiser Fleet, or Battle Cruiser Force, according to ones' predilections.

A little later on, Jonathan witnessed that tension at first hand.

9. GUNNERY PRACTICE AND REORGANISATION

The North British Hotel, Princes Street, Edinburgh, Saturday 27th May 1916, 9:30 PM

Jonathan and Frank had enjoyed their steaks. At Frank's suggestion, they washed it down with a decent bottle of burgundy. Then they had each enjoyed apple pie and cheese, followed by a cigar, coffee and a glass of brandy. Jonathan was beginning to learn from Frank's attitude towards alcohol. To Frank, alcohol was not just a stimulant, but an indispensible accompaniment to fine living. Each dish had its appropriate wine, and mixing and matching was part of the planning process, which seemed to comprise half the enjoyment.

Far from being the instrument of the Devil (which was in the back of Jonathan's Presbyterian mind) it was a foil and counterpoint to all aspects of life. His experience of socializing with Frank since Easter had made Jonathan begin to understand what a major sacrifice the Lenten fast was to his companion. He had vaguely heard the term 'gourmand' as one who understood and appreciated his food. He realized that this Englishman fitted the bill. He was a complex man, who was capable of deep thought, but on the other hand he could be very simple and direct when circumstances called for it.

At Frank's suggestion they moved on to a public house for what he referred to as a 'sundowner', which was not inappropriate given that the sun was only just setting, two and a half hours later than Jonathan was used to. Arriving at the pub, Jonathan finally learned that the Lounge Bar was where officers went, leaving the Public Bar for the men.

This particular bar was well furnished and quite crowded with young officers. Jonathan knew enough about the British way of doing things to realize that he had to fight his way to the bar, rather than relying on waiter service to his table. He bought two large malt whiskies ("Glenmorangie" Frank had stipulated. "You need the sweetness after the brandy.") Meanwhile by dint of his rank, Frank had secured a small table, already swimming in beer and adorned with an overflowing ashtray.

Jonathan found it curious that a middle-ranking officer such as Frank, would choose such a place, but he was aware of officers of a similar, and even more senior ranks sitting at the other tables. Not for the first time, he found that the stuffy Brits had rather more complex tribal distinctions than appeared at first glance. The seniors had seats, and the juniors stood around in noisy groups, nursing their drinks and talking.

Sipping his whisky, which was excellent, Jonathan looked around. Close to the bar was a rowdy group of young officers, clearly well in their cups. There was the same loud conversation that he had first experienced in Portsmouth, although these officers were obviously from the Battle Cruiser Force. Jonathan looked across at Frank, who was sitting back, enjoying the atmosphere. Their eyes met and both men smiled, remembering their first encounter in a place not unlike this in distant Portsmouth.

"No notes worth making Jonathan?" asked Frank. Jonathan had been taking notes of a rowdy conversation between young officers. He had been noticed and denounced as a spy. Frank had intervened to take charge. When Jonathan was reaching into his pocket for his billfold, Frank had said "If you take anything out of that pocket other than a wallet, I shall break your jaw for you, public place or not." The threat had been reinforced with an energetic fist, ready for a knockdown blow.

9. GUNNERY PRACTICE AND REORGANISATION

"No sir," said Jonathan, solemnly. "No state secrets on show here!"

And then, after a reflective draw on his pipe he said, "I sometimes wonder. What would you have done if I did, in fact, pull out a pistol that day?"

"Belted you as hard as I could and try and take the beastly thing."

"Even if I could have shot you?"

"Of course. *Dulce et decorum est pro Patria mori.*"

"Admirable" said Jonathan, mischievously, taking another draw on his pipe, "but isn't King George the head of a rival church to your own?" He had had enough alcohol to feel mellow enough to tease Frank a little.

"Indeed he is, in his ecclesial form," said Frank, who was not averse to a discussion about his religion. "But in his corporeal and legal form, he is my Sovereign and my Liege. He commands my allegiance, save and except where his commands, lawful under English Law, are in conflict with God's Law, as interpreted by the Traditions and Dogma of Holy Church."

As a doctrine, it had its points. Musing on that Jonathan became aware that Frank was being distracted. The young officers had begun to sing raucously, something, which his subconscious noticed, but did not flag up. Frank, on the other hand looked cross, and then as the song continued, furious.

Focusing, Jonathan heard a number of lusty young male voices singing

"Away, away with fife and drum
Here we come, full of rum
Looking for women who peddle their bum

In the Battle Cruiser Fleet

A-sailing up and down the coast,
Now here's the thing we love the most,
To fuck the girls and drink a toast

To the Battle Cruiser Fleet

Well, off the coast of Ard Druimm Mor
We took on board a floating whore.
We fucked her forty times or more

In the Battle Cruiser Fleet.

Frank put down his drink and stood up. In a quarterdeck voice he roared "STILL!" Jonathan could see that he was seething. The din stopped, but a whisper of voices continued.

"CEASE! BE SILENT!" came the quarterdeck voice again, and the suppressed buzz of conversation stopped. Frank had the undivided attention of the whole pub, including, Jonathan noted, some rather gaudily dressed females, some of whom were draped around the young officers. Their gaze was not friendly.

"How dare you sing such disgusting things in public!" said Frank in a voice only fractionally lower than a bellow. "You are officers of the Royal Navy. If you are not gentlemen, then please try and behave as such!"

There was a moment of silence, and then there was a casual drawl from somewhere at the back of the pub accompanied by a slow handclap. *"Ach! Quatsch! Halten Sie den Mund! Pompös Esel!"*

9. GUNNERY PRACTICE AND REORGANISATION

Stung, Frank turned around sharply. Jonathan, following his gaze, saw an officer in a Commander's uniform, with the tunic undone, nursing a whisky glass, flanked by two of the gaudily dressed females. The comment had obviously originated from him.

"I beg your pardon?" said Frank, taking in the scene with a cold eye. Jonathan could almost see his nostrils flaring. "Do you condone this...filthiness?"

"The people are relaxing. They are off duty. Don't be such a pompous ass." The voice was slurred and dismissive.

"And you are....?" Asked Frank, dangerously

"Murray. *Indefatigable*. And I should thank you to keep your opinions to yourself Hodgson. You aren't preaching at Mass here!"

"Murray...?" mused Frank. "Ah yes, I have it. *Dryad* in '10. I had cause to put in a report, if I remember it correctly. You were slack and out of order."

"So you said at the time. Your opinion was not upheld." And he tapped the three rings on his sleeve, which matched Frank's own.

"Well your attitude tonight, if I may say so suggests that my former view was correct. Are you seriously defending this juvenile music hall nonsense? Including, in case I am misunderstood, the sort of language that would not be out of place in a Singapore brothel." Frank's tone was hard, and it was a shock to Jonathan hearing him pronounce the word 'brothel' even if it was said with loathing.

"Oh stow it Hodgson! You're in the fighting navy now, no more of that skulking around in the north grounding on your own beef bones. Been to sea recently have you?"

Jonathan was quite shocked at the tone, which almost amounted to juvenile jeering. The young officers were moving, and whilst they weren't quite ready to join in an attack on a senior, Jonathan could sense that they were not far off it.

Frank stopped. His face was white. "I see." He said, shortly. "I had hoped to demonstrate the difference between our cause and that of the bosh to a neutral observer. Clearly I have failed. You appear to be, sir, as amoral and rapacious as those whom we fight. In those circumstances I am afraid that I cannot remain. Good evening to you." And he put on his cap, saluted and turned and walked out.

Jonathan followed. As they were well clear of the pub, Frank said, "I am sorry about that Jonathan. It was quite disgraceful. Clearly standards here are very slack indeed." He was still seething.

Jonathan's reaction was not straightforward. He had not liked the song, and agreed with Frank that it reflected badly on the Service. He was not sure that he would have intervened as Frank did, but he certainly respected his courage. It did, indeed, require guts to stand up as Frank had done in those circumstances. It required even more guts to deal with the fallout from the intervention. In Jonathan's mind, the salute as they left was a masterstroke. It reminded the other commander that they were both in the same service. And were supposed to follow the same standards.

Aberdour House, Monday 29th May, Forenoon

One of the advantages of Rosyth appeared to be a much quicker mail service. Jonathan had been delivered a package of no less than five letters, four of which had

9. GUNNERY PRACTICE AND REORGANISATION

been addressed to the US Embassy, and forwarded to Jonathan Marston Esq. HMS Warspite BFPO Ships.

First and foremost was a short letter from Benson, acknowledging his report. It was not written on official notepaper and bore an address that Jonathan did not recognize. With a thrill, he realized that it must be his private residence.

Congratulations Marston

Your letter addressed to my office reached me. As you know, I have recently moved and please address any further correspondence to this address.

I am very pleased to hear of your experiences, and I hope that you will have some decent hunting. I know the Master by reputation and I am of the view that if anyone can get the best out of the pack, he will.

On another topic, I see that you were dragooned into the Sussex *enquiry, even though you are on furlough. It seems that you have done some good work.*

Things here are the same as ever, but as always they will change in the fall. I do not wish to cut short your well-earned leave, but I should like to see you in person soon. Shall we say by August?

All the best

Benson

It was a very interesting letter, and gave him a date to work to. Presumably, Benson wanted to be ready for a change of direction and possibly a new President in November.

There was a simple and chatty letter from his mother, with a few lines from his father in his own unmistakable scrawl. Neither revealed that they knew anything about what he was doing or where he was. The closest was an imprecation to 'take care' from his mother.

There were two letters in a clear, feminine hand that he recognized as that of Clementina Fessenden. The first was obviously written before his own letter had been received and it was a pleasant surprise.

Jonathan

I had a note out of the blue from Cliff Carver, who wrote to tell me that he had seen you and that you were doing some very important work in Europe. I simply cannot tell you how hipped that made me.

I always figured that you were destined for great things: - Dad says that he has heard good reports about you and he says that your name is being mentioned in all the right places.

That was good to hear. The rest was her usual mix of the doings of her father, the weather and anodyne news from home.

The next was a revelation. His own letter had been guarded, but he had mentioned that he was taking a break in Scotland. Clementina's second letter was something else again. The first thing he saw was a small white cambric handkerchief with the initials CF embroidered on

9. GUNNERY PRACTICE AND REORGANISATION

it. He turned his attention to the letter itself. It was positively gushing

Oh My Dear!

I know where you are! And what you are doing! Don't ask me how, but I simply had to write and say how proud I am of you. You are doing something that other men can only dream about and I feel in the depths of my soul that you are doing the greatest service to your country that can be done.

I would give my eyeteeth to see what you are seeing and experience what you are experiencing. Daddy says that it is heartening to see someone in Authority actually grasping the nettle and acting for the greater good of the United States.

You know, of course, where my sympathies lie in this horrid war, especially after that dreadful affair with that ferry. Daddy says that he saw a report about it to which you contributed not a little.

I have to confess that I am now following the war news with that dreadful mix of pride and apprehension, which I guess must be the lot of anyone with a dear one in harm's way

Jonathan blinked at that, 'a dear one!' Jonathan had always cherished hopes about Clementina, but his career was not yet at a point where he could consider paying court to her with any sense of seriousness. He had been aware that she found him an interesting and stimulating companion, but they had never stepped over the bounds of propriety. They did, of course address each other by their first names, but they had been so closely involved with Reg's madcap schemes that they were colleagues rather than more formal young people. She was now addressing him as 'my dear' and confessing that he was, in fact, dear to her!

He read on

> *Daddy says that the threat from submarines is very great. I remember all those poor boys killed when a single submarine sank three great ships within an hour of each other. I want to tell you to take care, but I know you too well to expect you to take that advice when others are in danger.*
>
> *I try to get on with ordinary life, but I find myself at odd times looking at the ocean and thinking of you, so far away. I am finding a hitherto unknown, soppy part to my nature, which makes me want to sit at a window in some high tower waiting for my knight in shining armor to come and claim me. The closest that I can get is our attic room, which is rather dusty, but I should do it for you if I thought it would do any good.*
>
> *I heard the story of your funny uniform, and I should love to have a picture of you in it, can I beg you to send one? Then I can look at it and sigh pathetically at regular intervals. In the mean time, I can send you my favor in the form of this handkerchief, and beg you to keep it with you and think of your lady watching the lists from afar.*
>
> *Ever your affectionate friend*
>
> *Clementina*

9. GUNNERY PRACTICE AND REORGANISATION

Jonathan felt like shouting! Clementina cared for him! She had sent him a favour. A whole new future rose up in front of his eyes.

The final one was a short letter on thick, grey, official Admiralty notepaper, headed HMS Lion, 28th May 1916, written in a forceful scrawl. It read

Dear Lieutenant Marston

I have been told that you are to be here with us. I should be grateful if you would be kind enough to present yourself in 'Lion' at 1200 tomorrow. Please bring tennis gear.

It was signed 'Beatty, VABCF'

When he asked the Captain's permission to go ashore Philpotts said drily, "You are very privileged Mr Marston. As far as I am aware you are the *only* officer of this squadron to receive such an invitation, up to and including its admiral."

And here he was at Beatty's private residence ashore with a couple of other officers. They had all landed from *Lion* by the Admiral's barge at a dedicated pier. Coming alongside the flagship had been an impressive affair. *Warspite* was big, but this ship dwarfed her. The quarterdeck was high and narrow with that uncluttered look that Jonathan had come to associate with the latest British warships.

He was greeted respectfully and told that the Admiral would be with them shortly. When the Admiral bounced up the ladder, Jonathan was instantly impressed with a sense of suppressed energy. His cap was at a rakish angle and he was wearing a tunic of non-regulation cut. Everyone saluted. Returning the salute Beatty fixed a piercing gaze upon Jonathan and said, "You must be Marston! Very pleased to see you. Thank you for coming. Lady Beatty will be delighted" and his eyes moved on to the other members of the party, even though he was still speaking to Jonathan. They returned to him and their owner said, "She is always complaining that there are none of her fellow countrymen around.[61] We'll have lunch and then some tennis. Far better than chasing some damn' stupid ball over a grouse moor." And then addressing his Flag Lieutenant, a slightly rotund officer with a distracted air, "Come on Seymour, chop chop! Get to it then!"

Obviously the latter was used to the Admiral's moods and immediately indicated to Jonathan that they should descend to the Admiral's barge, which had seamlessly replaced *Warspite's* launch at the gangway.

Beatty started to interrogate Jonathan as soon as he was seated. He wanted to know all about him, who his people were and who he knew. He was interested to hear about his father and his friends. He was also interested to hear that Frederick Prince was a friend and appeared to know of the Lowell's. Jonathan felt that he had made an impression.

At the pier, an automobile was waiting for them. Jonathan, by now used to the ways of the RN was expecting a fancy welcome, but it was not to be. They were whisked away up a narrow road into another rather charming Scottish town without any ceremony at all. A narrow way led under an arch to a solid looking stone building, with roses climbing up it. The front door opened and a bekilted servant came out to open the car door for the Admiral and his party.

"Guid morning Sir David" he said. "Her Ladyship isnae come doon yet. But ah'll tell her ye're here."

9. GUNNERY PRACTICE AND REORGANISATION

"Thanks Hamilton. Gentlemen, come in." And they were ushered into a cool, dark hallway and from thence into a drawing room, with a well-stocked cocktail cabinet.

"What'll you have Marston?" asked the admiral, attending to the cabinet himself. "Lady Beatty is partial to a dry martini. Would you care for one?"

Jonathan was not at all sure what a dry martini was, but he was prepared to find out and indicated so. The procedure seemed quite elaborate, involving ice, a shiny metal cocktail shaker and various bottles of unnamed liquor. The Admiral himself took the shaker and shook it together with all the ingredients. The result was poured out into a series of small glasses, which were solemnly adorned with an olive on a stick.

"There you go Marston, down the hatch!"

Jonathan took a cautious sip of the concoction, which was, to his taste, marginally worse than the moonshine whiskey he had shared with an Irish officer on the way down from Liverpool. As he did so there was a female shout from upstairs

"Jaa-aaa-aack! Are you making cocktails?"

To Jonathan's attuned ear, the accent was pure Chicago.

"Yes Tata," shouted Beatty.

"Well save one for me, I'll be right down." The voice spoke of gin and cigarettes.

"Of course dear," said Beatty.

Shortly afterwards she appeared. She was quite the most fascinating woman that Jonathan had seen. Dark, aquiline features framed a pair of dark eyes and very red lips, obviously benefitting from artificial make up. As she made her entrance, she was carrying a long cigarette holder with an elegant cigarette in it. The paper was black, and the filter was gold. It looked, to Jonathan's eye, incredibly sophisticated. "Darling!" said Beatty, moving over to her with a gold lighter. He attempted to kiss her, but she turned aside so that his kiss landed lightly on her cheek.

Recovering quickly, he lit her cigarette.

She cupped her hands round his in an oddly intimate gesture, which contrasted with her previous behaviour. Straightening up and drawing on her cigarette, she took a look around. Her eyes swept over the assembly through the smoke. They lighted on Jonathan.

"Well hello there!" She said, with interest "and who's this?"

"Tata, this is Lieutenant Marston of the United States Navy. He is the surprise I promised you." The Admiral was like a schoolboy showing off. Jonathan was not quite sure that he liked to be described as a "surprise" but there was nothing he could do about it. "His mother is a Lowell."

"At last! A real man among all these stuffed shirt British faggots! You're very welcome." And she held out her hand to him palm down. Jonathan realized that she wanted him to kiss it. He disliked her language. At the same time he noticed that none of the men seemed to be offended and he wondered if the word meant something else in British English. The hand was shaken imperiously as if to tell him to get on with it.

He realized that there was really no alternative and carried the thing off with as much grace as possible.

"I can't tell you how bored I am here in this dead and alive hole with no decent company." She said, blowing out smoke from her cigarette, "Jack is so busy that he

9. GUNNERY PRACTICE AND REORGANISATION

neglects me terribly. It's just too bad being a war widow, especially when your husband is still alive!"

"Oh Tata, you know I get away when I can" said Beatty looking abashed "I am quite busy, you know."

"Oh yes, I do know. The thin blue line and all that guff. You are the boss. I should have thought that you could do what you like as long as the country's safe! You could sleep ashore occasionally, for instance."

Jonathan was beginning to dislike this woman intensely. Had she no idea of the responsibilities that her husband faced?

"Tata," said Beatty, almost apologetically "you know that we've talked about this. I can't sleep ashore when I have forbidden my men to do so. It's just not right"

"Aww Jack, you're simply too busy for me, admit it. If you weren't, you'd sleep ashore once in awhile. We know each other too well for that bullshit." She was like a demanding little girl.

"Tata, darling, you know that I am not, but I simply can't when my men can't."

She made a disagreeable face.

Jonathan was beginning to find that this exchange was acutely embarrassing. Casting sidelong glances at the other guests, he saw that most weren't happy about it, but no one was saying anything.

As an aside, he found it incredible that a senior admiral could be treated in this way by his wife. It went against every instinct that he had. In his book, part of the wifely duties was to support her husband, not belittle him. This woman clearly did not appreciate that.

Jonathan became aware of an RN Commander strolling into the room from the same door that Lady Beatty had entered as if he owned the place. Beatty noticed him and said "Hello Ryan[62]. Are you well settled in?" There was no irony in the tone whatsoever as far as Jonathan could see. "Oh yes, sir" said the man, easily. "Thank you so much for the billet. I am very grateful. It's such a bore not having anything decent to do. At least I'm close to the action here. Or should I say in-action." The man's attitude was rather dismissive. He was a little older than Jonathan, with dark, handsome looks and a knowing manner.

"I am sorry we can't oblige you Commander," said the Admiral. "Sadly Admiral Hipper doesn't want to come out to play. I appreciate, of course how much of a disappointment it must be after command of a torpedo boat, but there we are. The Bosh are not inclined to humour us. How long are you staying?"

There was a look of sheer murder in Lady Beatty's eyes directed at her husband as she watched this exchange. The Admiral appeared to flinch slightly and Ryan's *armour-propre* reasserted itself.

"I don't know sir, I don't have an appointment as yet" he drawled. "The clowns at the Admiralty don't seem to have shaken themselves down sufficiently yet to decide on the usefulness of a retired Commander, who is a member of the Awkward Squad, outside the Fishpond."[63]

Jonathan had learned that about ten years ago, the British Royal Navy had been seriously divided between those who followed Admiral Fisher, a modernizer and Admiral Beresford, a Conservative. That was the 'political' Navy that Brandon had referred to in that small, stuffy office not two months ago, but already, so distant in Jonathan's memory. This man must have been a Fisher opponent. Looking at his impeccably tailored uniform, and his faint air of superiority, Jonathan could well picture it.

9. GUNNERY PRACTICE AND REORGANISATION

"I understand." said the Admiral. "It must be so difficult for Mrs Ryan and the children. How is Percy by the way?" There was definitely an atmosphere between the men. Jonathan had his suspicions as to what it was but was not going to rush into any judgments.

"Oh he is fine, thank you, sir. Settling down well at school. Thank you for asking"

Jonathan took the view that both men were tearing chunks out of each other in an understated, very English way.

"You will stay as long as you like," said Lady Beatty firmly.

"Well, if the Admiral doesn't mind…" said the officer, languidly.

"Of course he doesn't mind. He's too busy for me these days anyway. He knows I enjoy the company of intelligent and personable people. Now, Lieutenant" she said, turning to Jonathan with a dazzling smile. "Tell me all about yourself."

"Not much to tell ma'am. I am just a regular Naval Officer. Quite boring really." Jonathan was uncomfortable. There was quite a lot that he wanted to tell this woman, but it wasn't his place to do so.

"Well you can't be a Naval Officer all the time. Do you ride?" Jonathan indicated that he did not.

"Do you dance?"

"When the occasion calls for it ma'am, I do."

"Great, let's have a dance! Jack, put some music on. Some decent music for a change." Obediently, her husband moved to the gramophone and picked up a record with a plain sleeve. When he put it on the turntable, wound it up and dropped the needle, a most extraordinary sound came out. Jonathan had frankly never heard anything like it. There was a cornet, but like no cornet Jonathan had ever heard, a clarinet, an insistent, frantic string accompaniment and a trombone. The beat was very rapid. Lady Beatty grabbed him and started a quickstep in time to the music; startled Jonathan tried to catch up. The dance style seemed to involve a considerable amount of rocking of the upper body. He couldn't help but be aware that Lady Beatty was not wearing any corsetry and his hands encountered warm flesh under the dress, as did his chest.

The whole thing felt wrong. "This is just the latest thing!" said Lady Beatty, pressing closer into him, "They are putting on a whole show next year, but Pop got them in to do a recording, just for us. This is hot off the press."[64]

Jonathan found it simultaneously disturbing and exhausting, especially when someone began to sing on the record. It included the line "I'm going to dance right off my shoes" which was just about right from Jonathan's point of view.

Happily the record finished allowing Jonathan to take a breath. He was aware of Ryan goggling at him in an unpleasant manner. Well that wasn't his problem. Conversely, the close and intimate embrace of Lady Beatty was. Jonathan was not used to such things and tried to distract himself with abstract algebra.

He was just succeeding when Lady Beatty said; "Again Jack!" and Jonathan had to go through the whole process again. Abstract algebra did not help him, and he found that he had to dance with his lower body well away from the Admiral's lady. It was ridiculous. He seriously disliked this woman and would never consider any form of friendship between them, let alone the closeness that his rebellious body seemed to desire. Desperately he asked

9. GUNNERY PRACTICE AND REORGANISATION

"Who are these people? The musicians, I mean. It sounds like Negro music."

"Stein's Dixieland Jass Band" was the reply, "Pop says they're going to be very big."

"Might have known they're Bosh" said Beatty to his staff, who laughed.

"Oh stoppit Jack!" said his wife "They're American through and through! Aren't they Cyril?"

"If you say so Lady Beatty," said Ryan, clearly amused. The music, if such it was, was not to Jonathan's taste. He didn't care for it and didn't care for the woman. Perversely, she seemed to be determined to monopolize him. She wanted to know all about his family and insisted on sitting next to him at lunch, much to Ryan's annoyance. Beatty seemed oblivious and was talking about hunting. "Do you hunt Marston?" asked the Admiral.

"No sir, never had the opportunity really" said Jonathan.

"Ah" said Lady Beatty, "You'll have to come out with us one day. That's how we met, Jack and I. Do you remember Jack?" Again, her tone was warm and intimate. This woman was a nightmare.

"Couldn't forget it my dear. The Warwick's. I had just got back from the Sudan, and saw you taking that enormous fence!" The Admiral was beaming.

"The unspeakable in pursuit of the uneatable" said Ryan, superciliously. That was unwise in Jonathan's opinion. "Oh shut up Cyril," said Lady Beatty, viciously "You don't know anything about it, so do keep quiet."

Clearly the extramarital beau had the same treatment as her lawful husband in Lady Beatty's book. To Jonathan's inexperienced eye, this was a seriously unusual situation. He was fairly sure that Ryan was more than a

247

'friend' of Lady Beatty, but Admiral Beatty seemed to be oblivious, apart from a couple of barbed asides. The men weren't very different in age, and were in the same service. Beatty was Vice Admiral in charge of the Battle Cruiser Force. Ryan appeared to be an unemployed torpedo boat captain. What did he have to attract the Admiral's wife?

And then, after some thought, he had it: - sophistication and style. If you can convince people that what you are producing is stylish, then you are home and dry! This man clearly had that gift.

Something in Jonathan rose up in revulsion. Ryan was clearly one of those 'oh-so-clever' officers who knew exactly what ought to be done and, by virtue of his intimate access to a senior officer's wife was attempting to put the Admiral down. Jonathan thought that was despicable.

He would have liked to say something, but Lady Beatty's retort had made it immaterial. Ryan subsided under her whip-like tongue and the expression on his face afforded Jonathan some small satisfaction.

The tennis match later was enjoyable. He was partnering the Admiral against the Flag lieutenant and Chatfield, the Flag Captain. Chatfield[65] was a worthy opponent and played skilful, aggressive tennis. The Flag Lieutenant, Seymour was hopeless, and suffered the wrong end of the Admiral's tongue on more than one occasion. To Jonathan's surprise, he acquitted himself quite well. His partner's play was accurate and enthusiastic. Indeed, he seemed to be thoroughly enjoying himself until Lady Beatty and Commander Ryan condescended to move out and watch the tennis match with their cocktails and fancy cigarettes. Jonathan was aware of them, but paid them no attention. The Admiral, by contrast, kept on casting

9. GUNNERY PRACTICE AND REORGANISATION

glances at his wife, which meant that he missed the occasional rally opportunity.

After a while, Jonathan began to find this irritating. There was, of course, nothing that he could do about it, but it was seriously spoiling his game. At one point, Lady Beatty and Ryan started laughing, it was not quite clear at what, but it got under the Admiral's armour. He was about to serve, but before doing so he turned directly towards Ryan and Lady Beatty saying

"I say Ryan. If you can't be quiet please go inside! You're putting me off!"

"Aw Jack! Stop being so cross. We're talking about something else," said Lady Beatty.

"Well damn well don't do it whilst I'm trying to play bloody tennis!" said the Admiral in exasperation.

"Don't take your filthy temper out on me Jack Beatty. I own you. Remember?"

"Oh Bollocks!" said the Admiral. Jonathan saw a faint, unpleasant smirk on the face of Ryan, just as Lady Beatty burst into tears and flounced indoors, which, to Jonathan, looked rather more theatrical than real.

"Tata, darling, please wait..." said the Admiral, throwing his racquet down and following his weeping wife. The men looked at each other uneasily.

Ryan contrived to look superior and said, "I had better go and see what can be done..." and gave every appearance of intending to follow the couple.

His arm was grabbed by Chatfield who said, "I would suggest, Commander, that this is a matter between the Admiral and his Lady. It is not appropriate for any of us to interfere." The voice was quiet, but authoritative and then, with greater emphasis, looking him directly in the eyes, "Any of us."

There was a distinct air of menace underneath the measured tone. "You, with the greatest respect, know nothing about the weight of responsibility that the Admiral bears. I would suggest, as one officer to another, that a period of silence would be appropriate."

Ryan looked as if he was about to protest, the look in Chatfield's eyes was enough for him.

"OK old man. Only trying to help."

"Do not call me 'Old Man'." The tone was like a whip. "I am your superior officer. You will address me as 'Sir' and you will refrain from any assumption that we were ever on intimate terms. Do you understand Commander?"

"Oh, I say…."

"Do you understand Commander?" the voice was pure steel.

"Aye aye sir."

Chatfield released Ryan's arm and said, in a lighter tone, "You do not have an appointment at the moment do you Ryan?"

"No sir" said the man tightly.

"You resigned in 1911 did you not?"

"I did sir. Politics, as you know."

"I do not know. And your last appointment was…?

'Commander of a TBD, sir" said the wretched man.

"When was that?"

"1911, sir." Shamefacedly.

Jonathan felt uncomfortable. This was torture of the most exquisite kind.

"In which case a period of silence from you is even more appropriate. Do you agree, *Commander?*" Chatfield made it sound like pure poison.

9. GUNNERY PRACTICE AND REORGANISATION

"Aye sir" was the barely audible reply.

"Very good." Said Chatfield. "Now Gentlemen," addressing the other two, "next set? Lieutenant Marston and me? Singles?" Ryan sloped off down the garden and stared moodily at the Forth.

The Wardroom, HMS Warspite a little later

Jonathan was not quite sure what to make of the afternoons' events. Lady Beatty was clearly a nightmare. She had reappeared with her husband a little later. She seemed to have got over her outburst, and was smoking quite contentedly. The Admiral, however was quiet and withdrawn and they returned to *Lion* in silence. Just before vanishing below, Beatty turned and said to Jonathan "A pleasure to meet you Marston. You must come again when we have time and leisure."

"Thank you for having me sir" said Jonathan, saluting. He had never been more relieved to return to his own mess. Frank took one look at his face and thrust a stiff gin into his hand. "Here you are old chap, you look as if you need it!"

"Thanks" said Jonathan, taking a swig.

"That bad eh?' said Frank

"There were Martinis. And Jazz."

"Oh you poor fellow. 'Nuff said. Here, have another!"

10. A New Sweep

Wednesday 31st May 1916, 1400 HMS Warspite, 56° 47' N, 4° 40' E

The 5th Battle Squadron was cruising in a dead calm heading east by north, otherwise 023 degrees. The water was like glass and the ships, screened by the cruiser *Fearless* and nine destroyers, were cutting their way smoothly through it.

In contrast to the general sea state, the wakes of their passing crossed and intersected leaving a miniature maelstrom behind them.

Five miles to the South were the battle cruisers. As always, Jonathan was on the fore bridge. Today, he was admiring the beauty of those ships. At easy speed, the sun lit up their light grey paintwork, which stood out clearly above their white wakes.

The orders were to turn north shortly after 1400 to close with the battleship squadrons and then return to base if nothing untoward happened.

Apart from the battle cruisers and their screen, there was nothing else of interest to see. At least, thought Jonathan to himself, the weather for this sweep was a huge improvement on the last one. Summer was finally coming.

"SOBCF[66] signalling sir!" sang out the lookout. Turning, Jonathan focused his binoculars on the sudden flash of colour at the *Lion's* foreyard.

"To turn north sir." The voice was from the Chief Yeoman of Signals who was apparently spending his time off watch on the Admiral's bridge a couple of levels below. He had a telescope to his eye as he watched the flagship of the Battle Cruiser Force.

"Very Good' said the officer of the watch. Moving to a voice pipe he said "Captain sir, preparative to turn north." A tinny acknowledgment could just be heard. The ladder behind Jonathan rattled as Frank came up.

"Turn North, preparative, sir" said the officer to Frank.

"Very good" said the latter.

"*Barham* acknowledging sir" said the lookout.

"Flag signal from *Barham*" said the Chief Yeoman, who was now watching their own flagship, "From SO 5th BS alter course together four points to port"

"Acknowledge." The procedure was for the Senior Officer of the Battle-Cruiser Force to signal to the Senior Officer of the 5th Battle Squadron who would, in turn, signal his own squadron.

As soon as each ship had identified the order from their own flagship, they would bend on the 'acknowledge' followed by a duplicate of the flag order on a different halyard. The flagship would then haul down the order (thereby making it executive). The acknowledgment and the executive would be hauled down together.

The ships sailed on with nothing but the hum of the ventilators and the hiss of the sea to divert them.

"Signal's down sir!"

"Very good!" said the officer of the watch. He turned to the voice pipe, "Starboard four, steer north." There was the usual acknowledgement and then a slight lean as the ship came round at the same time as the rest of

10. A NEW SWEEP

her squadron. It was like a ballet manoeuver. They were now in a shallow echelon.

"Ah well," said Frank to Jonathan. "Another happy jaunt with nothing to show for it. I'm getting fed up with this." He began to fill his pipe.

Jonathan was sympathetic. It was just so frustrating that the enemy wouldn't play ball. All those ships, all those men, all trained up and ready for action and nothing to take it out on.

"*Lion*, signalling again sir! Signal lamp!' Indeed a light was flashing from *Lion's* superstructure. Jonathan found that he was excited. Signal lights usually meant something urgent "From SOBCF to SO 5th BS Look out for advanced cruisers of GF when we turn north." Jonathan's excitement died within him. It was a routine signal, sent by the most urgent means.

"Yes, thank you Yeo," said the Officer of the Watch. Frank lit his pipe, shook out the match and said quietly to Jonathan "I expect the next one will have instructions on how to suck eggs. Sometimes I feel like signalling back and saying 'negative keep look out.' What on earth do they think we have been doing for the past couple of years?" He flicked the dead match overboard.

Frank drew on his pipe.

There was a sudden bustle as Captain Philpotts came up the ladder at a run, "I have the ship," he said to the officer of the watch. "Be ready for Action Stations please gentlemen, *Galatea* has found something."

"Aye aye sir. You have the ship." The formal phrase was charged with meaning.

Frank put his still lit pipe in his pocket and saluted. Jonathan and the erstwhile Officer of the Watch followed suit.

"Ship is yours sir," said the officer of the watch, confirming the handover.

"Very good. Course and speed as before. Connect all boilers."

Jonathan remembered that *Galatea* was one of the advance screen cruisers. Suddenly he heard the stirring bugle call for 'action' followed by the 'double'. The ship erupted like an ants' nest with people going to their stations, accompanied by the boatswain's whistles and shouts of "All hands to action stations. All hands to action stations."

Sounds came up the various voice pipes, "All boilers connected, engine room ready."

"Coxswain at the wheel sir, course North"

"Fore bridge, Spotting top manned and ready sir"

Jonathan, of course, had no formal station and so he thought he would remain on the fore bridge as long as he could so as to get the best idea of what was going on. Frank, with a wisp of smoke coming out of his jacket pocket slid quickly down the ladder to the conning tower, his post in action.

The Captain looked around himself thunderously. Something was not right. "Messenger! Get me the Commander please! At the double!"

"Aye aye sir. The Commander. At the double" he dashed below, sliding down the ladder like a child. The reports continued to come in.

"Bow torpedo room closed up."

"Damage control parties present and correct."

The Captain ignored them.

10. A NEW SWEEP

Within a very short time, Walwyn appeared, saluting the Captain. "You sent for me sir?"

"Indeed I did, Commander. What in Hell's name do you think you're doing?"

"You told me to get the hands up, sir. So I did."

"You blithering idiot! I want them to get some tea, not full blown stations! We don't know what's happening yet"

"Sorry sir," said Walwyn, apologetically, "but we are well on the way to clearing the ship. With respect, I should prefer to get cleared away as soon as possible. The people can get some tea afterwards if there's time."

Philpotts continued to glower.

"*Barham* signalling sir!' sang the Yeoman, interrupting the conversation. "Alter course in succession SSE, speed 22 knots"

"Acknowledge!" said the Captain over his shoulder. "Very well Walwyn," he said, subsiding a little, "you had better carry on." The Commander saluted. "Aye aye sir. To carry on."

The Flagship's hoist came down and *Warspite* turned back on herself following *Valiant* in succession. They began to accelerate. Jonathan could actually feel the ship going faster, pushing him onto his back foot as the stern dug in under the increased power. The funnels began to boil with smoke and the note of the turbines changed from a hum to a whine. Walwyn turned to go down the ladder, and as he did so he seemed to recollect himself. Locating Jonathan he said, "You had better come with me Marston. Things might get a little hectic. *Galatea* has sighted two cruisers, which are probably hostile."

Jonathan followed him down with alacrity. He felt the excitement building up inside him again. This might be the real thing.

Following Walwyn as he did his rounds was instructive. The Commander went round the mess decks to check all the stools and tables were on the deck, so they couldn't fall any further and that the emergency lighting (candles and oil lamps) were ready and lit, with the watertight doors closed. Special hoses with holes in them at intervals had been run out over the exposed decks and the water started. The holes allowed the water to run out over the decks to protect against fire. Battle ensigns and union flags were hoisted at both masts. There were cheery questions from the crew, "Wot is it sir? Are they out at last?"

"You had better hope so!" Walwyn replied, "Sounds like we have a couple of cruisers at least!"

"Sir! Sir!" A messenger came towards them at the run. "There's been another signal from *Galatea* 'Smoke seems to be seven vessels besides cruisers and destroyers'.

The compartment they were passing through (it was the starboard battery) erupted in cheers. There was no doubt about the eagerness of his Majesty's Royal Navy for a fight. "We'll get'em sir. Don't worry. At last!"

Jonathan was reminded of the old song that he had heard sung at the sods' opera 'We ne'er see our foes but we wish them to stay, they never see us but they wish us away' as true now as it ever was.

"Very good" said Walwyn. Turning to Jonathan he said, "We'd better let the Captain know that we're all closed up. Let's jump to it! Keeps you fit, all this

10. A NEW SWEEP

excitement!" Indeed it did as the Captain was still on the fore bridge, five steep ladders above their current position.

As he climbed in Walwyn's wake, Jonathan realized just how fast the ship was going. The ventilators were roaring and the wash overside was hissing like a thousand snakes. The ladder ways were vibrating in sympathy with the racing propellers and the wind of their passage was literally breath taking.

On the compass platform, Philpotts was staring out ahead through his binoculars. As they arrived the yeoman said "*Barham* signalling sir 'From SO 5th BS assume complete readiness for action in all respects'."

"Acknowledge."

Philpotts put down his glasses and turned to Walwyn with an expression of pure delight on his face. "We have them! That can only be Scheer's battle cruisers! Pass the word Walwyn. Now we'll see something!"

Seeing Jonathan, the Captain said, "Well Mr Marston, You wanted to see our methods. Now it looks as if you might have a chance!"

"Indeed sir" said Jonathan. He wanted to say something banal, like 'good luck' but it was totally superfluous in this atmosphere.

"Look after yourself Marston," said the Captain, "I don't fancy the paperwork if you get yourself killed, so try not to be, there's a good chap!" The conversation felt like a dream. Jonathan followed Walwyn down into 'B' turret, which they entered through the lower hatch. Griffiths greeted them with enthusiasm. "All Correct sir. Turret closed up and ready" he reported. And then "Is it 'it' sir?" he asked.

"Dunno Griffiths" was Walwyn's laconic reply, "but it sounds like it might be interesting!"

And then he asked, "Casualty preparation?"

"Morphine and syringes ready sir, as are bandages" a capable looking rating responded.

A cheeky looking mid said, "We shan't need that sir! We're insoluble, like the Pope"

"Shut up Walker" said Walwyn, without looking at him, or identifying the speaker. Walker was clearly the clown of the turret.

"Who sir?" said the lad "Me sir? No sir!"

"Walker. If you don't shut up you will be the first to see the enemy. I'll have you loaded and fired. You just see if I don't!"

"Aye aye sir. Always ready to do my duty!" The lad was irrepressible. Jonathan realized that this piece of byplay was incredibly valuable. Without any apparent planning, the exchange between a senior and a junior officer was keeping the turret crew amused and occupied, just as he had been telling his class a hundred years ago at Mare Island.

"Should we load sir?' asked the senior gun captain.

"Better wait for orders Curtess," said Walwyn. "No doubt someone will tell us when necessary" and he sat on his seat beside the rangefinder and looked through the periscope. "I can see damn' all at the moment" he said as he traversed the instrument.

The navy phone rang and Walwyn picked it up.

"Load and train red two zero" he said, "follow director". It was just like the practice the previous week. Jonathan was aware of the turret moving and heard the familiar clang and rattle as the projectiles and charges came up from below. He took his place at the port

10. A NEW SWEEP

periscope as before, and was conscious of a seaman proffering him some cotton waste to use as an earplug. Remembering his previous experience with these huge guns he took it gratefully and stuffed his ears.

He felt the vibration through his seat, even though his hearing was now muffled. He was suddenly conscious of his own heartbeat as he heard the blood pulsing like a drum. He was reminded of the negro music that he had heard at Admiral Beatty's house, *"I'll be there to get you in a taxi honey, better be ready 'bout half past eight, now baby don't be late, I want to be there when the band starts playing."*

Clearly the band was about to start playing, and, like it or not, Jonathan had no say over whether he was going to be late or not.

Looking through his periscope, Jonathan could see nothing apart from the next ahead, steaming hard with a huge white wake.

Then they heard a muffled rumble from a long way away. Gunfire! The Battle Cruiser Force was in action! The noise became continuous. Somewhere out there to the east a major action was taking place. He was conscious of the ship leaning as she turned at full speed.

The phone squawked, "Stand by."

Straining through the mist, Jonathan saw a thickening and a concentration of rather darker shades than were explained by the natural phenomena. As he watched they developed into four distinct columns of unnatural weather. Focusing the glasses of his periscope, he realized that these were the smoke plumes of ships steaming at full speed. The pressure of their boiler room fans was sending the smoke straight up for a considerable distance until the wind blew the plume aft, where it dispersed. These had to be the German cruisers.

They were heading slightly south, almost parallel to the track of *Warspite*. "Range one niner seven thousand yards," said the range taker, echoing the words in his ears from the fire control station above them.

"Bearing red one five. Target third ship." The turret adjusted itself slightly, the barrels just leading the second column of smoke and tracking it as the ships moved. It was almost as if the guns were alive, sniffing out their prey.

Nearly ten miles was just over the horizon from where he was sitting. Jonathan could see the smoke plumes through his periscope, but nothing else. The spotting top was fifty feet above him and could see further then he could. Calculating distances, Jonathan decided that from his position, at the top of 'B' turret he could see eight and a half miles or so (17,000 yards).

The spotting top could, in contrast, see about twelve and a half miles, i.e. 25,000 yards. This whole process was way outside Jonathan's experience. These ranges were unheard of. More prosaically, the guns that he was sitting behind were directed upon and were about to fire at, a target that he could only locate by a smoke plume. Suddenly, by way of a trick of the light, Jonathan saw some three-funnel cruisers with two masts through his periscope clearly. He knew that some atmospheric conditions allowed one to see a ship over the horizon. That must be what was happening.

The turret trained and Jonathan found himself looking straight at the second German cruiser from the front. It had three funnels and two masts. That was not a rig he recognized from Jane's. It must be something new.

10. A NEW SWEEP

"Range one niner three thousand yards" from the range taker. "Previously unknown type sir." The range was closing very rapidly as the ships rushed towards each other.

There was a burst of orange flame and brown smoke ahead, followed a few seconds later by a roar.

"*Barham* opened on first cruiser sir"

"Very good" said Walwyn. "Target third cruiser. Director firing. Time please?"

"Four oh five sir."

The fire gong sounded and the great gun below him exploded. Jonathan felt the familiar pressure enveloping him.

"Time of flight twenty-three seconds sir!"

"Very good."

"Range one niner thousand yards." The range taker sounded just as he did at practice. Calm and measured, almost soothing.

There! An unmistakable group of white splashes on the other side of the enemy cruiser, which was proceeding at high speed with thick smoke streaming from its funnels.

"Down two hundred" and the barrels lowered slightly. The gong sounded again and the right gun went off as the left gun was being reloaded. The splash this time was between the distant ship and the *Warspite*. The next one was a straddle and Jonathan distinctly saw a red glow as the massive shell exploded in the enemy ship. That was seriously good shooting.

"Target turning away sir. Range obscured."

The ship leaned again as they turned fast to starboard. He felt the turret training. "New target, smoke bearing red four zero, range two one thousand yards!" Ten and a half miles, still over his horizon.

This time he could see five distinct columns of black smoke. Those had to be the German battle cruisers. Jonathan became conscious of the continuous rumble from far ahead once more. He had obviously blanked it out as they were shooting at the cruisers. The British battle cruisers were still engaging the enemy. Those gentlemen were about to get the shock of their lives. The six British battle cruisers were about to be reinforced by thirty-two fifteen-inch guns from the 5th Battle Squadron.

"Target left hand ship. Range two oh five thousand yards."

Bong! And then the crash as the guns went off. Again the sequence of over and short, followed by "broadsides!" with both guns in each turret going off simultaneously. Jonathan was no longer conscious of the gun explosions; he was concentrating on that distant column of smoke. As he watched through the powerful instrument, he became aware of funnels and masts as the range closed. The hulls themselves were still below the horizon, but the individual ships were obvious.

The splashes of the British shells were high enough to see. They must be the best part of sixty or seventy feet high, thought Jonathan. The range continued to close and then he could see the massive stern waves of the enemy, bright against the murk. It was a strange sight, the thick black funnel smoke above the white wake, with the ships themselves quite difficult to make out. Suddenly he saw an explosion of bright orange from their target. They were firing back!

He could hear the shells over the din as they came. The sound was not unlike an express train at full speed.

10. A NEW SWEEP

The sea in front of him boiled as the shells hit, short of *Warspite* by a good five hundred yards.

Their own guns roared again. Jonathan saw an explosion amidships of their target ship. Unlike their gun flashes, this was altogether slower and more low key, almost like a haystack catching fire. The glow remained and grew, fanned by the speed of their passage. "Straddle. Enemy on fire sir" reported the range taker.

"Very good!" said Walwyn. It was seriously good shooting. The director firing method was working.

Jonathan could not imagine what it was like to be on the receiving end of these huge shells. Notwithstanding the fire, the enemy guns twinkled again, followed half a minute later by the noise of the shells arriving. The sea boiled once more. He felt *Warspite* tremble as she moved through the disturbed water.

"Enemy turning away sir!"

Jonathan could see for himself that the target ship was leaving the line under a cloud of black and white smoke, obviously hurt. Looking forward he could see other shells falling around *Valiant*, their next ahead, but couldn't see if any hit. They were themselves firing continuously and he saw that another enemy ship, which he thought might be *Von der Tann,* was burning brightly. The visibility, however, was worsening and it was difficult to make out the enemy ships, other than by their gun flashes.

"Range exceeded sir, guns against the stops."

"Thank you Curtess. Can't see anything to shoot at anyway." The guns fell silent for lack of targets.

Suddenly they were passing a stationary destroyer in the middle of a large patch of black water. Focusing his periscope, Jonathan realized that the destroyer was picking people out of the sea. He realized that he was looking at the grave of some great ship, British or German, he couldn't tell.

"What the…" exclaimed Walwyn.

Jonathan had to agree with him. Coming straight towards them at high speed was a squadron of large ships. They were firing off to their starboard, towards the Germans, so they must be British. As they closed rapidly he recognized the lead ship as *Lion,* steaming hard towards them on an opposite course. He noticed that she seemed to be on fire forward, and her side showed several black scars, which must have been from shell hits. Her central turret, 'Q' was pointing towards the disengaged side with the barrels askew. As she passed *Barham* Jonathan could see her hoist a flag signal, but he couldn't read it at all.

She was followed by *Princess Royal, Tiger* and one other, either *Indefatigable* or *New Zealand,* all of them apart from the last one showing some damage and all of them still firing on their quarter. They were surrounded by shell splashes from some as yet unseen enemy. He couldn't see the other two. The ships flashed past each other at a combined speed of some sixty knots. *Lion's* signal was still apeak.

"What does it say sir?" Walker asked Walwyn.

"Change of course. Turn 16 points in succession to starboard. As you should know by now, Wart. Keep closed up and watch the indicators, we'll be shifting soon."

"Aye aye sir." There was a huge noise and an immense splash close alongside as a heavy salvo just missed them. Jonathan ducked involuntarily

10. A NEW SWEEP

"There we go, *Barham* turning. Stand by for training" and the ship was swinging too, leaning hard through one hundred and eighty degrees under full helm at full speed. Jonathan could feel the turret training rapidly onto the other beam. The whole sensation was like being on some crazy fairground ride.

"Jesus Christ!" Walwyn swore as the horizon showed a forest of masts, funnels and a mass of black smoke lit by gun flashes. "It's the fucking High Seas Fleet! Heading straight for us!"

The salvoes arrived all together with an indescribable noise and tore up the water around the squadron again.

"Range one seven thousand yards. Bearing Green one two oh. New target, leading battleship. *König* class." The voice was not phased one jot.

Bong!!! ROAR!

"Salvoes!"

Jonathan was lost in a sea of noise and movement. Through his periscope he could see the distinctive shape of a German dreadnought leading a number of others, firing for all she was worth.

Warspite was shaking like a thing possessed as she sped through the water, also firing hard. Glancing aft Jonathan saw a German salvo hit their next astern, *Malaya,* with bright flashes and bursts of smoke. It must have done some damage as a plume of white steam came from the siren. A flair of fire erupted from the battery that looked like a serious hit A few seconds later he heard the siren itself, which was audible even over the tremendous din. She seemed to shake off the hits and continued to fire rapidly from her main armament as if nothing had happened.

In return, Jonathan saw that *Warspite's* fire was having an effect on the leading German dreadnought. Two salvoes landed almost simultaneously and a sheet of yellow flame flared up to her mastheads. They died down leaving a roaring red glow. The ship carried on, still firing, apparently unphased by the damage. These ships were amazing, taking great chunks out of each other, but still fighting back for all that they were worth.

"Keep it up men!" said Walwyn "We're hurting them! Keep going!"

The navy phone rang and Walwyn picked it up. "What?" he said, "Say again? Very good." He launched himself out of his chair and said to Curtess "Damage control call. Carry on here will you? OK Griffiths? Walker? Go below and join me on the mess deck."

"Aye aye sir!" was the response from the detail. Walwyn then turned to Marston and said

"Marston? Will you join us? I could do with another pair of eyes?"

There was only one answer that could properly be given. Jonathan grinned and said "with much pleasure sir!" Relinquishing his place he followed Walwyn through the top hatch of the turret into the middle of the battle.

"Christ Almighty!" Walwyn swore as they came out into the open through the top of the turret straight into Hell.

The first thing that hit them was the wind of their passage. It was wet and smelled of sea and burnt cordite. Walwyn made a dash for the ladder on the disengaged side, with Jonathan following as fast as he could. Just as Jonathan reached the head of the ladder, 'A' and 'B' turrets fired together, and he had to hang on to the rail to

10. A NEW SWEEP

avoid being blown overboard by the blast. He was just recovering when another enemy salvo landed close by, drenching them both.

Walwyn was already at the port door into the superstructure, which was, of course clipped shut in accordance with standing orders. "Bugger!" he said as Jonathan joined him. "Right!" he said, "Up and over it is" and he scrambled aft over the cutter heading for the door under the after funnel, which was not armoured and should therefore be open. Just as he dropped from the cutter the awful sound of an incoming salvo culminated in a huge noise as a shell struck the funnel above them and sprayed the area with lethal splinters.

Neither man was hit but they fell into the superstructure with gratitude. "More illusory than real" said Walwyn, gasping. "The security, that is." Jonathan had to agree; the thin roof and walls of the screen were perforated like a colander. "Lets get below quick!" he said as he threw himself down the hatch adjacent to the funnel casing.

It was almost peaceful below as they entered the battery on the upper deck. They were on the disengaged side, and apart from the sound of the turbines and the rush of the sea, the effect of their own gunfire seemed almost subdued in contrast to the awful noise and pressure that they had been experiencing in the open air. The ladderway came down facing the secondary six-inch guns in their casemates, each surrounded with dwarf walls about three feet high, lined with ready use ammunition.

The Lieutenant in charge greeted Walwyn. "Hello sir" he said. "How is it going? I can't see anything from here on this course."

"We're doing fine. Hitting them hard. Everything ok here?"

"Yes sir, no problems at all"

"Ok, I am off below. See you later." And he was off down the hatch to the main deck, where the crew had their messes. Jonathan followed. The main deck was a sensible choice for an HQ as it afforded access to all sorts of different compartments that were likely targets. It was also hidden behind the thickest armour on the ship, affording a secure base of operations.

All seemed quiet as they descended, moving aft they came across Walker grinning all over his face. "I say sir! What tremendous fun this all is!"

"Shut up Walker. Speak when you're spoken to" Said Walwyn

"Right gentlemen." He went on "The Captain seems to think that we have been hit badly aft. Have you seen anything Walker?"

"No sir," quite unabashed.

"Well we had better have a look around. Keep your eyes open." The ship trembled as the guns roared out again. "Let's get rid of the baggage" said Walwyn, taking the cotton wool out of his ears. Jonathan and Walker followed suit and Jonathan became aware just how noisy things still were without the earplugs. The turbines were whining, the enemy salvoes could be heard, but at this level, the noise of their own guns was merely loud, not overwhelming. The corollary was that whenever they fired the entire ship shook.

They went all the way along the portside messes, down and up into the Admiral's lobby, which was, of course the RC Chapel. All was relatively quiet, with no visible damage. One of the fire brigades was mustered

10. A NEW SWEEP

there and on enquiry told them that they had felt a shake, but could see nothing wrong.

Walwyn used a telephone point to phone the conning tower and tell the Captain that they couldn't see anything wrong at the moment. "Right, let's get forward," he said as he turned away from the phone.

They passed an ammunition supply party and Walwyn told them that they were doing a good job. As an aside, Jonathan realized how much it meant to these men, stuck below with nothing to tell them what was going on. He at least had an idea of what had happened and what was happening at this very moment. It was instructive to see how heartened they were by a few simple words.

The small party passed through the doors into the flat where the cooks prepared the food. All was in order, with the cooks standing by to make whatever was required in action. "May need some sandwiches boys," said Walwyn as they passed forward, into the mess spaces. " I don't think we shall be dressing for dinner."

"Any requests sir?"

"Anything but bloody sardines!" replied Walwyn, over his shoulder, "Too bloody greasy!"

"Ah but the grease is the best bit sir. Nourishing!"

"Not in my book it isn't. Give them to the Gunroom instead, they need loosening up!"

"Oh sir!" said Walker, "This is enough to loosen an elephant, let alone a poor mid!" They moved on through the watertight door in the bulkhead to laughter.

Eventually they reached the boys' mess forward, next to the massive shapes of 'A' and 'B' barbettes. In front of them was the armoured bulkhead embracing 'A' barbette. The mess tables and stools were all on the deck and the metal supports neatly folded up to the deck head.

The reading room curtains were folded back and the bookshelves neatly stowed with the restraining brackets folded up. All was as it should be, with no one around. They could hear the noise of another enemy salvo coming, just as their own guns fired directly above their heads.

CRASH! There was a terrible noise and a vivid sheet of orange flame right in front of them. Instantly the space was filled with screaming fragments of metal and wood, smoke, dust and a terrible choking smell. Jonathan could feel the searing heat on his face as he was nearly blown off his feet. He was temporarily blinded and deafened. The remains of mess kids, mugs and racks were thrown everywhere in confusion. The tables and mess stools were blasted away in all directions. Happily the small party was sheltered behind the massive armour of 'B" barbette, otherwise there would have been casualties.

The academic part of Jonathan's mind took note and was already analysing the forces unleashed by that shell. He wished he could see whether the fragments caught fire before they were blown away or afterwards. His numbed brain was trying to wrestle with the speed of fire and the speed of blast and was confounded by the whole experience.

Walwyn recovered first and shouted down the escape hatch "FIRE BRIGADE! At the double!" That brought Jonathan back to the present.

The nearest fire party came charging up the ladder and turned their hoses onto the blazing wreckage. Indeed, the very seawater seemed to be on fire. It was brought under control almost immediately. "Water Gas" said Walwyn to Jonathan, "seawater over hot carbon gives

10. A NEW SWEEP

you hydrogen, otherwise water gas. We don't want any of that thank you!"

As the smoke cleared, Jonathan could see that the armour – six inches of hardened steel - had been pierced neatly by a large shell which had broken off a substantial chunk from the rear face of the plates, scattering red hot bolts, fragments of metal and timber backing liberally across the flat, hitting the barbette, shredding the cabinet forward and the vent trunks aft.

Apart from a couple of bolts, which appeared to have embedded themselves in the barbette armour, the basic structure was unharmed. The cabinet was evidently a flood control point, filled with pipes and valves, all thoroughly mangled now. They were spurting high-pressure water all over the flat and the damage control party with extravagant abandon.

The deck below and the deck head above were full of holes. Smoke was seeping ominously from below. "Here, Walker" ordered Walwyn, "Nip below and get Pring to flood the HA magazine from the middle deck position."

And then "Oy! You lot! Knock it off you bloody idiots!"

Jonathan realized that some of the men were picking up bits and pieces of shell and broken armour, presumably for souvenirs.

"Here, turn the bloody hose on 'em!" which was no sooner said than done.

"That stopped 'em!" Walwyn said to Jonathan with satisfaction. "Half of those things are lethal, like picking up razor blades. Come on then, we had better get aft and see what's going on there." And he was off, just as Walker doubled up from below "Flooding HA magazine now sir" he saluted.

"Very good." Walwyn strode aft along the port side. "Just hope we don't get strafed by a zepp now since I've just ruined our high angle ammunition supply!"

When they got aft again, it was an entirely different story from before. There was water pouring into the flat from the church doors, rushing down the adjacent hatch to the deck below like a millrace. A group of men were trying to get control of the situation. They were fighting their way into the church against the flow, with shores and the rubber sheets that were used as temporary leak-stoppers.

"Stand fast there!" said Walwyn. "Let's have a look at it. He waded into the church himself, heading towards the after bulkhead which was spurting water throughout its length. Jonathan followed. It looked to him as if the bulkhead had been loosened at its junction with the deck.

As the reached it, the door burst under the pressure and Jonathan and Frank were nearly swept off their feet. Looking in, they saw that the water was spouting up from a hole in the floor like some sort of incongruous fountain, installed for the pleasure of an eccentric admiral.

Watching intently, they realized that the water wasn't gaining. It was a couple of feet deep and was ebbing as the ship pitched and surging as she came down again. Glancing out through the scuttles, Jonathan realized that she was steaming so fast that the stern was well tucked down, and the rushing wake was forcing the water into a hole below them and then up to the general water level, at the same height as the sea outside. It was quite clear that this flooding was going to stay at sea

10. A NEW SWEEP

level. He wasn't quite sure what was below them, but he did know that this far aft, even if the whole stern flooded, it wouldn't affect the safety of the ship one jot.

"Nothing we can do here," said Walwyn, evidently reaching the same conclusion. "Here, help me to shut this damn door. Brace it as best you can. Rubber across the deck seam." Whilst that was being done, Walwyn moved back into the lobby, which was still awash at the after end. After the sealing of the bulkhead, the water reduced to a level below the hatch coaming leading below, which meant that the sloshing water was an inconvenience, but not a danger.

"What's below here?" asked Jonathan.

"Writer's office immediately below the cabin." Said Walwyn. "That has clearly gone, but there shouldn't have been anyone in it anyway. Steering gear and submerged torpedo room forward of that. We had better go down and have a look." He went down the adjacent hatchway and found that the middle deck was relatively dry. Leaning over the coaming to the lower deck he shouted "Below there? Torpedo room? How are you doing?"

An officer appeared and looked up at them, "Thanks for the shower bath! We still have some water coming in, but not much. We're keeping an eye on it. We're fine really sir.'

"Very good, don't evacuate unless you have to, we might get a chance against the blighters yet."

They made their way up through the flat towards the battery again. They were just going up the hatch into the casemate lobby when a man came running up, "Sir! Sir! Captain's flat's been hit, can you come please sir?"

275

"Bugger!' said Walwyn, turning back at once, "if they've touched my cabin I shall do such things! What they are yet, I know not, but they shall be the terrors of the Earth!" Jonathan was uneasy as well. That was where his own cabin was. He didn't have very much that was precious, but his letters from Clementina were in there, and he didn't want to lose those.

As they arrived they realized that their cozy home was in an awful mess. Jonathan's cabin was burning, and there was a huge hole in the deck between it and the forward watertight bulkhead, which was itself spattered with splinters, but not pierced. It looked as if a shell had come in through the cabin from aft, diagonally forward, wrecking the night defence shelter above as it did so. The deck was covered in debris, and the whole place stank of the explosive that they had first experienced on the boy's mess deck. Walwyn's cabin had been shielded by Jonathan's and apart from a few splinter holes appeared to be largely intact.

"Lucky bugger!' Jonathan observed as Walwyn supervised the fire brigade pouring water into his erstwhile home and then "Oh, I say!" as he dashed into the wreckage to the desk, which was just catching fire. He was able to open the drawer before it caught and managed to rescue the letters. They were wet, and a bit singed, but otherwise legible. "That's a spot of luck! Wouldn't want to lose that!" He slipped it into his pocket.

Examining the mess when the fire was out, they ascertained that the armoured communication tube from the after director to the steering compartment was riddled and distorted over a large area, a couple of stanchions were cut through and the Captain's pantry would require serious re-organization. Jonathan's cabin was wrecked,

10. A NEW SWEEP

and all his goods burned or spoiled, but apart from inconvenience, nothing threatened the life of the ship. Again, there was nothing further to be done.

The next crisis was in the port battery. There was a huge hole in the deck above. The fire mains had been damaged and water was pouring out of them across the space, threatening to flood the boiler rooms below through the ventilation trunks. The armoured door in the centreline bulkhead had been blown off its hinges and the flat was pretty badly damaged, with everything black and sticky from the burned deck covering. The guns, however, on this disengaged side were still manned and ready. Mr Midshipman Fairthorne was stationed there and seeing Jonathan he beamed, "Hello sir! I trust you are enjoying yourself?"

"Not as much as you Mr Fairthorne, it would seem. Are you OK?"

"Oh capital sir, it's good to be doing something at least, even if I am not, at this particular moment, doing anything other than getting wet!"

Throughout all of this there was still a constant roar from the main battery, and the unrelenting sound of incoming shells. As far as Jonathan could tell, they were still steaming at their utmost speed, and not outrunning whoever was firing at them. Walwyn, Jonathan and Walker helped to plug the fire mains and stretch the rubber sheets over the vulnerable holes in the ventilating trunks.

Then it was aft again, this time to the Marine's mess deck where a shell had come through the side of the Sergeants' Mess and exploded. It had done extensive damage to the decks and stanchions. For the first time in all this madness *Warspite* suffered visible casualties. The explosion caught one of the fire brigades, killing several and wounding more. For the first time, the dread call "Stretcher bearers" was heard.

To Jonathan's surprise, Father Pollen appeared and moved from casualty to casualty, giving what words of comfort he could. Incongruously, he was wearing a purple stole.

The hole was another one at an awkward height. Their huge wake was pouring in through it, flooding the main deck and rushing below through the shell hole in the vent trunk straight into the wing turbine room below. This was a dangerous hit and needed to be dealt with swiftly. Walwyn directed the damage control party to cover the trunk with one of the rubber sheets, nailed down with wooden battens. "They might get a little hot, but at least they won't drown!" was his sensible remark.

Jonathan found that his admiration for this man was increasing. He was clearly not afraid of taking decisions, and Jonathan couldn't quarrel with his judgment. If something couldn't be done and it didn't matter, then there was no point in wasting time and energy on it. Conversely, if, as here the damage was dangerous, then he acted swiftly and decisively.

Leaving the marines trying to plug the hole in the side with hammocks they went off to the next job. The ship was taking hits, but nothing vital had been harmed and they were still steaming at full speed and engaging the enemy. This ship was living up to expectations and doing what she was designed to do, hit the enemy and take punishment.

As they moved about the ship, Walwyn was constantly making observations and dictating to Walker, who was taking them down in a pocket book. "Shell

10. A NEW SWEEP

blasts smash electric light bulbs. Candles work well. Oil lamps not worth the effort. Boots and gauntlets for all fire brigade and damage control personnel." Indeed, Jonathan was surprised at how much debris had accumulated all over the once spotless decks. The superstructure and all internal decks were covered with a form of corked linoleum called corticene. It was a very useful product, giving good grip and a pleasing light red-brown colour. The trouble was, when subjected to fire or explosion it produced an unpleasant black, sticky residue that stank, and more importantly, burned very well.

The electric light covers were thick glass, which shattered into lethal shards when hit, littering the decks with sparkling fragments, any of which were perfectly capable of piercing the shoes of unwary sailors. Added to that, the metal plates making up the ship's structure were twisted into extraordinary shapes by the violent explosions, with jagged edges that were every bit as dangerous as any number of razor blades.

The large quantities of electrical wiring that a modern ship required were an equal hazard for the unwary. Jonathan had seen several examples of cut wires sparking against torn metal. Some of the currents running through those wires were very strong indeed.

"Amend standing orders to forbid souvenir hunting." They had come across a ridiculous scenario where another shell had come through the Bandmaster's cabin without exploding. The filling was sticking out and a couple of stokers were trying to chip the fuse out of it.

There seemed to be a bit of a lull in the action. The party moved back to the cook's servery, where the Paymaster Commander was smoking. He had no action station and was wandering around in a life preserver, watching the action.

"Enjoying yourself Pay?" asked Walwyn, lighting a cigarette.

"Of course. Whole thing seems to be designed to amuse. That is until the bloody battleships turn up. I take it we are heading for them?"

"No idea old boy. I am, as you know a mushroom. Kept in the dark and fed on excrement. You must have a better idea of what is going on than I do, surely."

"No chance, chum. They're chasing me all over the blessed ship. I was in the wardroom lobby for a while, and thought I would have a turn about, so went off towards the gunroom just as the blasted thing hit. Some marines in the gunroom asked if I wanted to look through the scuttle at what was going on. No blooming fear I said, I don't want to see the damn things, I'm going below. And I did."

They all laughed. It was a release of tension. "Walker" said Walwyn, "Sir."

"Nip off to the phone and tell the Captain that all is under control. No serious damage."

"Aye aye sir" scampering off.

Looking at his watch, Jonathan realized that it was almost half past five. They had been fighting continuously for an hour and a half. They had been engaging the German battle-cruiser fleet AND the High Seas Fleet, been hit and were hitting back. All was under control and there was no serious damage. Thinking about it, it was an extraordinary achievement.

11. Battle

Wednesday 31st May, HMS Warspite, 1740, 56°40' N, 5°48' E

WhoOOOOOOOOOOOOOOOOOOOOOOOOOOOOOoh!

CLANK-CRASH! The incoming salvo landed and the ceiling exploded down on them in a maelstrom of flame and smoke. Jonathan was knocked down by the blast from the shell, which had hit the galley above them, and been deflected through the deck. The party in the cook's servery was scattered.

"Fuck! There goes my bleeding dinner!' said one of the ratings.

"FIRE PARTY! Take care of it. The rest of you, on top, double quick!" ordered Walwyn. Jonathan and Walker hopped up behind him into the six-inch battery above, which was curiously calm. The shell had apparently passed straight through and exploded on the deck where Jonathan and his party were, leaving the battery intact.

"A bit bumpy, but otherwise perfectly OK up here sir" said Hammill.

Looking around, that was true. There was a hole in the deck where the shell had exploded on the deck below, oozing smoke; but the port battery itself was intact and ready for action in all respects.

"Very Good Hammill" said Walwyn. "Come with me gentlemen," and led them around the after superstructure before turning forward through the Starboard battery on the engaged side. The gun crews were bunched up and talking to each other in spite of the noise. The enemy was well outside the range of their guns, so they had nothing in particular to do. These guns were designed to deal with enemy torpedo boats and as such were not currently employed as no torpedo boat attack had yet developed against the 5th Battle Squadron.

"Spread out there men" said Walwyn as he was moving forward. "You're too damn valuable to be wasted with one hit. Don't give the buggers a chance!"

"OK sir. Sorry sir! Spread out Mates! Listen to the hofficer." Jonathan realized that the speaker was Bond. "Hello Bond" said Jonathan, "How are you doing in your new rate?"

"Well hello yourself sir!" said Bond with enthusiasm, "Extremely well thank you sir. Gunner, 'e sez that I'm born for the position. Loving it sir. 3/9d a day now sir. Sweet."

Jonathan translated that as 75c a day; - good pay for an enlisted man.

"And what next Bond?" Jonathan asked. He was learning from the British way of doing things. Get to know the men and connect with them. They were all part of the same team.

"Well sir, I could make Gunner, they say. Warrant Officer. Coo! There's a thought. That'd be grand, sir. Me a bleeding WO wiv' me own mess and such."

"Well I am sure that you'll do that very well Bond. Carry on and enjoy it!"

'That I shall, sir. God bless you for asking!"

Feeling oddly uplifted, Jonathan moved forward with Walwyn and Walker.

They were just reaching the forward end of the battery when yet another runner came up: "bad hit port side aft sir, water coming in somethin' korful!" Jonathan hadn't noticed anything untoward in the noise and chaos of the

11. BATTLE

battle. It was extraordinary that they hadn't felt the hit, but then the noise and tempest was such that individual hits could no longer be isolated in the madness.

"Very good," said Walwyn, turning and he began to run aft again. Clearly the dignity of a Commander did not roll over to situations where his ship was in danger. Jonathan and Walker followed him with alacrity. This one was straight though the main belt into the Engineers' office about a foot above the water, which was rushing in. It was in the same hull compartment as the Sergeant of Marine's mess, which had been hit earlier. This time, to add to their difficulties, the oil tank directly below the office had been penetrated and the fuel oil was mingling with the incoming North Sea. It covered the labouring damage party with an iridescence that made them look like exotic seabirds, flashing colours in the uncertain light. There was the expected jumble of dust and mess over those parts of the compartment that were not under water.

Watching the men trying to plug the hole with hammocks, a Royal Marine observed to no one in particular "This will mean a drop of leave!"

"Shut up soldier!" said Walwyn, up to his arms in mess as he tried to see what the damage was, "and lend a hand here, or else the only leave you'll get will be to Davy Jones' Locker!"

"Aye aye sir!" said the man, springing into action. "Wouldn't want that sir."

"Let's try and plug it with hammocks!" said Walwyn and men went forward to the hammock stowage to bring other men's bedding to staunch the incoming torrent.

It was an almost impossible task. The hole in the side coincided with a standing wave of the ship's wake as she was pressing forward at almost twenty-five knots. That meant that the wake of their passage was spilling into the compartment and spreading out with enormous power. To add to that, the ash and soil shoots were ruptured, which meant that the heavy duty pumps designed to remove the detritus from the boiler furnaces with a flush of seawater were discharging an unpleasant slurry of ash and half burned oil directly into the chaos in the flat instead of safely overside as designed.

That, in turn, had consequences for the bilge pumps, trying to pump out the unwanted water. The boiler slurry was not as bad as it would be in a coal-fired ship, but it still could not be ignored. It meant clogged pumps and the inability to get rid of the excess North Sea pouring into the ship by way of the shell holes.

Jonathan was beginning to wish the incessant gunfire would stop, so that he could concentrate on the task in hand. Throughout all of this, *Warspite's* fire had not slackened noticeably, nor had her speed. The German salvoes were still coming in with regularity and were still hitting.

"Wing turbine room flooding sir!"

"Very Good. Martin, carry on here. Marston! Walker! 4th Fire Brigade! With me. Now!" And they were off again. There were four engine room vents in this compartment, two to the centre turbine room and one each to the wing turbine rooms. The vent to the starboard turbine room had been damaged by the hit to the Sergeant of Marine's mess, and now its fellow adjacent to the Engineers' Office was riddled as well. It was in that state that Jonathan had come to associate with collateral damage from shellfire, pockmarked with holes of various sizes, through which the water from the hoses was flowing

11. BATTLE

freely. One of the holes extended through the deck, so it was difficult to stop that from the outside.

If nothing was done, the ship was in danger of losing half of her motive power, with disastrous consequences.

"Right!" said Walwyn, "We'll have to plug that from inside. In you go Walker, Turn the sheet over and make an envelope to catch the water. We'll drop you from a bowline!"

Fascinated, Jonathan watched the lad being lowered through a shell hole, down the vent on a rope, where he helped to secure a rubber sheet, shored against the trunk so that the water influx could be minimized at the same time as maintaining the airflow to the turbine room. The roaring fans were not so far below him. Had he been dropped into them, the situation would not have been pleasant.

Once Walker was hauled back with the repair done. Walwyn was ready to move. "Port Battery again" he said and they were off. Jonathan couldn't help but admire the man's energy. They went forward, through the watertight compartment and up the ladder into the port battery again. Walwyn went forward and mounted the sighting hood just abaft gun P2.

There was a terrific shock, which echoed throughout the compartment, throwing people off their feet. Walwyn was violently ejected from his position and was smashed against the deck. Thick black smoke drifted across the space.

Jonathan, badly shaken himself, thought that Walwyn must have been killed and made his way forward on all fours to where he lay sprawled on the deck.

"Are you alright sir?" Jonathan asked, with concern.

Walwyn groaned and turned over, coughing. "I've been better Marston, but I'll live. I think. Where the hell was that? Must have been damn' close."

"Aft somewhere, sir" said Jonathan, "No way of locating it at the moment I am afraid."

"Well we'd better look at how they're doing below." and he rolled over onto his front and started to get up.

"Sorry sir" said Jonathan, alarmed, "Is that wise sir?"

"Probably not" said Walwyn, "but I'm doing it anyway. Any observations Lieutenant?"

"No sir." There was really no answer to that.

"In which case" said Walwyn coughing again, "let's see what's happening with that damn' great hole" and getting up, he led the way below to the engineers' office, hobbling slightly. The party was still stuffing hammocks into the hole. Whilst the inrush had been slowed, there was still quite a torrent of the cold North Sea coming inboard.

A rating reported as they passed through, "We're doing it sir, but it is a bit of a bugger. We keep on losing the bloody things to the wash" Again, there was nothing that Walwyn could usefully do, so he moved on forward, leaving the designated party to get on with it.

They were moving forward along the main deck. Jonathan found it helpful to think of the geography of this ship in terms of HMS *Victory*. There was a forecastle, running back to X turret, with the upper deck below that. The upper deck was the top deck of the ship proper, the forecastle being, strictly, an addition. Below the upper

11. BATTLE

deck was the main deck, where the people lived. That is were they were at the moment.

Originally, there had been embrasures for four six-inch guns right aft on that deck, but they had been proved to be useless, as being too close to the waterline and they had been plated over.

In *Warspite*, just like the Victory the main deck was just above the Middle Deck, which was, just about the level of the waterline.

The lower deck was below that and in contrast to HMS *Victory* was below the waterline. It was largely given over to stores and boiler space, with the transmitting station and its secret equipment forward.

They moved along the main deck to port of the funnel vents into number two mess. Like all of the messes on this level, it was a large open space with provision for tables and benches against the side. In accordance with standing orders, the benches and stools were flat on the deck, but the shelves supporting the mess traps and the small luxuries that made the sailors' lives bearable remained in place.

Again the terrible noise and flash above them and a sheet of flame came down through the sliding shutters of the light vent from the forecastle deck above. The battery had been hit.

They tried to open the shutter, but the result was an inferno of writhing flame. They could hear groans and screams above them, as well as a roaring sound as something burned with incredible intensity.

"That's cordite!' shouted Walwyn. "Come on you lot!' and dashed forward to the ladder up into the fore battery. As they arrived they could see that the after end was a mass of flame. There were long flares coming from number six, the after gun position, making it look like a battery of roman candles. Running towards the fire they could see that a shell had hit just above the gun and set light a charge in the arms of the loading number. He had been blown backwards and was now all but invisible under the inferno.

The flare had sprayed the other cartridge cases in the gun position, some of which were now themselves flaring in all directions. The flame was roiling over the dwarf wall to number five position.

The roaring sound that they had heard was the charges burning. Jonathan knew that the British used an explosive called cordite that burned very fiercely when allowed to do so. Deflagration was the technical term for it. When that burning was confined, it was a powerful explosive as the gases tried to make their way out. However, when it was allowed to burn, it flared, relatively harmlessly.

All of the crew were burned and dazed, lying around in and under the flame. The crew of number five was also pretty badly knocked about and not in a position to do very much to help themselves. Unless something was done quickly, the cartridges in number five position would be the next to go and the fire could knock out the whole battery.[67]

Acting on pure instinct, Jonathan dashed into number five gun place. Ducking under the deflected flame he grabbed the nearest six-inch charge, which was in a canvas bag stowed a shelf on the dwarf wall that was already glowing red with heat. There were others in the same position. The thing was hot under his hands as he cradled it in his arms. He ducked out of the space and lobbed it up through the shell hole onto the deck above,

11. BATTLE

where it could do no harm. Seeing the idea, others joined him and the charges were shifted in short order. There was one more left; Jonathan picked it up. It was very hot. Suddenly, the end blew off and the cordage within flared into a roaring flame that shot out of the end of the cartridge case as he was holding it.[68] He could feel the searing heat on his face and felt the charge case trembling under his fingers. The part that he was holding was heating up rapidly. Shifting his grip to the base he ran it to the shell hole and lobbed the flaring thing out after its fellows.

He was aware that the sleeves of his reefer jacket were hot and his face and neck were sore, but the fire brigade turned their hose onto him knocking him down and winding him but put the fire out.

"Are you OK Marston?" asked Walwyn.

Patting himself down and moving his arms, Jonathan realized that everything was working, and apart from a pain in his face, arms and fingers he was relatively unscathed.

"Yes sir" he said, "Pretty much, I think."

"Damn good show, anyway. You look a little pink. Better get the medicos to check you over when there's time.... Oh! I SAY!"

Following his gaze Jonathan saw the most extraordinary sight. The priest, Father Pollen, was running into the inferno of number six position, with his arms over his face to protect his eyes. Walwyn and Jonathan dashed to the entrance to try and see what was happening. It was very hot. They could see very little in the blaze, but suddenly there was the priest coming out backwards dragging someone by his collar. The victim was on fire and the two officers rolled him over to put him out. The victim was still alive, coughing and groaning. Looking round for the Priest they saw he had vanished into the inferno again and came out with another victim.

This time the priest was, himself on fire, or at least his clothes were, and he was subjected to the same treatment. His stole was still there, but the top part was burned and blackened. He appeared to have burns on his face and hands. His shock of grey hair was frizzled black. "Enough Father!" said Jonathan as the priest tried to get up again. "You can't do anything more in there!"

"Maybe you're right Mr Marston" he wheezed, through his blackened face, "I'm getting a bit to old for this." He rolled over and coughed. Jonathan could see that his hands were red and already beginning to erupt into black blisters as he pushed himself up into a kneeling position. He turned to the figure alongside him, who was clearly far-gone.

To Jonathan's surprise he recognized Bond. The Priest used his ruined hands to sign the cross on Bond's blackened forehead. Painfully, "Do you repent of all your sins my son? Signify if you can"

The eyelids flickered open and a voice from far away said "aye". A labouring breath and the eyes appeared to focus on the priest, "hello padre" he whispered. "Not one of yours 'm afraid."

"No matter my son" whispered the priest, who was in almost as bad a state as his subject, "God won't mind, I'm sure" and gasped "Absolvo te, in nomine Patris, et filio et spiritu sancto" trying to make another sign of the cross and falling back with the effort.

"Stretcher bearers!" was the cry again. By the time that they arrived, the fire was under control and the remnants of the guns' crews were being removed. As he was being loaded onto a stretcher, Bond's eyes caught

11. BATTLE

Jonathan's. "'Ello sir" he whispered, "Still got me eye on that there rate, sir."

"I am sure it's got your name on it Bond." Jonathan was impressed.

Looking around, he noted that the battery was still in good shape, with only number six unavailable. The remaining gun crews redistributed themselves to serve the other guns. It was amazing that this ship, having apparently suffered so much was still in full fighting condition, steaming at maximum speed and still firing her main armament regularly, as the trembling testified.

They moved forward and Walwyn led the way up the hatch to the superstructure. As they emerged into the open air of the battle, they realized that the whole fore part of the port shelter deck, the shelter for the searchlight and night gun control positions and the Navigator's sea cabin was ablaze. The fire was licking against the after part of the conning tower, from where the ship was being fought. The paint was blistering and Jonathan could see anxious faces looking out through the slits at what threatened to be their funeral pyre. He heard Frank's distinctive tones shouting, "Don't just stand there Walwyn, put the bloody fire out!"

"Oh shut up Hodgson! You're always complaining that it's too damned cold. Enjoy it for once!" There was a hose point close by, but once a hose was connected to it and the cock switched on, no water came out: - the fire main had been cut, as they should have realized.

The situation was complicated. It must have been clear to the people in the conning tower from the efforts of the fire brigade what the problem was. It had serious consequences, as the only access from the conning tower was through the blaze, which engulfed both decks. If the men within were cooked, it would take the ship's brain away.

"Well if you can't get the fire out, nip down to the mess and send up some beer, would you? There's a good chap! It's quite dry in here." Frank was obviously making the best of the situation for his men.

"You can get it yourself in a minute, just let me get these mains sorted out if you wouldn't mind?"

"Oh, my pleasure old chap. We'll just sit here and fry shall we? No rush."

"Fire Brigade below!" hailed Walwyn, "cross-connect to the steam main!" That was an ingenious solution, and it worked. Jonathan realized that there was no reason for water to be liquid to be effective at putting out fires; steam would do just as well. The fire was quickly subdued and the wreckage was revealed for the first time. Frank's sea cabin had gone the same way as Jonathan's and was completely gutted. The ship's store of swimming collars had gone up as well, leaving a filthy black mess of burned rubber.

The deck itself was warped and holed, as was the superstructure. The conning tower was blackened, but otherwise unharmed. Walwyn went to the still-hot door and opened it with gloved hands. Apart from the smell, the interior appeared to be in perfect order. The enamel was white and gleaming and the brass instruments still shone from their last polish. The inhabitants were clean and fresh in contrast to the singed, wet and dirty damage control party. Philpotts was on the sighting step, which ran round inside the tower, looking through his binoculars when he heard the door open. He turned away from the sighting slit, stepped down and took in the bedraggled appearance of his rescuers.

11. BATTLE

"You look as if you've been busy Walwyn. How is the ship?"

"We have a bit, sir," said Walwyn saluting. "Probably eight or nine heavy hits. No damage to main armament or propulsion. Starboard number six six-inch knocked out with its' crew. Casualties are remarkably light, considering. I would estimate no more than ten killed so far. We have some holes, but they are being dealt with. Ship still ready for action."

"Well done Walwyn, that is good to hear."

"Can you tell us what's going on sir?" asked Walwyn. Jonathan realized that he hadn't heard the guns for some time, neither theirs nor the enemy's.

"I think we've outrun them for the moment. Bloody difficult to see anything over there," indicating the murky horizon off to starboard. "We should be in touch with our fleet shortly.

"We followed the battle-cruisers south, they outran us. We found some enemy cruisers and then the German battle-cruisers"

"Yes sir, I saw that: - I was still taking notice at that time." Jonathan remembered the scene vividly.

"We then ran into the High Seas Fleet head on" went on the Captain. "The BCF turned around and we followed 'em. Seems the *Königs*[69] are faster than we thought and kept up with us for some time. They shouldn't have. I hope we're leading them straight under the guns of the Grand Fleet, the appearance of which, I might add, I am hourly expecting. Enemy is still over there in the murk, exchanging fire whenever there's a view."

"My I name Lieutenant Marston Sir?" said Walwyn; "he did very well in the starboard battery, shifted cordite charges on fire. An excellent show."

"Indeed?" said the captain turning to look at Jonathan with those direct eyes. "I shall make a note of that. Well done Mr Marston."

Jonathan was touched. He hadn't really thought about it, but in retrospect, it was rather a good thing to have done.

"Thank you sir." He said, "It seemed like the best thing to do at the time."

"I should like to name Father Pollen as well sir, he rescued some of the crew from the fire."

"Did he, by Jove! There's a genuinely good man. Is he alright?" Jonathan remembered that the Captain and Father Anthony played golf together.

"I am afraid that he has some burns, but I hope that he will be OK."

"Indeed. He's a pretty sound chap for a Roman."

Suddenly they heard the sound of guns again, somewhere up ahead and to starboard. Philpotts immediately went back to the sighting step, raising his glasses. "It's our battle cruisers sir," said the lookout, "They're turning east and engaging the enemy again. I can see shell splashes."

"Very good. Stand by to conform to the movements of the flagship." Jonathan knew that the Grand Fleet Standing Orders emphasized the need to follow the division leaders in action, where individual signals may not be visible.

"*Barham* turning east sir!"

"Very good. Turn in succession to *Valiant*."

"Enemy in sight sir. Bearing south-south-east!" Jonathan noted that there were several sets of binoculars lodged in a rack for the use of officers in the conning tower. He retrieved a set and stepped up onto a spare part

11. BATTLE

of the sighting platform. Focusing, he could see two of the German battle cruisers through the mist. They were firing, but not very frequently, nor with the accuracy that they had shown before. It looked as if they had been hit severely. There was a smoke trail that was not wholly due to their funnels

"I had better get back below and see how the damage is coming if you don't mind sir" said Walwyn.

"Very good Walwyn. Keep it up," said Philpotts. Jonathan put his glasses back in their case and made to follow Walwyn. "Don't worry Marston" said Walwyn. "I think I can manage for the moment. Why don't you wait here and see what's going on."

Jonathan was very pleased. He had been doing a necessary and stimulating task, but he really would like to see how the ship was handled in battle, and this was by far the best place to do it from.

"Yes, indeed" said the Captain. "I think you have done enough for the present. Now, let's see what those other fellows are doing."

Watching, Jonathan could see that the German battle cruisers were being supported by their battle fleet, which was just opening fire again. The British battle cruisers were cutting across the German line of advance, and he could see that the Germans were turning too, trying to keep broadly parallel to the British. It was almost as if the British battle cruisers were herding the German battle fleet.

The guns of their own squadron, following astern of the British battle cruiser force, opened up again, showering the German battle-fleet with fifteen-inch shells.

"Range increasing sir! One niner thousand yards and opening" an officer at the voice pipes reported to Philpotts. The Germans were turning away eastward.

"Keep following next ahead" said Philpotts. "Starboard thirty, new course north- east"

"Starboard thirty, new course north-east" said the quartermaster manning the wheel. He was just behind them, no more than five feet away. The conning tower was nothing if not cosy.

German salvoes were still falling, but with all the noise and movement it was quite impossible to tell whether they had been hit again or not.

Suddenly the port lookout shouted, "Our battle fleet in sight, sir, *Marlborough* bearing red 10, range three miles. Repeat, *Marlborough* bearing red 10, range three miles!" The report was electrifying.

"Is she by Jove!" said Philpotts spinning around to look. Jonathan followed suit. *Marlborough* led the right hand column of the British battle fleet, which was usually made up of six such columns, each of four or five ships. Now it was obvious what Beatty was doing. The battle cruisers and the Fifth Battle Squadron were leading the Germans straight under the guns of the entire British battle fleet. The gradual turn east was designed to mask the British fleet from the Germans, until they found themselves surrounded by the British. It was, in Jonathan's opinion, brilliant.

It was well known that the German plan was to cut down the British numerical superiority by cutting off and killing isolated squadrons of the Royal Navy. That was exactly what they must have thought they were doing when they lured the battle cruisers south into the arms of the

11. BATTLE

German High Seas Fleet. Well now the tables were turned. In spades.

"*Barham* turning East sir!"

"Very good. Follow in succession." They were giving the British battle fleet the opportunity to organize themselves ready to receive the Germans with open arms.

The usual procedure was that the six columns of battleships would transform themselves into a single line, by the column leaders turning ninety degrees, followed by their squadron mates, who would turn at the same spot. The column and line spacing was designed so that this could be accomplished automatically. It was not unlike soldiers carrying out close order drill. The question was whether *Marlborough* was still in cruising formation, leading the column furthest from the flagship to the southeast, or whether the fleet had already deployed and she was leading the entire fleet. There was no way of knowing.

If they had already changed into their fighting formation, the battle cruisers and the Fifth Battle Squadron were well on target to pass the fleet and take their proper station ahead of the main body. Beatty and the battle cruisers were heading straight for that position.

"*Agincourt* in sight astern of *Marlborough* sir" and there she was, the unmistakable shape of the "gin palace" following her flagship.

"Can you see anything beyond her?"

"Smoke sir, but not clear what it is."

"Foretop?" asked Philpotts into another voice pipe, "can you see anything beyond *Marlborough*?"

"Aye sir," Jonathan could just hear the tinny voice through the pipe. "*Revenge* and *Hercules* in echelon abaft sir." That was not helpful. Those two ships were the other part of the 6th Division and their position was normal in deployment on either wing and in cruising formation.

"Wait one!" the foretop again. "Heavy smoke in front of *Marlborough* sir, and further away. TWO TRIPOD MASTS sir!" That was significant. Only the older battleships had two tripod masts, and all of them were either with the 5th or 4th Division, which were normally to port of Marlborough's 6th Division.

Older ships forward and further away had to mean that the British battle fleet had not deployed and were still in cruising formation, with the two-masted ship being part of the second or third column beyond *Marlborough* from their point of view.

Jonathan took time out to consider what was happening. The battle cruisers and the Fifth Battle Squadron were heading almost due east. South-east of them, and turning to follow their course was the German High Seas Fleet, and what was left of the German battle cruisers. All ships were engaged.

On the Germans' blind side, the British battleships were heading southeast, straight towards them, but the British were still in their cruising formation of six columns of four ships. They would have to deploy one way or the other, either turning north-west to parallel the Germans, and then cross in front of them, or else turn south-east, which would allow them to cross the tail of the German line.

Turning northwest would cut the Germans off from their bases, but turning southeast would give them a better light for battle.

"*Marlborough* altering course sir!"

"Which way?"

Jonathan was straining to make that out himself

11. BATTLE

'Can't quite tell yet sir" and then, shortly afterwards, a shout

"*MARLBOROUGH* HOISTING FLAG SIGNAL, EQUAL SPEED CHARLIE LONDON!"[70]

"Fantastic!" said Philpotts to himself and then to everyone else "Battle Fleet deploying port, flagships together the rest in succession. Stand by for orders." Then again, almost to himself he said, "that's the best bloody deployment I have ever seen!"

Jellicoe was going to cut the Germans off from their bases. Jonathan noted that *Marlborough* had started the manoeuver as she was hoisting the signal, long before it would normally be executed. The Grand Fleet Battle Orders could be relied upon to remind captains to watch their squadron commander rather than wait for signals, which may not be seen in the fog of war.

As he watched, he could see the steam from her siren, and a little later he could hear the two blasts indicating that she was turning to port. It was strange to see the standard maritime signalling convention being used in this situation, but like everything else, it made sense to use basic signals, which had the virtue of being unmistakable.

And so the scene was set. The British battle fleet would be turning away from the Germans and forming up in a line, nearly seven miles long. They would then surround the German Fleet like a sack. The immediate problem was what to do with the Fifth Battle Squadron. Their primary position was as the first division of the battle fleet, immediately behind the battle cruisers, which meant that they should follow them across the front of the deploying Grand Fleet.

But that fleet was moving at twenty knots, which meant that the Squadron was not sufficiently fast to make such a deployment safe.

Suddenly there was a new diversion. The Grand Fleet's First Cruiser Squadron, made up of heavy cruisers, was headed down the engaged side of the line at full pelt. The lead ship passed so close to *Lion* that the latter had to flinch to avoid a collision. They seemed to be heading for a burning German cruiser on *Warspite's* starboard beam. Big, four-funnelled ships with distinctive fighting tops, they were flying.

They had not seen the German battle fleet in the murk to the east of the battlefield, but that fleet had seen them silhouetted against the light of the westering sun and acted accordingly. As the heavy cruiser flagship, *Defence*, passed *Warspite* she was straddled by the German battleships.

Jonathan watched as she took fire in a series of flashes all along her upper deck, followed by a most enormous explosion that wiped the ship out in front of his horrified eyes. It looked exactly like the famous painting of the Battle of the Nile, where the French Admiral's flagship erupted in the flame and smoke of a magazine explosion. Jonathan never imagined for one moment that he would be witnessing that scene in real life.

Her next astern was reduced to a hissing hulk, surrounded with steam and black smoke as she lost way through the troubled seas. The third reeled away, burning privately. Jonathan couldn't see what happened to the fourth. It was a seriously sobering sight. Each one of those ships carried eight hundred men and he had just seen the best part of them incinerated.

11. BATTLE

The plan for the battle fleet, however, was still working. *Barham* signalled that they should turn west, and then north to fit in with the end of the 6th division of the battle fleet, tucking in behind *Agincourt* the last ship of that division. That would mean that *Warspite* would be the second to last ship in the British line, with her squadron mate *Malaya* as the very last ship, closest to the enemy on this flank.

That meant that the drawstrings of the sack would be the Battle Cruiser Force to the east and the 5th Battle Squadron to the west. Together they could surround the German fleet and pound them into scrap iron.

That at least was the theory. Jonathan began to realize, as the signal was hauled down, that this particular area of sea was rapidly becoming very crowded. The battle cruisers and the Fifth Battle Squadron each had their own cruiser screen and destroyer outriders. The British main battle fleet had heavy cruisers, screening light cruisers and torpedo boat destroyer flotillas in abundance.

All of these were heading towards the same small area of sea at up to half a sea mile a minute. The 5th's own light cruisers were already turning away to avoid a direct collision with the battle fleet's cruiser screen. There were ships of all sizes heading in all directions at high speed. Jonathan was reminded of the situation a couple of weeks ago where airplanes and Torpedo Boat Destroyers were chasing each other all over the sea. If this went wrong, there would be more casualties than a single pilot.

If two dreadnoughts collided it would be bad enough, but if a cruiser or worse, a destroyer was rammed it would be all over very quickly for the unfortunate vessel. Whatever else was going to happen, what was going on at that moment was terrifying to any right-thinking sailor.

"*Malaya* getting close sir!" The voice was alarmed.

"What the...." Spinning round, Jonathan could see that *Malaya* was badly out of position. The drill book said that they should be in line ahead at this point, and the ships should turn ninety degrees west together, and then ninety degrees north, thus, theoretically keeping their station.

Something had happened. *Malaya*, instead of being comfortably on their beam, running parallel to them was still heading straight at their vulnerable side at full speed. She must have been almost a mile east of station. If nothing was done, *Warspite* would be rammed by her squadron mate. Thirty years ago a similar miscalculation had resulted in the loss of the first class British battleship *HMS Victoria* and over three hundred and fifty men.

Philpotts didn't hesitate. "Port 20" he ordered. That would swing *Warspite* parallel to *Malaya* and allow them to slip in to their allotted station when it was convenient to do so.

The coxswain spun the wheel rapidly "Twenty of the port wheel on Sir."

"Amidships"

"Amidships." The routine reply. Then suddenly

"HELM JAMMED SIR! Fifteen of the port wheel still on sir!"

It was a potential disaster. They were heading straight for their next ahead, *Valiant*, which was taking up her proper station. Suddenly there was a tremendous clang and a flash of fire outside the conning tower. Frank reeled back from the sighting slit with a cry, his binoculars flying as he fell to the floor.

Jonathan gathered his stunned senses and ran over to his friend "are you alright?" he asked.

11. BATTLE

"Dunno old boy." He muttered, "I can't see anything. Can't hear much either. Is that you Jonathan?"

"Sure is!"

"I'm not much use at the moment. Can't see. Can't hear. Tell the captain would you?"

"Of course" said Jonathan. And then aloud, "Medics here! At the double!" Then to Philpotts, "Beg to report sir that Commander (N) is out of action."

"Very good" said the captain in the time-honoured, if incongruous manner. "I have the ship. Steady as she goes!"

It was actually a nonsense. 'Steady as she goes' was an order designed as a standard handover where nothing was changing. It was redolent of blue-water sailing in sailing days. It had no applicability whatsoever to their current situation.

"Still turning starboard sir. Helm still jammed." The coxswain reported. Jonathan repeated the information instinctively. The noise was such that one couldn't rely on the Captain hearing the report without confirmation.

"Very good' said the captain, and with a sideways glance said to Jonathan, "Would you mind remaining for the moment Marston. It would be helpful. Take over from Commander Hodgson please."

"Aye aye sir. Take over from Commander Hodgson." It seemed to be the most natural thing in the world. He positioned himself behind the coxswain so he could see the compass revolving.

The turn had achieved its object. They were now clear of *Malaya* but were headed straight for *Valiant's* side at significant speed.

"Is the helm still jammed?"

"Still don't answer sir!" The coxswain had regained his composure.

"Stand by the telegraphs!" The captain was obviously thinking of using the engines to counter the useless steering.

"Half ahead both." Jonathan attended to the port telegraph and the captain himself took the starboard one. They rang down half speed simultaneously.

The ship was still turning to starboard, but not as quickly as before. It still looked as if they were going to hit *Valliant*.

"Stand by for full ahead port engines and stand fast starboard engines!" Phillpotts was also keeping his composure. Jonathan was impressed.

That would have the effect of swinging them away from *Valiant* but at the expense of heading faster straight at the German Battle Fleet.

As the scenario unfolded, it became clear that they were going to miss *Valiant* without having to use the engines.

"Clear sir!"

"Stop port." And then "Full astern port. Starboard full ahead!"

He was trying to keep them turning north.

"Still turning sir!" Jonathan as Frank's appointed replacement was keeping an eye on their course.

"How fast Lieutenant?" asked Philpotts.

"Equivalent to port 15 sir. Heading now passing due east."

Picking up Frank's dropped binoculars and looking out of the sighting slit, Jonathan could see the entire German battle fleet swinging in to view. *Warspite* was heading straight for them. The German battleships erupted

11. BATTLE

into flame as they realized that this impudent British battleship appeared to be challenging them entirely on her own. *Warspite's* fifteen-inch guns were still roaring out with regularity, but she was literally drenched with German salvoes.

The rational part of Jonathan's brain was remembering Sas's description of the Battle of the Yellow Sea, with the Russian flagship veering out of line because her bridge personnel had been killed, and the *Retvisan* holding off the entire Japanese Fleet to let her get clear. *Warspite's* position combined both scenarios.

It must have looked very strange to the Germans. There was an appreciable amount of smoke coming from her wounds, but she was apparently challenging the entire German Fleet to single combat.

"Heading south-east, sir. Still turning but rate slowing. Equivalent to port ten now sir. Speed dropping" he reported. They were slowing down and would end up heading straight into the German fleet. To his left a rating at an instrument reported "Target bearing green two oh sir! Rate of change diminishing!" Again the deadpan tone.

The 'target' was the lead ship of the German battle line. They were definitely heading right into the middle of it.

"Lead German battleship will be dead ahead very shortly sir. Rate of turn stabilizing. Our speed reducing sir." Jonathan said. Philpotts continued to look out of the sighting slit through his binoculars. What was he going to do? They surely couldn't take on the entire German battle fleet. Could they?

Lowering his glasses the Captain said, "Stop port. Full ahead when ready. Half ahead Starboard."

The telegraphs rang and the ship wallowed as the engines adjusted themselves: - they were turning towards the German fleet, but much faster then before. Jonathan realized that as the turn was inevitable, Philpotts was trying to do it as fast as possible so that he could return towards his own fleet after a foray towards the enemy.

"Contact after steering position if you can" Philpotts ordered Jonathan. "That voice pipe there. See how they are fixed."

"Aye aye sir!" With a sinking heart, Jonathan remembered that the after steering position was the compartment directly forward of the writers' office right aft under the chapel. He remembered that they had spoken to the after torpedo room forward of them but they had not spoken to the after steering position. He wondered if anyone was still alive in there.

The voice pipe was useless, clearly damaged by shellfire, but there was a telephone. He rang it apprehensively and to his surprise it was answered. "After steering position sir?"

"Conning tower" he said, "Report your situation please."

"We are flooding sir, the hatch is jammed and we can't get out." The voice was tight, but controlled as well it may be in that situation.

"How deep?"

"'Bout eighteen inches sir. Gaining slowly." They wouldn't drown just yet. If the hatch was jammed, the pressure would equalize and they should be able to live in the bubble for a while.

"Very good" said Jonathan "Stand Fast, we're on it. Can you take control of the helm from there?"

11. BATTLE

"No sir. Starboard steering engine is still connected and locked. It needs to be disconnected from the engine room for us to be any use." That was a nuisance. If that after steering position was like anything that Jonathan was used to, it had a direct connection to the rudder heads and could be used to correct their dangerous gyrations.

"Very good. Stand by for orders" said Jonathan. Turning to Philpotts, he gave his report:

"After steering position reports that they are functional, but starboard steering engine is overriding them. They suggest disconnecting the steering engine."

"Very good" said Philpotts, staring out of the sighting slit through his glasses. Without tuning round he said, "See to it would you Lieutenant."

"Aye aye sir."

Locating the appropriate voice pipe Jonathan got the central turbine room. "Centre turbine room? Conning tower here. Can you disconnect the starboard steering engine? It seems to be jammed!"

"Aye aye sir!"

Risking a quick glance out of the sighting slit, Jonathan could see nothing but shell splashes close alongside them. He was not aware of any hits, but then he supposed that the gyrations that they were undertaking were pretty unpredictable to the enemy.

There was a sudden whistle up the voice pipe: "Conning tower! Centre engine room here. Disconnecting port steering engine and connecting starboard. We should have you sorted shortly.

"Very good!" said the Captain. They were now heading directly away from the enemy. "Stop port. Full astern when ready. Starboard half ahead."

"Wheel's answering sir!" shouted the coxswain. "It's a bit stiff, but it is moving!"

"Very good" said the Captain, "keep the turn on for the moment." He was looking out for the correct moment to check their turn. They had passed the point of danger and were heading back towards their own squadron, a couple of mile ahead of them.

"Midships. Full ahead all. Course north" He was aiming to take station astern of *Malaya*.

"Midships sir" turning the wheel. Jonathan could see the effort that it was taking. "Wheel's amidships sir."

There was something wrong, the gyro repeater was still ticking round and they were still turning back towards the enemy.

"TURN STILL ON SIR!" said Jonathan.

"Starboard fifteen" ordered the captain. The coxswain repeated the order and started to turn the wheel back, sweating with the effort. "Here you!" said Jonathan to a hovering messenger, "help him would you!"

"Aye aye sir"

With two of them on the wheel, the effort was reduced. Jonathan was watching the repeater, which was slowing. "Turn stopped sir, stable on heading one three five."

"That's no bloody good!" said Philpotts, "That's straight back into the nasty people! Hard a-port!"

They were committed to another turn.

"Centre engine room, conning tower" said Jonathan into the voice-pipe. "We're still getting port helm when the wheel's amidships. Can you do anything?"

"Wait one." The tinny voice replied. Jonathan could hear a muffled conversation carried up the pipe. What seemed an age was passing. Glancing out through the

11. BATTLE

slit as he was listening, Jonathan could see that they were circling one of the damaged British cruisers. She was stopped and was blowing off steam. There were large holes in her side. They were close enough for Jonathan to see that the crew were apparently making rafts and clearing the boats. She was a sitting duck.

The Germans were, however, concentrating on *Warspite* as a much juicier target. It was hard to tell from this position whether they were being hit or not, as their own guns were firing regularly, and the sound and shock of shells exploding alongside were indistinguishable from actual hits.

There was no doubt in Jonathan's mind that this ship was extraordinary. He had seen the damage that she had already taken, and here she was, still steaming and fighting for all she was worth.

"Conning tower? Engine room here!"

"Yes Chief?" said Jonathan, recognizing the distinctive tones of the Engineer Commander, "Marston? Is that you?"

"Yes Chief. What can you tell us?"

"In the confusion we set neutral at port fifteen. We have sorted that out now. It should work fine."

"Very Good Chief, helm seems a tad stiff still."

"Ok, we'll look at it. Telemetry may be bent a bit, but you have a useable helm now."

"Thanks Chief!" Jonathan reported the position to Philpotts. "Course steady on two two five." They were heading straight away from the battle.

"Right!" said Philpotts "Stop engines. Pass the word for the Commander to report in. I want to see just what sort of shape we're in before we get back into it."

Shortly after one of the telephones rang. Jonathan answered it. "It's Walwyn Sir," he said. "I don't need a detailed report from him," said the Captain, "I just want to know how soon we can rejoin the line."

"Captain asks when we can rejoin?" repeated Jonathan.

"Any time you like, I think. All main armament is functioning. Fire control intact, boiler rooms intact, Engines working, Steering gear fixed. I am just a little worried about the leaks. We have two big holes abreast the engine room and the stern is flooded"

"What speed can we do?" asked the Captain, after the information was passed to him.

"Sixteen knots" was the answer.

"Excellent! Revolutions for sixteen knots, port twenty, steer due East. Yeoman? Make to *Barham*, 'To SO 5th BS *Warspite* has two big holes abreast engine room. 16 knots request position of battle fleet'. You had better use the W/T."

"Very good sir, two big holes abreast engine room, speed sixteen knots, where is Battle Fleet" and he was off outside to the flag deck.

Indeed, it was very difficult to see what was going on, the fleets had moved off out of sight, and there was no sound of firing that they could hear. *Warspite* was quite alone. The easterly course was an intelligent guess, but no more than that. To Jonathan's surprise it was nine o'clock in the evening. They had been fighting for five hours.

"W/t message sir! From SO 5th BS 'Proceed to Rosyth'." They were being sent home. It was desperately disappointing, but at least it meant that they had a fighting chance of survival.

12. Aftermath

Wednesday 31st May 1916, HMS Warspite, 2100, North Sea, position uncertain

"Acknowledge" said Philpotts. "Port twenty, steer two seven zero. Pass the word to the Commander that we are being sent home."

"Aye aye sir!" a midshipman saluted and left the conning tower. The men at the wheel strained and groaned trying to turn the helm against the resistance. There was no room for more than two or three helmsmen in the cramped control tower.

Watching them, Phillpotts made a sound of disgust. "This is no damn' good. Marston, direct steering from the engine room for the time being."

"Aye aye sir. Direct steering from engine room." That meant that the rudder would be controlled directly from the steering motor rather than either steering position.

"Now" said Philpotts, "where the hell are we?" Moving across to the communications tube with the lower position, four decks below, he shouted, "below there! Do you have a position for us?"

The normal arrangement was that Frank's deputy would be in the lower conning tower with a back up plot to cover the situation that had actually happened. The idea was that it would be updated with every change of course and speed to keep the dead reckoning position as correct as possible.

Sadly, that was not to be. They answered:

"No sir, not since 1830 when we were at 57° 03" N and 6° E near as we can make it out sir."

"Why on Earth haven't you kept it up to date?"

"No info sir. Commander Hodgson was attending to it himself. We haven't had anything since then." 1830 must have been when Frank was hit, which meant that after that no one else had thought to keep the plot. With a sickening sensation, Jonathan suddenly realized that it ought to have been his responsibility, if he was taking over Frank's position he should have done so. He hadn't thought of that aspect of his duties and he was mortified that he had not.

Reluctantly he faced Philpotts and said, "I am very sorry sir, I didn't know he was doing it so I didn't think to keep it up."

There was a moment of silence. Then Philpotts said, "That's alright Marston. I think you can be forgiven. Let's see what we can do. Can anyone see where Commander Hodgson was keeping his log?"

The logbook was swiftly located on the chart table. Picking it up, Jonathan could see that the last entry in Frank's neat handwriting was timed at 1830 and it was 'port 20'. Looking back through the entries, Jonathan could see that it was just as the helm jammed.

He reported that to the Captain, who said, "I see. We did two full circles did we not?"

"Yes sir, with a short period of northing as the steering engine was reconnected" said Jonathan.

"Do you agree Coxswain?" asked the Captain. Again, it was interesting that the Captain was asking for the recollection of an enlisted man. Thinking about it, Jonathan realized that the Coxswain was best placed to remember what he had been doing. It was another object lesson.

"Aye sir. I came amidships and we were still turning to starboard."

"Speed was dropping as you were working the engines sir," said Jonathan. "I would submit that we were

12. AFTERMATH

probably pretty close to the position that we were when the helm jammed at first."

" I agree," said the captain. "We then steered 225 for a few minutes at reduced speed, say ten knots until we heard that we could do sixteen knots. Where did we go then Coxswain?"

"Due east sir, sixteen knots."

"Time of receipt of the last signal?"

"2107 sir"

"Very good. Write that up please Mr Marston and drop it down the tube to the lower conning tower. Then go and find the commander please and get a report on our state."

"Aye sir." He noted it down in his pad and moved to the tube in front of the useless wheel. "Below there! Stand by to receive log!" A face appeared at the bottom of the tube thirty feet below him, "Buzz it down then would you?"

"Here, Catch! Said Jonathan dropping it into the void.

"Take over the log and give me a position please," Philpotts ordered down the tube.

"Aye sir."

"Right, on your way Marston! Tell the Commander that I shan't fall out from action for the moment, but I should like to try and get some food for the men if we can."

"Aye aye sir. Not to fall out from action, but try and get some food." He stepped out of the conning tower door onto what was left of the shelter deck.

Commander Walwyn's once smart ship was in a bit of a state. To his immediate left the torpedo shelter was burned out and all of the mysterious instruments were ruined. In front of him, the lower superstructure (which included Frank's sea cabin) was full of holes and stank of burned corticene. The deck was buckled and covered with a tarry black filth, the end result of burning the deck covering.

To his right, things were almost normal, but as he made his way aft he could see where the deck below him was torn up by shell hits over the starboard battery. There was a ladder, which led him down onto the forecastle. It ended very close to a large hole, through which he could see the starboard battery in almost indecent detail. The ladder had been bent sideways over the void, but he was able to step onto a firm surface. He noted that the teak planking had been blown away and he was landing on the scarred iron deck, painted an incongruous red.

The deck over the starboard battery was riddled with holes, and he could see the big one at the end, which had caused the fire. Large tracts of once spotless planking had been removed by high explosive, leaving indecently small remnants surrounding the bolts that had once secured the planking to the deck.

Moving aft towards the boat stowage he saw that the main derrick had been shot through and it was resting on what remained of Mr Midshipman Donald's picket boat, which would clearly never be caught speeding again. The still bright, polished brass fittings contrasted strangely with the ruin.

All the other boats were reduced to splinters.

Looking forward, he could see that the fore bridge was riddled with holes from hits. If anyone had been stationed there during the action, they would not have survived. He was reminded of Sas's story about the Battle of the Yellow Sea. Clearly the Russian Admiral had preferred to appear brave by remaining on his bridge, but was ultimately defeated by that vanity. Had he taken refuge in

12. AFTERMATH

the conning tower, he might have survived to direct his fleet to victory.

It was a profound thought. In some situations it was important to save oneself for the sake of others, who depended on you.

Reckless bravery was a noble concept, but it was ultimately self-defeating. If Witgeft had been wise enough to take cover, he might have won the battle, but since he was pig-headed enough to refuse to take shelter, his fleet lost it.

Moving aft, he saw a party of men trying to cover a big hole by the single 6-inch gun mounted there. As he half expected, Walwyn was in the thick of it, directing operations. The hole was efficiently covered with yet another collision mat nailed down to the surviving planking.

"Oh hullo Marston" Walwyn greeted him, "Come to see the fun?"

"Yes sir!" said Jonathan, "The Captain would like an update if convenient?"

Looking around him, Walwyn said, "Well, we are doing as well as can be expected. I can't do anything more for the moment. Very well, I shall come."

As they made their way forward they encountered the captain on his way up to the fore bridge from the conning tower. "Ah Commander!" said Philpotts, "I am off to where I can see what's going on. Come and tell me how we are doing."

Walwyn followed his captain up the ladders, filling him in as they went.

"All guns save P6 operative, engines and boilers fine. Boats less satisfactory though, sir. Launch absolutely smashed to blazes, all Carley rafts except two small ones broken up. Effectively no sound boat left. The first picket boat had just been painted, too, with new brass rails and round casings. All cut to pieces now. Both ladders to quarterdeck have gone and both life buoys blown away. That looks like blast from " X " turret to me though.

"All mainstays have been shot through except one the starboard side. Mast secure unless we have a gale. Searchlights haven't suffered too badly, save those on the after superstructure, which are only good for scrap iron. We should be OK if there is a night action, we can use the forward searchlights to cover the quarters. Lots of holes on the quarterdeck, I am afraid, they will be death traps to the unwary. I would recommend declaring it out of bounds for the moment."

"Very Good. Keep on it. Well done Commander. I shall remember it in the report."

"Sorry sir!" said a new voice. It was a matelot who made a sketchy salute to Walwyn, "bugger of a fire in the sick bay which we can't control. Can you come please sir?"

"Very good" said Walwyn. "With your permission sir?" looking at Philpotts expectantly.

"Of course Commander, please carry on." And Walwyn was off to the next challenge. Jonathan followed him.

An hour's strenuous effort got the fire under control, with the aid of some innovative thinking from Walwyn, involving taking the hoses outboard onto the fore battery embrasure to get at the seat of the fire.

They then went to report to the fleet surgeon who was at his fore distributing station on the middle deck. It was not a pleasant place to be. The electricity was off and oil lamps lighted the space. It was a timeless scene that would not have been out of place more than a hundred years ago at Trafalgar. There were moans and cries from the injured men, some of whom were writhing in agony in their cots. There

12. AFTERMATH

was an unpleasant combination of smells comprising of burned meat, blood and sweat, overlain with surgical spirit and anti-septic.

There were a number of men suffering from burns. Keir and his attendants were moving from one to the other in a never-ending pattern. To Jonathan's surprise he recognized the Royal Marines' Bandmaster among the group. He was surprisingly gentle for such a big man.

The patients included Father Anthony whose face, hands and legs were covered with bandages. Jonathan spoke to him and was recognized. The wheeze in the priest's voice was more pronounced, but he seemed to be his normal self under the bandages. "Sometimes" he quipped, "one should be careful what one preaches about. The Good Lord might hold one to it!"

"Are you in much pain, sir?" asked Jonathan

"I shall survive, Mr Marston." He said, "I am trying to offer it up."

Certainly some of the other injured were less equable. It looked as if the effect of the dressings was worse than the burns. They were being replaced with soothing ointment. As Jonathan watched, the Bandmaster was massaging a man's face. Great gobbets of burned flesh seemed to be coming away under his fingers. Jonathan couldn't imagine the pain.

He realized that he had been fortunate. He had forgotten about his smarting face and hands and decided not to mention them in this company.

Frank was also bandaged, but was protesting that he was perfectly fit for duty and wanted to go back to his post. The Fleet Surgeon, a formidable character, dealt with him in short order. "You have concussion, shell splinters about the eyes, and until such time as I can remove them I am not taking responsibility for blinding you. Be told." And then, as Jonathan appeared out of the lamp lit gloom, "What do you want?" It was not a welcoming greeting.

"Come to report to Commander (N) sir."

"Be quick then. He's next."

Turning to the bandaged figure of his friend Jonathan said "Hello Frank. How goes it?"

"Jonathan? Is that you?" the voice was sturdy. "Can you tell the PMO that I am perfectly fit and I am needed at my station!"

"Don't worry about that old man" said Jonathan, grasping his hand. "We managed to update the plot and we are headed home. I guess we'll hit the coast somewhere in due course."

"That's what I am worried about. It's a tricky coast if you don't know what you are doing." For Frank, he was almost peevish.

"We'll manage. You just get yourself sorted out, will you?"

"Right! Enough" said the Fleet Surgeon. "Your turn now Hodgson. Be a good chap and co-operate will you" and he rolled up Frank's sleeve, swabbed his arm and jabbed it with a needle. Still protesting, Frank went to sleep.

"Ok, through there!" said the surgeon to his crew and they began to wheel Frank into a makeshift theatre behind a curtain rigged up between a shell hoist and the bulkhead.

"Out of the way please Marston, you can see him tomorrow, but at the moment I am a bit busy." Jonathan complied immediately.

He also saw Bond, who was in a very bad way, completely sedated. "Sad about that'n" said a sick berth attendant "Doubt he'll make it. Sixty percent burns. Not

12. AFTERMATH

survivable." Jonathan's eyes prickled, thinking of Bond's cheery greeting at the station and his pride in his rate. He would certainly have his own mess now, just not the one he was expecting. Muttering a brief prayer he moved on.

Passing through the compartment he saw a number of shrouded forms, neatly stowed out of the way. There were not many of them. He counted six. A swift count of the wounded being cared for showed that they numbered about twenty. That was extraordinary for the pasting the ship had received.

HMS Warspite, 31st May 1916, 2130, 57°30' N, 5°3' East

The sun was setting and dusk was beginning to fall. Walwyn was trying to darken the ship, which was difficult given the number of holes in the structure. "We're bound to be a target for the submarines and torpedo boats on our way home," he told Jonathan. "We have to make it as difficult for the buggers as we can."

There was another messenger. "Lower steering position says that they are still flooding sir!"

"Blast!" said Walwyn, "I had forgotten about them!" Indeed they had been reported as flooding early in the action. With a guilty start, Jonathan realized that he had remembered them but had omitted to remind Walwyn. They went aft and tried to open the hatch, but couldn't get it to budge. Some energetic work with crowbars and sledgehammers allowed the hatch to be forced open just enough to let the men out, who were pretty cheery, considering that had been stuck below in a half-submerged flat for about eight hours.

"Bloody cheek!" said Walwyn privately to Jonathan "They said that they were three feet under, but they damn' never got deeper than eighteen inches!"

Jonathan thought that even eighteen inches of cold seawater for eight hours was unpleasant enough.

The Wardroom a little later

"Aaah! That's better. First time I've sat down for a long time" said Walwyn relaxing into an armchair with a large brandy.

The wardroom was a little different to the cosy space that they were used to. There was a tarpaulin pinned across a bulkhead leading outboard and the remains of the piano were neatly gathered together under another tarpaulin bound with cordage. One of the wardroom tables had a hole in it where a shell had pierced it, bounced off the deck and demolished the stove and piano. There was a lingering smell of high explosive and burned corticene, but also a distinctive whiff of toast and sardines, overlain with the warm, comforting smell of spirits.

Jonathan had joined Walwyn in a brandy, and now, he was beginning to feel the relaxing spirit invigorating his veins.

"They got Single I am afraid," said Walwyn. "The marines mess deck hit cut him in half. Shame. He had the makings of a good officer."

Jonathan was too tired to be shocked, but he did remember the young sub Lieutenant from the train, and felt a sense of sadness that such a lively lad could have been wiped out in a moment. But still, he thought, he would have known nothing much about it and certainly would not have suffered.

"A good lad" said Jonathan. He was tempted to tell the story of Mr Midshipman Brown and the height restriction, but frankly he was too exhausted to want to make

12. AFTERMATH

the effort. He sipped his brandy. "What was the butcher's bill?" he asked.

"Just eight in so far as I can see, but there are a few who may not make it over the next few days. Mind you, WE may not make it after tomorrow. The Bosh will be waiting to try and pick us off as we go home." He tapped out his pipe on an ashtray and said,

"I am going to try and get some sleep. We had better turn to early and see what we can do about the boats and make some rafts. Dawn will be about 0330 so I shall aim to be up and about then. I would be grateful if you could join me. No pressure, but we seem to make a decent team. 0330 tomorrow?"

"Ok" said Jonathan. "Assuming I can find a place to sleep tonight."

'I should make yourself comfortable here" said Walwyn. "No-one else is around, and the only other refugee is Hodgson, and he's in no condition to join you."

As he was going out of the door, he turned back to Jonathan and said, "You put up a good show today old man. I just want to say 'well done' and I hope you get the recognition you deserve."

"Why, thank you sir. That's much appreciated." And he was off, leaving Jonathan alone.

Jonathan thought that Walwyn had done pretty well himself. From the beginning of the action he had been in the thick of it and had kept his head in some very trying circumstances. He raised his glass to the door, drained it in his honour. He then took off his shoes and tie, followed by his reefer. He swung his legs up onto the settee and used the scorched and salt stained thing as a makeshift blanket. Within minutes he was asleep.

HMS Warspite, North Sea, 0330 Thursday 1ˢᵗ June 1916

Jonathan was aware of someone shaking him. Opening his eyes he was immediately conscious that he was stiff and sore. His face and hands were smarting and the feel of his salt stiffened reefer was unpleasant. The smell of burned things was strong. He could hear the rushing wake, indecently loud through the tarpaulin covering the shell hole in the outer bulkhead, and an unfamiliar breeze. It was almost like camping under canvas.

To his surprise the shaker was Brown. "0330 sir, sunrise shortly. I have taken the liberty of securing a shift of uniform for you sir. RN buttons I am afraid, but at least it's clean."

Wonderingly, Jonathan saw that he was holding a neatly folded pile of clothes, topped off with a clean shirt and collar.

"Where did you get that Brown?" He said swinging his feet down and unbuttoning his shirt.

"It belonged to Mr Single sir. Gunroom steward thought you might like to make the usual arrangement sir."

"Usual arrangement?"

"Aye sir. Dead man's belongings auctioned off and proceeds to the family." It was positively Nelsonic. But at least it was a fresh uniform. And a clean shirt. Brown had contrived to bring a bowl of water and shaving things, which he placed on the counter for Jonathan to wash in.

Five minutes later he was on the upper deck in the early light of a North Sea dawn. Walwyn, of course was there contemplating the damage. He too had been able to shift into a fresh uniform and had had a shave. It was somehow indicative of the attitude of the Royal Navy.

"Morning Marston" he said cheerily. 'I see you've changed ready for another dunking!"

12. AFTERMATH

"Do you think we'll have one sir?"

"Well, we're doing eighteen knots and zigzagging. But then so was the *Lusitania*. I think we'll get some rafts built. We can use some of this damn' planking. Let's have a look at the boats and see what we can do."

An examination of the boats showed that the only possible candidate that could be made to swim was the first cutter. "We'll get chips on that straight away when the hands are called."

A messenger appeared and saluted. "0345 sir" he said.

"Very Good messenger. Call the Morning Watch."

"Aye aye sir" and he made his way forward to rouse the duty watch. Normally the day would start with washing down the decks, but this particular morning there was a bit more than that to do.

When the watch was mustered in their various positions the senior NCO or each division reported to Walwyn. "Duty watch mustered sir." Walwyn had them wait until all were present and said, "We are in a bit of a mess I am afraid. Priority is to ensure that gangways and hatches are clear and safe. We may have to get off her in a hurry. The general rule is 'if it's in the way, chuck it overboard unless it floats'. If it does, I want as much wood and floatables on the boat deck as possible. Boats crews? Apart from the first cutter your boats are useless. Collect as much as you can and make rafts. Use the deck planking where it is started.

"Quarterdeck men and top men? I want you to proceed with caution. There are some nasty holes there. Dismiss."

The carpenter appeared and reported that he had already investigated the damage and thought that he could repair the first cutter. Walwyn gave him the go ahead to try it.

By 0530, the normal time for calling all hands, some considerable progress had been made. They had ascertained that the ship was steaming at eighteen knots quite safely, gradually being pumped out. They were zigzagging and apart from the standard compass being off by about ten degrees they were fully under control and ready for anything.

Walwyn stood the men down for cocoa and to wash, resuming the work with both watches at the normal time of 0600. "It's good to keep to routine if we can. It settles everybody."

Walwyn and Jonathan went to report to Philpotts, who was sure that they would be attacked. They closed up the six-inch gun crews and carried on building rafts. Lookouts were doubled. Many off duty officers crowded the various vantage places adding their skills to the lookouts.

Sure enough, a little later when they were steaming at nineteen knots through a choppy sea, the dread cry "Torpedo to port!" was heard. Jonathan, at his usual post on the compass platform turned instantly to see the sinister thing heading straight towards them.

"Hard a port!" ordered Philpotts down the line to the engine room speaking tube. He was turning the ship to comb the tracks in the approved manner. It was working! The torpedo was going to pass ahead of them.

And then "Torpedo track to starboard!" from the other lookout. Some anxious observation over the next few seconds revealed that this one was going to pass them harmlessly as well.

"Anyone see a periscope?"

"No sir, too many white horses."

12. AFTERMATH

"Very good. Increase speed to 21 knots. Signal Flag at Rosyth by w/t 'Zigzagging at 19 knots missed by two torpedoes at. Give DR position. Returning to Rosyth alone.'

"Walwyn, you had better see about getting the wounded up on deck, just in case and shut all doors please."

"Very good sir."

And so they proceeded anxiously back towards Rosyth. They were told that some TBD's were coming to escort them in, but just as they appeared over the horizon, there was a sudden sighting of a periscope close under the bow. Philpotts turned to try and ram, but, because they were still steering from the engine room, the submarine got away, pursued by a couple of six inch shells. At least she did not do any more damage to *Warspite*. That little episode warranted a burst of full speed, but the strain on the bulkheads was such that Philpotts realized that this was not a good idea and dropped back to twenty-one knots, which seemed to be relatively safe.

Some hours later, as they passed slowly under the Forth Bridge, Jonathan was astonished to hear jeers coming from the railway workers lined up on the bridge above them. Something landed just beside him with a crack. Then another that skittered away into the scuppers. Soon there was a veritable hail of the things. Looking at a piece of black, shiny material, Jonathan realized that the railway men were throwing lumps of coal at them!

He heard shouts of "cowards! You ran away!" among the jeers.

Jonathan was shaken to the core. Given everything that the ship and her crew had been through in the last twenty-four hours this was too much. The other men were clearly feeling it as well.

Philpotts was stony faced as they proceeded under the bridge and began the tricky business of docking the damaged vessel. Some of the matelots, drawn up on the decks were looking murderous. No one reacted, but Jonathan could feel the tension. He would make a point of avoiding the Edinburgh pubs that evening.

The dockyard crew was also uncharacteristically silent. Jonathan realized that many of the men were wearing black mourning bands on their arms.

It was only later, as he was relaxing in the wardroom of *HMS Dreadought* (which, together with the *Queen Elizabeth* had been in dockyard hands and so missed the battle) that he got to the bottom of it.

"The Germans have claimed a great victory," said a hospitable officer, "They said that they sunk you, the *Queen Mary, Indefatigable* and two armoured cruisers as well as numerous TBD's and a submarine. They also said they damaged a number of our battleships and torpedoed *Marlborough.*"

"Well they damn' well didn't sink us." Jonathan was nettled. "What do they say about their own casualties?"

"One cruiser and a battleship torpedoed last night."

"Well that's a lot of bull for a start!" Jonathan fumed. "I saw heavy damage to their line with my own eyes!" He was furious.

'How dare they?' he thought to himself. He had clearly seen German battle cruisers and dreadnoughts burning under the onslaught of the Fifth Battle Squadrons' massive and concentrated guns. They could not possibly have escaped undamaged. It made him mad that they should make such statements, which were demonstrably untrue.

12. AFTERMATH

HMS Dreadnought, Rosyth Dockyard, Friday 2nd June 1916

Over the next few days the situation began to unfold, but it was very confusing. It looked as if the British had indeed lost a number of great ships, but were still looking for a fight. According to the London Times, the German High Seas Fleet 'aided by low visibility' avoided prolonged contact with the British Grand Fleet and returned to port as soon as it appeared, but, the British said, not before receiving severe damage.

That sounded more like the battle that Jonathan had witnessed. He had vivid memories of watching those huge shells landing on the German ships and the flare of the fires. The British said that at least one battle cruiser was destroyed and another severely damaged, with a battleship sunk by a torpedo at night.

On the other hand, the British battle-cruiser force was severely handled, with *Queen Mary, Indefatigable* and *Invincible* sunk, along with the heavy cruisers *Defence* and *Black Prince*. Jonathan had a vivid flashback of one of those ships erupting almost under his nose. He remembered the frantic dash of the First Cruiser Squadron, dodging around the British battle cruisers only to run slap-bang into the arms of the German High Seas Fleet. To his mind, it epitomized the British fighting spirit. He was reminded of Farragut's injunction fifty years ago: - "damn the torpedoes, Drayton, Full ahead!"

He was enjoying himself in *Dreadnought* and was fascinated to be a guest in the first of the many, now a little quaint to one used to the *Warspite*. This ship was only ten years old and had been the wonder of the world when she was launched, but like the poor old *Wisconsin* outmoded. The wardrooms of the two ships made the wardroom of *Warspite* very welcome. Their officers were mortified to have missed the big show and wanted to bask in the reflected glory of those who had been there.

As the story unfolded in the newspapers over the weekend the situation became marginally clearer. Neutral reports suggested that the German Fleet had returned to its bases, but was dispersed and severely damaged. The German Admiralty came close to admitting the same with a cautious statement to the effect that 'of course a portion of our ships was severely damaged.'

A name caught Jonathan's eye, Winston Churchill wrote a thoughtful piece in a Sunday paper in which he pointed out that the German Fleet had only escaped destruction by flight. Control of the sea depended on dreadnought battleships and that the British supremacy was undiminished. Yes, they had lost the *Queen Mary* but the Germans had lost *Lutzöw,* their latest battle cruiser, less than a year old. As for the rest, the losses were regrettable, but far from crippling.

The Germans continued to claim that *Warspite* was sunk, despite British denials, and to Jonathan's distress, that claim was repeated to the German Embassy at Washington. In the absence of Father Anthony, Jonathan was subject to the same rules as everyone else, one postcard with two letters only allowed, just 'OK'. He sent that to Cliff at the Embassy, knowing that it would be passed on.[71]

To his surprise, a couple of days later, he was summoned to Scapa Flow to see Jellicoe. Philpotts, on learning that, entrusted his formal report to Jonathan for onward transmission to the c-in-c.

Some while later, Jonathan found that he was sharing the flagship's tender (a specially modified TBD, painted white) from Thurso to Scapa with a group of soldiers headed by a very familiar figure indeed: - the British

12. AFTERMATH

Minister of War, Lord Kitchener, whose extravagant moustaches adorned any number of recruiting billboards that Jonathan had been seeing ever since his arrival in Britain.

In the *Oak's* cramped wardroom he found himself in close proximity to the great man who fixed him with a piercing gaze. "Young man. Why are you wearing an odd cap badge?"

"Because I am an American sir."

"Indeed? And what do you think you are doing here?"

"I am reporting to Admiral Jellicoe sir."

"Why?"

Jonathan was not very comfortable in this company. The weather was rough and the wardroom crowded with soldiers all being thrown about by the lively motion of the small ship. The minister did not seem to be very friendly. "He has asked for me sir. I suspect that it was because I was involved in the battle sir."

"You were WHAT?" The explosion was nearly as bad as some of those that Jonathan had experienced the previous week.

"HOW were you involved? Why were you involved? Who the devil is responsible for it?" and then to his aide "Fitzgerald, do we know anything about this?"

A Lieutenant Colonel said "No sir. We know nothing about neutrals being involved in the battle" and then turning to Jonathan accusingly "What do you mean by it young feller? What? What?"

"Yes. What do you mean by it eh? Speak up man! Speak up!" The minister was clearly not a patient man.

Jonathan took a breath, and thought rapidly. This was a serious problem. After some thought, he said, "I hold the post of Supernumerary Naval Attaché and was directed to *HMS Warspite* as an observer." The reaction was rather worrying.

"*WARSPITE!*" expostulated Kitchener, "As an OBSERVER? Whose bloody stupid idea was that?" The question was clearly rhetorical and Jonathan decided that he didn't want to dip his toe into what was clearly a British problem.

And then turning to his staff the general said, "Some blasted civilian I'll be bound." The companions started muttering among themselves like some absurd Gilbert and Sullivan chorus: ….an observer…..an attaché…..how dare they….how dare they!

And then, after a short pause, Kitchener again, but quieter, "Have you met Jellicoe before?"

"Yes sir. On more than one occasion. He was fully supportive sir."

"Was he bigad?" The minister was subsiding. Suddenly Jonathan realized that this man was old and tired. "Well I suppose if it's good enough for Jellicoe it's good enough for me." He sank into the soft armchair, and then looked at Jonathan questioningly. "So you smelt powder did ye? Did ye see what happened?"

"Some, sir. I saw the opening and a bit of the main clash, but we got a few knocks and I was rather busy. I still don't know much about what happened after we got sent home. I am hoping to find out."

"Harrumph!" said the Field Marshall.[72]

The rest of the trip was quiet, as far as Jonathan was concerned. The Army officers obviously knew each other well and made a close-knit team, from which Jonathan was excluded. He would like to have left the wardroom, but thought it might look rude to do so.

12. AFTERMATH

Admiral's day cabin HMS Iron Duke, Scapa Flow, Forenoon Monday 5th June 1916

"Sit down Mr Marston. Thank you for coming all this way." Jellicoe was his usual unassuming self. "I sent for you because I wanted to hear what happened at your end of things first hand. Thank you for the Captain's report by the way. He mentions you by name. Jolly well done."

Jonathan glowed.

"I can't do anything official about it of course, because you are not a member of the Royal Navy, but I shall do what I can. A letter, perhaps. Now, to business. Tell me what you observed."

Jonathan reflected. He had been pretty well occupied throughout those momentous hours, but he clearly remembered Philpott's succinct summary of what was going on.

"Well sir. It was a confusing affair, but when we left it looked as if you had them in the bag." He stopped, awkwardly, realizing that could be misconstrued.

"We did," said Jellicoe. "They turned sixteen points and vanished into the murk going west, away from their base. They tried to get through three times and turned away each time. We were barring their way home so I expected to get them in the morning but they seem to have slipped through the tail of the line during the night."

"Were there any surprises sir?" asked Jonathan.

"Not really Mr Marston. The torpedo attacks were pretty much as we had anticipated and rehearsed for. I was disappointed with the performance of some of our armour. We need more deck protection. We also need to do something about the charges of small guns being ignited by shells. Those battery fires in *Warspite* and *Malaya* were worrying."

"Indeed sir.' Said Jonathan thinking of the inferno.

"We also need to make sure that if a turret is penetrated, the flash doesn't go down to the magazine. I am sure that is why we lost the *Invincible* and probably the *Queen Mary.*"

"I am very sorry about them sir. I saw one of the cruisers blow up. It was not very nice to watch." Jonathan was not a sensitive individual, but over the past few days he had been wondering what it must have been like to be in one of those ships as it blew up. Having been close to some of the shell burst below deck, he supposed that if you were hit, you wouldn't know much about it: - a bit like poor Single, whose uniform he was wearing (with the USN buttons transferred by the ever-faithful Brown).

Much worse would be the fate of people trapped in compartments like the after steering position. They would be in a bubble of ever worsening air at the bottom of the sea, with no alternative but to die of slow suffocation.

"I am sending you home, Marston," said Jellicoe. "I think you have seen us at our best, and possibly at our worst. I think that we have no more to show you. *HMS Roxburgh* is heading across to Halifax in the next few days; you can have a passage in her if you wish. Do you have any dunnage? Would you like it sent up from Rosyth?"

"Sadly, no sir. Most of it was destroyed by a German shell the other day."

Jellicoe smiled a sad little smile and said, "Well let us see what we can do about that. Fare well Marston, it has been a pleasure knowing you." And he stood up and shook Marston's hand.

Unexpectedly, Jonathan felt a rush of emotion. He could feel tears welling up in his eyes and he stifled a gulp. This man, with all the cares of the world on his shoulders

12. AFTERMATH

had taken time out to talk to a junior officer from a foreign service.

"I don't know how to thank you sir" he managed, squeezing the Admiral's hand. "I have had been made most welcome. I am sure that it is all down to you sir. I am most grateful. Truly I am."

"There will be a boat to *Roxborough* shortly. I am sure that the wardroom will give you shelter for the time being. Give my regards to Captain Sims will you?"

Jonathan remembered not to salute, as they were below decks without hats, turned and left the office. He was having some difficulty in seeing.

Up on the quarterdeck, the weather was turning nasty. It had been lumpy enough on the way over, but now it was turning into a filthy afternoon, with horizontal rain and a rising gale. The weather suited his mood. He had not, up until that moment, realized what a strain he was under. Vivid memories of the recent battle jockeyed for position with others. That moment when he thought he was going to be shot as a spy, Amparo dancing flamenco, the sheet of flame from the six-inch battery as Father Anthony dashed in to it, Bond's cheerful face, blackened and burned, the pathetic remains of the *Sussex* and worst of all, the firecracker chain of explosions culminating in the complete obliteration of *Defence* right before his very eyes.

Jonathan wept.

ENTRE'ACTE

Report of Lt. Jonathan J Marston USN

HMS ROXBOROUGH, AT SEA THURSDAY 8TH JUNE 1916

SIR

I HAVE THE HONOR TO REPORT THAT PURSUANT TO YOUR ORDERS OF THE 16TH OF MARCH 1916, VIZ.

1. *TO OBSERVE AND REPORT ON HOW THE ROYAL NAVY OPERATES ON A DAY-BY-DAY BASIS*
2. *TO REVIEW THE TACTICS AND KNOW-HOW OF THE SAID NAVY*
3. *TO REPORT ON THE MORALE OF THE COUNTRY AND THE FORCES*

I duly proceeded to London by way of SS City of New York *(American Flag) where I met with Commander Symington, US Naval attaché to the Court of St. James and, having obtained the necessary clearances from His Britannic Majesty's Royal Navy, I was directed to* HMS Warspite, *a dreadnought battleship of the said navy, arriving in her on the 21st of April 1916, where I remained until the 4th inst.*

This report follows on from my endorsement of the findings of the Inquiry into the damage of SS Sussex, *channel packet (French Flag).*

I should like to record that I have had the co-operation of His Britannic Majesty's Royal Navy at a very high level and have had a number of private conversations with Admiral Jellicoe, the Commander-in-Chief of the Grand Fleet of the said navy and have had extensive day-to-day experience of the operation of the said fleet over a six week period, during which I experienced three full scale sorties, a seaplane raid and the late battle in the North Sea against the High Seas Fleet of His Imperial Majesty, the German Emperor.

<u>Day to day Operations</u>

The Royal Navy is a highly organized operation, relying on detailed standing orders with scope for individual flag officers to meet any envisaged move by their opponents. The late battle, although perceived by some as indecisive was, in fact, anticipated by the command and the procedures (both tactical and strategic) appeared to work in a satisfactory manner. It should be held firmly in mind that whatever the differences in material losses, the simple fact is that the Royal Navy remained in command of the battlefield at the end of the operation and the forces of Imperial Germany took the opportunity of thick weather to escape to their bases. I personally observed damage to the High Seas Fleet, which was far in excess of the damage admitted by them.

By contrast, I note with some diffidence that the vessel in which I was borne was claimed to have been sunk by the said forces, whereas in actuality it was in full fighting form, with all main armament, boilers, engines and fire control equipment fully operational, able to steam at a speed in excess of the designed fighting speed of the US battle fleet. She was detached to her home base as being surplus to the requirements of the moment.

The objection was that she was only able (temporarily) to make sixteen knots in contrast to the fleet speed of twenty or twenty-one knots. I believe that she had received hits from some fifteen heavy shells and also some lighter ones as she circled within range of the German secondary armament without affecting her fighting efficiency in any material way.

The claim to have sunk her may be related to the difficulties of observing opposing fleets at the ranges involved in unfavorable weather conditions. It should be born in mind that the extreme range of action was anything up to 19,000 yards, which is over the horizon from most of the gun positions and was the subject of director firing (as to which see my observations below.)

Observations by subject

1. Materièle

Battleships:

The latest generation of dreadnought battleships requires considerable rethinking as to their use and *employment in war. The speeds are substantially in excess of pre-war standards and the range at which combat is undertaken exceed previous practice by a substantial margin. In turn, this requires adequate scouting resources (as to which see below).*

These vessels demonstrate excellent protection and survivability to surface fire Provided *fire discipline and safety are not compromised by the desire to attain a rapid rate of fire. Their vulnerability to torpedoes is an unknown quantity, save that it is noted that* HMS Marlborough *appears to have taken a torpedo hit which did not affect her ability to remain in the line and continue the fight.*

The use of oil fuel has major advantages over coal in that it is more efficient, cleaner and quicker to fuel and leaves the majority of the ship's company free for other tasks during refueling. An example is that after returning from patrol, an urgent call was made for a new sortie. The oil-fueled vessels were able to fuel and exit much faster than the coal-fired ships to the significant advantage of the fleet as a whole.

It is clear that larger caliber armament is to be favored. The British fifteen-inch caliber gun is a formidable weapon, possessing significant advantages over the thirteen point five or fourteen-inch guns. The Japanese (see below) are considering a move to a sixteen-inch caliber gun and we may have to do the same.

Similarly, it is clear that ever increasing speed will be a requirement of future capital ships. Although the ships of the Queen Elizabeth *class are fast (25 knots) the German*

König *class is not much slower, having kept up with the* Queen Elizabeth *class for a considerable period, under heavy fire from the latter.*

I was able to observe a new, previously unknown, British battle cruiser version of the Queen Elizabeth, *which was proceeding at a speed in excess of thirty knots, which observation was confirmed by Commander Kenji Sasai of the Imperial Japanese Navy. We estimated the guns to be fifteen-inch, six in number.*

Fire Control

Is essential. At the ranges at which the late action was fought it was difficult, if not impossible to aim ordnance by conventional means. Because of its secret nature, I was not party to fire control as currently practiced in the Royal Navy, but I was able to observe the effects in practice and subsequently in action. The results were impressive. Consistent grouping of shots on target at extreme range was normal, and expected.

In the latest batch of dreadnoughts, even the secondary (anti-torpedo boat) armament has dedicated fire control positions, as does the torpedo armament itself.

Scouting vessels

The importance of scouting vessels of adequate force and speed was forcibly demonstrated. I understand that fast light cruisers of the 'c' type acquitted themselves well, being able to observe the enemy at close quarters and use their high speed to great advantage. At the time of writing, I do not have final figures, but losses in this class of vessel were surprisingly light for the information received.

By contrast, the losses in the battle cruiser force were appreciable, albeit not such as to affect the superiority in numbers available to the royal navy. I personally observed the fall off in performance by the German battle cruisers as the action proceeded, which suggests that these vessels suffered badly at the hands of the British forces. I was able to observe at least three German vessels forced out of line by British fire. It should, perhaps be noted that they came under very heavy fire from the fast battleships of the Queen Elizabeth *type (15-inch guns).*

The losses amongst the British battle cruiser forces may be as a result of factors unrelated to their design, namely poor fire prevention discipline and possibly over-confidence. That said, all scouting forces were distinguished by gallant leadership and aggressive handling at all levels which was most marked.

It should be noted that the older type of armored cruiser (such as Defence *and* Warrior*) are no longer fit for their purpose and cannot stand against fast dreadnought battleships, let alone battle cruisers.*

Torpedo boat destroyers

Appear to have been well and aggressively deployed on both sides. The tactics of the Royal Navy for dealing with attacks by these vessels were effective. I have no information on the results from British attacks on the opposing forces, but suffice it to say that I cannot see that these vessels have reached a sufficient state of development to warrant the abandonment of the battle fleet as a means of obtaining naval supremacy.

Submarines

Remain a danger, especially to a damaged and retreating fleet. At the present state of development, these vessels cannot operate with the battle fleet as being too slow for fleet work. I am aware that the Royal Navy is developing a class of very large steam-powered submarines, which are capable of operating in this role. It is noteworthy that HMS Warspite *was able to avoid two attacks on her (unescorted) way home and was able to make an attack of her own on one of the attackers. It was only a lack of nimbleness (as a result of battle damage) that allowed the submarine to escape.* Warspite *had the speed advantage to ram, but was operating the helm from the engine room and could not turn fast enough to engage. The submarine made good her escape submerged.*

Aircraft

I was privileged to observe at first hand the use of seaplanes in war as an attack weapon. My view is that these weapons are worthy of attention as being potentially devastating. Much faster (and cheaper) than a torpedo boat they would appear to be very hard to bring down. They have the potential for delivering bombs or torpedoes into a hostile force from several directions at once.

The seaplane raid that I observed was unsuccessful, in part as a result of adverse weather conditions, but I was informed that the use of land planes from flying off platforms fitted to dedicated aircraft carriers is a promising way forward, especially if those vessels are endowed with high speed. I am even led to believe that it may be possible to launch and recover land planes at sea, in company with the fleet.

Such airplanes can also be used for scouting in suitable weather. In the late battle I am given to understand that a scout plane was used to determine the position of the German fleet and reported it by radio at a time that the relevant commanders were in ignorance of it but owing to unfamiliarity with the medium, and possibly distrust of innovation, the position was not transmitted to the appropriate commanders, which was a great shame.

I witnessed a raid by zeppelin airships, but found the raid inconclusive, and noted that the raider was brought down by the defending forces.

2. Organization

The Grand Fleet maintains a detailed set of standing orders that attempt to anticipate all probable moves by the enemy. Recognizing that war is full of uncertainty, individual commanders are enjoined to watch their squadron flagship and conform to observed manoeuvres.

The establishment of a Naval Staff is an interesting development, but there needs to be a clear demarcation between orders given to the commanders in the field and their discretion to deal with what they see in front of them.

3. Communications

Signals by flag are hard to read in these conditions. Wireless telegraphy has obvious dangers. Light signals appear to work well.

4. Establishment and infrastructure

The infrastructure and establishment is impressive. The civilian rail structure is used to its full advantage, meaning that supplies are well organized; communications (by coded telegram) are attended to promptly. The arrangements for coaling in particular are efficient, with each capital ship allocated a dedicated collier. Supplies seem plentiful.

Domestic supplies from home at remote bases are a great contributor to maintaining good morale. It was most marked that every effort was made to keep large numbers of men entertained and happy in a hostile environment. Indeed, it seemed to me that the portion of the fleet that was housed in that location fared rather better in fighting efficiency and morale than those other divisions that based in a major city, with all the distractions that such a base contains.

I mention in particular the presence of a floating department store and a theatre ship, as well as the provision of wholesome entertainment, football, boxing, regattas and similar competitive sports.

5. Morale

Is and remains high. There is a considerable frustration at the fact that the German Fleet refuses to engage, and when engaged invariably tries to disengage as rapidly as possible. This appears to be so even when a raiding force of battle cruisers is spotted and engaged by light forces as happened at the bombardment of Scarborough and the east coast in April. In general the officers and men of the Royal Navy are very much aware of the burden being born by the Army and would like to shoulder their share.

There is no question but that the Royal Navy is prepared to fight, wants to fight and is bitterly disappointed when there is no opportunity to fight. After the late battle, there is a strong desire to 'finish the job' and the next encounter is eagerly awaited.

6. Domestic morale

Whilst waiting for authorization to proceed to the Fleet I had ample opportunity to observe the civilian population closely. There are no shortages, and indeed, trade seems to be booming. In many ways the populace is continuing as if there was no war, with vacations being taken and theatres and restaurants open. Such economies as there are appear to be voluntarily undertaken.

The casualty lists are a source of sorrow and regret, but are, in general, being born stoically. There is genuine outrage at aerial and naval bombardment, which is a source of much anger, not only against the perpetrators, but also against the authorities for failing to prevent it. Such discontent, however, is more of a symptom of a healthy and skeptical society than anything more sinister.

A particular aspect to notice is that with so many men away in the services, women, even gentlewomen, are taking up the vacancies. I have encountered women clerks, bellhops, hotel proprietors and trolley-car conductors, all of who appeared to function well, without regard to their sex. Of note is the employment by the Admiralty of a whole corps of women auxiliaries, who, in addition to clerical duties even go as far as running picket boats.

7. Other matters

In the course of my duties, I was able to spend some time with officers of the Imperial Japanese Navy, as well as *highly placed personages from Australia. From the Japanese I received information about the organization of their navy, their plans for the future as well as personal recollections of the war with Russia and the progress of submarines in that navy. I was favorably impressed with their expertise and morale.*

The Australians are concerned that Japanese ambitions in the Pacific may be a problem in the future. Having been in the company of senior Japanese officers, I am forced to the conclusion that such concerns are not groundless.

8. Recommendations

1. *We should consider that the new generation of dreadnought battleships is likely to be (a) fast and (b) armed with heavier main armament.*
2. *Care should be taken to subdivide the secondary armament, so that damage to one gun does not spill over into other positions.*
3. *We should urgently address the issue of fire control.*
4. *Fast scouting vessels are a must for any balanced fleet. Indeed, I am of the view that such vessels should have priority at this time.*
5. *Our new generation of torpedo boat destroyers is of a satisfactory size and design, standing up well to contemporary European practice.*

6. Aviation, both heavier than air and lighter than air should be developed. It has the potential to be a game-changer in future naval warfare.

Jonathan J. Marston
Lieutenant USN

Author's Note

The Battle of Jutland is probably one of the most controversial sea battles in the last hundred years. The British public was expecting their beloved navy to knock the Germans into a cocked hat: - it expected another Trafalgar and was bitterly disappointed when the German fleet was not annihilated. Jellicoe, however, had to cope with factors that Nelson never did. Submarines and torpedo boats were only two differences. There was also the question of the enormous ranges at which early twentieth century battles were fought, at speeds unheard of in Nelson's day.

Jellicoe was not given to blowing his own trumpet and in general considered the press to be a pernicious institution. He did not 'do' public relations in the same way as the charismatic and media-savvy Beatty did. The Germans, by contrast did 'get' propaganda and were announcing a famous victory whilst Jellicoe and Beatty were still in the field, searching in vain for their late opponent.

The reality was, however, different. A senior German Naval officer remarked "we must never do that again" and whilst the High Seas Fleet did come out again in August, they never strayed far from their bases and were effectively reduced to a fleet in being.

The damage to the German fleet was much greater than is generally credited and many of their ships, including all but one of their battle cruisers were out of action for the next two months.

Notwithstanding a hundred years of dissection and analysis, Jonathan's conclusions are broadly correct.

AUTHOR'S NOTE

Jellicoe said exactly what he was going to do and did it. Beatty and the Admiralty were in complete agreement with his ideas, whatever was said later on. In fairness, Jellicoe knew that his actions might not satisfy the public, but he was of an age and generation where he preferred to do the right thing rather than the popular thing. The politicians, by contrast (including one W.S. Churchill and another David Lloyd George)) preferred to advocate the popular rather than the correct.

Based on extensive original research and eye witness accounts, many of the eccentric characters who feature in this story are real people, and the events portrayed, however unlikely they seem a hundred years later, actually happened. The politics (US and British) are as accurate as the commentators can make it.

Comment has been made that the characters are more like caricatures of the British stiff upper lip, but the attitudes (especially with regard to death and injury) are correct for that time and class. It was, after all, only a hundred years since Lord Uxbridge, at the Battle of Waterloo, said to Wellington "By God, I've lost my leg!" to which Wellington replied "By God sir, so you have!"

The experiences of Jonathan during the battle are largely taken from Commander Walwyn's first hand account, reproduced in "The Fighting at Jutland" (Macmillan 1921). Philpotts, Walwyn, Hammill and many others were forcibly retired in 1921 under the post war Geddes axe. Frank, however carved out a career as a hydrographer, being promoted to Captain. He died at a Catholic nursing Home in Crediton in 1965. His charts of the East Indies are still the basis for the Charts today.

Father Anthony Pollen stayed in *Warspite* until she was decommissioned in 1924, whereupon he translated

AUTHOR'S NOTE

to the Birmingham Oratory. He insisted on keeping seagoing hours, and was often getting up at the same time as his fellow Jesuits were going to bed after their midnight devotions. He was the only chaplain to be decorated for gallantry in that war, receiving the DSO.

Jonathan, his family and Clementina Fessenden are fictional. I have taken one or two liberties with the history. The Granados did not sail on SS New York, neither did Jamie but both crossed the Atlantic at that time. The new British battle cruiser, *HMS Renown* did not start her trials until two months later, although completion was scheduled for March 1916. Ironically the Japanese sank her in 1941.

Jonathan's Mission is fiction, but Billy Sims and his subordinate crossed the Atlantic by civilian steamer in disguise in April 1917 exactly as Jonathan does.

HMS Roxburgh was not actually allocated to the Atlantic and North American station until September 1916, but Jonathan has pressing business back in the States that warrants some liberties.

The Book cover photograph records *HMS Warspite* and *HMS Valiant* at the opening of Chapter 10, taken from *HMS Malaya*.

AUTHOR'S NOTE

Notes

1   Richard H. Dana junior (August 1, 1815 – January 6, 1882) an American lawyer and politician from Massachusetts, who gained renown as the author of the American classic, the memoir Two Years Before the Mast, which recorded his time as a merchant seaman between 1834 and 1836

2   HMS Dreadnought built in 1905 was bigger, faster and had more guns than any other battleship in the world. She gave her name to all of the new battleships of the early 20th century and made all other battleships obsolete

3   Later Admiral Arthur W. Radford, a pioneer naval aviator.

4   The Veracruz invasion (otherwise the Tampico incident) was set off when nine American sailors were arrested by the Mexican government for entering off-limit areas in Tampico, Tamaulipas.

5   A landing party under Capt. E. A. Anderson had gone ashore and been caught in a murderous fire from the cadets in the Naval Academy. Jonathan was with that party.

6   Three large British cruisers, the *Aboukir, Cressy* and *Hogue* were sunk by the same German submarine on the same day in September 1914. They were supposed to be on anti submarine patrol, but found themselves victims rather than attackers. 1,450 British sailors (mostly reservists and boys) lost their lives. It was a major wake-up call to the value of submarines.

7   The battles of Coronel and the Falklands in 1914, which gave the British a false appreciation of the value of battle cruisers.

8   Later Admiral Sellers, Commander-in-Chief United States Fleet.

9   William Shepherd Benson (25 September 1855 – 20 May 1932) was an admiral in the United States Navy and the first Chief of Naval Operations (CNO), holding the post throughout World War I.

10 The American Civil War was "The War" for Jonathan's generation

11 Alfred Thayer Mahan (September 27, 1840 – December 1, 1914) was a United States naval officer and historian, whom John Keegan called "the most important American strategist of the nineteenth century."[1] His book The Influence of Sea Power Upon History, 1660–1783 (1890) won immediate recognition, especially in Europe,

12 The strongest elements of the German Pacific fleet. They were sunk

NOTES

by British battle cruisers in the Battle of the Falklands in December 1914

13 February 15, 1845 – February 7, 1937) was an American lawyer and statesman who served as the Secretary of State under President Theodore Roosevelt and as Secretary of War under Roosevelt and President William McKinley.

14 Henry Cabot Lodge (May 12, 1850 – November 9, 1924) was an American Republican Congressman and historian from Massachusetts. A member of the prominent Lodge family, he received his PhD in history from Harvard University. He is best known for his positions on foreign policy, especially his battle with President Woodrow Wilson in 1919 over the Treaty of Versailles. The failure of that treaty ensured that the United States never joined the League of Nations.

15 April 11, 1860 – July 12, 1926 was an American politician in the Republican Party. He served as the Mayor of Newton, Massachusetts from 1902 to 1903, and a United States Representative for Massachusetts from 1905 to 1913, as a United States Senator from 1913 to 1919, and as Secretary of War from 1921 to 1925.

16 Edward Mandell House (July 26, 1858 – March 28, 1938) was an American diplomat, politician, and an adviser to President Woodrow Wilson. He was known by the nickname Colonel House, although he had performed no military service. He was the principal mouthpiece of President Wilson between 1916 and 1922

17 German cavalry

18 1 Samuel 14:10

19 Geymjio Sasai was a Japanese Naval officer in WW 1. An engineering specialist, his son Junichi Sasai (1918-42) was a Naval fighter pilot in WW 2 and earned the undying affection of the Japanese Ace of Aces Saburo Sakai for his care and compassion when the latter was ill

20 Enrique Granados Campiña, was a Spanish pianist and Composer, heavily influenced by Spanish Nationalism (notwithstanding the fact that he was of Catalan extraction). He was a friend and contemporary of Maurice Ravel, Claude Debussy and Camille Saint-Saens with whom he studied in Paris

21 James Norman Hall (1887 –1951) was an American author best known for the novel Mutiny on the Bounty with co-author Charles Nordhoff. During World War I, Hall had the distinction of serving in the militaries of three Western allies: Great Britain as an

NOTES

infantryman and then flying for France for the Lafayette Escadrille and later the United States Army Air Force

22 The Russo-Japanese War of 1904-5 was a revelation. Barely forty years after emerging from medieval isolationism, the Japanese Empire took their military instruction from the best in the world as they saw it: The British Royal Navy and the Imperial German Army. They decisively defeated Russia on land and at sea. The conflict was watched eagerly by the rest of the developed world, especially by the naval pundits.

23 William Sowden Sims (October 15, 1858 – September 25, 1936) an Admiral in the United States Navy who fought during the late 19th and early 20th centuries to modernize the navy. During World War I he commanded all United States naval forces operating in Europe. He also served twice as president of the Naval War College. At this time, he was commissioning the latest US dreadnought battleship, USS Nevada

24 The latest American and Japanese battleships

25 The last pre war dreadnoughts ordered for the Royal Navy

26 The Battle cruiser equivalent

27 *HMS Renown* was indeed a battle cruiser *Queen Elizabeth,* capable of thirty-two knots, unheard of at that time (and pretty impressive today). Her problem was lack of armour, but, conversely her anti-torpedo protection allowed her to survive somewhat longer than her consort, the 1940 battleship *Prince of Wales* in the face of concerted Japanese air attacks in November 1941

28 Edward Bell (1882–1924), American diplomat was the Second Secretary at the time. Later on he was involved in the notorious Zimmerman Telegram that brought the Unites States into the War

29 Clifford Nickels Carver 1891-1965. Secretary to American ambassador, London, 1914-1915. Secretary to Colonel E. M. House on mission to Europe for President, 1915-1916. Assistant to Bernard M. Baruch in Council National Defence, 1917.

30 Commander Vivian Brandon was one of the first Intelligence Officers in the RN. He carried out a number of covert operations against the Germans in the years leading up to the First World War.

31 Winston Churchill, who had been the First Lord of the Admiralty, but had been removed after the Dardanelles debacle

32 Detective Inspector Percy Savage was a policeman in the Special Branch of the Metropolitan Police. He was a very successful spy catcher in the years leading up to the First World War and worked

NOTES

very closely with the embryonic Military and Naval Intelligence services that became MI5. His proud boast was that on the outbreak of war "so effectively had the [German] espionage system been demolished that not a single item of military news got through to the enemy"

33 The Zeppelin L15 (*Kapitanleutnant* Brethaupt) was brought down off Margate on the night of the 2nd of April 1916. It was attacked and damaged by anti-aircraft guns at Purfleet. Further damage was caused by 2nd Lieutenant A de B Brandon in a BE 2c biplane.

34 Later Admiral Sir William Reginald Hall KCMG CB (28 June 1870 – 22 October 1943), known as Blinker Hall, was the British Director of Naval Intelligence (DNI) from 1914 to 1919

35 Janes Fighting Ships was, and is the bible for any sea officer wanting to know about other navies and their ships

36 Karl May (25 February 1842 – 30 March 1912) was a German writer best known for his adventure novels set in the American Old West.

37 Thurso railway station is not very different today: the space taken up by the wartime platforms is now occupied by a builders' merchant, but the former extent is very clear

38 Baggage

39 The WW1 equivalent of a Bedford Lorry

40 Half a sea mile a minute

41 Originally *HMS Audacious* launched 1869, one of the first generation ironclads

42 Like most people in this tale, Donald was retired as a junior Lieutenant in 1922, but unlike everyone else, he was actually recalled to the colours in 1941 and managed a Canadian Naval Base in the Second World War

43 A compound not unlike linoleum, used as a deck covering

44 Lavatories

45 Whilst this epithet was spelled 'Boche' in World War 2 the British (and American) usage in World War 1 was 'Bosh"

46 "Our separated Bretheren" The approved reference for non Catholics in 1916

47 Battle cruisers of the Dominions serving in the Grand Fleet, members of their namesakes' Navy

48 Bloody Fools

NOTES

49 Schoolmaster

50 Clementina's father, Reg Fessenden was an inventor and scientist. With the aid of his remarkable family he had sent the first radio broadcast from Brant Rock Massachusetts to Machrihanish in Scotland

51 It is a curiosity of RN practice, only recently rediscovered, that the dark red boot topping is set at about 3' high in the parts of the ship occupied by the lower deck, reduced to about eighteen inches for the petty officers and six inches for the officers. Unkind researchers have suggested that the reason is that the higher up the social scale you were, the less likely you were to get your food over the walls!

52 Father Anthony Hungerford Pollen was one of a remarkable family. His father was an architect and artist in the pre-Raphaelite movement. His brother Arthur JH Pollen was a Barrister, Writer and Businessman who was at the centre of controversy over Royal Navy Gunnery Fire Control systems for over a decade. Two other brothers were Jesuits, and their only sister was the model for the Beggar Maid in Burne-Jones' famous painting.

53 The Ness of Brodgar is one of the most extraordinary archaeological finds of recent years. It appears to be a vast temple complex, nearly two thousand years older than Stonehenge. This description is, of course contemporary with 1916 information and assessment

54 Fred Rutland (DSC & Bar, AM (21 October 1886 – 28 January 1949) was a British pioneer of naval aviation, especially flying off, and later landing on, ships at sea.

55 The Short Seaplane was a remarkable achievement. It served throughout the First World War and was actually capable of launching torpedoes from the air. The trouble was, the state of the art at the time was not up to providing it with an adequate range with a torpedo. Most were later converted to carry bombs only.

56 *RMS Campania* was, in the 1890's one of the fastest liners in the world. In 1914, she was due to be broken up. While awaiting demolition, the Admiralty stepped in at the last minute and bought her with a view to converting her to an armed merchant cruiser that could carry seaplanes. The conversion was completed in 1915, and trials took place under Captain Oliver Schwann of the Royal Navy, with Charles H. Lightoller (formerly second officer of RMS Titanic) as the first officer. Two weeks later she joined the fleet at Scapa Flow as HMS Campania, and subsequently began manoeuvres in the North Sea. Her job was to send aeroplanes ahead to scout for the German fleet.

After a short period, it was decided to add 160 ft (49 m) flight deck

NOTES

at the front of the ship, to enable aircraft to take off directly from the ship without being lowered into the water. Trials following this conversion indicated that the deck was too short, so it was extended to 220 ft (67 m). The alterations required the removal of the forward part of the superstructure, and the first funnel (which was replaced by two narrower funnels on each side). The aft deck was cleared and the aft mast removed, so that she could also serve as an Observation Balloon Ship.

57 Kōsaburō Oguri (1868-1944) was the Japanese Naval attaché to Great Britain during the First World War. He was a pioneer submariner and the first commander of the Japanese submarine fleet

58 Odd though it sounds to our post WW2 generation, this is exactly true. I am indebted to Fred Jane for his portrait of the Imperial Japanese Navy and its traditions from this time. Would be officers had to pass three exams in English before proceeding to the Naval Academy. On the ships, English food was served to all three days a week, with Japanese food on the other four. Sas's anecdote is a true one!

59 A famous hotel in the Centre of Edinburgh. Now the Balmoral

60 A battle between the German and British battle cruiser squadrons in which poor signaling by the British allowed the Germans to get away

61 Ethel Beatty was the daughter of the American retail magnate Marshall Field. She married Arthur Tree, son of Lambert Tree, in an opulent ceremony held at the home of her parents, 1905 Prairie Avenue, Chicago; on 1 January 1891.They had one child, Ronald born on 26 September 1897. She had a secret affair with Beatty, and married him on 22 May 1901 ten days after her divorce from Tree was made public. Famously, when Beatty was in trouble for hazarding his ship before the war she said "Pooh! If the Admiralty are worried about David, I'll buy them another stupid battleship!"

62 Commander Cyril Ryan (1874-1940) was a hydrophone specialist and famously the lover of Ethel Beatty, who prevailed upon her husband to appoint him to his staff

63 A reference to the famous feud between Admirals Fisher and Beresford at the turn of the twentieth century that divided the Navy. Fisher, and his favoured members of the "Fishpond" prevailed

64 Stein's Dixieland Jass (*sic*) Band was the sensation of 1917, with their rendition of "The Darktown Strutter's Ball, which introduced Jazz to the wider public. This would have been an early proof.

65 Later, Admiral of the Fleet Alfred Ernle Montacute Chatfield, 1st

NOTES

Baron Chatfield, GCB, OM, KCMG, CVO, PC, DL (1873 – 1967)

66 Senior Officer Battle Cruiser Force

67 Which is exactly what happened in *HMS Malaya* as a result of the hit noticed by Jonathan at page 267

68 Cordite consisted of a bag of explosive cords, not unlike spaghetti in appearance (hence cordite). It is technically a low explosive which works by producing large amounts of expanding gas very quickly rather than explosive detonation like high explosive

69 The latest German battleships

70 The code for deployment to port. "Charlie London" was the phonetic alphabet of the time. Today we would say "Charlie Lima"

71 In fact there were rumours in the United States that Symington, the Naval Attaché himself had gone to sea with the Battle cruiser Force and had been sunk on *HMS Indefatigable*

72 Kitchener and his staff had less than a day to live. That very evening the was proceeding to Russia on HMS Hampshire, which hit a mine off Marwick Head and sank with the loss of 737 men, including Kitchener and all his staff

Printed in Great Britain
by Amazon